HENRY WILLIAMSON

THE GALE OF THE WORLD

Introduction by Anne Williamson

SUTTON PUBLISHING

First published in 1969 by Macdonald & Co (Publishers) Ltd

First published in this edition in the United Kingdom in 1999
Sutton Publishing Limited
Phoenix Mill • Thrupp • Stroud • Gloucestershire

British Library Cataloguing-in-Publication Data

A catalogue record for this book is available from the British Library.

ISBN 0-7509-2155-2

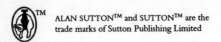

ALAN SUTTON™ and SUTTON™ are the
trade marks of Sutton Publishing Limited

Printed in Great Britain by
The Guernsey Press Company Limited,
Guernsey, Channel Islands.

To Kenneth Allsop

ACKNOWLEDGEMENTS

The author is indebted to Mrs Farrar for leave to print some prose and peoms by her son, James Farrar, R.A.F., killed in action in July, 1944. The verse, and some prose pieces are taken from *The Unreturning Spring*, published by Chatto & Windus.

The author gives thanks also to Sir Oswald Mosley, for permission to quote from *The Alternative*, a work written in 1946 and privately published in 1947; and herein ascribed to a character in *A Chronicle of Ancient Sunlight* called Sir Hereward Birkin.

INTRODUCTION

HENRY WILLIAMSON was a writer of tremendous energy and tenacity. He wrote over fifty books, innumerable short stories and articles in newspapers and magazines, and literally thousands of lengthy letters. Most of his books were long and there were several typescript versions for each one. His compulsion and need to write ruled the whole of his life.

His first book *The Beautiful Years* was published in 1921. In 1951, thirty years and thirty-five books later, there appeared the first volume of his long novel in fifteen volumes, *A Chronicle of Ancient Sunlight*, whose hero, Phillip Maddison, is based on Henry Williamson himself. Apart from being an absorbing story of the life of an extraordinary man, the entire *Chronicle* is a fictionalized social history of the first half of the twentieth century.

The first volume, *The Dark Lantern,* opens with a scene where a man called Richard Maddison is out collecting moths on a summer night when he is set upon by two ruffians. Richard Maddison is based on Henry Williamson's own father, William Leopold Williamson, and this scene and most of the characters and incidents throughout the entire series are based on real scenes, characters and incidents from Henry Williamson's own life, and that of his family and friends. The element of fiction and transposing of real events with imagined ones does, however, mean that nothing can be taken for granted.

William Leopold Williamson was a bank clerk by profession who, in May 1893, married Gertrude Eliza Leaver in a secret ceremony. This dramatic tale is to be found in *The Dark Lantern*. Their first child, Kathleen Gertrude, was born in 1894, while Henry William Williamson was born on 1 December 1895 at 66 Braxfield Road in Brockley, south-east London. A third child, Doris Mary, was born in 1898. Soon after, William Leopold bought one of the new houses being built next to 'Hilly Fields' in Lewisham, and so the family moved to 11 [now 21] Eastern Road, where the main part of Henry Williamson's childhood and adolescence was spent. A blue commemorative plaque was placed here in 1984 under the aegis of The Henry Williamson Society and Lewisham Council.

Henry Williamson's mother came from a family who had been farmers in Bedfordshire and the young Henry was very friendly with his Bedfordshire cousins in whose home he felt more relaxed; we find all the relations woven into the tapestry of the *Chronicle*. An earlier branch of the family had originated from Devon, which Henry Williamson always claimed as his spiritual home and where he was to live for the greater part of his life.

In 1907 he obtained a scholarship to Colfe's Grammar School in Lewisham. He was not psychologically suited to the strict discipline of school life, preferring to roam the countryside collecting birds' eggs, but he was not a disgrace either: he became Captain of Harriers [cross-country running] and was in the school rifle team. His feelings, friendships and adventures gave him plenty of writing material and are marvellously captured in an early book, *Dandelion Days,* and later in *Young Phillip Maddison*, the third volume of the *Chronicle*.

On leaving school in the summer of 1913 Henry Williamson became a clerk in the Sun Fire Insurance Company, which becomes the 'Moon' Fire Office in the *Chronicle*. In the early summer of 1914 he went on holiday to stay with his Aunt Mary Leopoldina [Theodora in the novels], who rented a cottage in the tiny village of Georgeham in North Devon. This holiday made a great and lasting impression on the young Henry Williamson. He loved the wild coastal scenery of the nearby Braunton Burrows and the cliff promontory known as Baggy Point. This idyllic impression was further reinforced because shortly afterwards the First World War broke out and soon Henry Williamson was a soldier in the battlefields of Flanders.

He had enlisted into the ranks of the London Rifle Brigade the previous January, and was mobilized on 5 August 1914, embarking for the battlefields at the beginning of November. This period is related in the fourth volume of the *Chronicle*, *How Dear is Life,* where Phillip actually joins The London Highlanders, who also leave for the horror of the trenches. The ensuing volumes, *A Fox Under My Cloak*, *The Golden Virgin*, *Love and the Loveless* and *A Test To Destruction,* are all devoted to coverage of the war, interspersed with scenes of amorous and hilarious adventures of home leave, and service in this country training to be an officer, many of them episodes which were personally experienced by Henry Williamson himself. These books are considered by many critics to be some of the best that have ever been written about the First World War.

The war affected him greatly, particularly the extraordinary Christmas Truce of 1914, when he discovered that the German soldiers – the enemy – were fighting for the same ideals as the British: God and their country. He realized the futility and destruction of war and this determined his life's work: to show the world, through writing, that truth and peace lay in beauty and the open air. This was reinforced when, in 1919, stationed in Folkestone with the Dispersal Unit, he discovered a copy of Richard Jefferies' book, *The Story of my Heart,* and read in rapt attention what was to him 'a revelation of total truth'. He began to write seriously from then onwards.

After demobilization in September 1919, Henry Williamson returned to live at his parents' house, where he behaved rather wildly for a few months. At the beginning of 1920 he obtained a job as motoring correspondent for the *Weekly Dispatch* and was soon having short nature sketches published in various newspapers and periodicals while he worked on his first novel. But he found life in the family home too narrow and frustrating because his father disapproved of everything he did. Finally they quarrelled irrevocably, and in March 1921 Henry left home for the cottage in Georgeham whose lease he took over for £5 a year. This period of his life is related in *The Innocent Moon,* the ninth volume of the *Chronicle,* although Phillip's courtship and marriage with 'Barley' and her subsequent death in childbirth soon after is a fictionalized version of what in real life was a frustrated love affair.

The Beautiful Years, the first volume of his tetralogy *The Flax of Dream,* was published that autumn. From then on Henry Williamson wrote and published a book (sometimes two books) more or less every year, almost to the very end of his long life.

In 1924 he embarked on an ambitious project: a novel depicting the life story of an otter. To procure material he joined the Cheriton Otter Hounds and at one of their meets he saw a beautiful young woman, Ida Loetitia Hibbert, whom he soon decided was his ideal partner. They were married in May 1925. She is Lucy Copplestone in the *Chronicle* and we first read about their courtship and subsequent marriage (and Henry's quarrels with her brothers) in the tenth volume, *It was the Nightingale.*

Tarka the Otter was published in October 1927 to much acclaim, especially after it was awarded the Hawthornden Prize for Literature the following year. A letter arrived from T.E. Lawrence, Lawrence of Arabia, who wrote to say he had 'sizzled with joy' on reading it, thus starting a correspondence and friendship between the two men. With the £100 prize money Henry Williamson bought a field on the hill above Georgeham and built himself a Writing Hut which was to be his refuge throughout his life.

In *The Power of the Dead* Phillip goes off to learn farming from his uncle, Sir Hilary Maddison, who owns twelve hundred acres of downland with its own trout stream. In real life Henry and his wife and two sons moved to Shallowford in the village of Filleigh near South Molton in Devon, where there are, of course, several hundred acres of farmland and a trout stream. Henry set to work to improve the trout fishing and to write a book about another water creature, to be called *Salar the Salmon*. He published several more books and made two long visits to America, where his books had always been well received, at this time. His family increased and was complicated by the fact that his secretary, known in the novels as Felicity, also bore him a child.

In early May 1935 he wrote a letter to T.E. Lawrence asking if he might visit him to discuss a writing project for a friend, Victor Yeates, who had just died; Lawrence rushed out on his motorbike to send him a telegram in reply and as he returned had an accident from which he subsequently died. Later that year Henry was invited to visit his great friend Sir John Heygate, who was working in a film studio in Germany, and to attend the huge Nüremburg Rally being addressed by Adolf Hitler. Henry also saw and was greatly impressed by the German Youth Movement and the agricultural and industrial reforms Hitler was instigating. We must remember here that Henry had a German grandmother, and that his own ideas that 'truth and peace lay in beauty and the open air' coincided with what he saw happening in Germany. Later he was to call Hitler 'Lucifer', the fallen angel. This era is covered in *The Phoenix Generation*, the twelfth volume of the *Chronicle*.

Once *Salar* was published Henry Williamson felt he needed to move on to find fresh material. Two books, the charming *The Children of Shallowford* and the factual *Goodbye West Country*, relate the family's life at Shallowford in an interesting saga. Having seen the portents of war looming, he decided now to become a farmer and in 1937 bought a very run-down farm on the north Norfolk coast to which, amid much turmoil, the family moved. *A Solitary War* relates Phillip's [and Henry's] struggles to turn the 'bad lands' into a viable farming unit. Once in Norfolk Henry Williamson was persuaded to attend a meeting of the British Union of Fascists where he met its leader Sir Oswald Mosley. As a new farmer Henry felt the BUF's agricultural policy held the answer to the country's troubles, and Mosley became his new hero. Mosley is Sir Hereward Birkin in the *Chronicle* novels. *Lucifer Before Sunrise* continues the story of the farming struggle in wartime England. He also covers the farming era in *The Story of a Norfolk Farm* and *The Phasian Bird*.

It was a harrowing time for the family. Henry was exhausted and irritable, trying both to run the farm as a perfect system and to write to earn enough money to keep everything going. At the end of the war it was obvious that things could not continue as they were. The farm was sold but the tensions were so great that the family broke up. Henry returned to his field in Devon alone, although he always maintained close touch with his ex-wife and his children.

The last volume of *A Chronicle of Ancient Sunlight* also has Phillip returned to Devon, living alone on Exmoor. This tremendous novel, *The Gale of the World*, culminates in an epic description of the storm that led to the flooding and devastation of Lynmouth in 1953. Afterwards, Phillip, finding himself still alive, decides that he can at last start to write his Chronicle – opening with a shy young man out with his dark lantern mothing on 'the Hill' and including all his friends in ancient sunlight . . .

In real life, on his return to Devon Henry Williamson met and soon married his second wife, Christine Duffield, and their son was born in 1950. He built a larger studio in the Field, and bought a large, comfortable and convenient caravan, but eventually also bought a cottage in nearby Ilfracombe. And he began in earnest to write *A Chronicle of Ancient Sunlight*, publishing one volume almost every year between 1951 and 1969. His second marriage could not withstand the pressure of his difficult personality and this tremendous workload, and he and Christine were divorced in 1964.

Despite the attentions of friends and family Henry was then permanently lonely. His last book *The Scandaroon*, the story of a racing pigeon, was published in 1972. Many years previously he had drawn up plans to build a large house in the Field and he now achieved that ambition although he never lived in it. He finally gave permission for a film to be made of *Tarka the Otter*. With his life's purpose over he was now tired and ill and eventually was taken into a nursing home on the outskirts of London run by Alexian monks. The filming of *Tarka* went ahead unknown to him. He died aged nearly eighty-two years old on 13 August 1977 on the very same day that the death scene of Tarka was being filmed in the exact spot that he had placed it over fifty years previously, and a few days later he was buried in a simple grave in the churchyard at Georgeham, in a plot he had bought many years before.

ANNE WILLIAMSON

Readers who are interested in the life and work of Henry Williamson might like to know that there is a Henry Williamson Society. Meetings are held twice a year and the Society's *Journal*, with a wide range of articles on his life and work, is published in the spring and autumn of each year. For further information please contact the Membership Secretary:

Mrs Margaret Murphy, 16 Doran Drive, Redhill, Surrey,
RH1 6AX.

Further Reading: *Henry Williamson: Tarka and the Last Romantic*, an illustrated biography, written by Anne Williamson, was published by Alan Sutton Publishing Limited in August 1995.

A CHRONICLE OF ANCIENT SUNLIGHT

CONTENTS

PART ONE

MOON OF THE HOMELESS GHOSTS

'We are all living under the harrow
        Sir Winston Churchill
        to H.R.H. The Duke of Windsor,
        May, 1946

Chapter 1

SHEP COT

The tides which flow and lapse in the Bristol Channel are often distained by the freshets of many streams falling through wooded coombes below the moor. This tableland, covered by low, wind-bullied plants of heather, furze, and whortleberry is dissolved by clouds when the south-west gales are blowing. It is a sea country. Westward lies the Atlantic, open to far Labrador.

The flow of the streams rushing down from the moor is short. The longest is the river Lyn, which has two wide-gathering arms —the East Lyn and the West Lyn—embracing roughly a hundred square miles of catchment area. There are three score tributary streams in the area, or waters as moormen speak of them. These waters start as runners from the upland bogs, which are of peat, or turf, overlying rock.

The highest area of Exmoor is called the Forest. Here the turf, which is brown to black, lies many feet deep, veritable graveyard of millenia of rooted plants; but never a tree. The Forest is one vast sponge. Annually sixty inches of rain fall there.

Throughout long summer days the Forest yields its tribute waves to both Severn Sea on the north and English Channel on the south coast of England, 'the precious stone set in a silver sea' of Shakespeare; and, at the time of the opening of this tale, 'a disused aircraft-carrier lying off the continent of Asia', in the words of a once German Ambassador about to be hanged by the neck, with Field-Marshals and others who had held high office in a defeated country.

The high moor, the Forest, is no place for husbandry. In the 19th century a rich Worcestershire ironmaster had the idea of converting Exmoor into an arable estate. He planted belts of Scots fir and beech to shield his crops-to-be from the prevailing south-west winds. He built farmhouses and thus attracted Scots highlanders who could endure life upon the incult moor ... until

11

it should become, in the eye of the new squire, a fertile region
of waving corn, mangolds and roots for winter keep, and hay
for fodder to see through the horned stock during the dark
months of late autumn and winter. The squire also mined for
iron—the successful ironmaster did this, where there was no coal;
and where the lanes were steep to the little ports of the Severn
Sea.

Today the beech hedges stand along the verges of motor roads;
nearly all the pines are dead, and remote cottages derelict.
Heather, ling and rush have returned upon thousands of acres of
moorland once ploughed and cultivated; where seldom a corn crop
ripened. Arab stallions let run among the herds of shaggy, semi-
wild ponies improved the breed but not the weather. As for the
iron-mines, they had no commercial value, costs of haulage alone
were prohibitive. The would-be squire lost a fortune, made near
the Welsh marches, in a cloud-capped dream; for he was no
Victorian Prospero. Inevitably the moor returned to Ariel.

The topmost hills of the Forest, with its draving wet winds, are
no place for either tree or man. There is no mother-earth, no
meat soil, no Demētēr to bring forth food for man; but her
daughter Persĕphŏne is known to wander there, for in her foot-
steps spring the flowers of a sparse wilderness, the white blossoms
of cotton grass, wind-shaken among mosses and seed-tufts of sedge
grass empurpled under summer clouds smouldering in an Atlantic
sunset.

And when the sun had gone beyond the rim of the ocean, there
comes upon the solitary writer, who has come to live in a long-
disused shepherd's cot below The Chains, a sense of great loneliness ... until Night yields its secrets, with planets in glow among
the starry constellations—immortal friends guiding mariners upon
the waste spaces of the sea : steady Polaris, around which the
universe appears to turn; Andromeda, more beautiful than the
Nāïdes, nymphs of running water; Cygnus the swan, lying wing-
spread on its side to the east; Bootës the waggoner, to whom
slide those silent meteors of the summer night, by their dazed and
wan fires of estrangement seeking lost love; Ursa major and Ursa
minor, Big Bear and Little Bear; while Antares, most passionate
of summer stars, blushes above the southern horizon.

And the summer dawn coming up beyond the beacon of high
Dunkery brings the curlews into air, to fly in circles above their
young walking among the bedraggled white blooms of the cotton

grass, their parents crying warning that the carrion crow is searching, searching; a cry to hide among the clumps of sedge-grass,
to quit the bare patches of peat until rapine blackness has flapped
away.

Wild deer live in the wooded coombes below. At night they
travel to farmlands below the moors, to feed on the crops grown
by farmers. They are seldom seen by day; but occasionally a stag
is perceived, diminutive antler'd, momentarily against the sky as it
crosses the horizon of the Forest. Then the moving speck is gone;
minutes pass; a cry from the onlookers, far below, as a smaller
speck followed by another, another, another in line astern, goes
over the horizon. These are the stag-hounds running mute on the
line of the deer, following scent from slot-marks in the peat, and
brushed upon the leaves of sedge.

Hounds and quarry have been known to travel sixty miles
from the stag's day-time harbour to where the quarry stands at
bay in water, its last refuge.

The stag-hunting season begins in August. By the beginning of
October, as rutting time approaches, it is ending.

One early October morning, when hounds were kennel'd, no
longer on a hunting diet of cooked horse-flesh or offal (with oat-
meal baked in square tins) but on meal only—the tiny figures of
two riders appeared on the skyline of The Chains. As they descended the steep northern slope, and came near to the common
below, it could be seen that one was an elderly man on a hunter,
breeched and jacket'd but wearing a pre-1914 velour hat at a
jaunty angle; while his companion was a young girl on a cob.
She wore blue jeans and jersey, while her long dark hair was
left to fall about her shoulders. Following the cob was a white
goat.

"Nobody makes good cyder in the farmhouses nowadays,
Miranda. At best it was a wry business. The trees gone to canker
and lichen growing on unpruned branches. Unwashed hogsheads
turned the juices to acid, otherwise vinegar, thus giving some
substance to the local name of 'tanglilegs'. One wasn't so much
tipsy as full of acid. But everything's changed since the war. Even
painting's gone to hell. Look at those layabouts in Chelsea—their
work's as formless as their lives. The war's got a lot to answer
for. However, it's saved the red deer from extinction, since thumping farm-profits have turned many tenant farmers to owner-
occupiers. And since deer, both stag and hind, are crop-thieves,

damaging more than they eat, hunting flourishes. Without hunting, they'd be poached to death, maimed by shot-guns, their wounds a fester of maggots. The Hunt Committee is the deers' patron. That's why the deer have lived here since before William Rufus. There's the shep cot! See it?"

The descent from The Chains was fairly steep. "Steady, gel!" he said to his mare.

Frederick Riversmill, the painter, had a great store of country lore, like most people with the seeing eye and sense of form. "I've seen Ernest Bawdon the huntsman galloping down here, all his mounts had cat-feet. Go easy, now. It's a bit boggy below, source of the West Lyn, so walk your cob."

They dismounted before a small building, which Riversmill had come to view. "What d'you think of it for a pied-à-terre, to keep canvases and painting clobber? Good place for picnics, too, during our swampy summers. One of half-a-dozen similar shepherds' cots built by John Knight during the last century. Like Hitler in Russia, he was defeated by General Winter. Almost as bad are the tempests that break upon this high ground. Ever seen a thunderstorm on The Chains? One lightning bolt split the Hoar Oak in the valley over there." He pointed with his riding whip. "Struck it a stunning blow one August morning."

"General Zeus, pourer of rains, hurler of thunderbolts," said Miranda. "The Greeks couldn't have known that it's the intense heat of a lightning flash which splits the trunk of a tree."

"Golly, is that what they teach you at school?"

"The sap boils, and steam bursts the trunk."

"Well I'm damned. It would never have occurred to me."

A remarkable kid, thought the painter. Molly Bucentaur had certainly thrown a good filly in Miranda. If she was any criterion, a dam' fine generation was on the way, provided they kept their heads and didn't fling themselves to the devil.

"I wonder if they have the key in the farmhouse over there. This place is in better shape than I'd imagined."

The cot had a mason'd wall of stone. Riversmill took a spare shoe from its leather case attached to a saddle ring, and using it for hammer struck a projecting lump of mortar. It was soft.

While he was doing this, a little dog was standing still, watching him from a distance of about ten yards. It took no notice of the goat, which wore a crimson collar around its neck.

"The builder skimped his job, Miranda. He should have used Welsh lime, brought to the kiln at Lynmouth from the pebble ridge near Barry. That makes the hardest mortar, the Normans knew that. They were craftsmen. Their walls will be dry, their cathedrals still be standing when the jerry-built farmhouses and cottages of Ironmaster Knight are forgotten."

"What about Westminster Abbey? The stone is wasting away."

"They didn't foresee the Industrial revolution, with its filthy acid smoke, and later carbon monoxide and diesel fumes."

"Is it true there is oil under the moor?"

"What! Oil under Exmoor! Oil rigs and new concrete roads! If the Americans hear of it, they'll be on to it like a shot. We've already lost enough to them in the war, by God!"

He looked through the window. Table with paper, bottle of ink, pens, books. Pile of small, slim magazines with yellow covers. "'The New Horizon', " he said. "That's Wallington Christie's quarterly. Someone's forestalled us, Miranda! Let's go to the farmhouse yonder and find out who it is."

The dog followed them at a distance. It stopped a dozen yards from the house, unmoving spectator of Riversmill knocking at the door. "Is that your dog?" he asked, of the farm-wife.

"He belong to Aaron Kedd down the coombe, zur. The gennulman what has rented the cot took a vancy to the little dog, who be waiting for'n to return."

"What's his name, d'you know?"

"He gave me his address, on a card with printing on it. I'll fetch'n, zur."

"'Barbarian Club'," read Riversmill. Then, "Good God, it's 'the Norfolk Hero', Phillip Maddison!"

"Who wrote 'The Water Wanderer'?"

"That's the chap, Miranda."

"But why 'the Norfolk Hero'?"

"'Buster' Cloudesley's name for Maddison, after he was shot by commandos on his own meadows. They were there without notice, doing a practice assault, with live ammunition. When 'Buster' went to apologise to him in hospital, Maddison apologised to 'Buster', saying he had forgotten he was no longer on the Western Front, where no one in khaki ever shot at him or his men."

The girl laughed. "It's like in a play by Oscar Wilde!"

Riversmill asked the farm-wife when he was coming back.

"He only said he had to go up to help a friend what was in trouble."

During these exchanges the dog had remained still, listening to what was being said. The goat went to inspect it in the friendly manner of one who had been the companion of children since kidhood. The dog recognised this, and gave a wag of its tail.

"That dog's intelligent," remarked Riversmill, watching the girl stroking it. "Foxhound in'm somewhere."

"That's right, zur. His mother came from the varxdog kennels, his father was Nip, the hunter terrier."

"Get's his brain from his dam. Well, we must be going," and touching brim of his ancient hat, Riversmill mounted the hunter and the two rode away, followed by the goat.

Chapter 2

BROTHER BARBARIANS

Taking long strides, forcing himself against fatigue to pass other figures in the shabby, half-starved London masses moving almost automatically on wide pavements to bus-stop and underground station, Phillip missed the turning and found himself in a narrow passage between Piccadilly and Regent Street. He saw the name-plate on the wall with a shock: Man-in-Moon Street: he had come too far: and hastening down the short passage, turned west and soon recognised where he was by the bombed church on the south side of Piccadilly and the gap before him where the V1 rocket, fired from Holland, had fallen. Over the ruins hung the wraith of the moon in full shadow of the earth. He hurried up another lane in gathering darkness, lit by one solitary street-lamp, and there was the dugout entrance to the Swallow Dive. Down steps of frayed linoleum, porter sorting envelopes.

"Any message for me?"

"None that I know of. I've only just come on duty, sir."

"Have you seen Sir Piers Tofield recently?"

"I have," replied the porter, "very much so."

"Was he all right?"

"In a manner of speaking, in that he's not dead, so far as I know."

"What's happened?"

"Did you notice any glass in the gutter when you came in? Anyway, the police took most of it away as evidence. And," he added, "the bold, bad bart's Aston-Martin."

"Did he have an accident?"

The porter put down the letters, and looked at Phillip. "You're a friend of Sir Piers, sir?"

"Yes."

"Then you know his little ways," and the sorting of letters was resumed.

"Do tell me what happened."

17

"It's none of my business, but between ourselves, your friend was asked to leave this club last night, and I understood the lady with him insisted on takin' 'im home, and Sir Piers didn't want to go, so to settle the argument, he fired a burst into the engine. And up come the police, and round to Vine Street went Sir Piers and the lady. Haven't you seen the evening paper?"

"I've only just come up from Devon."

"You might find something about it in here."

Banner-line across page one,

LAST PLEAS AT NUREMBERG

He turned pages, and found

'BANDIT' BARONET FREED ON BAIL

"He won't come here tonight," said the porter. "My orders are not to let 'im in, tommy gun or no tommy gun. Not after last night. Sorry, sir," as Phillip gave him half-a-crown before hurrying away up the steps. He must eat; nothing since breakfast.

Food was short, rationing of Utility clothes still in force, London partly in ruins. Sitting at the dinner table of the Barbarian Club he heard with deepening aloofness what the others were saying. Why all this farce of a trial of war criminals? Why hadn't they been shot out of hand, or strung up as the Russians had done? He shut himself away with the paper, reading a report of the last day of the Trial.

Row of white-helmeted· military police behind them,·defence counsel a solid phalanx in front, defendants in two rows, pale under Kleig lights, smartly groomed, uniforms specially brushed and pressed. Reichsmarschal Göring, two stone lighter after six months in prison, called on to speak first by Lord Justice Lawrence.

Göring's voice quiet, "Only motive behind actions ardent love for his people and its fortunes, freedom and life." Complained the prosecution accepted as truth every statement supporting indictment, rejecting as perjury all evidence refuting it. "One day history will justify that we never wanted war. What Germany did in France, Belgium, Holland, Norway and Greece bears no comparison with what occupying powers are doing in Germany now—dismantling industry, confiscating money of millions, interfering with the people's freedom."

Rudolf Hess cadaverous, craggy-brow'd, ashen face, deep sunk eyes like two black holes, pouring out spate of words, often incoherent, spoken at such speed he often had to pause for breath. Nudged by Göring and Ribbentrop to shut up. "It was my pleasure that many years of my life were spent working under the brightest sun which the history of my people had known for a thousand years. I regret nothing.

If I was now at the beginning, I would act as I did, even if at the end I knew I would meet death on a funeral pyre."

The old waiter, flat-footed and exhausted, who sometimes wore the ribands of the Boer War and the 1914 Star, was waiting.
"Mutton hotpot is off, sir. There's whale-meat casserole."
"No thanks. I'll have the sausages and mash."
"Sausages all gone, sir. There's the main dish available. Hotpot à la Carlton."
"What's that?"
"Mainly offals, sir."
"I'll have Carlton hotpot, please."

Albert Speer, former Armaments Minister, did not defend himself but devoted his statement to the horrors of the next war. "The war ended with radio-controlled rockets and aircraft developing the speed of sound, submarine torpedoes which could find their own targets, atom bombs, and chemical warfare. Through the smashing of the atom the world will be in a position to destroy one million people in New York in a matter of seconds." For the rest, a few were unrepentant. Funk and Saukel broke down while protesting innocence. Frank and Fritsche admitted guilt. "I did not know of Hitler's crimes," sobbed Funk, former Reichsbank President. "Had I known of them I would not be here."
Ribbentrop put the blame for the war on Hitler. "Foreign policy was determined by another before I knew of it" he averred, while some of his fellow-prisoners removed their head-phones. "I devoted twenty years trying to prevent a war by removing the evils of Versailles. Never did this policy embrace plans for world domination."

A member coming into the room sat beside Phillip. He was a professor, appropriately dressed in short vicuna jacket and striped trousers. His head was large and partly bald, he had eyes that stared as though he had meditated much. Half-Spanish, half-Italian, he had been naturalised British for many years, and fought as a young man in a county regiment during the Great War. Since then he had become a physicist, Fellow of the Royal Society, and one of the leading 'back room boys' of Professor Lindemann, the 'grey eminence' of Churchill during the war.
Phillip's upheld paper had been casting a partial shadow on an unused space of tablecloth. An electric light in another direction overlaid the shadow with a second shadow from a silver flower-bowl in the centre of the table. The double shadow was darker,

he vaguely wondered why before lowering the paper out of consideration for the professor next to him.

Frank, former Governor-General of Poland. "Hitler is the chief accused here. We turned from God, and were doomed. It was not technical hitches and shortages which lost us the war; God pronounced judgment on Hitler and his system, which we, our minds turned from God, served. More and more it degenerated into a political adventure, without truth or conscience."

"But the terrible deeds committed by our enemies, which are still going on, particularly in Silesia, Pomerania, East Prussia and the Sudetenland—all these atrocious crimes against humanity, which have been carefully kept out of this trial—have long ago expunged any guilt our people may have incurred."

The flat-footed waiter, sensitive, delicate, aware of life's end—everything was beyond him—put a plate before Phillip, having first polished it with a napkin; then he brought a small casserole dish of offal stewed with grey potato slices.

"I don't think I'm very hungry. Would you mind?"

"I can take it back, sir."

"I'll have it," said the professor. "Are you sure you don't want it?"

"No, really, thank you. May I have some sandwiches please?"

When the waiter had served him, the professor said, "I suppose you farmers live on the fat of the land, and regard the townsman's food as uneatable? You were wise to foresee what was coming, and buy land before the war, Maddison."

Phillip raised his paper. "I was wondering why a shadow can darken a shadow. See, on the tablecloth. It looks blue, while the shadows all around look grey."

"Two sources of light are deprived simultaneously," replied the professor, munching vehemently.

"Like this trial, according to Frank. Atrocities induce atrocities —all those civilians burned by our phosphorus bombs on German towns—all those Jews burned in revenge."

There was no reply, so Phillip returned to the paper.

Rosenberg, the Nazi Philosopher, and Streicher, the Jew-baiter, both protested personal innocence while blaming Hitler for mass-murders and atrocities. Kaltenbrunner, ex-chief of the Security Police, denounced anti-Semitism as barbarism in which he had no part. Von Schirach, Nazi youth leader, appealed to the tribunal to declare

German youth guiltless of the excesses and degeneracies of the Hitler regime.

Only Seyss-Inquart, Hitler's aide in the rape of Austria, remained faithful to his idol, declaring: "I served him and remained loyal to him. I cannot today cry 'Crucify him' when yesterday I cried 'Hosannah'."

Finally, Lord Justice Lawrence expressed the appreciation of the Tribunal to both prosecution and defence counsel. Revealing that some of the German defence lawyers had received threatening letters from Germans, he said they would have the protection of the Tribunal and of the Allied Control Council.

The waiter brought sandwiches which seemed to be made of flavoured wood-paste of the kind the Germans were living on. Phillip felt suddenly exhausted. The voice of Osgood Nilsson across the table saying the whole trial was a farce, everyone knew the Boches were bloody-minded sadists and butchers, thieves and gangsters.

"I wonder," said Phillip, looking across to Nilsson, "I wonder if, when the history of this war ever comes to be written impartially, it will be learned, for example, that the art treasures found in German salt-mines were put there to be out of the way of the Allied bombing?"

At this the professor sitting beside him jumped up, exclaiming, "I refuse to sit at the same table with you! I shall complain immediately to the Committee! I come here to eat my dinner in peace!" and explosively left the room.

Phillip followed him downstairs, ready to explain that he was sorry he had spoiled the other man's dinner. In the hall the professor was making for the library and silence room. The door closed behind him. Phillip hesitated to follow him there. Leaving the club he hurried across Pall Mall and walked rapidly through St. James' Square and so to Piccadilly and the Swallow Dive.

"No message for you, sir."

Up the stairs again and out of the cellar, back to the half-light of Regent Street, feeling himself to be hurrying from nowhere to nowhere down the subway steps to the Underground.

"South Kensington, please."

A Le Mans Bentley parked outside the Medicean Club. He went up the stairs, remembering his visit there during the phoney war—Melissa and her painting of the night of phosphoric waves and fish and seals on the East Coast, the last bathe before the war. Still a painter's studio, thank God, same two bars, pianist and drummer, candlelight, quietude, laughter. O'Callogan declaring he had turned his studio into a refuge from the war in which art would lose its heart, so at least let it remain a refuge from form-lessness and the tyranny of what was coming. Here Apollo would rule, and give the boot to Mars if any of his myrmidons tried to get in!

Good intentions. Irish lyricism had wilted, the painter had not painted, the Great Vacuum had arrived with riff-raff splurging on canvas imitations of Picasso and selling their daubs to rich and foolish Yanks. One phoney went about London in a Rolls with buffalo horns across the front of the roof, a Cockney with a fudge-up dialect supposedly from Greenwich Village —he having helped Al Capone (he declared) to blast New York's bootleggers from their headquarters in the Bowery.

Overcome by so much fake, so much untruth, O'Callogan, the London-Irish painter, hadn't painted. Who could paint in this bloody war, he had repeated amidst raised glasses and the thud of bombs, until he believed it and was finished.

Phillip looked around the curtain at the top of the stairs, but could not see Piers. At the far end of the room O'Callogan stood talking to an officer in uniform standing upright, reading a book. He was, apart from this detail, the picture of military rectitude. And vaguely familiar—where had he seen him before? No, it must have been someone else.

In fact it was someone Phillip had seen in hospital during the war; but without the parade ground stiffness which was due to the spine being held rigid, under the uniform, within a steel corset. The facial complexion was pink, the waxen effect emphasised by a wide ginger moustache below a very straight nose grafted on a face which had partly perished in the heat and flare of a flame-thrower in the Reichwald, after the body had received the disrup-tion of a mortar shell.

Sitting beside this living effigy, on a stool, was a girl with short black hair, rose-pink complexion, and when she turned his way, large and dark-blue eyes. She was smiling—at him? Had he met her somewhere? He felt weak. Was this the beginning of mental disease—a split mind? When she turned her head to speak to her Madame Tussaud companion, Phillip crossed the floor to a table at the other end of the room, near the piano where sat the same blind pianist with apparently the same fag hanging from his lower lip, as during the last visit there, in the middle of the war, with Piers on overseas leave before embarking for the Far East, and the 'forgotten' Fourteenth Army. Less substantial than shadows, weak saline in the sea.

The drummer, aged and white-haired like himself, bowed his head. He at least was real. "Glad to see you back, sir!" Carnation in button-hole of frayed but clean dinner jacket with no breast-pocket, relic of the 'twenties, when one put a handkerchief in one's cuff, later a middle-class solecism. That jacket was a relic of pre-war upper-middle class grandeurs of S.W.1, before the black-market boys came out of the East End, when young ladies still ignored, at least in public, the commonplace four-letter words. The disintegration had come after the bombings, following a we're-all-in-this-together-boys camaraderie in the Medicean Club : the blitz pulled people together when it didn't bury or tear them to bits. Thereafter the wide boys, the spivs, had taken over.

The drummer caught Phillip's eye again, gave another little salute and smile. He remembered Phillip as one of the original founder-members with Sir Piers Tofield, Mr. Archibald Plugge. and other gentlemen of what he called the ancient régime of the pre-war. He watched Phillip sit down at a table, unfold the evening paper, glance again at the front page; put the paper aside. The drummer thereupon leaned over and said to the pianist, "Variations on a Theme by Paganini."

Hearing the music, Phillip re-entered the present. So the drummer remembered! He ordered a pint of bitter and a bottle of brown ale; put down the glasses on the top of the piano, and stood there, smiling.

"Good to see you again, sir!" said the drummer, taking the brown ale. "One of our stalwarts, if I may say so."

"Thank you for remembering my favourite tune!"

The pianist drank from his pot, and then came Rachmaninov's marvellous white music. Gone black thoughts of the ebb-tide swirling down under Chelsea Bridge to deep oblivion of Thames estuary. No, never yield to grief. Never hurt Lucy and the children. The divorce was to be heard in two days' time. Empty formality, dead words, no contesting the charges of desertion and cruelty. The ghost of old times, when I lost my heart. I must see Lucy when it's all over—if it will ever be all over—

O'Callogan came across the floor. "You're wanted on the telephone, my boyo."

The hall porter of the Barbarian. "Sir Piers Tofield has just called in. He says will you meet him at the Swallow Dive, sir."

"How was he, George?"

"Seemed all right to me, sir. Shivering a bit, coming from the Far East, so I took him up to the bar where he had one drink and then left, sir."

Phillip got on the wrong train. Charing Cross. Take taxi. Quick, quick! Down the stairs. German dugouts on the Somme had forty steps. Intelligence reports of thirty yards depth never reached Army staff. "The preliminary bombardments will destroy all enemy field-works." They didn't. Hence sixty thousand casualties on July the First. History hadn't yet caught up with that. I must write my war novels—

"Sorry, sir, but your friend is barred after last night. Told me he was going down to your club, sir, the Barbarian, is it?"

When Phillip returned, the professor was handing an envelope, addressed to the Chairman of Committee, to the night porter who had just come on duty. Phillip said, "May I speak to you a moment, privately? I want to apologise for spoiling your supper."

Whereupon the professor asked for the envelope to be returned, tore it to pieces, and turning to the younger man, said, "Say no more, my dear fellow! I must tell you that the war hit hard many of my friends who died in the concentration camps. Their genius lies in ashes."

"I do assure you, Professor, that had I been in Germany during the war and seen little children being thrown into crematoria flames, I'd have gone in after them."

The professor thought this to be of the lunatic fringe of the fascist attitude compounded of 1914-18 war-exhaustion, whence death-wish, megalomania and exhibitionism; but offered his hand warmly, having seen tears in the younger man's eyes. Then he went to the lift, to play poker.

Jubilantly Phillip leapt up the wide main stairway, two and three red-carpet'd treads at a time, to the bar. He entered quietly, and so heard what a labour M.P. was saying.

"We've got Maddison! I've two witnesses who heard him saying that the horrors of Belsen were caused by Allied bombing, which destroyed all public utility systems including sewerage, transport, and food haulage which led to typhus! As peace isn't yet signed, this is giving comfort to the King's enemies, so he's virtually in the same category as 'Lord Haw-Haw'!"

Phillip returned down the stairs, quietly, to spend the next hour and a half—with several interruptions—composing a letter.

*　　*　　*

My Dear Professor,

I was much moved by your magnanimity towards me in the Club tonight. I thought your words had a Churchillian quality. Did he not say, after the Boer War, when speaking up for our (then) late enemies, Botha, Smuts, and others, *"The grass grows green again upon the battlefield; but on the scaffold, never."*

Churchill has written some of the splendid prose of the century, which means that he has received some of its finest thoughts.

In the days before the nominal rule of the commonplace, uncommon men were able to be uncommonly chivalrous; and thus the rancours of the South African war were transmuted into respect and amity—and loyalty. How proud I am as an old soldier that Smuts is now a Field-Marshal of the British Army!

He was preparing to continue when the door into the Silence Room opened and a tenor voice was heard singing softly,

"Your tiny hand is frozen
Let me warm it into life"

and the tall figure of the night porter, who had just come on duty, entered. Phillip ignored him. That night bird, who called himself Globe-Mornington, could be a nuisance. He was an oddment of the times, which were in polluted flux. Before the war a minor operetta star, the night porter now cleaned the club premises, and some of the members' boots outside bedroom doors, in an erratic manner. Thus sometimes he was to be seen, by some late reveller, wearing a grey-blue Ruritanian hussar's jacket and dolman, together with trousers of the same shade, with broad red stripes down the outside seams. While he did not treat those members of the club who had been elected under Drama (which included all sorts from Shakespearean actors to panto comics) with incivility or in an over-bearing manner, Globe-Mornington was wont to assume the air of a superior *artiste*, with added advice to members to enjoy themselves on all nocturnal occasions. (He sold miniature bottles of black-market spirits). Sometimes snatches of Italian opera were to be heard about the corridors of the upper bedrooms, once attics occupied by the servants of a most noble marquess.

"Bless your heart, you're working late, aren't you? What is it this time, seagulls behind your plough, or your defence as a club criminal? Though it's none of my business, of course. I suppose I'm paging you, one of your friends has just rung you up, I couldn't quite make out what he was saying, seemed a little incoherent. Sears or Cheers I think he said his name was, anyway he's on his way to some club or other, what was it now? You know more about these places than I do, the Medical Club I think it was. He says if you've nothing better to do will you meet him at Piccadilly station at half-past eleven. He doesn't want to miss you this time."

"Thank you", said Phillip, and went on writing; while the porter picked up a copy of *The New Horizon,* saying, "May I look at this, sir? I heard from Mr. Osgood Nilsson that Wallington Christie, the editor and pacifist, wrote in here that the atom bomb should be dropped on Moscow and the sooner the better."

"I'm going to edit it now."

"My word, sir, aren't you taking on another load of mischief?"

"Of course I don't agree with that! May I read what I've just written? 'O, if the war could have been stopped when Hitler went into Russia! Hereward Birkin, then in prison, wrote to me to ask Churchill to consider withdrawing from the war, arming with the might of the British Empire, and then await the victor of the Russo-German clash—if any. For myself, I did not want any nation to lose the war; I wanted all the peoples of Europe to be friends, to be purged of their intolerances. And yet it seems that I, in my own small orbit, have not only failed in harmony as the head of a small family, but I have despoiled what I set myself to create on a few hundred acres of a farm in East Anglia'."

"You're trying to save the world, I can see that, sir. Well, the best of luck to you. Now about that telephone call. I think it was the Medicine Club, or something like that. To tell the truth, I couldn't make head or tail what he said. Of course, the call may not have been for you at all, the lines get so crossed these days. It's all these Americans in London, they will put florins and half-crowns into the telephone booth boxes. I got a haul one day when I went to telephone and pressed button B. Showers of silver, nearly half a quid, not bad considering."

With the patience of the defeated, Phillip made a show of listening.

"Yes, as I was saying, the telephone system has more or less had it," went on the night porter. "The other night someone asked me if I was Attlee the Prime Minister, would you believe it, and told me to scramble. Still, members of the Government are like anyone else I suppose, liable to fits of absent-mindedness. It's the awful food we get, don't you think? Though you as a farmer are doing pretty well, I suppose. Anyway, just in case, I thought I'd ask you if you knew Attlee. Perhaps it was his personal secretary who wanted to ask you to accept a Cee Bee Eee. Like many other famous writers, I suppose. Commanders of the British Empire. Well, as there's practically nothing left of the British Empire, it means you'll be a Commander of Nothing. Not very polite is it, to infer that so many writers are as good as Nothing? Anyway, if the call was for you, this fellow said he'd meet you at Piccadilly tube station—there's a place for queers if you like, and he'd wait there for you. Glad it's you going and not me, at this time of night. London's full of spivs and cosh boys, isn't it?"

"You appear to know more about it than I do."

"I say, you referring to me? Well, I suppose I am a bit of a spiv. I've got something to drink if that's what you mean. How about a nip of brandy, or whisky?"

"I'll have brandy, please. Don't bother to come up with it now, I'll come down to you."

"Your consideration touches my heart, sir, but I cannot take advantage of your generosity. One double brandy. That's set you back ten bob. Cash first, please. Thanks."

"I'll come down for it," said Phillip, taking the lift to his bed-room.

Do you remember the events of December, 1944, when the Prime Minister, then Winston Churchill, flew to Greece, having left his bed where he was convalescent after pneumonia? *The Times,* and most of the other British papers reproved him for interfering in the war of liberation in Central Europe. I had a card at that time from Birkin, then ill and under house arrest. He, too, like Churchill, was a man anguished for his country, lest it 'sink into eternal night'. The card said, *Trust Churchill; he knows.* For Stalin is a dictator more terrible than any that has arisen in Europe for centuries; and owing to American inexperience it looks as though there is nothing to stop the 200-odd Soviet divisions now in Poland and East Germany from advancing to the northern coast of France, There were 11,000 guns bombarding Berlin during the last battle. When the city fell, rape and sadism preceded slow murder. Neither those 'war criminals' nor their Russian Generals are being tried at Nuremberg.

A knock on the door. Mr. Globe-Mornington entering with tray holding tumbler, miniature bottle, and large jug of water.

"Don't let me interrupt your love letter."

And singing *The flowers that bloom in the spring, tra-la!* the night porter left the room.

What of the so-called Allied War aims? We are impotent to do anything about the loss of Poland's integrity; Czechoslovakia also is absorbed; and Jugo-Slavia (by correlation). Greece, going that way, through civil war, meant the end of Great Britain, or her spheres of trade and influence maintained by her naval and other powers.

From the view-point of those who feel that such powers as finance and service-strength are the only realities and basis of life, of Britain ruling the waves, the signs were, to both Churchill and Birkin, alarming. For if a Napoleon, a Hitler, or a Stalin, unites the economy of Europe and makes it self-supporting, independent of bills of lading and loans and imports, it spells the doom of Great Britain. For this is what the war was about; it was not directly about Synagogues burned down or heads shaved or Catholics saying Mass or anything else which the man in the street was told, since that was ALL he can comprehend. The war, was, and remains, an economic war; and historically speaking, the misery of a generation is less in eternity than a wave expending itself on a rock. The European wave breaks; and is no more.

A whistle pierced the attic. It was the blower—relic of servants' quarters from the butler's pantry in the days of the most noble marquess. Phillip pulled out the whistle and listened at the rim of the pipe.

"Globe-Mornington here, sir, from the bowels of the building. I'm worried about your friend Squeers—someone has just rung up to say he's about to resume his ride of the Inner Circle—all on the same fourpenny ticket, round and round, I gather, until closing time. Marvellous isn't it what you can do underground on fourpence. Anyway, Steers will look out periodically for you at Piccadilly, on the Inner Circle, he'll wave a banana at you from the open door of his carriage. Right? Right!'

The pipe ceased to whisper, and Phillip plugged back the whistle, before reading aloud what he had written.

" 'With Stalin holding the Dardanelles and Gibraltar, Britain becomes 'a disused air-craft carrier lying off the coast of Asia', its power minimised, its ports decaying, its factories idle, its people in civil war. Where will the socialistic sympathisers of the 'gentle classes' be then? Where was the tolerant Kerensky in 1918?' "

The whistle gave a bleak note.

"Sorry for troubling you, sir, but I feel I must correct a faulty impression I think I gave you—to wit, in one word—banana! Shows how reading the papers brain-washes you, doesn't it? Bananas are 'news' just now. It was a *bandanna* Squeers said he'd wave to you. Bandanna—an Irish potato-picker's handkerchief, I think is the right description."

"Yes, he used to wear them, with his friends of the Bright Young People."

"Talking of bright young people, there's been a little to-do in the bar just now—Dylan Thomas throwing a bottle at Osgood Nilsson, who called him a fake and a no-good man. I'm about fed up with this club, honest I am. I suppose you don't know of a country gentleman down your way who wants a major domo, do you? A butler—valet—chef? House-parlourman is the modest term used nowadays among the new-poor, I believe."

"I'll let you know if I come across a country gentleman. There's Mr. Osgood Nilsson, of course. He lives not far from me, in North Devon. Shall I ask him on your behalf?", and Phillip let the whistle-plug dangle as he took up his pen.

And but for Churchill's intervention during that Christmas of 1944 every male German, from six months upwards, might now be dead, with every Polish bourgeois, every Czech and Slovak likewise; and in turn every Dutch, Belgian, French and Spanish tradesman, priest, banker, etc., gone down before the Tartar hordes. And to think Stalin, despite the humanitarian-dreams of our parlour bolsheviks, is other than the sworn and dedicated enemy of Great Britain is to have a very short memory. Hitler was never the real enemy of Great Britain; and my belief in Hereward Birkin is all the firmer when I remember something else he wrote to me; 'It took a man of genius to frustrate another man of genius; but Churchill could not build.'

There was a knock at the door.

"Excuse my coming once again, sir, but I felt you would want to read about your friend in the Late Night Final. If Sir Piers Tofield needs help, and he surely does, I'm his man. I can cook, mend, clean, sing, cut the lawn and do the gardening, so do remember me, won't you? This is positively my last appearance. I hope it won't be your lady's after getting that letter!"

"It's to Professor da Silva Hendrade, perhaps you'll give it to him when you see him." And signing the letter, *Yours in Brotherly Barbarianship, Phillip Maddison,* he stuck up the envelope and went down the lift with the porter.

Once again through St. James' Square to Piccadilly. It was 11.25 p.m.: he must find Piers. Down the escalator to meet the last train from South Kensington. It roared in; he hurried up the platform : a few tired-looking people got off, he hurried down the platform, thinking that when he had been there during the war the platform had hundreds of metal bunk beds along the wall, filled by bombed-out families. Perhaps Piers was asleep? All passengers to the station appeared to have got off. The engine pulled out before he could get to the end of the train. Carriages flashed by with a roar of shaken metal and he could not discern faces, his left eye, which had been stinging while he wrote the letter, was now sharply hurting. It had been like that, when he was tired, ever since Billy had driven his fist into it. Whenever he thought of his eldest son, it was as though he was speaking to Billy's image : Never worry, if you are near me, Boy Billy, it was all my own fault. We were both breaking down on the farm, the war was within us. I love you dearly, Boy Billy; I love you.

Chapter 3

LAURA

He was about to return up the escalator when he was touched on the arm. The girl who had been sitting beside the Commando colonel in the Medicean Club said softly, "Hullo. I don't expect you to recognise the grub who crawled to see you at your farm six years ago. I was dumb, now I have wings! How are you Phillip Maddison?"

"Laura Wissilcraft!"

"You *do* remember?"

"Yes, to my shame! You rode on your bicycle miles up the coast to my farm, and I was bloody to you. You see, I was horribly frustrated, because the war with the old Alleyman, as we called him in nineteen fourteen, had come again. So I was no good to anyone. I was particularly bleak to you, I remember."

"That's all you remember?"

"And your eyes. I must find a friend I missed at the Medicean."

"Piers?"

"You *know* him?"

"Yes."

"He may be upstairs."

"He is. Or was."

Piers falling down the ascending escalator, turning over and over, first one leg uppermost then an arm. He managed to get to his feet and began to run down, a treadmill action in reverse. Then he got across the dividing barrier, but slipped on a descending tread and fell, tumbling to the bottom, where he got on his feet laughing with that sudden loud laugh remembered by Phillip: Piers then seeming to be clear and enjoying life fully, living outwardly as he had seldom been able to do in the constrictions of his father's home, overlooked by a mother dedicated to the higher life of a Victorian heaven, after the death, in a seizure, of her elder son, who had passed on when eight years old. So little Piers had always been part of her grief. When Piers laughed like that he was outside the penumbra of childhood and school, thought Phillip, now face to face with his friend after nearly four years : a face sharply thin, dark spaces under eyes, hair grey above ears. Half the front teeth were gone.

"How are you, Piers?"

"Oh, not so bad. Hullo, Laura. I must apologise for spluttering, my upper denture must now be somewhere in the machinery. How's the farm, Phil?"

"Gone. *Force majeur.*"

"Where are you living now?"

"Shepherd's cot on Exmoor."

"You've travelled in a circle. How about Lucy and the children?"

"They're in Suffolk. I bought a house for them."

"Your shepherd's cot sounds ideal for a writer. I must find one, having found myself homeless."

"Have you given up the flat?"

So far Piers had been avoiding Phillip's gaze. Now after a quick glance at his friend he went on, "I see you're in the picture, as they say in the army, with the Wissilcraft. Well, I mustn't keep you."

"We've been looking for you."

"I'm practically on the run. Deserter. However, that's enough of me. If you've nothing better to do, shall we all go back to the Medicean?"

They returned up the escalator. At the top Piers said, "I must go to the lavatory, you won't mind waiting."

"So must I. See you in a minute, Laura."

Standing side by side, Piers said, "She's quite a girl. She found me lying in the gutter in Soho, stripped of nearly everything. If you don't want her, I'll take her on. Where did you meet her?"

"Six years ago in a Suffolk pub, one evening. Daughter of a smallholder on the heavy clay of Suffolk. Later she bicycled all the way up to my farm. Was almost entirely silent during the twelve-hours she was there. All I could do was to urge her to write."

"If that's all you urged her to do, no wonder she was silent."

"It was rather a difficult time. Others were involved."

"People always did revolve round you."

"How long have you been home, Piers?"

"Three days. Sent a signal to Gillian telling her when the troop-ship I jumped at Rangoon was due to berth, and she promptly skipped. The morning of the day I arrived, in fact. With some

American colonel who dug himself a foxhole on the beach at Arramanches on D-day as soon as he got ashore. and remained there, saying he had battle-shock. Never stirred, not one thought for his men. So a commando type who hangs out in the Medicean tells me. Back came the American colonel with a Purple Heart decoration and not only slept with my wife in my flat and at my home at Field Place, but drank my port, wore my suits, and didn't even bother to send my shirts to the laundry. I found them chucked in one corner of the bedroom."

"Oh Piers, I'm sorry."

"I don't blame him. Looting is traditional in war. I gave Gillian power of attorney when I went out, and you know my woods going down to the Benbow Fishponds? She had all the timber thrown, and paid the nine thousand pounds from the timber merchant into her private account. That was two months ago. Well, it's good to be with you again, Phil."

Piers began to cry.

Phillip waited, hoping that Laura would not have gone when they got outside.

Piers' longing for love, while fighting in the jungle with the Fourteenth Army, had made him idealise his wife, who had been his mistress before Virginia, his first wife, had divorced him while still loving him. Piers was what the Victorians called 'two people'. His mind had a deeper bifurcation than most men of imagination marred by the prison house of an Edwardian childhood. The darkened Piers came out when he was drunk, the thwarted child of a stiff-starched nanny behind the discipline of his grace and awareness of the feelings of others. Thus his wives, first Virginia, and to a lesser depth Gillian, had been unable to remain with him.

Piers' despair on finding himself forsaken had found no relief, certainly no solace or satisfaction, with the anonymous tart he had taken to his flat the night before, there to try to impose on her personality the image of the wife who had left him. Being unable to conjoin with her body he had begged her to whip him, but without the desired result : so he had beaten her in the hope of sadistic erection—in vain. Then to the brandy bottle, oblivion, and waking to find the flat pillaged. Even the unwashed shirts in the corner of the bedroom had gone. So he had sought to find another image of love. The same thing had happened; and he had come-to in the gutter, to see a gentle face above him. She had helped him upstairs to a room, he had awakened to find her writing in a book of bound foolscap paper. She had looked at him and said quietly, "I am Laura."

The three stood in Piccadilly waiting for a taxi. Tarts, male and female, hung about in darkened doorways, one little more than fourteen years old, hoping to meet American soldiers, black for preference, they were honeys, their skins soft, like a baby's. But almost all had gone home to the U.S.A.

"Where are you sleeping tonight, Piers?" Phillip asked, as a taxi drew up.

"God knows. You remember my Ulster one-and-a-half litre? That American colonel Gillian hooked drove my motor until the canvas showed through the tyre treads. Didn't use the right engine oil either. The bores were badly worn, you could drop pennies past the rings, the plugs oil up every few miles. That Aston was my real wife. I'm going to get her put in order, then build a pantheon for her near the house in the woods beside the lake, with a plaque. God!" he shouted. "I haven't got any woods! That bitch Gillian sold them all!"

The taxi drove away.

"Come down to the Medicean, and have some supper, Piers. Then we'll get your 'bus repaired, and go down to Exmoor and write."

"A hard life, that's a soldier's end. You know it, too, Phil. Everything is money now! You can sell old rope in Bond Street. A faked Picasso was bought by Gillian's colonel, ha! ha! Sold to him by Archie Plugge, for a thousand dollars in cash. I left Archie, dead drunk on the sitting-room carpet, plugged full of surgical spirit. Remember Archie? He's a major, or was; fought the war at desks all over India and Ceylon, never without a glass in his hand. Good old Archie, he has an infallible instinct for where the going's good. I wasn't back in my flat an hour, with one call at the Medicean before unlocking my door, when Archie turned up. Fatter than ever. After the collapse of Germany he got a job as British Gauleiter in some Rhineland town or other, was sacked after a week—dead drunk most of the time, when he wasn't fraternising with the enemy. Monty was hot on fraternising, so Archie got the push. He got as far as Southampton with a camouflaged B.M.W. motorcar he'd looted, left it there before questions were asked. Don't tell him about your shepherd's hut on Exmoor, or he'll smell you out. Tells me he may get a job as public relations to an American Doctor of sorts, called Schwenkfelder, who hangs out at Oldstone Castle, near Lynton. A new religion, I gather, based on a sort of psychology of the psychic mind, plus vegetarianism. That won't suit Archie, I fancy. God, look at all the tarts. Is there a decent woman left in London?"

Laura looked unhappy, Phillip saw. Had Piers forgotten the good Samaritan who had picked him up from the gutter?

"What's happened to that tommy gun, Piers?"

"The police took it. In fact I asked them to take it. Taxi!"

On the way down the Cromwell Road he said, "I may be arrested as soon as they find out who Bombardier Tofield is. I jumped a troopship when I got Gillian's letter saying she wanted to marry her American hero, so I'm now posted as a deserter. I suppose you saw the evening papers?"

"Yes."

"They've got my photograph now, and will be able to check up. So I can't very well go back to the flat."

"You can sleep on my floor if you like," said Laura.

"Ah, back on the old rug! No promotion for bombardiers, I see!"

Phillip felt relief that his old friend was present. He was afraid of Laura: he feared to put himself into a situation of courting betrayal.

The Medicean still had a possibility of life. Rows of lighted candles, faces. Ginger-moustached Commando lieutenant-colonel still upright by the bar, reading his book. Pianist playing Paganini theme. Thank you, sir. Your health sir! Glad to see you back, sir. Did the drummer say that to everyone?

O'Callogan asked them to have a drink.

"Coffee please," said Laura.

"I'm not drinking any more fusil spirit just now, thanks all the same, O'Callogan," said Piers.

"Right you are, my boyo. Have brandy. What's for you, Phillip?"

"Oh, brandy, please."

"I think they're rather hungry," said Laura.

"How about eggs and bacon?"

"Sounds good to me, 'old boy', as Archie Plugge would say."

Sitting at one of the small tables along the wall, Phillip glanced towards the longer bar. The Commando colonel smiled. Laura went to him.

"Go and talk to 'Buster'," said Piers. "I'm going to have a nap."
He closed his eyes.

"Phillip," said Laura Wissilcraft, "do you know my friend
'Buster' Cloudesley?"

"Yes, indeed," replied Phillip recognising a suggestion in the
face of the soldier from the Battle School who had come to apologise for the unannounced use of live ammunition on the farm
meadows during the war.

"You came to see me when I was in hospital, I remember."

"I do indeed, sir. You became a legend of chivalry in the Battle
School."

"An accident of an accident, Colonel."

"May I offer you a drink, sir?"

After the brandies Piers collapsed. No food. O'Callogan told
Phillip that he would put up Piers in his flat adjoining the studio.
After the meal Phillip walked along the Embankment with Laura,
hand in hand: a new Laura; the gentlest eyes which had seen
suffering that transcended her own.

The black tide below the Embankment was lapsing fast, silently.

"How far are you going?"

"How far are you?"

"I've a long way to go."

"So have I."

"How far is that, Laura?"

"You should know, my Prospero. I am your Ariel."

"Don't dream of me, Ariel. I am no Prospero."

"Then what are you, Phillip?"

"I think I must be like Francis Thompson—'I am an icicle,
whose thawing is its dying'."

"Music comes from an icicle as it melts, to live again as spring
water. Do not sigh, my dear. The dream of resurgence is over."

"How did you know what I was thinking?"

"Because you kept looking at the evening paper. 'Buster' found
a photograph in Berlin of him lying dead, clutching his mother's
photo across his breast. I suppose someone put it there before
they poured petrol on the body and burned it in the Chancery
garden. You know about it, I expect?"

"Yes. Are you writing, as I urged you to do?"

"Writing is all my life."

"It's all mine too, I suppose, when I can start—"

"You told Piers you had a shepherd's hut on Exmoor. Where

is it? I know Exmoor, a little of it, anyway."

"On the side of a coombe, among bracken and heather."

"Do you know The Eyrie in the woods below Lynton?"

"No."

" 'Buster,' " she went on almost timidly, "is really Lord Cloudesley. He wants to use his place as a guest house for writers and painters."

"Does *he* write?"

"He wants to. We're going to write together a biography of his father, who tried to fly the Atlantic in an old one-engined aeroplane, and fell into the sea. Have you heard," she went on softly, "of Manfred Carew-Fiennes-Manfred? That's the family name. He was in your war."

"Yes, indeed. He won the Victoria Cross in nineteen eighteen when he took on Göring's squadron over their own aerodrome in Havrincourt Wood—called 'Mossy Face' because it was the shape of the ace of spades—and although wounded again and again, he continued to fight until he had shot down nine of their Fokkers."

"Really, my Prospero, that doesn't show much respect for your 'Old Alleyman', does it?"

"A Fokker, you fu— you funny idiot, was a fighter aircraft, designed by a Dutchman called Fokker. That was his born name!"

"A better name for a man I can't imagine."

She clung to his arm.

"Oh Phillip, I love you so. You were a bastard to me, you know, when I cycled all the way up the East Coast to see you, nearly five years ago! Why do you shut yourself away from women? Did you do the same thing to Melissa? Ah, you didn't know I knew her, did you? We were at the same hospital together in, of all places, Calcutta. She saw me reading one of your books, and we became friends. Where are you taking me to? Are you going to abduct me?"

"How's Melissa? I haven't heard for ages."

"Nor have I."

After awhile he said, "Where are you sleeping tonight?"

"With you, if you like."

"I'm afraid ladies aren't allowed in the Barbarian Club at night."

"Oo-er! Fancy that, now! What orgies you Brother Barbarians indulge in! Well, I've got a room in Old Compton Street. If you're tired, you needn't see me home."

"How long have you known Piers?"

"Since last night."

"You're not in the old clothes trade by any chance, are you?"

"Oh yes, I am! I stripped him, and pinched everything I could, before he woke up! I only helped him to my room to get his pants, vest, and socks! Didn't you know I was in the Rag Trade? Oh yes! I'm known as the Female Totter of Tottenham! I buy rags, bottles, and old bones. I'll buy yours if you like! Oo, I'd like to have you stuffed!"

"So you've only known Piers twenty four hours, then? Fast work, Wissilcraft."

"I've spent more time with him than you ever let me spend with you, you prickly old Merlin."

"Well, this is my club."

"Aren't you grand!"

"No, we're squatters." He kissed her cheek. "The prickly old Merlin will walk with you to Old Compton Street, if you like."

"No, you're tired, my Prospero," she said, suddenly gentle. "I can take care of myself. I learned judo in the army. When shall we meet again?"

"I'm engaged tomorrow, and the next day am due at the Divorce Court."

"Oh Phillip, I'm sorry. Really I am. I heard about Lucy from Melissa. She said she was very sweet."

"I was a brute."

"Yes, you can be the wrong sort of brute, I know. That's what 'Buster' says of himself. Why do you men of intelligence and sensibility always condemn yourselves? Anyway, he's divorcing his wife in two days' time, so you may meet. Shall I come and hold both your hands? How is Boy Billy? I took quite a fancy to him, when I came to your farm. He must be almost grown up now. He was so sweet!" She saw his staring eyes in the light of one of the tall gas-lanterns. "O, Phillip! What happened?"

"He was killed in the last week of the war."

"Oh no!" Her eyes filled with tears, her sympathy was swimming towards him, her arms went round his chest, she laid her cheek against his neck, holding him. "O, not that sweet, sweet, boy!"

Laura was lying in her small iron-framed bed in her attic room. Phillip lay beside her. Both were in their day clothes, less their shoes. Each was trying to find comfort in the presence of the other.

Laura was thinking that Caliban was one's subliminal self, that
Ariel was the spirit's aspiration; and all human beings were lost
in the dark chasm of hopeless hope between the two elements of
nature. Phillip was thinking, I cannot lose myself in her, with her.
What is it that is holding me back? Perhaps it is all romantic
love, no more real in nature than the transfer of a crude picture
on the back of a child's hand. I am afraid, not of her, but of her
desire for me, which I cannot fulfil.

The ghost of the moon, distained by London air, was going
down behind black chimney pots.

"What are you thinking, Phillip?"

"I was wondering if you were comfortable."

"Oh, were you, now. Well, since you've mentioned it, I wonder
if you could move your arm a little. It's pressing on my ribs. Oh
no, don't go away," she sighed. "Come closer. Be *with* me, my
sweet. Just be yourself."

"I feel you want me to make love to you."

She sighed. "Don't you have any other feeling?"

"I'm like men coming out of battle. They can't change over,
they feel lost to themselves, they drop to the ground, crying."

"Must you talk of the war? *Your* war?" She got off the bed
and filling a glass with water, swallowed two tablets almost
violently, then threw the rest of the water away. He heard her
unlocking the chest in the corner by the window, saw her taking
out a large book with millboard covers. Then she sat down, and
using a knee for desk, began to write. He thought this was himself
all over again. But age had sublimated the strain of selfishness in
him. There was no jag to make her pregnant. No opposing
masochism in her.

Footfalls were coming up the stairs, between pauses. A man's
boots. Coming to see Laura? Perhaps she's a tart, I'll leave.
Double knock on door. Laura capped her pen, shut the book,
put it under an arm and in stocking'd feet went to the door.

"I hope you don't mind my coming," said the voice of Piers.
"Couldn't stand the snoring in O'Callogan's annexe. May have
been my own." He saw Phillip. "Ah, already at roost, I see. What's
the book, Laura?"

"My one and only true companion, the love of my life."

Phillip got off the bed and reached for his shoes. "I must be
going. I've got to deliver an article tomorrow morning."

"Oh no, you're too tired! I can sleep on the floor," said Laura.

"How about going back to my flat? Plenty of room there, if

you don't mind American food packs and medals lying about," said Piers.

"I really must go," said Phillip.

"In that case, I'll take the bed," replied Piers.

When Phillip was gone Piers pulled Laura to him and then began an imitation of a man supposedly in love, so that she turned away from his face and then wished she hadn't because he began to cry. His mental rupture changed with her compassion, and thereafter she submitted to a variant of mental lust; and then, caught up by frantic despair, felt erotic and tried to enliven him. When he stopped her to ask if she had any brandy, she felt revulsion.

"I haven't any brandy."

"Then whip me!"

"No, not that," she said, and turning him on his side, lay against his back, saying, "Try and sleep. You're exhausted."

Thus relieved of the fear of impotence he lifted her hand and kissed it. She felt a stir of desire at the tenderness but lay still, her thoughts on Phillip. When Piers began to snore she moved slowly off the bed, and wrapping her gown around her, lit a candle and began to write a letter.

Piers was still snoring when she returned from posting the letter, two hours later. She did not mind the snoring; Phillip would get the letter at his Club by the second post that morning, it had caught the 4.30 a.m. collection, and if he was truly the one she had been waiting for, he would come to her.

Thus, gentle within, Laura fell asleep.

Chapter 4

THREE LETTERS, ONE TELEGRAM

Phillip looked in the card-room on the way to his bedroom, and found the professor still playing poker with his cronies. Trays of self-cremating cigarette stubs, piles of silver money, intent faces, cards. No-one spoke to him. He went on up to bed. Should he take back the letter from the porter's lodge? Get it tomorrow; too tired. Bed in all his clothes; eyes shut tight against stare of light-bulb.

In the morning three letters came up with the tea-tray.

"My goodness," said the night porter. "You're not undressed. You looked a proper tired man when you came in last night. Did you find your friend? You did. Good for you."

My Dear Brother Barbarian Maddison,

Thank you for your letter. It is true, I suppose, that there are considerable Russian forces mobilised in Europe, east of central Berlin. May I, however, suggest one point that you appear to have missed. The Western powers have the atom bomb and Stalin hasn't.

At the same time, I have little sympathy for those who misled our late enemies. When British parachutists, the maternal relatives of patriotic young Frenchmen, and others, have been tortured and shot; when prisoners-of-war, notably several R.A.F. pilots, were likewise shot *after* recapture, having escaped from a certain *Stalag*—then I hold, with all good soldiers, including many in the Wehrmacht, that these are acts of murder, and that the perpetrators should be brought to justice.

A Committee member has asked me to confirm certain statements alleged to have been made by you last night at the dinner table. I told him that you did not say what is alleged, in my hearing: I told him that one-sidedness is a vice of great virtue; and that the war has been fought and won for free expression of opinion.

Ever yours,
Bruno da S. Hendrade

Phillip opened very carefully the next envelope. Every aspect of it was suddenly precious.

41

Old Compton Street.

My Prospero!

Physicians can often save others when they can't look after themselves, so this. You are in the low state of a shrinking icicle and all
cold thoughts are bogus in that they are not of the stream of spring-
water but stagnant, enslaved, abysmal. You—and I—we all—
Europeans—Asiatics—soon-to-be Africans—Americans—Russians—
have had a hell of a time and feel all to hell and death or revenge
the only forked ways forward.

I am a dark soul but I go to the light, you a bright soul sometimes,
filling me with terror and darkness, being not so well just now, but
nothing considering what you've had to bear. Mine was a mere high
temperature and pain for a few days, my head a battered ram, and
leaching away tears at the slightest bit of poetry or some sad tale of
the death of loyal soldiers and sailors since there are almost no more
kings, as thou knowest, O my Prospero, Shakespeare's loveliest creation.

Will you come and eat something with me in my shepherd's hut,
you said. Yes please. Irish blue eyes and the youngest face I know.
Fifty you said, sixteen I thought. Then God, what am I doing, looking
into Prospero's fathoms-deep sea? I willed you to look at me in the
Medicean, for I recognised you from the Wooltod Inn meeting all
those long years ago, when I said, *That* is the man. Since then I've
given to others but never given myself. Please be kind to me this time.
You were so hard and away when I saw you on your farm, but no
longer. Gentleness, mutual gentleness. Relief. But what sort of a girl
am I now. Can I be Ariel again, I who am also Kundry? And you see
with paradise clearness. That's a phrase from your very first letter
to me, written in 1939, urging me to write. *Learn to see all things with
paradise-clearness,* you said. Are you still in love with Melissa? Am
I being non-paradisaical, impertinent? I feel no reserve whatsoever
with you. But you are so young, and I am so OLD. Tell me, I beg of
you, where do you get the dye for your hair? Such soft
hair, so beautifully white. I must dye mine, too. Some said in Ypern,
my village, I was a black witch. Am I? To be burned at some stake?
I have always, as Francis Thompson wrote in his *Shelley* essay,
burned at the stake of my own heart. But now the fire warms, no
longer scorches. I shall dye white my black witch's hair, it shall turn
white overnight through courage, which is, you told me, love.
Comradeship equates with the social instinct, the centre is personal
love, I'll come any time you want me and serve you in your shepherd's
hut on the moor. And we'll have a routine, never meet until noon
every day. At night I'll creep up to you from the foot of your bed and
slither away at dawn while you are still sleeping. And write my prose,
and you yours, so we won't fight through frustration and try and
Calibanise each other. Have you a bit of wild heather near, where I can
lie and hear the lizards and mice creeping about? I'll go barefoot

and cook for you, or you for me sometimes to give balance. Only I can't do arithmetic, you must do your own accounts and taxes and all that. I don't expect you to love me now, so don't try, you've been so long in the wilderness. You are almost all saint. But you mustn't let the tears drip so much. I do, I know, but you mustn't. I'll look after you, and guard you, but please never shout at me or I'll die.

Piers said you had been an awfully good friend to him and I can see how you are about half of one another to each other, but not more. He is not a steady boy just now, but will recover.

Darling, it may be a difficult time for us both, we are as it were both reprieved. O Phillip, my Prospero, you are such a fine person. Lucky me. Yours for ever and ever, Laura.

River Cottage,
Drakenford,
Dorset.

Dear Phillip,

I am writing to tell you that our Father is very ill and has had an operation which confines him to a nursing home near here. Will you please come down as soon as you can and help me prepare for the worst. I read in the paper that you have given up your farm, so I am sending this to your club in the hope of reaching you as soon as possible.

I still have my job in the City, but shall retire in three years, meanwhile something must be done about looking after Father, who is asking all the time to be allowed to go home. The doctor says he is old and his mind is wandering. I don't accept this, for when we are alone he is normal, though as you know a very neurotic man. As you are the head of the family now, at least actively the head, I think you should come at once and discuss the matter with me at your very earliest convenience. I know you don't like me, but this is a case of duty, I hope and trust you will realise.

Your sister (whether you like it or not)
Elizabeth.

P.S. Doris can't come, she is still teaching, or rather a headmistress in Cross Aulton, she chose to go there because our dear Mother was, as you know, born there. Please be a sport and help.

He telephoned Laura, he would be away for the night, and why. If she saw Piers would she tell him. A telegram to his sister. Then away in the Silver Eagle, which had been standing under a plane tree opposite the club, to Hammersmith and the Great West Road to Staines, making for the New Forest.

He had been going a couple of hours when, at a village before

Ringwood a butcher boy on a bicycle swerved into the front of the car, touched a wing, and fell clear; but the front wheel of the bike was crushed. One rusty spoke had pierced the cracked wall of the near front tyre. Air was hissing out. New tyres were still unobtainable, except by permit; the spare wheel, fitted into the offside wing, had long since been stolen. He rolled the wheel by hand to the nearest garage, three miles away, and when it was mended, back again. This delayed him four hours. It was twilight when he reached Drakenford, to hear from a neighbour that Elizabeth had gone to the nursing home to await his arrival there. Did the neighbour know the name of the home? The woman shook her head. It was ten o'clock when Elizabeth appeared, on the last 'bus. She was querulous from lack of food.

"I've been twice to meet the London train! Why didn't you tell me you were coming anyway? No, I didn't get any telegram!"

There was a notice in the letter-box that a telegram could not be delivered, so it awaited collection in the village post office; which was then shut.

"I hope you've brought your own food! We're not like farmers, you know, we're still rationed!"

"Perhaps we can go into the town, and get supper?"

"What, at this time of night? The place will be all closed up!"

"I'll put up at the Railway Inn."

"Yes, and leave me all alone in an empty cottage!"

"Shall I try to get some bread and cheese at the pub?"

"It's closed. Why didn't you come earlier?"

"I'm afraid a puncture delayed me." They went into the cottage. It had electric light.

She made some tea. "I'm afraid there's no sugar. Father's ration card is at the nursing home."

"I never have sugar in tea, thanks."

They talked about the situation; and he proposed that he pay her £150 a year for life, the amount of her pension-to-be, if she left the office to look after their father.

"But he'll need two trained nurses, and none are available! There aren't enough to go round. And they'll want someone to cook and clean for them. I've been into all that. I can't do it all by myself, how can I? He'll need constant attention!"

"What is the matter with him?"

"Didn't you know? His prostrate gland has been removed."

"Was it cancer?"

"Oh no, nothing like that. But he's old, he's over eighty, and senile. He won't be able to contain his water. I couldn't possibly look after him!"

"But he has some capital, why can't he live on that? And surely a good parish nurse can come in once a day?"

"He's afraid that if that's all the help he has, they'll soon have him in an old people's home, which means the Infirmary. He dreads that. No, he expects me to look after him, and it's too much for me. And as I said, there's a shortage of trained nurses around here. The district is full of retired business people, so all doctors, dentists and nurses find themselves overworked. And you know what a stickler he is for having things done properly. Matron says he's always complaining, so they take little notice of him, having other things to do. Then there's that girl he had in his house, Myra, he calls her, she comes and wants to see him, but they won't let her in. Quite right, too, she's only after what she can get. Silly old man, he thinks she's in love with him, he wants to marry her, can you believe it! Of course it's old age, he's gaga! Isn't that what they call it?" she said, suddenly laughing.

"I think I'll go to bed, Elizabeth, if you don't mind. Have you done with the newspaper?"

"I never read them, they're left here for Father. Anyway, you can't read in bed. Electricity is rationed. It's the same everywhere today. Well, how are you? You never write, so I've not the slightest idea of how you are or what you're doing. But you never did care about your family, did you? Father thinks you're ashamed of us. Anyway, I'll show you to your room."

If only he had bought a candle. Or the dark lantern Father had given him.

To make a fresh start, Phillip had made over to a trust all proceeds of the farm sale—nearly twelve thousand pounds—together with the copyrights of his books. The royalties from the books were small, under one hundred pounds a year. His publisher had told him that his public had gone, owing to his views on the war and also because he had 'burned up' his children upon the farm, that is, had made them work so hard that the eldest boy had run away. Then he had taken the second boy, aged sixteen, away from school to replace his brother. These things, the publisher declared, were generally known, and had lost him his reading public. Therefore, he was sorry to say, he had decided not to accept Phillip's autobiography, with regret for what he could only describe as the misuse of a splendid talent.

Phillip had four hundred pounds, his motorcar and his typewriter. He would start again. All income from the trust, paid to Lucy, was not enough to pay boarding school fees for Peter, Roz, David and Jonny. Another six hundred a year was required. He had hopes from *The New Horizon*. Now, lying in bed, he wondered if he could look after his father as well as write and edit the magazine. It would mean keeping regular hours, and a strict schedule. His thoughts returned to Laura. Perhaps the three of them, in his father's cottage? No, it wouldn't work. Also, he mustn't get involved with her. Lost girl with lost man would mean—disaster. Two stars, each needing a satellite to reflect its light, leaving lonely orbits to conjoin. Explosion. Darkness. No, he mustn't involve Laura. That lost girl blazing with her own chaos, must not conjoin in orbit with a lost old man. He must start his novel at once. He thought of 'Buster', living near him on Exmoor. He would have a friend. Now to think about the first novel of his series.

General Mihailovitch's last words, before being shot in front of one of his daughters—a Communist; the father a Fascist, greybearded, manacle'd. *I and all my works were caught in the gale of the world.* The hail of bullets cutting bone and flesh. O fortunatus tu, mon general! If only I had died of my wounds on the Somme. Morbid thoughts no good. Breathe in slowly; as slowly respire; twenty times.

'Be still, and know that I am God.'

A few miles away, in Bournemouth, Richard was lying in bed, groaning to himself as he thought that he was going to die, that his daughter intended that he should die, now that he had signed the new will in her favour. Why didn't she come? Where was the nurse? He had rung the bell once, and again after waiting five minutes exactly, by his watch. He had said to himself, five minutes, in order to make himself ring again. He was afraid of the nurse. She had complained that he was fussy, just because he had asked for his roll of lavatory paper to be returned. He wouldn't have to ring for her if only she would let him get out of the bed to sit on the commode. It was spite, that was it, pure spite! He was quite capable of attending to his own motions, and of removing the apparatus for urination. O, why hadn't Elizabeth engaged the two nurses, it would only be for a month at most, and would cost well under a hundred pounds. Life afterwards would be fairly comfortable, only he would have to regulate his intake, as the doctors called it, of liquids.

For a week Elizabeth had been living in his cottage, and had come to see him only twice in that period, after the will had been signed. Everything to her, everything! A simple will, revoking all other wills, including the last one, leaving all to Phillip. Now, according to Elizabeth, Phillip was being divorced, and for cruelty. What could have happened? When he had seen him with Lucy, and her brother and his wife, during the war—a visit as unexpected as it was delightful—they had seemed to be the best of friends. Ah, well, one can never tell. Cruelty, too. Phillip had always been a wild boy, but never cruel.

Ah! No! Had he not pushed little Mavis in the nursery fire, when he was not yet three years old? He had grown up to be a little coward, going round with his bully boy, urging him to fight for him! There was that boy in the Backfield, what was his name —never mind, his father had come up from Randiswell later in the afternoon, with his boy whose face was covered in blood and his nose swollen. Phillip had said it was because Mavis had been lying in the long grass of the Backfield with the boy. So Phillip had only been protecting her honour. The whole thing was disgraceful, Hetty said there was no harm in it at all, the boy was very shy—and so he had hidden himself, beside Mavis, in the long grass!

His sigh ended in a groan. Mavis had turned against him ever afterwards, and used her second name, Elizabeth. Ah, the christening, his dear little daughter, his best girl! And then to behave like that, and hardly having reached the age of twelve! It was as though it happened yesterday. That was the point when he had found himself alone in his own house. Hetty and the children taking sides against him. Work, work, work for the family—and what had been his reward—to be regarded as an ogre in his own home.

His thought returned to little Myra. She had written him such a loving letter before his operation, and again when he was back in his room. And the two letters, kept under his pillow, had gone! Then his talisman had been taken from him : his lavatory paper roll! Had Myra been to call at the home? You could not trust that Matron. She was almost brutally rude, refusing to listen to his just complaint that no-one came when he rang the bell for a bed-pan, and saying abruptly that it was against the rules for patients after abdominal operations to use the commode 'on their own'. An uneducated woman : 'to use the commode' was sufficient. How else would one use a commode? While anyone else, and most certainly a woman, was in the room?

Richard was in pain. Sometimes the pain arose up like a great tooth-ache and at times the pain came in waves. It was after the doctor had given him injections of penicillin. And spots had broken out all over his legs and chest, followed by throbbing headaches. The doctor said it was the penicillin fighting an infection, and had given him another dose, with worse headaches, and vomiting, to follow. And his lavatory roll, kept hidden halfway down the bed, had been taken away. His sheet-anchor! Almost his only friend, a comforter during the sleepless hours of the night. For then in an emergency he could use the commode, and not disgrace himself. As he had when at boarding school, by wetting the bed. And been caned every time that happened, in school at Slough. Still, he had been only a bit of a boy, no doubt it was done for the best.

And now the same terror was with him in the dark hours of the night.

Even sunlight through the window had no power to help him now.

Voices along the corridor. No-one, he told himself, was coming to see him. No-one. Indeed, he did not want to see anyone. Certainly not Miss Myra! He was of no more use to her. No more tea parties, with his weekly ration of boiled egg, four minutes precisely, given to her, and also his sweet-meat ration. He did not want anyone to visit him. If only he had died when the Zeppelin bomb had blown him across the road, his clothes and beard covered with powdered glass. So Master Phillip, according to Elizabeth, was planning to write a family chronicle, was he? And, no doubt satirize his own people, as Thomas Morland had done in *The Crouchend Saga!* Would he write that he had not allowed his children to see their grandfather? Oh no—Master Phillip would not show himself up like that!

Footfalls along the corridor. Not for him. The footfalls would go past, and a good thing too.

Tap on door. A voice, who could it be. "May I come in?" and a face peering.

"Who is it, pray?"

"Phillip, Father!"

"Well, this is a surprise, I must say!"

"Glad to see you looking well, Father. The flowers are from a friend of yours I met outside, Myra. I remembered her from my visit to you during the war. She asked me to give them to you with her love."

"Oh did she now!" Richard felt a glow of hope. So little Myra did care after all! He lay back, and sighed with happiness, his eyes closed; then drew a deep breath, smiled at Phillip, and the weak voice, hollow and reedy said, "How kind of you to come to see me, old man."

I must make another will, with something for Myra. Phillip should have the family plate, and other *lares et penates*, whatever happened. Oh, if Myra would marry me! For that was Richard's dream. In the young girl's company the cark and care of the years fell away, as a London plane tree shed its sooty bark every year with the rising of the sap. Other men had re-married at his age, and even given their young wives children. Was there not the great Coke of Norfolk, made a widower when he was over eighty, who had married a young girl of eighteen and lived to raise another large family, and die at the age of one hundred and ten?

"What did you think of little Myra, old chap?"

"I like her, Father. She's as pretty as she's intelligent."

Poor Father. Shrunken arms, drawn face, thin white beard, scraggy neck, blue eyes almost faded of colour. Was he dying?

"Have you seen your sister Elizabeth?"

"Yes. I stayed in your cottage last night."

"Am I going home, Phillip?"

"She did say something about getting a nurse, Father."

"Thank God!"

Richard lay back on the pillow, looking less haggard. He breathed deeply, respiring as slowly, and smiled at his son. "So I'm going home at last," he said. He raised himself on an elbow. The room had lost its menace. The Michaelmas daisies suddenly took on a deeper mauve colour.

"I wonder if they came from my garden, old chap. Perhaps Elizabeth asked Myra to bring them. But I suppose you would not know."

"I'll come down and see you and Elizabeth, Father, if I may, from time to time. You will forgive me if I don't stay this time very long, won't you? I've got to get back to London before dark. My battery is rather dud, it's gone all through the war, and you can't buy new ones yet."

"Well, don't let me detain you, old man. Oh, before I forget, did you see Matron downstairs, before you came up?"

"I walked straight in, Father. Your friend Myra told me the number of your room."

"Well, I must warn you that the matron here is not always in a pleasant mood, Phillip. So if she says anything about me, take it with a grain of salt, old man."

Matron was waiting in the hall. "Who let you up?" she demanded.

"I didn't see anyone here, and knowing my father's room number, I walked up, Matron."

"Well, don't do it again, if you please. I am in charge of the patients here, and Mr. Maddison is on a restricted diet, and so I hope you did not bring in any food for him?"

"No."

"I would have warned you, had you rung the bell—the notice is prominently displayed on the board there!—that your father is mentally deranged, and any complaints he may have made should be taken with a grain of salt."

"I understand from my sister that he suffered only from an enlarged prostate, and that has been put right, Matron."

"He's over eighty and has delusions, which are not unusual at his age."

"What sort of delusions are they?"

"He keeps asking for some young girl he says has promised to marry him, when she's older. Why, it's positively indecent!" she cried; a short woman, imprisoned within fourteen stone of muscle, bone, fat and offal, held within a grey uniform in places nearly bursting, after half a century's stuffing with the wrong foods. "Why she is barely sixteen! I won't let her into my Home, not likely!"

"Is it his delusion that he is having penicillin, Matron?"

"Dr. Manassa is treating him with penicillin, yes, but that will not arrest the deterioration of his mind."

"Is he well enough to go home, do you consider?"

"That's for the doctor to say, Mr. Maddison."

Phillip got the address of Dr. Manassa. He lived in a mock-Tudor house, of the style built in the early 'twenties, standing in grounds of about an acre, set with flowering and other shrubs. Seeing no-one about the front door, Phillip went round to the kitchen where he saw an elderly short man with nicotine-stained moustache washing out a bottle. He asked if he were Doctor Manassa, and the man shouted, "What the bloody hell are you doing at my kitchen door? Go round to the front and ring the bell if you want to see me!"

This Phillip did, and waited awhile. The door was drab with cracked and blistered paint, the brass knocker and letter-box flap dull with a greenish tinge. Obviously the doctor was overworked in a town full of elderly retired people, and so an incipient spirit of Belsen prevailed about the nursing home. It was the war, which had brought exhaustion and excess everywhere. And criminals to an almost honoured position. How many thousand French shopkeepers had been murdered, their entire stock looted for the black market, and a note *Il fut collaborateur* beside the body? Veritably a cads' war, a war of the spiritually damaged.

"Sir, I am Mr. Maddison's son."

"Oh well, that's a different matter. There are a lot of bloody thieves in this town now, and how was I to know you weren't a decoy to keep me talking while others entered my house and pinched what they could? You can sell old rope now."

"I am sorry, I am a writer, not a totter. How ill is my father?"

"He didn't let me know he was ill until complications set in. After the operation he got out of bed when the nurse's back was turned and picked up an infection. I'm giving him penicillin. Some people are alergic to penicillin as you may know, but it was either that or the infection spreading. If he had come to me two years ago, it might have made things easier. But he's turned eighty, and there's not much more can be done."

Phillip went back to the nursing home. Richard turned imploring eyes to his son standing by the bed, but managed to keep his feelings back sufficiently to ask how his grand-children were.

"Very well, Father."

"I never knew them, you know. Ah well. I knew Billy, of course, what a bright little boy he was. He's quite a man, now, I suppose."

"He was killed in the war, Father."

"Billy? Killed? Oh dear! I didn't know. Oh dear!" The voice more reedy, fretted away. The old man lay back, weak eyes closed, tears dripping. Then he managed to say, "Elizabeth tells me you and Lucy have parted. Is that so? Oh well."

"We are still friends, Father. She'll feel free without me. You know, I think we men demand too much from our wives. I'm afraid I've disturbed you. I'm sorry."

"Well, what is done is done, I suppose." Richard sighed inaudibly, and murmured, "Well, I did my best, and now I begin to see I failed. Oh well, my father and mother fell out, now history repeats itself." He half-sat up, levering himself on elbows that revealed forearms almost all yellow skin. His eyes seemed larger. "Don't bother about me any further, old chap! I'm a goner, and I know it. But Billy—he was such a bright little chap. We used to play chess of an evening. Very good he was, too. I'll miss Billy," he murmured, lying back with his mouth open.

The son put a hand on the father's forehead. God help this poor lost father of mine. I ought to stay with him, Laura. What will you think if I do not return this night? Might we look after him together?

And Lucy, he must see her on the morrow. My poor father. Are you watching by us now, Mother, as you in a dream saw Grannie waiting to take Hughie away, when he died when I was a boy? And Father mocked your tears, when you told us at breakfast that you knew your brother was dead, and we three children sat silent at the table.

His father seemed to be sleeping. Phillip crept out of the room. As he was closing the door he heard his father utter a deep prolonged groan of despair. He went back to the bedside. Richard's eyes were open.

"Father, I know it's no consolation, but think of Billy, he and his crew had to bail out over the Alps, and Billy was held by his parachute on a crag, and frozen to death. Your grandson was a brave boy, Father."

Richard turned his face to the wall, and Phillip heard what were to be the last words from his father.

"I begin to see you are against me too, are you? Well, you must be on your way—I must not keep you."

FATHER DIED THIS MORNING
FUNERAL FRIDAY ELIZABETH

Chapter 5

GOTHIC INTERLUDE

Michaelmas Law Sitting of the Court of Admiralty, Probate, and Divorce. Gothic arches of black, acid-eaten stone. Everything, animate and inanimate suffers ruin; changes; dies. Corridors dim with musty smell. The writing room. People sitting at little tables, some with solicitors. Men in neat suits, women subdued, pairs of hands clenched, one dabbing eyes with twisted handkerchief. Save for the orderliness it might have been an Aid Post in some church after an air-raid, without blood, without dust, without rubble. Yet in spirit all was there, on the battlefield; the desperate and aggressive were now in retreat, some ruined in name—others to be, by petrifaction.

His solicitor was approaching. "You have not changed your mind?"

"No. My literary reputation is gone anyway. My publisher says, 'You have lost your public'. So I shall not contest."

"Your wife's solicitor tells me the Judge will hear the case in chambers before the court opens. At nine o'clock reporters won't be here, so there should be no publicity."

"Shall I be able to see her afterwards?"

"It's not altogether advisable. Judge Aaronson is fairly hot on anything that looks like collusion."

When the solicitor had left, Phillip wandered about in the hope of seeing Lucy. He would raise his hat and smile, no more. Where was chambers? The robing room behind the Court? It was five minutes to nine.

The man called 'Buster', now in plain clothes, was standing by a table, listening to be-wigged Counsel with his solicitor. Replies in monosyllables, lips hardly moving, he looked straight ahead, sometimes nodding. When the barrister went away, brief bag slung over shoulder, followed by the solicitor, he remained standing there, looking neither to left nor right. Phillip went over to him and said good-morning.

53

"Good-morning to you, sir."

"Laura told me you are writing a book." A lame enough remark; stupid; verging on the personal.

"Well, I'm trying my 'prentice hand at biography. The trouble is I find words a little difficult. Well, how are you? We're all in the melting pot, I suppose. The old forms are gone."

"It was the same in nineteen nineteen."

"History repeating itself, what?"

Phillip felt foolish. He had obtruded on another, who might well be in pain, mental and physical. He was about to make an excuse to go away when Lord Cloudesley turned to him and said,

"After the politicians have killed off the soldiers, what next? We'll be run by heroes of the New Statesmen. Then God help us all." His impassivity broke, he flashed a sudden grin, gentlemen into fox. He brushed up his moustaches, as he had done at the bar of the Medicean after putting a pint pot under his nose.

"I believe that you have written somewhere that Hess, when he flew over in nineteen forty one, fell among thieves. Do you still agree? Not that I'm all that struck on 'the old Hun' as he was respectfully called in my father's day, but I don't find myself standing with the politicians in this matter. If we are out for justice, why did we sit with the Russians? They should be in the dock, too. There are eighteen million slaves working in Russian labour camps, sixteen hours a day. They talk of 'genocide', but what about the massacres of Polish officers in Katyn forest?"

The speaker again brushed up his moustaches, while looking casually around the room by moving his head in sections, as it were : examining first one section then another, then a third and a fourth, as though descending under a parachute. "Surveying the form what?"

"Or the formlessness."

"Ah, yes." The glance was no longer guarded, the eyes impersonal; there was sadness, friendliness, gentleness in the glance. There was communication. "I must look you up when you return to Exmoor, Maddison. We must foregather." He appeared to be searching again, then turning to Phillip he said, "It is probably a foolish question, but do you happen to know anyone who has a four-and-a-half-litre supercharged Bentley cylinder block for sale?"

"I can think only of a certain maltings on the coast of North Norfolk, in a village where some of the Bentley boys had their workshop. It was the headquarters of one of the Le Mans team who died of burns, after his motorcar had crashed in a race."

"I know who you mean, and I know the village. Thank you so much. I'll do a recce there, and let you know if I have any luck. Well, I think it's about time I did my drill in order to retain some semblance of what I'm supposed to say. God bless."

Lucy in chambers. Dark grey coat and skirt, her one hoarded pair of black silk stockings, black shoes, small close-fitting hat of black straw with grey goose feather to match her eyes.

"Pray come forward, Mrs. Maddison." Lucy swore on the Bible. "Now, learned Counsel, will you be so good as to proceed."

It was the young barrister's first brief.

"M'Lord, I have the honour to represent this lady. Mrs. Maddison—"

Lucy heard it all as from another world—even her voice seemed to be coming from far away—Skirr Farm and the division in her husband's mind, deepened by his inability to forget his first wife—yes, she died in childbirth, and he was really a writer, but was always trying to help other people—yes, she was afraid it was usually to the disadvantage of, well, himself and therefore of those near him. Yes, he had given up sleeping with her. Lucy blushed, hesitated, sought for words that would not hurt him too much, well yes, there was someone else. At Flumen Monachorum, yes. Yes, she had condoned the adultery. Flumen Monachorum, yes happy sometimes, yes, she was made to feel apart.

"Why did you condone the adultery? Were you greatly unhappy at this intrusion of another woman in your home? Tell his Lordship."

"I tried to conceal it." Should she say, "My lord"?

"Why did you conceal your distaste at the intrusion?"

"For the sake of his happiness, my lord."

"Pray continue with your questions, Mr. Strangeways."

"Thank you, m'lud. Now Mrs. Maddison, I must, with regret, ask you if there was any issue from this liaison with your husband and this woman."

"You mean issue in the sense of a child or children, Mr. Strangeways?"

"Yes, m'lud. I understand that there was one child, Mrs. Maddison?"

"Yes." Lucy breathed deeply, and told the truth. "I thought a child would be good for her, she was unhappy at the idea of not having it. My husband," said Lucy blushing again, "was the direct means of the child being born."

"Does that mean that he wanted the child, to acknowledge it as the father? Pray tell his Lordship."

"He didn't want it to grow up feeling without a father, I think, my lord," faltered Lucy.

"And did he bring his child into his household with you, Mrs. Maddison?"

"Only when he was a grown boy, my lord. It was on the farm we had in East Anglia, so that he should know his brothers and sisters."

"Did the mother come too?" interposed Counsel. "Reply to his Lordship."

"No, my lord. She had married, and lived in another district."

"I see," said the judge, making a note. "Now Mr. Strangeways, may we come to the evidence of your case for cruelty, if you find you can present the case within the short time that remains with us before we go into Court."

More and more irritable as the war went on; moody; constantly complaining that she was hindering his life; spoiling it by her presence; until the neighbours had to close their windows to avoid hearing his chronic shouting; and finally he used violence against her in the presence of the children and threatened to shoot them all and then himself, so that she began to believe that this might happen and when he was away she left home and took the younger children with her, feeling that she could not go on any longer.

Lucy's face was pale, almost sallow, when the judge asked, "And has the plaintive remained apart from her husband, Mr. Strangeways?"

"M'lud, my client wishes to ask for the discretion of your Lordship—"

"Does that mean the discretion of the Court, Mr. Strangeways?"

"With great respect, Yes, m'lud, in that my client returned to her husband, but did not share the matrimonial bed, because the farm had declined, with the ending of the war, to a standstill."

"What is the connection between sharing a matrimonial bed and a farm which has come to a standstill?"

"M'lud, with all respect due to the Court, I am trying to establish the point that both the farm and the matrimonial bed had come to a standstill. After the war the farm was sold, and a trust made for my client and her children. The husband then departed, and has paid only a couple of visits since."

"To the farm which had come to a standstill, Mr. Strangeways?"

"My client's spouse, m'lud, included in the trust a house elsewhere, but has not shared the matrimonial home for a year and more."

"Where does your husband live?" the judge asked Lucy.

"On Exmoor, my lord."

"Does he write to you?"

"Yes, he does, my lord."

"Has he shown violence towards you since giving up the farm, during the two visits he has made to your new home?"

"No, my lord."

"Where is your new home?"

"In Suffolk, my lord."

"And he is supporting you, and the children, by the income from the trust he made in your favour, and that of the children?"

"He also sends extra money, from his writing, my lord."

"Is he living with anyone else, any other woman on Exmoor?"

"My lord, with great respect, I was coming to that point."

"I have already come to it, Mr. Strangeways. Perhaps you will be good enough not to interrupt any remarks from this direction. Now, Mrs. Maddison. Is your husband living with another woman?"

"I don't think so. It's only a tumbledown shepherd's hut, my lord."

"Does he live there alone?"

"Yes."

The judge made notes. "Pray proceed, Mr. Strangeways."

"M'lud, I have here several letters which he wrote to my client's brother, a Mr. Timothy Copleston."

"*He*, Mr. Strangeways?"

"The husband under discussion, m'lord."

"I am not aware of any discussion, Mr. Strangeways."

"Yes, m'lud. I mean no, m'lud."

"Make up your mind, Mr. Strangeways."

"Thank you, m'lud. Well, as I was saying, or attempting to say, with the greatest respect, m'lud."

"That is better, Mr. Strangeways."

"Yes, m'lud. I have here several letters which my client's husband wrote to his wife's brother, who reveals a morbid frame of mind—or rather, the letters reveal the morbid frame of mind, in that they virtually disclose—"

"What is the distinction between virtually disclosing a morbid frame of mind and revealing a morbid frame of mind, Mr. Strangeways?"

"In this case, m'lud, it is my intention to prove cruelty arising from a morbid condition of mind, in that the writer of the letters, my client's husband, clearly reveals sympathy with the fate of one of our late enemies of the first rank, Hitler's Deputy, Rudolf Hess, and has declared in the letter that Hess flew to England on an angelic impulse."

A British-born Jew, the judge looked severe. "Mr. Strangeways, you have introduced, indeed you have strayed from your argument into political propaganda which does the plaintiffs case no real service. I have heard what you have had to say, and although this case comes before me in the nature of an uncontested case I am bound to say that your argument for alienation by cruelty has not been established."

The judge bowed to Lucy. "In the circumstances, Mrs. Maddison, I must dismiss your plea because, from what I have heard, there is no case. I understand that your husband has suitably provided for your support and that of your children, by this means showing that he is not without regard for your joint welfare. I will go further, and say that he has shown concern for your welfare. It has been a difficult war, the world is strewn with the wreckage of human hopes and ambitions, and before I leave you, as I must immediately, I must remark that I have perceived a feeling of loyalty remaining in you for your husband's well-being. May you come together again as a family, to the easement and happiness of yourselves and particularly of your children."

Phillip saw Lucy leaving chambers, and followed at what Tim would have described as a discreet distance. Phillip had written to Lucy's brother, giving him permission to use his letters in any way he, Tim, thought fit; thus to allow himself not to feel critical of Tim for what, among some men, would have been considered to be a breach of confidence. After all, Tim's Pa had been an old man when Tim was born, and Tim was only twelve when his mother had died, leaving Tim and Pa alone in Down Close. Lucy was seventeen, and had left school at once to go home and look after 'the two poors', as she thought of them when she saw them, standing side by side, looking entirely lost, by the garden gate, watching for her. It was in 1917, during the war in which many of her cousins had been killed. Seven years later she had met Phillip, and his little motherless son, also 'two poors', and from a deep compassionate nature decided to look after them—if he wanted her, as he seemed, at first, to do.

Lucy walked slower, but Phillip did not catch up with her. Doubt suddenly appalled her. Supposing he had *wanted*, after all, to be free of her? Perhaps he could divorce her for cruelty, she had, in a way, caused him to suffer by not trying harder to understand the things he wanted to talk about with her, Wagner and other composers and authors like Dostoieffsky and all those war books. That was mental cruelty, but not allowed in divorce. Oh dear, she had let him down again. What would he think of her?

She stopped, and moved to one side to be out of the way of people hurrying past. She saw he had stopped, too. So, summoning up resolution she walked towards him, feeling the dreaded colour coming into her face, and smiling nervously, but maintaining her fortitude. He was looking as though he hadn't seen her when she stopped by him.

"I haven't seen you," he said, out of the corner of his mouth. "Every peeler, bluebottle, copper, bogey or slop is an agent of the King's Proctor. Maintain a stiff upper lip, harden your eyes, be remote. Like me!" he said, turning to her with a smile. "I'm awfully sorry to have put you to all this inconvenience, but in six months you should be entirely free of me, when your decree nisi is made absolute. Why do you look so sad?"

"You'll never forgive me, Pip, but I didn't get a divorce. The judge said I did not make out a case."

"Well, now we can have some coffee in the Strand together! And if you've nothing better to do, will you come with me afterwards to St. Paul's Cathedral? I want to make notes, also to hear a service; for it was there, in November nineteen fourteen, my mother and Grandfather Thomas Turney attended the memorial service for the funeral of Lord Roberts who died in France. It was also a service in mourning for those of the original B.E.F. who were killed during the first battle of Ypres. I could not be present, for I was one of the survivors."

Lucy thought, This is a new Phillip. How quietly he talks. They went down some stairs. Sitting at a table, he went on, "Altogether in my territorial battalion we lost more than five hundred of our chaps, when the battle ended on the fourteenth of November." He sighed. "But that war is now as far away as Waterloo or Hastings. Perhaps no-one will ever want to read about it again."

During a second cup of coffee in the Mecca basement room he

told her about meeting Laura Wissilcraft. "She's rather a wonderful girl, you know. She seems to know everything I am thinking. Almost we don't need to speak. We've got the same sort of
eyes, only her's are young and beautiful, unlike mine now, one of
them dead, and the other misty at times."

"Do try to do less, and not strain your sight, Pip. We're all
rather worried about you, you know. You seemed to bear the
whole war, *both* sides that is, when we lived at Banyards. Do you
know," she said, turning to him and speaking with a decisiveness
he had never seen in her before, "I used to hate Luke, the
steward! It was *he* who led Billy to be untruthful! He was what
they call two-faced. He used to say one thing to you, and then
behind your back tell the men to do another!"

"Poor old Luke, he felt awfully frustrated by me, I feel sure. He
was always anxious lest we were getting in a muddle. After all, he
knew only what he knew. And he was but a labourer, suddenly
promoted. And had never left the village. That was his entire
world. No, I can't blame Luke. I failed as a leader, and I know
it. Look how I was always shouting—not at him, thank God—
but usually when I was alone—like an overheated threshing
machine!"

"Poor Pip, you had always far too much to do."

This use of his intimate name before marriage made him wary,
which in turn made him feel mean. Poor Lucy. Then he thought
how she had always strained to interest herself in what he was
writing, the music he loved—far beyond her capacity as a mother
happy with her children.

Lucy divined what he was feeling, and said, "Well, perhaps you
will find someone cleverer than I am, and then you can divorce *me*
for desertion. I shall be quite happy with the children at Hill
House, with Tim and Brenda and their little family."

"And wash your hands of me, Lucy?" he said gently.

"Not at all, my dear. But if you are free, we shall be able to
meet as friends, won't we? Anyway, do let's see St. Paul's
Cathedral! I've never been inside, and I would so like to."

Laura Wissilcraft came down the stairs. She saw Phillip at
once, but went to sit alone at a table.

"It's the girl I told you about. Would you like to meet her?
She knows your cousin Melissa, they were nursing in India together."

"Are you sure she isn't waiting for you?"

"She came with a friend of hers, an ex-Commando who was

hit rather badly in the war. Of course, you know him! He came with you to the hospital after I was hit by a stray bullet on the farm. 'Buster' Cloudesley!"

"Oh yes, of course! What a small world it is, after all!"

"His wife skipped while he was in hospital."

"Well, perhaps he's well rid of her," she replied, blushing.

"You seem to be quite resolute, all of a sudden."

"Well, I liked Lord Cloudesley. He had manners. He's a sort of connection—a cousin of my cousin, Molly Bucentaur—who lives somewhere in Somerset, I think."

"By the way, Piers is very much on his own now. He's back from the Far East. His wife skipped the day before he returned. She went off with some American."

"Oh dear, everyone seems to be in a mess, don't they? I wonder *which* wife it was, now. I liked Virginia, the first one. Then there was the girl who came to luncheon once, do you remember, the time when you and Felicity went on to the Yacht Club? What *was* her name, now? Gillian, of course! Well, I hope things will come right for Piers in the end. He was so charming, I always thought. Do introduce me to your friend."

Laura was shy at first, but when Lucy spoke of Melissa, light came into her face.

"She was wonderful," she said, in a soft voice. "When she was slashed by the—" She stopped, feeling Phillip's shock pass through her. "It was only her face, her cheeks. Oh, I'm sorry if I've said what I shouldn't. Didn't you know, Phillip?"

"Did *you* know?" he asked Lucy, whose cheeks were again colouring.

"Well, yes, I did hear something, when George Abeline called in as he was passing the other day. He told us she's going to have skin-grafting done by McIndoe, you know, the man who has done such wonders with pilots burned in the R.A.F."

"Yes," said Laura. " 'Buster' was much more badly damaged than Melissa. Anyway it's my fault for speaking out of turn. And perhaps Melissa didn't want you to know, so you mustn't blame Lucy!"

Phillip said, sharply, "Of course I'm not blaming Lucy! What happened? No need to mince matters!"

"I never mince matters!" she replied as sharply. Then, softly, "Melissa happened to be off duty, and was walking in the garden. It was a hospital in Calcutta, where we had many Indian soldiers back from Jap prison camps, where they had been tortured.

Melissa was walking under a deodar tree on the lawn when a Sikh soldier who'd been hiding round the trunk sprang out and stroked both cheeks with his razor. When she was stitched up," Laura went on, "there was an identification parade, but she would not say who it was, because she could not be sure, and an innocent man might have suffered for her mistake. She *did* know who it was, and *I* knew, too, but he had been one of the tortured, and was beyond himself, mistaking her for me, for I had let him make love to me." She went on quietly, "After that, the men in the wards couldn't do enough to help the sisters and nurses, but I had to go to another hospital, for white soldiers. Do you mind if I smoke, Lucy?"

"Please do."

"I'm sorry I was so gauche."

"I suppose people during the Crimean War thought that Florence Nightingale was gauche," said Phillip. "Well, au revoir, Lucy. Enjoy yourself—and give my love to all at Hill House, especially to Tim."

"Oh, aren't we going to St. Paul's Cathedral?"

"Yes, of course! Won't you come with us, Laura?"

"I don't think I will, but thank you for asking me. I promised to wait for 'Buster', who's rather upset at the idea of seeing his wife again, although it's in Court." She fumbled in her handbag, while Lucy went on slowly, to let them have a word together. "Here's my telephone number. You will see me, won't you?" With upward glance of eyes filled with blue light, and, "Say goodbye to Lucy for me, isn't she sweet?"

They sat in the nave. Lucy prayed on a hassock, Phillip knelt on the stone. She was surprised to see tears running down his face when he sat up; she dared to take his hand. He showed her the telegram of his father's death, while the organ began to play a fugue by Bach.

"How are you getting on with your brother Tim and his wife?" he asked, as they went down the broad steps of the cathedral.

"Oh, quite happily! We all fit in very well. They have one wing of the house to themselves, but we find it easier to have our meals in the kitchen together. Tim has one room for his special workshop, making things on Pa's old lathe. And how are you getting on?"

"Oh, I'm still living. I hope to settle down soon to writing again, then I'll be able to send you some more money for the little boys' schooling. How are the children? Do they like the new house?"

"Oh, yes. There's plenty of room for everyone, and it's a lovely house to play hide-and-seek in, with its three staircases. Jonathan has what he calls a hidey-hole under the rafters, which is his den. He likes to watch the bats up there, hibernating upside down as they hang from the rafters."

"May I come and see them one day? I won't stay long."

"Stay as long as you like, my dear!"

"Thank you, Lucy. Have you any luggage, now I mean?"

"Only this hand-bag. I came up on a cheap day-return ticket. They've started again, it will be so easy to spend a day in town now. Which reminds me, I must be getting back soon."

"I'll take you to Liverpool Street Station in a taxi."

Nearly a year had gone by since Lucy and the children had moved into the house in the quiet Suffolk village, together with brother Tim and his family. Tim loved Hill House. He and his comely young wife never crossed one another; she was an Australian girl, with none of the complications of a European civilisation exhausted by industrialism and its internecine wars. So Tim, with a quiet, slow mind which accepted all that happened as part of normal life, was deeply happy. Since his wartime job in an aircraft factory had ended, any worries he had had about how to earn a living were gone when he and his family had been invited to live as Lucy's guests in her new home. There Tim had had a splendid idea. He had his father's wood-turning lathe, a rare Holtzappfel, one of the delights of Tim's life, and capable of turning every kind of small object, from a steel or brass screw to three hollow ivory balls, one inside the other. When Pa had bought it there were only ten such lathes in England: machines of hobby-work for rich Victorian country gentlemen, costing six hundred pounds each.

In one of the larger ground-floor rooms Tim had his own machine-shop, fitted with a large coke-burning stove; as well as the workshop in the courtyard behind the house, where stood a full-size carpenter's bench brought down by Phillip from the farm. The workshop adjoined a loose-box and coach-house. Pottering about these buildings, Tim was thoroughly at home, feeling to be his own master. But best of all he liked working the lathe, making *objets d'art* in ivory for a Bond Street shopkeeper.

Ivory, he told David and Jonathan, whenever they came to

watch him, was one hundred pounds a ton, a price which had not varied since the ending of the Great War.

So in Hill House, standing on high ground and adjoining an old coach road through the heart of Suffolk, never a cross word was heard, or intrusive reminder of the late war.

Chapter 6

BRUDERSCHAFT

Well, not entirely. For there remained the prisoner-of-war camp in the park of a local land-owner. At night the sky north of the village glowed with neon lighting, although the tall platforms around the electrified barbed-wire fencing were no longer manned by armed sentries. For the camp was now occupied by Displaced Persons, nearly all of them ex-soldiers of a Ukrainian Division which had fought beside the Germans against Soviet troops: and such men could not be allowed to return to the Ukraine, their home. If they went back, all would be executed by the Russians.

Within the park, which extended upon some hundreds of acres, stood a large country house, which had been uninhabited during the years between the wars, when its old life had gone, and a new life not yet come to being. During the second war it had been used as an American hospital for airmen. While the war was on, the hospital had not been guarded, other than by the normal team of doctors, nurses, and orderlies on duty. But now it was guarded; for within the hospital was the German Feld-Marschall von Rundstedt, together with some of the *aides-de-camp,* including his doctor. And that doctor, who had been at Stalingrad and escaped being taken prisoner by the Russians, occasionally sat with Tim, Lucy and Brenda at the supper table of Hill House.

It had come about this way. Lucy and the others had gone to the village hall to attend a concert given by members of the Ukrainian division. There had been dancing and singing—strange dancing, some of it—done almost sitting down on the stage, and shooting out jack-booted feet—before an audience of local people; but the majority of the listeners were Ukrainians. It had been for them an occasion of deep emotion, for they had heard nothing of their wives and families left—to what fate?—behind what was now called the Iron Curtain.

And during the concert Tim has spoken to the doctor sitting next to him, who had mentioned that he had read, in the hospital library, a book about a man called Donkin, an old soldier who, like Hitler after the 1914–18 war, had striven for clarity of thought between England and Germany; and perished because of his dream of *Bruderschaft*. And Tim, who normally had guarded feelings about Phillip, replied modestly, "I know the man who wrote that book. As a matter of fact," his voice dropped with modesty, together with his eye-lids, "he is my brother-in-law."

This led to a call at Hill House from the doctor, who with some punctilio explained that his wife had died during the Russian invasion of East Prussia, his home. Now, he said, he had made great friends with an English nurse, and hoped in time to marry her. He begged that his request, which he made after great hesitance, was not offensive. But might he bring the lady to meet Mrs. Maddison?

Lucy was agreeable; and thus had begun a series of visits for supper, after which the two were left alone, before a fire of oak logs which Phillip had brought from the farm the previous year.

One evening, as they sat at Table, the doctor told them that Hitler had ordered Feld-Marschall Rundstedt to halt the German tanks before Dunkerque, declaring that he had no quarrel with the English, and wished not to invade or injure in any way a 'cousin nation'.

"Ah," said Tim.

"The Führer said that if the British Empire went down, the Germans, although they would win the war in Europe, would go down under Bolshevism. Because we did not command the sea as well."

"Ah," said Tim again. He was a little embarrassed, for it was outside his experience.

Through the curtain'd window came a slow but steady beat of iron-shod boots as pairs of Ukrainians slowly passed in the twilight up and down the street, as they passed every night, upon the narrow cobbled foot-way below the window.

These were men lost forever to their native land—their wives, parents, sweethearts, children. There was talk of emigration to Australia, Canada, even the United States, after 're-education'.

"All Europe is in passive despair, dear Mr. Copleston! The old way of life is in ruins like the cities in all countries!"

And the Russians, went on the doctor, speaking as though words to him were as broken glass, together with the look in his eyes, would soon have the atom bomb.

"Ah," said Tim, nodding his head slowly. He wanted to go on with his lathe-work in the adjoining room.

"If your General Montgomery had gone through at Arnhem, Stalin would now not have any of the German scientists what you say 'in the bag', Mr. Copleston."

Tim had worked ten hours that day at his Holtzappfel lathe, turning circular boxes of teak and sandalwood, to be inlaid with ivory. Phillip had promised to buy two, at ten guineas each. That was Phillip's price : Tim would gladly have given them to him.

The meal ended. The nurse offered to help clear away, to wash up. The doctor stood up, respectfully.

"Oh," said Lucy, "Brenda and I can manage, thank you. Will you forgive us if we leave you? We're both making clothes for the younger children in the nursery."

The doctor clicked heels, and bowed; the nurse smiled. Tim led them to the sitting room. Lucy came in to say,

"Do please make up the fire if you feel cold. The logs are in this basket. Would you like some tea later on? Oh no, it's no trouble at all, I do assure you."

Later, when she brought a tea-tray, Lucy said, "I must write and tell my husband, for I know he will be glad to hear that you came to see us. He was a soldier in the first war, and has the highest opinion of German soldiers. He was in the truce in no-man's land on Christmas Day, nineteen fourteen, and it left a great mark on his life ever afterwards." She coloured as she said this, and with a nervous smile, went out of the room.

Chapter 7

ARIEL CONFINED

"I suppose I'm what's called a bird," Laura said aloud, as she lay in the bath. "A farmyard hen, to be trodden by any old cock! O Phillip, I need you so much. Will you write to me, I wonder? No, you won't. Why should you?"

But if I drown myself then they will see my body—

The bath was a Victorian pattern of cast iron on three lion paws almost wholly hidden under coats of paint. The fourth paw was replaced by a broken brick. The bath itself was a scabby affair, showing scars of violence, for the house had suffered from bomb blast. Half the roof was still covered by a tarpaulin. On a wall above the bath was a copper geyser the barrel of which was as green inside as it was outside, judging by the pale layers of drippings down one end of the bath. The course of the cold tap drippings were brown from rust, she supposed—an iron pipe. The bath might symbolise the war. Green—brown—red. Red for the blood of abortion, she left alone after the 'doctor' and his felt hat, which never left his head, had gone. Leaving her with fear of bleeding to death, alone. Looking at three streams, two mere water-courses, dead cascades, and blood's dull drip-drop in the plug-hole.

Ever since that time, whenever she had lain in the bath, Laura had been possessed by the same thoughts, turning her against her true feelings.

I hope he won't write or phone. I never want to see him again, I am only good for writing—traumatic escape from the blood and cloaca shed in the bases of life. I don't want to see Phillip, it is always the same pattern with every man.

Life was, as Shakespeare wrote, 'a tale told by an idiot'. And told to an idiot. A woman was a forked ex-quadruped, with breasts like bags slung from her collar-bones. By which the parasitism of human life was maintained. She would never have a child. Not in this bloody world. Supposing it had been Phillip's

child. No! Romantic delusion was death. She lifted a leg and put
her hands, tips of thumbs and fingers together, round the thigh.
The tips just met. She was not running to fat. Sexy legs, men
always looked at them, imagining what was at the top. Was that
all love was? The water was getting cold. I could drown in the
bath and no-one would know. Painful to breathe-in water.
Swallow aspirins, and fade out. No, he won't telephone. I'm no
good anyway. No-one ever waited, made love so that I really
wanted it. Or stayed afterwards. Perhaps she was a repressed
homosexual, men unconsciously wanting revenge? What made
female cats attack a eunuch tom-cat? Because it was a peeping
tom, and if strong, pounced on other courting toms—scratched,
bit them, likewise females. Out of spite? Am I like that, really?
Wanting revenge, because my father raped me when I was a
child, was it punishment for coming on him when he was frigging
the nanny goat behind the hedge? If I wrote that, no-one would
believe it. Mother found out and I had to sleep with Grannie ever
afterwards. The torture of her snoring. Could she use the phrase
in that 1918 war-book about flying, which 'Buster' had given her
to read, when the pilot was in hospital, sleepless . . . 'the hours
were black monarchs who ruled by torture'. She must get out,
and write the scene. White bags and all. Was it when we started
to walk upright? Animals are shapely, compared with women
after twenty five. Black brassieres and French knickers—trap for
John Thomas, Esquire—and finally cancer of the breast, from too
much mauling. God, I am human bait, nothing more, for
Klingfor's purpose.

The telephone bell shocked, thrilled and sickened her. Not for
me. Anyway, I don't want him to ring, or anyone else. She ran
down the seven treads to the landing below, half-covered in her
wrap, and trailing a thin old towel.

"Yes?"

"Yes! It's Phillip. It's rather early, I'm afraid, but may I come
round and take you as I find you?"

"That would be delicious."

"Why are you laughing?"

"I think it's because it's suddenly such a beautiful morning.
Isn't it St. Martin's Little Summer? I'll get you some breakfast
right away." She put down the receiver, saying to herself, "O,
my love—" Then, after waiting to prolong the vision, she leapt
up the stairs to her room, and put on a record of *Parsifal*. O, I
am Kundry, led back by your light to the Grail! I am all spirit

now, I am Ariel, my master is coming!

She threw off the towel of Bombay cotton pinched from the hospital in Calcutta, adjusted her wrap and prepared breakfast. Would something happen to prevent his coming? Suddenly, with a sick feeling, she heard the door-bell ringing below.

Through the letter-box slit Phillip saw a tousled old woman coming along the passage. She said grumpily that Miss Wisselcraft's room was at the top, so ring the top bell next time.

He went up three flights of brown linoleum. Three attic doors. On one a label with the words—held by drawing pins—*Laura. Hello.* He tapped and waited. The latch clicked, the door opened a few inches. He waited, tapped again, expecting word to enter. Hearing no movement he said, "Good morning." Her voice said, "Come in." He went inside, expecting to be greeted. She stood at the far side of a round mahogany table laid for two, about to put on a gramophone record. He felt blank.

"Parsifal—Klingfor's Magic Garden," she said softly, putting down the tone arm.

During waking hours of the night he had imagined her happy smiling face, her gaiety and frankness.

"I'm afraid I'm rather early."

"I was in my bath when you telephoned. You came quickly."

"I rang you from round the corner."

"I thought so."

Other visitors used that box, then. The gramophone became efflorescent with voices, love in hopeful bud. Klingfor's Flower Maidens—

"Would you like some coffee?"

"Thank you."

A portable Bijou typewriter stood on the table, a half-typed page under the roller. The room was heated by a gas-fire. On a cooking ring a tinned kettle steamed. In one corner the bed, covered by a flaccid counterpane.

When the record was ended she said, "I could see you summing it all up. Well, I rent this room furnished for thirty shillings a week, and I'm not a professional whore."

"It's a jolly nice room. High up. Faces south, too."

She poured boiling water into two mugs. "It's only sawdust, coloured by rust. I hope you can drink ersatz coffee."

"I have it in my shepherd's hut."

" 'Buster' was wondering where exactly it is."

"North of the Lyn valley, rather high up on the map, near one of the so-called Hut Circles marked in Gothic letters."

She gave him a mug of Kenyan coffee, and sat on a stool at one side of the gas fire, he on the other side in a lopsided wicker chair. He wondered if heavy men had sat in it.

"I bought it for half-a-crown in Soho market," she said.

"You seem to read my thoughts, Laura."

"Darling, I am *with* you."

Stool, chair, bed and table were the only furniture, with a corner top from which was hung a curtain on rings.

"It's enough for me," she said. "How did you like living in that pill-box on your hill in South Devon—the 'Gartenfeste'?"

"Melissa told you, I suppose."

"Yes," she said in her breathing voice.

"It's blown up. That South Devon country was a battle-practice area. The Americans played hell with it. In some houses they slid down the stairs, using torn-out baths as toboggans. Then used them as latrines."

"They must have been very unhappy. What made you think of Exmoor?"

"I walked all over it when I was a boy, just before the out-break of the first war."

" 'A la recherche du temps perdu'. Poor Phillip, must you always live in the past? That's what Jane Williams wrote to Shelley, just before he was drowned. But *I* write in the idiom of the future —I leave out what most other writers put in. I get at the real, spasmodic thoughts of my characters, so that you can hear them *breathing* as they think words to themselves." She moved across the shabby carpet and, kneeling, put her arms round him and hid her face against his chest. He stroked the dark hair, his fingers moving down the skull to the neck, then up again to touch with a finger the lobes of her small delicate ears. If eyes were the windows of the soul, ears revealed the perceptiveness of the spirit. She had ears like his mother's, and his sister Elizabeth, that lost girl who had sought refuge in the Catholic Church.

Abruptly she stopped the music, saying, "I was brought up in a Catholic school. The nuns were like Gogol's dead souls, festering."

"I suppose we all live in the past, Laura." He thought of Barley; and Laura became lifeless to him.

"Don't you know your William Blake? He knew it all before Freud. 'The genitals—beauty'." She went away from him, say-ing, "O set me free! I must be free!"

"I'm sorry. I'm—I'm rather tired."

"I don't mean *that*! I'm not ready anyway. And I'm only good to sleep with anyone when I'm in love. You found that with Barley, didn't you?'

"Yes. Head-devoted heart; Heart-devoted head. Tristan and Isolde. 'True love is likeness of thought,' wrote Jefferies. You see, Laura, wild animals' bonds are natural. They work together, are devoted to one another, each has his or her job, and in season they love, to fulfil themselves, in service to their race or species."

" 'We are born to die for Germany'—the motto of the Hitler Youth. Hitler and his mother-fixation, dreaming of the beauty of heroism and self-sacrifice. I have a photograph of Hitler, with the last of his faithful boys, outside the bunker in Berlin. He looks worn-out, but he is so gentle and kind to those twelve and thirteen-year-old boys."

"Too gentle and kind, Laura. All that fell backwards in a rage of impotence upon himself, and so upon others. Now the faithful will be hanged."

Laura said in a low voice, " 'Buster' went to see the Commander-in-Chief, British Zone of Occupied Germany, Sholto Douglas. He told 'Buster' he'd been ordered by Bevin not to make any recommendations for mercy. Douglas is furious, and wants to chuck up his job."

"Bevin threatened to bring down the Government in the autumn of nineteen forty three, when Churchill released Birkin from Brixton gaol, owing to Birkin's illness! Bevin should have done his whack on the Western Front as a foot soldier."

"It's the politicians who start wars."

"Or Geography. Geopolitics!"

"I don't know what you're talking about," she replied shortly. Then, " 'Buster' said he saw the Russian Generals when they called on Sholto Douglas—great square shoulders—granite faces —'Buster' said 'God help us if they ever become our enemies'."

"Don't forget we've got the atom bomb Laura."

"Oh, go to hell, you bloody Geopolitician!" She turned away her face; then slid to him and pulled down his head to hold to her breast. "No," she whispered, "No, my master, no! 'For, lo! The winter is past, the rain is over and gone, the flowers appear on the earth; the time of the singing of birds is come, and the voice of the turtle is heard in the land'." She led him by the hand to a corner. "Lie you down on my bed, and I'll play you something.

Do you know, in *Parsifal*, where the Grail music glows and throbs as the pilgrims are going through the forest?" She knelt by the bed, hands on his shoulders, cheek to chest. "I am Kundry, you are Parsifal. Don't let me die alone at the end! You know, Phillip, that poor girl didn't want to be bad. She had no one to love her. If she had, she would have seen God plain. No, no, *you* must not swim with your eyes! *You* must not be like me." She covered him with a blanket, and going behind a curtain, dressed in her day clothes; while Phillip lay on the bed, wanting to relax, but depressed because he did not feel able to make love to her—or want to.

She came to the bed, and almost hopped beside him. The way to the genitals, Blake's 'beauty', was through a woman's hair. Clasp her head, stroke her hair, feeling her sweetness. Such tenderness. How different from his other meetings with her years ago. Then she who was locked fast; now, unlocked.

"Have you ever been in love, Laura? I mean apart from the Sikh soldier?"

"Of course I've had lovers! But each time something in me seems to repel men. When I first left home I used to sleep with any boy who wanted me. Sometimes I didn't even know his Christian name. In the morning I'd leave him, and never want to see him again. The man I really loved was that Sikh from the Punjab, who mistook Melissa for me. He was sweet. But in the end he wanted to own me, as his possession. So I broke it off. Like you, my real life is my imagination."

"So is everyone's."

"Men want to own a woman. They want to be supported. A blood transfusion to keep them alive in their activities, careers, ambitions. I suppose what I want is a wife, like you want one. I can be friends with women—one is free, then. I really love Melissa, she's free, too. She understands that women are people. She loves you. I know, although she never said so. Phillip, when you see her, you won't tell her what I said, will you?"

He shook his head. She curled herself beside him. "Oh, I do love you so. Let's go to sleep, and then I'll get some lunch and we'll go for a walk to Kensington Gardens, shall we? I go there most days. It's so lovely, to be able to walk on grass."

She sighed deeply, put an arm round him, and snuggled up, murmuring, "Your Ariel feels safe, O my master. And Kundry need not die now," she sighed.

"Do you, too, want to die sometimes?"

"Often. O my love, you are the air I breathe." A few moments later, "What are you thinking now. I can feel you thinking. You have shut yourself away from me."

He was thinking of Billy, who had loved him, and how he had alienated Billy's love, and was Billy crying out to him when he fell from his aircraft returning from Eastern Europe and knew he would never see his home again? And from Billy he thought of Jewish boys and girls, white-faced and quiet, being herded into gas-chambers; and of German boys being shot or hanged as the soul of Germany entered upon its dark travail, and accepted that all had been in vain, in 1945 as in 1918. The old battalions now a scatter of brown bones upon the Steppes of Russia, and the sandy plains of North Germany, as once upon the chalk uplands of Somme; melting into the wet, the treeless, the grave-set plain of Flanders. He must write; the only thing left to live for: a dedication known and accepted, even though leading to spoliation and dereliction of life ever since the miracle of that Christmas day in no-man's land in 1914.

"What are you thinking, my master?"

When he did not answer she felt with her finger-tips the tears upon his cheeks, and a cry of knowledge subdued, and of pain, came from her.

"I know now! You are thinking of Billy, and others like him sacrificed by the old men who have died while living, and grown hard because they could no longer love! And so sent their sons to war! O, I cannot bear to feel you grieving!"

"You have the advantage of me, because you have read my books."

She sat up and regarded him sharply. "*I* have the advantage of *you*! O God, I like that! You have haunted me for years, so that at times I have wanted to kill myself! And now you say 'You have the advantage of me!' Well take it, take me, beat me, rape me! Anything but this hypocritical gentle-Jesus stuff! I want your very essence, I don't want your little-boy fears of my body, or your dreams of the boobs women have to carry around like pouter pigeons—for that's all they are—I want to communicate with you, the true-self you—the *free* you—"

He was alarmed, for she had reverted to the dark aspect of herself that had repelled him in the past. For now she was not only angry, but her face seemed to have changed, particularly the eyes, which were round and protruding, and the mouth no longer gentle and pliant, but a thin line.

And as abruptly as she had reverted, her face became relaxed and gentle, then falling upon him she acted like a man, kissing and biting his neck, covering him like a man, holding his head by a handful of hair while giving little kisses on his lips and cheeks, before going limp upon him, and releasing a profound sigh followed by a murmur of "O, my master, why wasn't I born a man, and you a woman, to take you now and make you my wife?"

"I hope you feel better Laura!" he said, mildly ironic.

"I do. I've restored the balance symbolically, if not bolically, between the sexes."

"Now may I have the promised eggs and bacon?"

"You may, my master. Then let's leave my turret room, and go and see the little boats on the Round Pond."

"Well, for a little while, Laura. Then I must go back to Dorset for my father's funeral."

"Oh, I'm sorry," she said, entirely without feeling.

Kensington Gardens. Small boys and retired Naval Officers sailing their craft on the Round Pond. Dogs racing over leaf-bestrewn grass. Laura seemed to melt in the mellow sunshine. He told her his plans for *The New Horizon*, and invited her to help him edit it, and to write for it.

"I'll live with you and be your love, and we will all the pleasures prove, my Prospero. I'll be your tidy secretary, sub-editor, reviewer, and general drudge. What fun it will be!"

"You'll have to go up to London for a week every quarter, and cadge advertisements. The mag. will pay all expenses, and five pounds a week. How's that?"

"Then may I keep on my room? The rent is thirty shillings a week."

"Yes, if you can post off the copies from there, and make your selections as well. It can be *The New Horizon* office! How about it?"

"Yes, my master!"

"There's just one little thing I should perhaps, tell you—in his last number Christie proposed that the atom bomb be dropped on Moscow."

"Instead, the bomb fell on the magazine?"

"More or less. Christie gave me the unexpired portions of

annual subscriptions, plus roneograph plates with names and addresses."

"How much is the unexpired portion of subscriptions did you say?"

"I didn't say. But it comes to nine pounds and eight shillings."

"O my master, what an orgy we'll have on that!"

Chapter 8

FAMILY REUNION

On the way to Bournemouth Phillip called at Field Place, the home of Piers Tofield. Would he be there? The lodge garden was untidy. Trees felled in park. Branches—loppings and toppings—left to rot among brambles, thistles, docks. Grassy drive, house unpainted, rows of moving whiteness in upper windows. When he stopped before the Palladian pillars at the entrance he saw hundreds of Wyandotte hens looking down from what appeared to be bedrooms. Was the house a ruin? He walked under a high stone wall, and entered the courtyard by the postern gate.

The remembered fountain was still playing in courtyard pond. Weeds between cobbles, fresh heaps of dung of heavy-draught horses. The open coach-house door revealed a black flywheel revolving in darkness. *Thump—thump—thump,* charging batteries in an adjoining room for electric light.

On doors of the buildings around the courtyard someone appeared to have experimented with paint : red streaks and green blobs—doodling art. On a large rainwater trough was the picture of a yellow steamship. Relics of soldier occupation; or Pier's attempts to escape reality? There was a full garbage can outside the kitchen door, under a lean-to iron roof. He knocked.

Piers, clad in deciduous tweeds, semi-buttonless jacket, loosely corrugated trousers, opened the door. Glittering, evasive eyes, peaky unshaven face, Etonian politeness. "Glad to see you again, Phil. Come in. You'll find it a bit of a mess, but an improvement on Berlin, I believe. Only part of the roof has fallen in. I live in the kitchen, a comfortable wolf's lair."

After a cup of tea which was half whisky they went outside.

"The first floor is let off to a farmer, who asked me if I'd mind him 'havin' a foo guests' to stay with him. Apparently he murders his guests periodically, for I hear squawks and other cries of distress at all hours before market day. The smell is somewhat over-powering upstairs, I'm afraid, for I haven't so far removed the

77

'manners', as he calls the chicken dung—to the kitchen garden.
I've plans to start it up again—always tomorrow, so far. The
greenhouses haven't much glass left, apparently the troops cele-
brated V.J. day by smashing all they could see. Can't blame them,
really, after all the boring years of home service. Good to see the
old Silver Eagle again. My Aston isn't mobile at the moment,
needs a rebuilt engine among other things. Left it in London."

The walled garden was a wilderness. "Two acres. Take some
doing to get it all back into shape."

They walked down to the water-meadows. "No trout in the
Benbow ponds. Troops cleared them with hand grenades."

Back to the house. Little trees growing among chimney stacks.
Family portraits awry on faded dining and drawing room walls.
Pallid empty patches where pictures had hung. Rows of empty
whisky bottles along wainscotings.

"A London business man used to come down with fusil spirit,
bartering ersatz whisky for china and plate. Told him to help
himself. He did. He and his wife emptied the butler's pantry. How
my mother would have been upset. All her Jacobean, Caroline,
and Georgian silver going into the back of an S.S. saloon to
Whitechapel. Took all the china-ware too. Heard he sold some
of it to an American dealer for ten thousand dollars. When I
break a cup now I replace it from Woolworth's. He must have
made a small fortune—combines kerb-stone stock-broking with
deals in the Black Market. He also bought most of the house
for demolition, leaving the central rooms and walls of the original
farmhouse barton. I can't wait to see the house-breakers start."

"Piers, I can only say that all of us now living have been
'caught in the gale of the world'! Let's keep in touch, old friend.
I must now go on my way, for my father's funeral."

Phillip was prepared to tell Elizabeth that he would honour his
promise made during the war to their sister Doris : when Father's
estate was wound up, each sister would receive in cash one third
of the probate value. He would tell them after the cremation,
before the will was read.

As soon as he arrived down the lane, his younger sister came
out of the cottage. "Thank God you've come, Phil! Elizabeth is
unbearable. I've been here since last night, and have had to put
up with her. So I thought I'd come out and warn you what to
expect."

At the door Elizabeth said, "Isn't it awful! I had to face it all

alone! Here, in the hall! He died on the sofa two minutes after
the ambulance brought him here! Aunt Viccy had refused to visit
poor Dads in the nursing home. Her own brother! Aunt Viccy
hates me because I've become a Roman Catholic. Why shouldn't
I, if I wanted to? Mumsie wanted to be one you know, but
Father wouldn't let her! Of course the Maddisons hate Catholics,
they got it from their mother, a German Protestant!"

"Would you like some tea?" asked Doris.

"I would rather, I've driven rather fast after calling on an old
friend near Colham."

"Yes, the Maddisons hate Catholics," went on Elizabeth.
"Father said they're all after other people's money to build
cathedrals while poor people starved."

"The cathedrals were built to give employment to masons and
craftsmen, surely?"

"I know!" cried Elizabeth, as though she had thought of it
herself. "But Father could never see that. He said that novices in
Ireland shadowed young couples, ready to pounce if they saw
any spooning. And yet he himself hated to see couples lying on
the grass on the Hill! He knew about your illegitimate son, you
know that, don't you?"

"I wonder who told him."

"Aunt Viccy did. She says she won't come to the funeral, if
'the black sheep of the family' is going to be there. That's you!"
She laughed hysterically. "Also they know all about you in the
office. It's not very nice for me, you know. After all, they know
I'm your sister! But I shan't go back there! No fear! They've
agreed to give me my pension. I had a letter this morning! Anyway, I don't think I can live here now, after these past few weeks.
That awful Dr. Manassa! He turned out poor Dads as soon
as he saw he was dying! And do you know what I think he died
of? Penicillin poisoning! He broke out all over in a red rash
after you'd left. It's my belief he was dying when they carried him
out on a stretcher. I was just about to leave here, to visit him,
when there was a ring at the bell. I opened the door, and there
he was, on the stretcher, his eyes staring past me! They just
lifted him on to the sofa, waited for me to tip them, but when
they saw he was dying they hurried out. I was left all alone with
him! Then his mouth opened to say something, and his eyes
looked up, and I knew he had recognised me. He stared and
stared. He tried to say something. Then his head went back, and
his eyes closed ever so slowly, as though he knew he would be

forgiven for the way he treated us all. Well, don't stand there without a word, looking at the floor! Don't you care for anyone but yourself? Why don't you say something? Don't you realise that poor Dads is dead? No, don't touch me!" as Phillip went to take her hand. "I know you only came here to see what you could get!" and she went out of the room.

"She's been going on like that ever since I arrived," said Doris, wearily. She sat down and held her head. "I feel quite worn out. It's this goitre on my neck, you know—you can't see it, it's under my scarf. I'm having iodine injections for it. And they always make me feel funny."

"Are you sure it's a goitre?"

"Yes. My first doctor said it was, then when I was appointed to be headmistress of another school, I had to change my doctor. *He* said it wasn't a goitre, but a cyst. He wanted me to have an operation, but I believe in homoeopathy, and iodine as you know comes from seaweed, which is natural. People live on certain kinds of seaweed, laver for example. Anyway, the doctor wouldn't give me injections, so I found one who would."

"Well, I hope it's all right. Some commandos in the war lived on seaweed for days, on the coast of Italy. Congratulations on being a headmistress. By the way, what I said about sharing the estate with you and Elizabeth still stands."

"Can you afford to, now that you've made over all you had from the farm sale into a trust?"

"Oh, I need very little for myself—food, clothes, and petrol. I'm going to write the novels I wanted to write a quarter of a century ago."

"What's that?" said Elizabeth, coming into the room with a bottle of gin. "Novels, eh? Aunt Viccy says your Donkin novels are rotten."

"Oh."

"She could have come and sat with Father, only she's utterly selfish, living all alone in a seven-bedroom'd house. Even her daughter Adele won't see her any more. I've visited her sometimes, and come away feeling quite ill. Viccy says horrible things about my poor little mother, and how Grandpa Turney was a Jew, and ruined Father's life by coming to live next door at Wakenham. Well, why do you look like that?"

Phillip put down his untasted cup of tea. "I think I'll go for a walk and get some fresh air. I may be the black sheep of the family, but I don't want to hear what my aunt and godmother

says about me or the Turneys, or anyone else. Even if Grandpa
was a Jew—which he was not—the Turney's have been Gaultshire
yeomen for centuries—what does it matter? He was damned
good to his family, perhaps that's what made the Maddisons
think he was Jewish? Do you remember how Grandpa, when
Hugh developed locomotor attaxia from syphilis, kept him at
home, and had a man to look after him for years, and only put
him into a Nursing Home when his mind was gone, properly
gone—not like Father's mind, which was clear and reasonable.
My protesting godmother got rid of *her* husband, George Lemon,
when he got syphilis, and *her* brother Hilary shipped him off to
Australia, to get him out of the way. There's your Christian
Protestant for you! Now *I'm* ranting, so I'll shut up!" He seized
the bottle. "Did you say help myself? You didn't? Well, it'll all
be the same in a hundred years time, so I will!" He filled three-
quarters of a tumbler, and drank half of it. "That's better!
Petrol for the old engine! That'll put up my revs! Now come
with me, dear sisters, and we'll have dinner at a Bournemouth
hotel."

"What, and leave poor Dads all alone?" cried Elizabeth.

"We can take him with us if you like."

"Isn't he awful?" Elizabeth appealed to Doris.

"Well, perhaps you're right. After all, this isn't Ireland, and I
don't suppose they'd welcome a wake in a 'respectable' middle-
class hotel. Sure, the sight of the ould gintleman, all stiffly formal,
would liven up the company, himsilf standin' up in a corner,
dressed in frock coat, top hat and holding a butterfly net! I could
tell the company his last words—'It isn't so bad dying, the trouble
is that one is so confoundedly stiff the next day!'" He refilled
the tumbler. "All right, I'll buy you another bottle! No, I haven't
had too much, I haven't had enough! By the way, is the coffin
screwed down? What a pity: we should drink a toast to your
poor old Dads. No, I'm not sneering. He used to be your dearest
Dads, I know, but he was never mine. He liked you, not me. And
I let him down, you know, just as you have done. I asked him
to come and live with us on the farm, but I never followed it up.
For one thing, our accommodation was pretty awful. So was I.
Worse than he ever was at his worst. He was only a nagger, he
never struck Mother. I bashed Lucy. So I'd like to see him before
he goes into the flames tomorrow. He had some tools here, I'll
find a screwdriver."

"You're tipsy," said Elizabeth, seizing the bottle. "And if you dare to take off the lid, I shall telephone for the police. I warn you, now!"

"You sound just like Father in the old days, dear sister. But I must not be rude to a guest in my house."

"*Your* house? I like that!"

"Well, I must tell you that, during the war, when Lucy and I, with her brother Tim Copleston and his wife, called here one day, he told me that I was his sole heir. I wrote to Doris shortly afterwards, saying that I intended, when he died, to share everything with you two. And so I'll keep my promise."

"Well," replied Elizabeth, "you're a bit behind the times! Father made a new will while he was in the nursing home, leaving all to me! And there's a clause in the will saying that if anyone tries to contest it, he or she will automatically be excluded from any benefit from the will."

"I'm not a lawyer, but I should say that if there be only one beneficiary from a will, that clause is invalid. Any crook could force someone to make a will under duress, and there would be no appeal against such an act, if your clause were legal!"

"So you're thinking of going to law, are you? Haven't you got enough already? Anyway, if you're going to threaten me, I'll call the police, as I warned you!" And with that she left the room.

"No, of course I'd never go to law, Doris. I spoke too hastily. She must think me pretty awful."

"She's the awful one, Phil. I've had her going on like this ever since I arrived." She looked at her brother intently. "Now I know what cousin Maude meant when she told me that Elizabeth had asked her to live with her here and look after Father! She said she'd pay for her services, but when Maude told her she couldn't come, as she was nursing at the London Hospital, Elizabeth said that she'd have 'to stall', because she couldn't look after him all by herself, or get anyone else. You see what I mean? She must have promised Father to take him home, if he made a will in her favour, for if she left her office before a pension was due, she would have nothing to live on."

Elizabeth, coming back into the room, cried, "Well, now you two conspirators know that this cottage, and all its contents, are mine. Father's last will leaves everything to me. Including the family plate! So if you try to take it away Phil, I'll telephone the police!"

"I'm afraid I was tactless and stupid in saying what I did say, Elizabeth. Of course I won't think of contesting Father's will.

But the family plate should go on down, you know, to the heir. There's Peter, now that Billy's gone. And I hope you won't mind my saying it, but you might like to consider leaving the set of books I gave Mother, to Peter—or sell them to me—"

"They're not worth much, anyway! They're in the sitting room. Come and see for yourself."

There stood the mahogany bookcase remembered from faraway Hillside Road. Along the top shelves were the volumes, each in its dust cover, all in what collectors would call mint condition.

"They'll be valuable one day, Elizabeth."

"That's what you say. I had a second-hand bookseller in yesterday, and all he offered me was ten bob for the lot."

"I'll give you fifty pounds for them. I'd like Peter to have them."

"I may want to read them myself. But why do you talk of money at this time? That's all you think about, isn't it? And our Father lying in his coffin!" she cried with rising hysteria. "Is that all you came for, to try and get what belongs to *me*? You've got everything that matters—children—what have *I* got? No-one cares whether I live or die! *You've* had two wives! What have *I* had? The boy I loved, Alfred Hawkins, what happened to him? Yes, you may well look guilty! You got your friend Peter Wallace to thrash him, didn't you? Poor little Alfie, who could not defend himself, who loved poetry, and watching butterflies, and looking up into the blue sky, while lying on his back among the grasses, in the Backfield! What happened to him? Do you remember? I do, if you don't! You told Father I'd been lying in the long grass with him, meaning we were spooning, when we weren't! Father turned against me from that moment! Alfie was killed in the war, and you came back. Alfie was ready to go, he was a pure spirit. You weren't, and you know it!"

"Yes, I know it. I assure you I've thought about that, many many times."

"Then don't try and take those books away from me! I know you don't like me, you never did like me! And you didn't really like Father, either. Do you know what he said to me once while he was lying in the nursing home? 'Do you think Phillip is ashamed of me, he has never invited me to stay with his family.' Then he said, 'I suppose that must be it, for I am not allowed to see my grandchildren.' That's what Father said, and that's why Aunt Viccy called you the black sheep of the family! You heard her say that Phillip was the black sheep of the family, didn't you Doris?"

"If you don't mind, I prefer to remain out of it. And I must remind you that I haven't yet seen the will."

"I've told you, Father left everything to me!"

"Look here," said Phillip, "we're all over-wrought. Let's go into Bournemouth, and have dinner. I don't think Father would mind. In fact, I don't believe he's here. I remember my great friend in the army, 'Spectre' West, telling me how it felt when he was unconscious after being hit. He saw himself from the air, in clear azure space, looking down at his body lying there—it was on Passchendaele Ridge—and he was clear thought or an idea, only that, just looking down, the idea being, *That isn't me, it's poor little body.* I'm not adding to his words, I give you my word of honour. He told me that after he'd recovered in hospital." He gave a shout. "Oh God! *That's* where I got that from, in my dream of seeing Billy lying dead, among the Alps! That's the source of what I believed was a vision the night before we heard he was killed!"

"There you are, you see!" cried Elizabeth, who had only half listened. "That's what I felt about poor Dads—his eyes looked up as though hearing a voice from above—then he looked amazed. That was when his soul left the body!"

"Yes," said Phillip, taking her hand. "I believe that is truth." He put his other arm round Doris. "Now that we are clear, dear sisters, let us look after what Hamlet called 'this machine'. Put on your coats, and we'll dine together! I'll drive carefully, I'm not tight, alcohol is a pure form of food."

They went to the Wrangaton Towers, and sat among pallid elderly people. There was whale meat or jugged hare for the main dish. The jugged hare looked remarkably like a cat, he thought, after a double whisky and soda, laughing to himself.

Phillip, staring through closed lids, legs crossed at ankles, arms folded—crusader in stone upon a tomb of lost hopes. Father in the early 'nineties bicycling to see mother on his Starley Rover, up the Rise to Sydenham Hill and down past the Crystal Palace. Stolen meetings in the summerhouse of the garden at Cross Aulton; the shuttered light of the lantern. Father and his butterflies, the rare Camberwell Beauty seen on his rum-impregnated cloth strips pinned to one of the elms on the Hill, in the circular light of his beloved dark lantern. The secret register-office marriage; Grandpa Turney finding out, knocking down Mother; departure to Wakenham and the little house above the railway cutting, once the Sydenham Canal. My birthplace. Father's life one long grind in the City. Office shadow'd in summer, befogged in winter. Slow wilting of butterfly-dreaming youth to bitter parenthood and final aloneness. Always the Faustian dream of ideal love. Myra walking slowly away, after putting down her bunch of Michaelmas daisies. He felt a sudden desperate need to go to her. I want to be loved by you, Myra, I want to love you.

Coffin going down in the lift to the furnace, parson's conventional words over. Yes, I'd like the ashes in an urn, please. Father's holiday at Lynmouth towards the end of the nineteenth century, so happy with his elder brother John, and Jenny his wife. You were only a baby, Phillip, we were all so happy, Aunt Dora was with us, it was her cottage, before she moved lower down the hill to be by the river. She loved the song of the river on its way to the sea. I stayed in Ionian cottage just before the war. I must scatter Father's ashes on The Chains of the high moor—

Grey shreds of calcined bone swept from one side of the oven —handful of Heraclitan grey ashes—mixed with coffin nails oxidised umber-red in furnace flames. German ashes in the suburbs of industrial towns, after Churchills' bombings; Jewish ashes at Belsen and Ravensbruck after Hitler's retaliation—phosphate and potash for wheat and potato fertiliser. Better that than the common sewer. Wheatfields on the Somme uplands, after one million German-British-French casualties, gave heavy yields of corn between the two wars. Dust to dust, ashes to ashes—great Jacobean poetry, the Bible.

The parson surprised that I asked that the nails be left in. Christ on the cross, nailed by Pharisean Establishment. Love thy enemy in the desert, and your tribe is soon extinct. Ring out the old, ring in the new, for God fulfils Himself in many ways, lest one good custom should corrupt the world. Hitler burned at his own stake. I must begin my novel series, or I'll die.

"Thank you. Please send the bill to me. Here is my address."

Father, I am sorry, truly I am. Is there revelation after death? If so, you will know all things, Father—

He felt to be at one with his father.

But not with Mother. And yet Mother was in spirit like himself—

He could not sleep. Elizabeth had said that as electricity was rationed, he must not switch on the light in his bedroom. He sat up in bed and wrote by his flash-light torch.

In my young childhood my mother, one night, came, dressed for going out, into my dark bedroom. "I am going away, Father does not want me any more, little son." I lay still. When she had gone I felt a sort of invisible darkness come upon me. I lay there without any feeling. When Mother came back, and knelt by the bed and asked me if I wanted to kiss her I said, "No thank you". I did not kiss her, nor do I remember ever kissing her again. I avoided all her attempts to kiss me. When she was dying of cancer I kissed her on the brow, without emotion. After her burial I prayed to go down into the grave with her. At the same time I silently shouted within myself that she leave me alone. And in times of stress my thoughts of her have been impatient: that she was so afraid of father, that she extended his nervousness: the result being that I grew up in fear of him, and a coward.

In the morning Phillip thought to present himself to his godmother, Aunt Victoria. He asked Elizabeth for her address.

"Don't blame me if you get a cold shoulder. Have you forgotten that she looks on you as the black sheep of the family?"

One of the older, Victorian houses among pines. Garden a wilderness. Weedy carriage sweep, overgrown rhododendrons, door green with dusty algae. The bell pull. A jangle below. Waiting. Windows barely visible through branches of laurel. Then a curtain corner moved, glimpse of white face, curtain dropping back.

When there was no further movement he thought to write a note and drop it through the letter-box. Was seeking paper when a quiet voice said, "The door is screwed up, will you come round to the kitchen door, by the lower gate?"

He found the way to a pale and rather beautiful ghost, dignified and thin, composed. He bowed to the ghost, who responded with the least inclination of the head, and led the way to what had been, in the old days, the housekeeper's room.

"Well, Phillip, this is a surprise."

"I could not leave without calling to pay my respects, Aunt Victoria. I've never forgotten the book you gave me when I was a boy, 'Our Bird Friends', by Richard Kearton. It changed my life."

"Oh," she said; and after a pause, "I did not feel equal to going to the funeral of my brother Dickie."

"I—I feel I should have come to offer escort, Aunt Viccy."

At the mention of her familiar name she smiled wanly. "We were such a happy family when we were young, you know. Your father was so kind to Dora and Effie and me, the younger ones. It was a *jolly* family, you must know. At least, when we were all together at Fawley." She sighed. "You should jolly well have stuck it out there, you know, when your Uncle Hilary bought back the land, Phillip! Hilary looked upon you as the *heir*." She looked at him steadily, "What is it in you, Phillip, that made you always so perverse, so 'agin' what ordinary decent people regard as the right thing?" She shook her head, and sighed. "Dora says you were the unhappiest small boy she ever knew, but *what* was it in you that got up against your father?"

"I think we were all just a little afraid of him. He was usually —well—irritable, and liable to be angry."

"It was the lies, Phillip that upset him. He could never rely on Hetty's word. She used to—what is the word—well, *prevaricate*. And you seldom told the truth to him, did you, Phillip? Come now, old chap, speak like a man!"

"I was a thief, a liar, a coward, and a mischief-maker on all planes, Aunt Viccy. Also I was, as you said just now, usually very unhappy."

"But that surely does not *explain* everything? Many of us have been unhappy at times, and had our cross to bear, but we did not, well, we did not behave *oddly* on that account. You were always what your father called the *wild boy*, you know, and caused him much grief and unhappiness. Punishment did not seem to alter you in any way."

"I suppose I was what he called a 'throw-back'. But the point is that the book you gave me helped enormously, in that I came to love the countryside, and particularly wild birds. They—they were almost my only love."

"I must say I enjoy your country books, you are certainly at your best there, as a writer. But your Donkin novels I found dull and dreary. You should not try to write novels, you know. It is not your line. Hilary, Dora and Dickie are all agreed about that. But why, oh why, did you put in that Donkin's grandfather died of drink? Surely that was muckraking, Phillip?"

"Well, you know, some people do take to drink. A wrong marriage—let me see now—how can I say it—well, a square peg in a round hole—"

God in heaven, what am I saying, I'm back in the Land of Victorian clichés.

"But *my* parents were ideally happy, Phillip, at least when we were young! It was the trouble with the land, you know, and

the depression of the 'eighties in farming, and the loss of tenantry.
Papa had to forego rents, even then, the farmers had to give up.
So mortgages had to be arranged. My father was by no means
alone, you know; many other landowners were forced to sell
their properties about that time. And my father's family had held
their land for more than five centuries. And yet, when Hilary
bought a considerable part of it back, you virtually refused it
from Hilary. Why, why, why?"

"I suppose because I'm a throwback, Aunt Viccy."

"It comes from your *mother*, Phillip! I am sorry, but it is the
truth. It was a case of mixed blood. The Jews, you know, have
been the cause of the ruin of our country. Not that I hold with
Hitler, he was an Austrian upstart, and took advantage of the
defeat of Germany to impose his own evil will upon dissident
elements, in alliance with the Catholics and Freemasons! Of
course he used both on the way up, then turned against them
when he had achieved what he set out to do. And what caused
him to be a wild man, Phillip? Shall I tell you? It was his Jewish
blood!" Leaning forward in her chair she said earnestly, looking
almost with appeal into his face, "Once a Jew, always a Jew!
The leopard cannot change its spots, remember." Then she said,
"Well, now tell me something cheerful about yourself, Phillip.
Come on, show a leg, as Hilary would say!"

He thought to lie back in the chair, hold up a leg, and waggle
it, but all he did was to say, "I don't want to say anything to
hurt *your* feelings, Aunt Viccy."

"I see you have begun to learn your lesson, Phillip. Other
people's feelings are as important as one's own."

Well, well, well! he thought, feeling Tim's face upon his own.
"Well, Aunt Viccy, I have *tried* to know my *own* defects."

"That is something, Phillip," she said earnestly.

"My sort is really alone. And my needs are simple. I've got a
shepherd's cot on Exmoor, and shall earn my own living by
writing, as I did in my cottage at Malandine after the first war.
Well, I am so glad I dared to call on you." He got up and kissed
her on the cheek, summoning resolution against upwelling
emotion to say, "I am taking Father's ashes to scatter on the
the Chains of Exmoor, he too was a wild boy locked up in duty,
he was happiest alone in wild places."

There was just time to call at the bank, to see a copy of his
father's will made during his illness. A local branch, had, accord-

ing to Elizabeth, been appointed executor and trustee.

St. Martin's Little Summer appeared to be the time for the migration of souls in that town of the near-spent and the aged : for in the room marked *Trustee Department* several people were waiting as in a dentist's ante-room, but without bestrewn and dated copies of *Punch,* diminutive *Strand Magazine,* and *Tatler.* A man, apparently a bank official, in his late 'twenties, and wearing a suit appropriately dark, was standing in one corner, explaining something to a customer. When Phillip's turn came the official, before attending to someone else, gave him a copy of the will to read, together with some papers which related to money due to him from a trust made by his mother, the income of which capital sum having gone to his father for life, was now to be divided among her three children.

The will was brief and clear. It had been signed and witness'd three weeks previously. Cottage and all its contents, together with all moneys to Mavis Elizabeth Maddison. Nothing for his 'little friend' Myra. Having read the two-page document, Phillip signed the trust papers, to save time. The official was standing near him, but when some minutes later he gave the papers to the official he was told that the signatures were not valid.

"You signed your name without being witness'd. You must sign again."

"I thought that as you were in the room—"

"I can't see to everyone at once. You'll have to write your signature again. No, not now, I am called to the telephone."

When the official returned he said, "Your sister, Miss Maddison, has just telephoned to enquire if you have seen a copy of your father's will. Now, if you will sign your name again, I shall be able to act in the capacity of witness."

When this was done Phillip said, "I hope I was not out of order in asking to see the will?"

"You have, I understand, seen a typescript copy. If you wish to see the will, you should follow the procedure laid down by my department, and apply through your solicitor for a certified copy. The alternative is to wait until the will is proved, when a copy will be available at Somerset House in London. Good afternoon."

Poor young clerk. Your hopeful flesh battered by the words, words, words of old flesh. Young flesh reserved from the services, denied freedom from civilian servitude. Better the chop than the slow mortification of an office saturated by the fears and anxieties of the living dead. Laura and himself. Laura crying, *I must be free*—from the power of the past : the dead. Where can I go to be saved. Where can I die, and my body never seen again? The sea's priestlike ablution—the salt, estranging sea—the deep, the green, the serpent-haunted sea.

That night when he saw Laura in her room in Old Compton Street he asked her if she would return with him to Exmoor.

"What now, Phillip? I'm afraid I can't, I must look after Beth, my friend who is in trouble. I'm sorry. And I *must* finish my novel before I come to you. I'll write to you. You will write to me, won't you? And when I come down to 'Buster's' place, you will be near, and we shall see each other, won't we? I am with you, always."

Chapter 9

MEETING WITH RIVERSMILL

I wish I had kept my Norton motor-bicycle, my 'Brooklands Road Special' model, belt-driven with Phillipson automatic expanding pulley. Why did I let cousin Arthur swindle me out of it, he was my best friend in those days after the old war. God, it's a quarter of a century ago that I and my lovely bike bounded up this narrow road for the first time, up and up to the Great Plain, with its barrows and beech hangers, grey grass and air of lonely space and almost primeval wildness. My hair was black in those days, I returned so hopefully to the West Country in 1919, just after the war. Then, two years later, Valerian Cottage with Julian Warbeck. What books would we write, what fame seek together! But Julian wrote his books, as they said in the pub, with a pint pot; *ergo*, Julian arrogant and quarrelsome. That marvellous summer of 1921! The footprints from the sea, I followed them with my head held low, playing a game, and they led across the sands to my first sight of Barley sitting beside her mother, their backs to a rock above the tide-line.

Long brassy summer of 1921, no rain falling between April and September. On the rough grazing above Valhalla maggot-loosened skins of mad sheep flapping as their feet rattled on hot shale scree, always moving on but never escaping the foetid buzz of blowflies. Flies were merciful on the summer battlefields. The Yorkshireman with arm blown off in wide no-man's land between Croiselles and Bullecount in the Hindenburg Line. Wound cleaned of suppurating flesh by maggots. He lifting arm-stump above elbow void of proud flesh, happy to be back, grateful for 'them fookin maggots'. I must write, write, write, for the night cometh.

Shall I turn south for Exeter, and the Channel Coast? Malandine Village and Barley's grave? How shall I my true love know, from another one, save in words, words, words? Only by words shall I see myself again beside her, transformed, sharing all day the unnumbered smile of ocean with Aeschylus, while we walked home above the wine-dark evening sea of Homer.

Or turn north to Lynmouth, and Aunt Theodora in her cottage beside the rushing Lyn? How old is she now—well over seventy. Perhaps she won't want to see me, she turned against the Germans —her mother's people—in the war. And against me too, according to Elizabeth. *She knows about your illegitimate son, by that girl. So did Father. That's why he left you out of his will!* Still, I mustn't let that stop me doing my duty. I'll go by Minehead and Porlock and stay only a couple of minutes.

True love is like sunlight; it casts no shadow on the soul. The feeling between Laura and me is not love, it comes from the blue halls of Dis. Are we 'dead souls' seeking resurrection through the non-existing inner peace of the other? You say you have never been at ease with any man, Laura; nor have I with any woman save Barley. No, not really with Melissa. What was it that stopped me? Made all feeling blank? She offering her natural love, revealing the compassion of her body, all gentleness—and courage. For she was virgin. Yet I was never 'withdrawn' from Lucy. Because I did not love Lucy? I was sealed off *entirely* from Lucy, my selfish little ego practically raped her on the marriage night. My personality was decayed—scattered—in dark fragments. Is it the same with Laura? A woman corroded by fear, or despair, crying save me, save me, from fear of loneliness. Yet who am I to talk? Am I a disintegrating old man needing a young woman, almost any young woman who is comely—to sacrifice on my altar of fear?

If personality—essence—is reality, then I am but an apparition from the Western Front, *which was in being for millions of other youths long before August 1914.* For we were the heirs of our fathers' and grandfathers' minds; our bodies purged their sins on the battlefield. We that were left grew old, for age to weary and the years to condemn, and at the going down of the sun, and in the morning, no-one to remember them.

And yet—in a way, yes—I enjoyed the war, by and large. For the war did not maim me, it released me. For it was the Greater Love War!

Down the hill : mind the sharp bend to the left : slow down to fifty : there on the right lies bleak Stonehenge. If only I was on my Norton, lying along the tank, arms spread to wide handle-bars, moulding my body to the breast-like swellings of these hills, bracing myself to accept the sudden plunging hollows lying all

Danäe to the stars. God, I had hope in those early days after the war!

The Great Plain like the Somme country: eroded landsherds —lychetts—lanchetts where flints had fallen from chalk-breaks in the turf acidulated by the centuries' rains. John Masefield's *The Old Front Line* one of the great books of the 1916 Big Push. Machine gun nests on the landsherds of those wider downs above the Somme, Moonrakers and Back-to-Fores—Wiltshire Regiment and Dorsets—mucking the aerated wheat-fields of Piccardy. Six-foot subsoiling, all free—Somme cornlands in heart for a century, the composted lost heart of England. O my friends, come home, come home!—be with me, Baldwin and 'Grannie' Henshaw, 'Spectre' West and 'the boy General'—Colonel Kingsman and the Iron Colonel—Lance-Corporal Hitler shepherding his sixteen-year students, arm-in-arm across the Menin road and through Sanctuary Wood, to be shot down in stumbling masses. Zandevoorde and the Brown Wood Line, and Cranmere yelling *Up ve old Blood'ounds.* Jesu Christus, help me with your compassion to write my Greater Love War!

Onwards to the West, by Mere and Wincanton, Langport and Taunton, turn north down the valley under the Quantocks for Dunster with its brown-stone castle on a motte, or hill; left-handed to Minehead and the road winding through coastal meadows to Porlock. Here, petrol and oil for the Eagle, beer for the driver. Now I'm for it! Porlock hill and its two steep bends, the second said to be one in four, but more like one in three. Before the first turn, change to bottom gear. This turn is right-handed, it must be charged, one is well away up: now for the left-handed bend, looming steep as the wall of a house. The Silver Eagle takes it in its flight! And on and up and up, second gear now, third— faster—faster—change to top gear, passing the thousand-foot contour to see an embered sun, and the charred ruins of sulky nimbus strewing the world's rim upon the Atlantic. The moon is over my shoulder, the hosts of heaven are there to greet me! Wonderful how much better an engine runs when the driver has had a pint!

Mechanical man and metal eagle flying along through heather and furze, seeing twinkling lights along the Welsh coast across the Severn Sea. The sun's disgust mouldering to little pieces of dying ember. We are all more or less in ruin. Poor old Eagle, the springing isn't what it was, shackle-bolts worn, shimmer in the steering: and suddenly they were descending from the moor, and there was the Blue Ball Inn before them. *It's a poor heart that never rejoices,* battle cry of Julian Warbeck, armed with a pewter pint-pot! That voice, out of the past.

Phillip longed to see old Julian. And having toasted the imagined arrogant face he went into Devon, round and about the snaking road until, abruptly, there was Lynmouth far down below. Now he was down, and turning right over the bridge. I haven't seen Aunt Dora since before the war. Ionian Cottage, named after her beloved Greece visited during Edwardian days. It was somewhere beside the river. Can this be it? A wilderness garden, astrew with waste paper blossoms of dead summer days? Unpainted door and window frames, curtains seeming fixed behind dull bubbled glass panes. Sad. He tried to knock, the knocker resisted. It was set in rust. He tapped. Nothing. Wrenched free knocker, it banged unexpectedly loud and hollow. Had she gone away, died? Elizabeth would have told him. Rapped with his knuckles. Knelt to peer through letter box. A globe of light approaching, oil lamp borne by a ghost. A voice, weak as the pith of a reed saying,

"Is that you, Elizabeth?"

"I'm Phillip. Phillip Maddison, Aunt Dora," he replied, still kneeling by the open letter-slit.

"I thought you were not coming until next month, Elizabeth. I must ask you to wait until I can set down the lamp."

Bolts slowly withdrawn, slow rattle of chain, key squeaking. He stood up. The third family apparition he had seen that month stood beside four feet of *The Times Literary Supplement* piled against the wall.

"Who are you?"

"I'm Phillip, Aunt Dora. Your nephew."

"It is very late to call. I am just going to bed."

"I'm so sorry. May I call sometime during the day—any day to suit you. I have come to live on the moor, near the hut circles."

"Why have you come here?"

"I must not keep you, Aunt Dora. Goodnight."

He drove over the high-arched bridge which spanned the river, and at once before him was the remembered hill which rose left-handed up and up through trees growing on the almost sheer sides of the glen footed by white foaming waters far below. He was making for Barbrook and the remembered narrow lane past a water mill which led to the heather common across which stood the shepherd's cot. It was bottom-gear work, he must be careful not to over-rev the old engine. He stopped past the sharp right-hand bend to Lynton, and leaned on the stone-wall, listening to the dull roar of unseen waters.

There was a strange, chuckling noise rising out of the glen, perhaps of multitudinous echoes from unfallen leaves among the oaks and beeches of that dark abysmal place, where Shelley had walked with Harriet Westbrook, a wife magnanimously married to save her from a harsh father—but not strong enough to save from a suicide's death by drowning when the poet had gone off with Mary Woostonecroft to Italy—and his own death in the waters of the Gulf of Spezzia. Poor innocents all.

That dark chuckle coming up from the Glen : he remembered the same unearthly sounds arising from the Pass of Roncesvalles during that moonlit walk with friends, years ago, from Spain into France : the year he had found Barley. The same innocent moon was shining over the high peaks of the Pyrenees—which in the following year drew upon the estuary of the Two Rivers that great tide which drowned cousin Willie, a few miles from where I am standing now. This is my land and sea of ghosts, an extension of my greater phantasmagoria of the Western Front, where only the wan light by which poets live can transcend terrible nights of fire and flare upon that livid wound across Europe's no-man's land which drained, then, and once again as now, all Europe.

"It's all too much for me alone!" he shouted to the wind. "How can I hold to the old war in one head, *and* the terrors of mass-man of the second war! Blood calling to blood, not for resurrection, but for revenge! And when the whole world may be destroyed, become as the moon, the tottering lady of Shelley's prophetic imagination."

Farther on, at the head of the glen, now a small coombe with lesser trees of willow and alder beside rock-white waters glittering with the pale fires of the crookback moon, Phillip came to the grey stone straddle of a pack bridge. In his exhausted state he missed the way, by turning left-handed over the bridge instead of to the right : to find before him a sheer stony lane, no more than an ancient sled-track, rising on naked rock to the appalling summit called Beggar's Roost. If the engine blew up, it blew up. Slithering and slewing at full throttle, with tyres near-burning, he flogged the engine in a skidding slow crawl, sometimes crab-wise, to the summit, and over the last hump, stopped to the thundering boil of the fanless-engine. The Silver Eagle relied on speed into rush of cold air through honeycomb of radiator, to cool block bored for the six cylinders and pistons. He waited until the boiling ceased, and only then did he dare to press the starter button. Was the magneto burned out, or the platinum points of the contact-breaker? Or the spring? His heart waited. The engine fired! Onward slowly: chassis springs laid, resilience gone, steel become iron. Even steel dies, returning to ancestral crystals.

Sirius shaking rainbow fires over the black line of the moor, so he must be going south, but whither, dimly knew. Down and down, skidding on shillets, coming to another pack-bridge over one of the many brooks, or waters, breaking down from the northern slopes of the moor. Uphill once again, until he topped the rise and descended to a wider, wooded valley noisy with swift confluent streams. The stars swung round, Orion was bright before him over the roof of a grist-mill.

Round a rising bend, and abruptly a chess-board of window lights in what appeared to be a castellated building. And driving on slowly in second gear, he came to the end of the stony track, and by the dim farmhouse on the left knew where he was. Dare he risk the springs—or engine sump—over the heather and furze of the remembered common? What if he hit a concealed rock? Why hadn't he reconnoitred the way during his first visit? Very slowly, in bottom gear, engine little more than idling, driving on hand-throttle, feet on clutch and brake pedals ready to stop. And so, without mischief, he passed the site of a group of Bronze Age hut circles, beyond which stood the shepherd's cot.

And there was a pale glow upon the heather. He watched the rising of the eclipsed and fretted ruin of the moon while recalling with melancholy its shaded rim seen rising over London rooftops from Laura's attic window—then with the shock of memory cried "Bloody fool!" at himself. For, standing beside her, he had started to tell her how he had seen the same moon when full, rising out of the Flanders plain to silhouette the Bavarians coming up in masses to attack Messines ridge on Hallowe'en, 1914. He meant to tell her how the moon *had* been an object of terror, of his world lost ... but no longer—because he had met *her:* that when she came down to the shepherd's cot it would be shining with a gentle, companion light, for both of them, warm flesh and clear spirit together. But she had broken away, crying *You are dead and don't know it* while pulling open the door to run down into the street. He had followed her, walked beside her on the pavement, she unspeaking all the way back to her street door; let herself in with her key and leaving him outside.

There was a bottle of whisky in the corner cupboard. He drank from it; and feeling better returned outside to say aloud to the moon, "Attend me, all my dear comrades of the Greater Love War!" Then to write in his note book.

I must never allow my personal constrictions with Elizabeth to occlude the truth that she is lonely because loveless as the hunch-backed moon. Did Richard Crookback stutter? My poor moon, deprived of its full light by mother earth—withered, dead. Stutter-stumbles eternally through the sky; lifeless, childless.

Open door casting wan shadow on lime-ash floor. He lit the cold wick of the candle in its latten stick : faithful friend. The moon gave her wasted light, rising to challenge taper. Match to dry furze sticks in open hearth. Kettle on lapping crook. Thank God I washed up plate, cup, knife, fork and spoon before I left. I must eat, a duty to keep the mind calm. Lay supper, be tidy—plate, knife, mug, spoon—I and my father, Richard Maddison—are you with me, poor father, from your glass jar of ashes and coffin nails on the chimney shelf?

Then another shot of whisky, imagining Cousin Willie to be with him—"Your health, old boy!"

Switch on radio.

Late night news from the American radio in Occupied Germany, facing the Russians.

Ten Nazi leaders, 'not one uttering a word of regret as he went to his death on the scaffold', hanged at Nuremberg. Scaffolds erected in gymnasium under ten fierce electric lights. *Ribbentrop* held his head high. Handcuffs removed, hands tied behind back. At scaffold, "State your name!" Followed American officer up steps. Feet bound. "Have you any last words to say?" In ringing voice cried, "God protect Germany!" Black hood over head. Noose adjusted Crash—bump. Rope hung tautly through open trap. Eerie sounds as rope cracking as it swung to and fro. Twenty minutes passed, then doctor pronounced death.

Three scaffolds; one used, two held in reserve. *Field-Marshal Keitel.* As on parade. Shaved, washed. "I call on the Almighty that He may have mercy on the German people. Over two million went to their death before me. I now follow my sons. All for Germany!"

Interval for smoking. French and Russians exchanged cigarettes, Americans puffed at their own.

Kaltenbrunner. Slow walk. Efforts made to save his life after a cranial haemorrhage were unsuccessful. Dressed all anyhow. "I have served my German people and Fatherland with willing heart. I regret crimes committed in which I had no part. Good luck, Germany".

Alfred Rosenberg. Followed by two padres but declined their services.

Frick in check sporting suit, scowled at guards, yelled, "Long live eternal Germany".

Streicher burst through the door, and was thereafter held and forced across floor to scaffold. Roared, "Heil, Hitler!" and later, "Now to God! The Bolsheviks will get you next!", to the guards. Then, "Adele, my loving wife!"

Sauckel refused to dress, taken to scaffold screaming, "I pay my respects to American soldiers and officers but not to American Jews! I die innocent! God protect Germany, and my family!"

Field-Marshal Jodl. Smart, soldier-like. "I salute you, my Germany!"

Seyess-Inquart. Limping, tired, formal. Executioners were Woods of U.S. Army; Pierrepoint the elder, Britain's own.

Having made a fair copy of hastily scribbled notes, Phillip went to bed supperless, thus failing to sleep except in snatches, and lying open to the Furies. The only thing to do was to light a candle, and write.

Herman Göring shot down Manfred Cloudesley over Mossy Face wood at Havrincourt in 1918. He saw that his enemy, who had killed nine of his Richthofen Staffel pilots, had the best surgeons and treatment in hospital. This morning Göring committed suicide. Better to have died on the cross, old Knight of the *Ordre pour le Mérite*.

The same moon hung above the broken roofs of London as 'Buster' Cloudesley left his club in St. James' Street and walked in the direction of Old Compton Street. There was little traffic. Petrol was still rationed; old motor cars had yet to make top prices in a sellers' market. He had some stored in various places in the Home Counties, having bought half-a-dozen Rolls and Bentleys during the 1940–41 blitz on London, paying no more than £200 each, at their various mews and garages. Their owners' insurance policies did not cover the risk of damage by riot, civil commotion, or war.

"What a 'Peace'!" he said aloud. Bananas were news. There was a half-page photograph of a bunch in *The Daily Crusader*.

Ah, the whirligig of time! There was Wallington Christie, once of the original Peace Pledge Union, urging, in his literary-philosophical quarterly magazine *The New Horizon* that the Allies drop the atom bomb on Moscow!

'Buster' had read the article while flying back from Norway, and thought it was merely the swing of the pendulum in the life of a man starting out as pacifist and ending up prang-merchant. Herbert Morrison, Home Secretary, pacifist in War One and fire-eater in War Two. There was an old Tolstoyian type living on Exmoor, vegetarian conscientious objector when young, Home Guard hero in War Two (given an all-wooden dummy rifle lest he knock off one of his chums). My father, who collected five gongs in War One—including the Cross for his lone fight against the Richthofen squadron in 1918—threw them out after the Armistice, and went into reverse to a watery grave.

'Buster's' pale moon-shadow slanted away from his moving feet, a Doppelgänger knocked askew, moving always apart from his marionette-like walk. I am encaged like the remains of Europe.

Those emigrant Yanks letting Russia into Eastern Europe—strategical ignorance of top-brass Pentagon, following the tactical ineptitude of Eisenhower, desk major when the shooting war started. Stalin sitting pretty with most of the German scientists of the Baltic experimental station in the bag. Soon the Ruskies will have the know-how about rockets, and then—a fallen-out England carcinomatical sans all mammalian life—birdless, treeless, even flealess, surrounded by a bitter sea.

'Buster' stopped, regarding his shadow. An ever-torturing mental picture inhibited all his hopes of Laura. He saw her blue eyes bulging with sexual frustration as she got out of bed to take benzedrine pills, she coming back quietly to say *Darling it doesn't matter. I want to look after you, but will you mind if I make love to Phillip?*

She make love! He cursed her image: and moving his feet into reverse, returned to his club.

Ah well, matriarchy was on the way. Maybe there would be foxes, birds, trees and fleas again in Old England!

In the morning Phillip walked down to Lynmouth to buy his weekly rations and collect letters marked *Poste restante*. He sat on a stone wall, below which the river rushed amidst great boulders.

My Prospero!

I must be honest with you, and myself, if I am to be good for you. Why, perhaps, I am difficult in that I am like Brunnhilde, ringed in flame; and perhaps charred within. You have read Scott Fitzgerald's *Tender is the Night,* and so you will know the cause of the problem of Nicole, the schizophrenic wife of Dick Diver. Well, the same cause here. Although Nicole was paternally raped at sixteen years, I was at eight. But truly, I did not pick you from a father-fix, but because I knew you were me inside. I knew it at a glance, and I hoped you would penetrate behind my Gorgon-mask.

Darling, I hope to join you soon, when the moon, which I talk to every night as I retrace our foot-steps along the Embankment, is full. O, Dian's heavenly light, so serene, so calm with all wisdom! I thought of you as I watched it rising, and your poor little lost-boy stutterings to me, so war-bloody-minded the other night! I hope to see you soon, for I must earn my bread and margarine, and by so doing help my dear 'Buster' as his part-time secretary. At the moment I am looking after a little friend, who looks like sixteen but is twenty-eight. She may, later, go to work at 'Buster's' place with me. Beth married a sadist who broke her, he aborted her again and again, she wanted a child, he forced her to take a lover and she pretended to have one, while he used to whip his mistresses. Then he gave her drugs to stop her worrying but really because he wanted her to die. Her baby was started before she fled from him and it died last year when it was four. A darling little girl, and ever since my friend has been suicidal.

Now for a secret (I know I can trust you, a *prieux chevalier*). This morning I stood outside a London prison where they were to hang my little friend's husband. We both wore slacks, she with her long brushed hair hanging down her back, sobbing and wringing her hands. I wept too. When we hang others we hang ourselves.

You would like Beth, Phillip. As I said, she may come down with me shortly, but for the time being I must remain in London. I know you will regard all I've written in confidence. There are many girls like Beth in London, alone and dying for want of loving kindness. She is so sweet and kind, she still grieves for her husband even after his sadistic murder of that poor prostitute whom he got to write a suicide note before he turned on the gas, after he'd given her those pills, but he left his finger-prints on the tap as you may have read in the papers.

There's something very wrong with our civilisation. Perhaps if we had lost the war we might have revived as Germany did under Hitler in the 'thirties. London is now a terrible jungle, the jackals are on top.

When I first came here, after the war, I got a job with a man who said he was a photographer. I knew nothing of London. He had a studio and one day he appeared in a black brassière and things and begged me to whip him. He cried when I stopped. He grovelled! I

fled, while he screamed at me to be a Christian! London is full of
fairies, queens, and oddments. No, I don't intend to put them in my
books, not like that anyway. I see them through a prism, not as you do,
through a glass darkly. That sort of art died in your war, it died
before the big battalions began to disinherit the earth. You are really
the unknown soldier, miraculously reprieved—or are you the Flying
Dutchman? O I love you so, I'll die if ever you leave me. I don't care
if you're ninety or nineteen, you're my sweet darling Phillip and I
want to be with you in the country. I love the sea and walks, and to
live a very quiet private life, very slow tempo. Do you know I prayed,
after I met you, to God to thank Him for sending you to me.

Piers, poor boy, is in deep trouble. He is sleeping in my bed while
I write this by my candle, a solitary gleam meditatively moving
its light slightly one way then the other as though in unison with your
presence hovering about me. No, Piers and I didn't make love, or
rather try momentarily to out-range our derangements and tensions
through coitus. What a word! Snaky. Poor boy, he is broken by his wife
having left him. He spoke so restrainedly to me in the Medicean, and
mentioned you, and I told him of my ride on my cycle up to your farm
during the phoney war and back again next day after I'd flung the
food-money you gave me at you, or rather I skidded the coin, what
was it, a crown, over your shiny refectory table. I went to London soon
afterwards, and later, during the blitz, joined the Q.A.N.S. I loved
living in a community of nurses, and men being healed after wounds
and burns. Didn't you like your war, too, because you were with the
chaps?

All my love, darling Phillip, from Laura.

P.S. I have just heard on the wireless that they have hanged all those
loyal generals and others at Nuremberg. Weep no more, my Prospero,
for the sins of the world! Your staff shall never be broken, your books
never sink deeper than plummet sound: never, never, never while
this machine is to your Laura.

Sitting on the wall, wondering whether or no he should call on
Aunt Dora, Phillip saw a man he had known in East Anglia
looking down at the river. Riversmill, the horse painter, greeted
him cheerily with,

"Well, my lad, I heard you'd travelled in a circle, and come
back to the West Country! You can't beat Somerset, Devon and
Cornwall, now East Anglia's all derelict airfields and rusty wire
barriers along the coast from Lincolnshire to Kent. I know your
shepherd's cot, thought of it myself for a studio, but it's just a
little too far up the coombe. And dam' sight too near that American who calls himself among other things Caspar Schwenkfelder,
Doctor of Diaphany of Little Rock Academy. All a money-making

racket, like spiritualism and all the usual sort of nonsense that
starts up, like a virus, after every war. Lynmouth's full of cranks
these days. There's a chap going around, calling himself Piston,
who believes in flying saucers!"

"I wonder if it's the same Piston who was here in nineteen sixteen, after July the First? He was a crazy sort of chap."

"He's crazy all right. But harmless. But that fellow calling
himself 'Doctor of Diaphany' is a menace. Lives in that Victorian
Castle—it lies on the coombe-side east of your cot. It was built by
the Sugar King who went bust playing the organ all day and
night when the bailiffs were in. But that was before your time,
when I was a young Edwardian buck of sorts."

The sharp eye of the painter saw that Phillip looked tired.
He changed his manner. "How's the family? Still in East Anglia.
Well, you'll need to be on your own, until you're bedded down in
your novels. Come and dine with us tonight at Molly
Bucentaur's. She knows your books, and likes 'em, so do I. 'Buster'
Cloudesley's coming, he's a great man! Spends his time gliding. We can give you a shake-down for the night in our cottage
at Willowpool. Be there at seven and we'll take you on to Molly's.
No, of course don't dress. Come as you are. I'm going up the
glen to paint now, the light changes every minute under those
beeches. Right, see you later."

Phillip was jubilant. The perplexity—a sort of double-dealing
of the mind—over Laura was gone for the moment. He had somewhere to go that evening, something to look forward to! He took
new interest in the river, seeing it as a score of separate streams
bursting out of the great turf-sponge of the high moor: he must
explore all the threads and runners which had channered im-
memorially the faces of the rocks. Salmon would now be moving
up to spawn in little runners clear of silt, and bright with oxygen
absorbed from the pure air. He had heard that sixty brooks, or
waters as they were called, fed the East and West Lyn rivers in
their confluent descents to the Severn Sea.

PART TWO

LADIES OBSERVED

'The work in progress becomes the poet's fate and determines his development. It is not Goethe who creates Faust, but Faust who creates Goethe.'

Jung

Chapter 10

AT COUSIN MOLLY'S

Shortly before seven o'clock that evening Phillip arrived at Willowpool. After a couple of glasses of sherry, Mrs. Riversmill drove them to Molly Bucentaur's. The last lane before they arrived was steep, and loose with shillets of stone. It was dark when they arrived. A diesel engine thumped upon the night air. Two rounded pillars of shillet and a seven-barred gate of oak. New, he felt, as he got out to hold it open. Mrs. Riversmill wanted to drive in backwards, the easier to get out again. He thought to guide her by standing between the nearside pillar and tail of the motor, to give soundings.

"Two feet clear of the post this side! Come on back! You'll clear it on that lock."

There was a smell of goats upon the night air. The driver seemed to lose her nerve. "I can't see!" she cried. So he ran round and shone a torch downwards on the offside pillar.

"I'm not an idiot! I can see what I'm doing this side!"

He returned to his original stance. "All clear on your near-side."

"What good's that to me? I can't see *my* side now you've gone away," so he darted behind the car, and as she went back slowly, moved the beam first one side then the other.

"What's the good of that? You're just dazzling me! Why the hell don't you let me get in my own way? What are all those yellow eyes looking at me? Switch off your torch, you fool!"

"They're goats!" cried Riversmill.

The driver went forward, before reversing once more. There followed a scraping sound and a bump. The engine stalled. The driver yelled, "There you are, you see, you've mucked me up completely, so that I don't know what I'm doing! Why don't you mind your own business?" as she went forward again into the lane.

Something pushed Phillip from behind. It was a goat. He flashed the torch away from the car. Several other goats were

105

standing about. Bleats arose as a light was switched on to illumine
the area before a white-washed cottage front. A door opened and
a girlish voice said, "Do I hear sounds of revelry by night?"
There was much bleating while many apparitions clustered around
a spry young woman walking towards them, hair *au page boy,*
rosy cheeks and smiling lips. She and the goats leapt nimbly
aside as the car drove fast backwards and stopped with a lurch.
"So glad you could come, my dears. And at last I have met 'the
water wanderer'! Tilly darling, how sweet of you to bring Cousin
Phillip to our little shack! Freddie, did you paint the Glen, or
was the light bad? Now do come in, everybody. No, not you,
King Billy!" she cried, addressing a large horned goat. "Take
your wives back to the paddock."

She turned to Phillip. "The last of the Brockholes herd. How
do you like Exmoor after East Anglia?"

"It's like coming home."

"How is Lucy? I'm longing to meet her again—and the children. D'you know, I've never seen them? Time flies!"

"What a sight East Anglia is now," said Riversmill. "Rows and
rows of Halifaxes and Lancasters, all along a couple of hundred
miles of the Eastern Counties, the perching places for rooks and
crows. In some, squatters are living. Great cruciform runways a
mile long each way, ruining the countryside."

"Come into our shack!" she replied. To Phillip, "We built it
ourselves, all cardboard and corrugated iron, tied together by
string," as they entered what to Phillip was a new, well-propor-
tioned room, lit by concealed lights revealing panel'd walls, parquet floor, tables and chairs all of some pinkish wood.

"We threw two cottages into one, and knocked this up ourselves," said the hostess, seen now to be white-haired with
enamelled cheeks and lustrous eyes above mascara'd lashes. "I'm
Molly Bucentaur" she said with a smile showing splendid teeth.
"Lucy and I share a grandmother. So you and I are cousins!"
she said, glowing before him.

"How perfectly splendid!" he replied, with sudden happiness.

"We've read all your books. Miranda, my elder daughter, knows
every word by heart. I've promised to take you up after you've
had a drink. Do help yourself from the sideboard."

"What lovely wood."

"It's Brockholes yew, Phillip. Bring your glass with you."

She led him up open stairs. Within a bedroom two girls and
a small boy were lying, each in a separate bed with reading lamp

at bed-head. The boy, seeing round his book who had come, immediately went under the bedclothes.

"Imogen, this is Cousin Phillip."

The younger of the two girls continued to lie back, murmuring, 'How do you do,' while her sister sat up, a mass of dark hair falling on shoulders and pyjama jacket which revealed the curves of a fully developed bust.

"I've brought Cousin Phillip! Isn't he good to come all this way to see us?"

A muffled "No!" came from under blankets.

"Yes!" cried the dark girl, as Molly turned to Phillip, saying, "Miranda's mad about anything to do with the Great War." She turned to her daughter. "Well, I've captured your hero at last! No, Anda darling, I won't say any more, I'm going now." With an arch look from the open door she said, "Don't let her tire you, will you, Phillip?"

"I feel like Parsifal among the Flower Maidens."

"There, now, isn't that charming, Anda?" She returned to kiss her; then the younger daughter. The boy ducked the embrace, with a stern "Mother!", as he leapt out of bed to hide beneath it. She playfully smacked his bottom, and left.

Phillip, standing with a smile near the dark girl, said, "Thank you for reading my books."

"Well, you know, Cousin Phillip, you're a pretty good writer. You're the only English author I know who can present the truth objectively in all dimensions. 'Buster' and I are agreed about that. He says that the folly of England's leadership throughout the past fifty years, which your writings illustrate in their own right, reminds him of Goethe's *Zauberlehrling*, except that there remains no magician to undo the spell now leading the white races to ruin and their civilisation to extinction."

"Unless the magician, or rather the prophet, is Hereward Birkin."

"I haven't heard of Hereward Birkin."

"You will."

There was a pause. Then she said, "We've all read your *Water Wanderer*. I've wept enough to 'water heaven with my tears', over that book. Wasn't your otter really a woman, Cousin Phillip?"

She gazed at him with large brown eyes.

Molly said in the doorway, "Is she a swan, Phillip, or just a young goose?"

"Both are beautiful birds, perhaps she has something of the swan. And if all her generation has the fidelity of both swan and goose, the human race will cease to be predatory and cannibalistic."

"*There*, Anda, you heard what Cousin Phillip said? Isn't he a sweet man? I must flee. 'Buster' has just arrived."

The boy shouted, "Send up 'Buster', Mummie, won't you, to say goodnight? I must know if he's got his new glider," and disappeared.

"Gliding—they do that on the Dunstable Downs," said Phillip.

"Do you glide, sir?"

"I want to, Roger."

"How wizard!"

"I must go now, young cousins."

Miranda held out her arms, hugged him, touched him on the cheek with her lips; then, a little overcome by her temerity, turned round to bump her pillow violently before sitting back in position as before the visitation.

That morning in London 'Buster' had gone to see Laura. He found her tender, compassionate, a true friend. Even so, he said au revoir to her with relief. His wounds had been severe and terminal. He dreamed vaguely of some heroic occasion when he might lose his life by self-sacrifice. He found some relief in driving an open four-and-a-half-litre super-charged Bentley on full throttle across the Great Plain, while he ruminated upon an idea that had almost become a dedication since a meeting with Hereward Birkin, who had given him a copy of a book, composed in prison during the war, declaring that both Fascism and its opponent, Financial Democracy, had failed; and that the nations of Europe must unite, all grievances and revengeful feelings changed to brotherhood, in 'Europe a Nation'.

'Buster' knew the opening passage of Birkin's book by heart, after several readings, or rather incantations. *"We were divided, and we were conquered. That is the tragic epitaph of two war generations. Those words alone should adorn the grave of the youth of Europe—"*

During the battle of the Reichswald, when he had been badly wounded, 'Buster' was taken prisoner and treated with chivalry by the enemy. Reichsmarschall Hermann Göring, learning of the prisoner's name, visited him in hospital, to ask if he was related to the Major Manfred Cloudesley who was one of his heroes of the Great War. "Such bravery, such courage in the air, Colonel!" He was delighted to learn that this Lord Cloudesley was Manfred's son. And the Führer had a high admiration for dutiful English soldiers, he declared. He had, indeed, offered to put the Wehrmacht at the disposal of the English, should the British Empire ever be attacked. Yes, he had made that offer, and when the English Government had declared war in September 1939, over a matter of the lost provinces in East Prussia returning to the Reich, the Führer had been as surprised as he was distressed.

Now and again, since the disastrous end of 'the Brother's War', 'Buster' had wondered if it would be possible, by employing gliders one moonlit night, to descend upon Spandau prison and rescue Rudolf Hess—who had been Göring's adjutant when his father had been shot down in October, 1918, over Mossy Face Wood—the Bois d'Havrincourt. It would be a gesture equal in magnanimity with that of the young Winston Churchill towards the Boer generals, Smuts and Botha, after the South African war.

The R.A.F., pranging Fresnes prison in France during the war, had breached one wall with bombs, in order to release partisan prisoners due to be shot ...

Bombs useless for Spandau. Silence and moonlight, black gliders, the only possible tactics ...

'Buster' lifted his foot from the throttle until the engine of the Bentley was little more than idling along at 50 m.p.h. He considered: First, the General Idea. The guard duties were in mutation every month—Russian, American, British. Silence, moonlight. The British month. British guards. Gliders. Softly, softly, catchee monkey. His right hand brushed up his moustaches. Spandau prison was beside the road to West Berlin. Gliders might drop steel wires to fuse the electric fence. During some future International Gliding competition? Moonlight. That raw-carrot-painted monstrosity beyond (a) mesh fence, (b) electric fence, and (c) seven-yard high wall. Prison fifty yards back from road. Barred moon-glazed windows. Descent by parachute would be visible. Black gliders landing near the prison. Commandos. Get some of the boys together. Trusties. He could imagine no further; until—Ah, start a gliding club! Based on the marsh grazings behind the pebble ridge at Porlock! Likelihood of European championship being held in West Germany, *out*. Ah, gliding club with the Army of Occupation! H'm. He yawned, suddenly weary. No proper breakfast. Laura's vegetarian food—uncooked tomatoes, chopped olives, sardines, black pumpernickel bread gave no stay-ing power. Laura mortifying the flesh. God, if only he could give her what she wanted : what *he* wanted; an heir.

He pulled up before the inn at Mere and went in to drink beer at the bar with gentleman farmers who were ploughing up the Plain to grow barley to fatten calves for baby beef. There he had luncheon, including a fillet steak, and went on his journey feeling optimistic. He was staying the night at Molly Bucentaur's cottage up by Bewick down.

"Darling Hugh, do go up and say goodnight to the children. They're all *so* looking forward to seeing you. Roger wants to know if you found a new block for your motor, whatever that is."

"Thanks entirely to Maddison, whom I met in the Medicean, I was fortunate in finding one in a disused maltings on the East Coast. It was one in a million chance. I spotted it, rusted up, in a corner. Probably the only unused Bentley four-and-a-half-litre block left in Europe."

"Wasn't it frightfully rusty?"

"All the better for being seasoned. I rather fancy, when the new models of any make come again on the market, their engines won't last. A cylinder block of cast iron requires a couple of years, normally, to harden and weather in the open."

"How clever of you to know such things, darling."

"Entirely due to a chance meeting with Phillip Maddison."

A voice called from the top of the stairs, "Cousin Hugh, don't forget to come up and say goodnight!"

"Yes," said Miranda's voice. "I want to ask you something, Cousin Hugh."

"I asked first!", cried the boy, pattering on bare feet down the open stairs which led directly into the living room. He flung himself at 'Buster', who turned half-sideways to receive the im-pact, while Miranda stood at the top of the stairs, wearing one of her grandmother's evening dresses of the early twentieth century. Seeing her there, Molly went up the yew-wood treads to lift her hair back upon the shoulders.

"What a picture!" exclaimed Riversmill, holding head on one side. "My God, I must paint her just as she is, Molly. That neck! Look at those shoulders—and the line of the collar bone!"

"It's for Shaw's 'Pygmalion'—we're doing it at school. I put it on because it was all I could find, and I must say goodnight to Capella."

"You're Liza, of course, in the play?"

"Yes."

"Why aren't you at school?"

"She's a day girl at Lynmouth." said Molly. "The school isn't back in Cheltenham yet—the Americans took over all the buildings during the war. Now Roger my sweet, trot up to bed, and Cousin Hugh will come and say goodnight, then I'll tuck you up. And no more heavy reading at night, Miranda."

There was a bump on the hall door, a series of bleats. "That's Capella, I haven't said good night to her."

"What's the heavy reading?" asked Riversmill.

"Schopenhauer. I'll just say good night to Capella," replied Miranda, coming down the stairs.

"Schopenhauer? Ye Gods, what's the new generation coming to, Molly?"

The hall door opened, a white goat with a red collar bounded into the room. Miranda said, "Schopenhauer sees the world as Idea, and life as ceaseless conflict and strife," as she stroked her pet.

"All artists see the world as Idea," replied Riversmill, while the goat lay down with the cats before the hearth. Miranda said, "He says the life-urge of nature is intrinsically cruel and destructive, and it is necessary to attain pure knowledge by standing to it in relation to dialogue. Mummy, may Capella have an orange? A blood orange, if there's one left."

"Golly," said Riversmill. "Do *you* understand that jargon?"

"Yes, of course."

"Put it in simple language."

"I can illustrate it better by saying that I read a chapter of Schopenhauer, then a chapter of *The Water Wanderer*. Both stand up to each other." She looked at Phillip, who felt her beauty upon him.

"Of course I know Phillip's book, but I can't see its relationship to philosophy," said Riversmill.

"O please shut up, Anda!" said the boy. "I want to talk to Cousin Hugh about his Bentley."

"Come on upstairs with me, Roger, and I'll tell you all about it."

Molly gave her daughter an orange. The girl rolled it over the floor, cats and goat sprang up, and slithered about on the polished parquet. The goat picked it up in its mouth and brought the orange to Miranda.

"The goat retrieves!" cried Riversmill. "Well I'm damned!"

"Capella likes cricket, Cousin Phillip," said Miranda. "So do all the other goats—the young ones, I mean."

"Goats, like all animals, have a sense of fun."

"Darling, we can't have Capella in here," said Molly. With the orange in its mouth, the goat was led to the door and put outside.

"I'm still in the dark," complained Riversmill.

"You're in good company then, with your friend Moses," said Mrs. Riversmill.

This was a needling reference to her husband's everlasting tirade against the iniquity of art-dealers.

"Who asked you to speak? Go on, Miranda. Tell me why Phillip's book is philosophical."

Miranda continued softly, "In *The Water Wanderer* Cousin Phillip puts his own subjectivity upon Lutra, the otter. But to become whole one must pass through nature fully aware, then one can perceive an aspect of eternity, as Richard Jefferies did in *The Story of My Heart*. That way he by-passed the unreal self which is only identifiable by dialogue—"

"What's this confounded 'dialogue', Miranda?"

"Argument."

"There you are, you argue from your unreal self, Riversmill," remarked the painter's wife.

"I'm not arguing, you fathead! Go on, Miranda."

"Well, by passing beyond subjectivism, man gains the essential relationship between the totality of the world and the whole being."

"Beats me," said Riversmill.

"In accepting the world as it is, he accepts himself as he is," said Phillip. "He becomes calm—a spiritual being—an artist in action."

"Bravo!" cried Riversmill. "If Phillip edited Bradshaw's Railway Guide, he'd make it interesting."

"Miranda cleared the way," said Phillip. "I've never read a word of Schopenhauer."

"That's dialogue," said Molly, putting an arm round her daughter. She said to Riversmill, "Anda's won an Exhibition at Oxford, haven't you, my cygnet?", as she kissed her before standing back to admire the happy girl.

Riversmill was admiring her, too. "Look at that figure under the gown! By God, I'd like to paint you as you are now, young woman."

"You're a horse painter!" cried Mrs. Riversmill.

"What are you going to read in college?" asked 'Buster', coming down the open stairs. "Philosophy?"

"Modern history, Cousin Hugh. The last fifty years, from the late Victorians to the Edwardian and Georgian periods—from nineteen hundred to nineteen forty-five—the beginning and the end of the British conspiracy to destroy Germany."

After hesitation, Phillip looked at her and said, "That's the period to be covered by my novel series."

"I know," replied Miranda, as quietly. "That's why I've just chosen it."

"How did you know?"

"Because it is your life."

In the silence which followed, 'Buster' took from his pocket the book he had been reading when Phillip had first seen him in the Medicean.

"I wonder, Molly, if I may read you something from this book? It has a bearing on what has been said, I think."

"Who wrote it?" asked Riversmill.

"I'll leave you to guess."

"Come round the hearth, everybody," said Molly.

They sat down on the floor, the three children staring into beechwood flames.

"I may as well start here. I quote—'Nature works always to higher forms on earth. If one purpose of life in this world be individual development with a view to immortality, or successive incarnations directed to the same purpose, the most effective process of that individual development in this life is clearly the service of God's purpose in this world as revealed by nature : which is the evolution to higher forms on earth'."

"You're right!" cried Riversmill. "And the present anti-life craze is served by formless daubers exploited by the art dealers' rackets to feather their own nests!"

"Hold your hobby-horse!" demanded his wife.

"And you hold yours! Go on, 'Buster'."

'Buster' smiled at Mrs. Riversmill, as much as to say, These temperamental artists.

" 'It is by service that man both develops his own character and aids this purpose of God. No conflict exists between individual development and service of humanity : that was the error of the brilliant Nietzsche in posing a conflict between the character of his higher type of man and the interests of the people. On the contrary, the type beyond his Will to Power, which is the Will to Achievement, finds his self-development under the impulse of the derided compassion in his long striving to lift all earthly existence to a higher level, at which the attainment of a higher form is possible. In this sense, the purpose of life is not self-development, *in vacuo,* but the development of self in Achievement, as an artist in action and life, who creates, also, for humanity. The proud words, 'I serve', are to such a man also the highest expression of self-development'."

"Bravo!" cried Riversmill. " 'The hero of Norfolk' wrote that!"

"No, 'The hero of Brixton'," replied Phillip.

'Buster' said, "Roger, I feel I've left you entirely out in the cold."

"No, go on, Cousin Hugh, I like it. Honestly, I do. I like what you write!"

'Buster' smiled as he turned pages. "This is at the end of the book, wherein the whole Idea is worked out—the analysis of failure through European conflict—the failure both of Fascism and of its opponent, Financial Democracy. This is how the book ends:— 'So, we approach the conclusion of a practical creed, which is, at once, a creed of dynamic action, summoned into existence by the urgent necessity of a great and decisive epoch; a creed of science which is based on the observed operation of a higher purpose on earth, as revealed by modern knowledge in an intelligible pattern—' "

"Space ships!" cried Roger, from the top of the stairs.

"Well, yes; but first the space ships of the mind, Roger. This, you see, is a sort of blue print. To continue—'and the creed of a spiritual movement, which is derived from the accumulated culture and original faith of Europe. Our creed is both a religion and a science, the final synthesis : nothing less can meet the challenge of the greatest age within known time'.

" 'Our task is to preserve and to build. If the Fatherland of Europe is lost, all is lost. That home of the soul of man must be saved by any sacrifice. First, the world of the spirit must unite to resist that final doom of material victory. But, beyond lies the grave duty imposed by the new Science.' "

"I want to be a new scientist," said Roger.

"Well, it will be up to you to become one of the new men, Roger," said 'Buster', with quiet patience.

"Roger darling, it's past your bed-time," said Molly.

"Oh Mummy, this is part of my education, really it is!"

"Well, try to listen, darling, while Cousin Hugh reads to us."

" 'It is not only to build a world worthy of the new genius of man's mind, and secure from present menace. It is to evoke from the womb of the future a race of men fit to live in that new age. We must deliberately accelerate evolution : it is no longer a matter of volition but of necessity. Is it a sin to strive in union with the revealed purpose of God? Is it a crime to hasten the coming in time of the force which in the long slow term of unassisted nature, may come too late? We go with nature : but we aid her : is that not nearer the purpose of God than the instinct to frustrate instead of to fulfil? Is not the hastening of our labouring nature the purpose for which this great efflorescence in man's intelligence has been allowed to him? How wonderfully the means has coincided with the necessity. Will man now use it? A new dynamism in the will to higher forms is the hard and practical requirement of an age which commands him to rise higher or to sink for ever. He can no longer stand still : he must transcend himself; this deed will contain both the glory of sacrifice and the triumph of fulfilment. It is the age of decision in which the long striving of the European soul will reach to fulfilment, or plunge to final death. Great it is to live in this moment of Fate, because it means this generation is summoned to greatness in the service of high purpose. From the dust we rise to see a vision that came not before. All things are now possible; and all will be achieved by the final order of the European.' "

'Buster' closed the book.

"Cousin Phillip wrote it," said Miranda.

"No," replied 'Buster'. "As Phillip inferred, it was written in Brixton prison by the Englishman most despised and hated in England during the war, Hereward Birkin."

"If you lend me your copy, I'll review it in *The New Horizon*," said Phillip. "Just before I came here, Wallington Christie gave the magazine to me, and I'm going to edit it."

"Bravo !" cried Riversmill. "Hereward Birkin is a great man. I heard him speak once at the Corn Hall in Fenton just before the war. Phillip was there—weren't you? Birkin was all for developing the Empire then, and creating the Welfare State people are now talking about. Indeed, he had the same ideas soon after the Armistice of nineteen eighteen. And Phillip has had the guts to stick to him all through, like Kurvenal to Tristan."

"Who's Tristan ?" asked the boy.

"The hero of a Cornish legend," said Miranda.

"A man in whom an immovable sense of honour was struck by the irresistible force of a love potion," said Phillip, keeping his eyes from Miranda, while feeling her spirit upon him.

"Sir Hereward Birkin," Phillip went on, "was released from prison only when he was seen to be dying. And if Ernest Bevin had had his way, he—Bevin—would have brought down the Government by calling out the Trades Union, and getting rid of Churchill. It was Winston, you see, who insisted that Birkin be let out of prison, where he had been held during three and a half years without charge, and without trial. He was released while Churchill was in the United States. Attlee sent Winston a signal."

"Good for Winston!" cried Riversmill. "When I was president of the Painters Guild, Winston was my guest at the inaugural banquet. We had a long talk."

"Yes, and you got drunk, you idiot," remarked the painter's wife. "You tried to drag Winston into agreeing with your tirade against Picasso! But Winston had far too much sense to be dragged into anything by a screeching old jay like yourself!"

"Who asked you to speak?" the painter yelled.

"Who asked *you* to speak for Winston, you mean! Go on, 'Buster', don't let Riversmill drag you into an argument." She looked at her husband. "If it hadn't been for me looking after your money, you'd have been in the gutter by now, you mouldy old dog-fox!"

At this Riversmill pointed his nose at the ceiling and let out a prolonged high-pitched scream, as of a vixen calling a dog-fox under the moon. Everyone laughed. Peace was restored.

"Talking about goats, Molly," said Mrs. Riversmill, "What are you going to do with the Brockholes herd? You surely can't keep them all here."

"Perry wrote the other day and said he'd offered them to the Devon County Council. Peregrine", she went on, turning to Phillip, "is my husband, at present in Kenya, shooting big game. The goats used to live in the park at Brockholes, but now the place is sold, we've no scope for them."

Riversmill said, "Lynton will want them, Molly, I fancy. All the other goats in the Valley of Rocks disappeared during the war. Poached, of course, and sent up to London hotels as venison. Some venison! Still, we ate anything in those days." Then turning to Phillip, he said, "Where's Birkin now, d'you know?"

"Living in Berkshire, under police protection, or rather surveillance."

"Good God! Can't the Government let him alone now the war's over?"

"They don't want him murdered by some fanatic," said 'Buster'.

Riversmill looked at Phillip. "Some madman may track *you* down to your shepherd's cot one day, and then—"

"Oh no!" cried Miranda, sitting on the floor, swaddled in the long gown, as she turned to hide her face against her mother's knees.

Chapter 11

THE NEW HORIZON

Chimney smoke veering to the south-west. Dragging nimbus overcast; water running everywhere. Runners a-splash with hen salmon, colour of bronze, attended by cock-fish with flanks of copper, some yellow-patched with fungus. Females extruding eggs while male fish shed their milt in water so shallow that their back-fins were exposed.

One morning a man with clotted hair arrived, in a butt drawn by a moorland pony, beside the head-waters. With a four-tined dung fork he began a search for fish. Soon he had transfixed a decayed salmon, and jerked it into his small cart.

So this was Aaron Kedd, owner of the little dog. Phillip had heard of him from the farmer's wife across the common : a 'local preacher' of no denomination whose mind had turned to hell rather than to salvation : a most unhappy man, living alone, his moods varying between bitter silence and near-raving distress. Rather like one of the men on his war-time farm, Jack the Jackdaw, thought Phillip; but Jack never took it out on horse or dog. Jack had kind moments; he could still weep, whereas Kedd seemed to be charred beyond tears.

Phillip went to talk to him, thinking that perhaps he might be able to aid him in some way or other, and so directly help the odd little dog which stood watching each action of its master in an attitude of detachment and without cocked ears, as though it were thinking about what it saw.

"These fish have spawned by the look of them, Mr. Kedd. And they're too far up to be able to get back to the sea, judging by their condition."

"Aiy, they'm unclane!" cried the fellow. "They brocks and varxes, aiy, and they craws, wull get'm if I don't!", while with turns of wrists he flipped fish after fish into his butt. "They'm unclane, I tell 'ee, like the swine of Gadarene!"

"What are you going to do with these fish? Rot them down for compost?"

"What be thaccy?"

"Dressing."

"Noomye! Feed pigs on'm."

"That yellow fungus on salmon is the same kind that grows on dying trees."

"I don't know naught about thaccy! I ban't no 'igh-class gentry, with their flim-flam talking."

"Otters come so far up the water, I suppose?"

"Aiy, they arrters be hellers! They be! One of they girt mousey-coloured fitches stole one of my ducks t'other night! The bliddy dog beside 'ee stood watchin' of 'n, didn't even holler!'A be no more use than a mommet!" He made as if to throw the dung fork at the dog. "You'm no flamin' gude to me! Yar!" he yelled at the animal cringing among rushes. "Tes no bliddy use to me! Hangin' around where nought be doin' save idleness."

"A writer works hard, too, in his own way."

"I ban't blind, midear. I see what be goin' on wi' visitors."

"I'll give you ten shillings for this dog."

The man touched his arm. "Done!"

The dog stood still as Phillip approached, and wagged its tail stump. It followed him up the slope, and waited in the doorway. It had never been inside a cottage. When Phillip called, it remained outside, the line of its back curved. It looked pitiful, so he picked it up, while it held itself stiff, trembling. He nursed it on his lap. It remained still for awhile, then slowly got off and walked away to a far corner. It returned, with a couple of stump-wags, to a saucer of milk. But it stopped lapping when Phillip felt the lumps on its ribs. Had kicks broken the bones, which had set irregularly? He spread a corn sack in front of the hearth. BODGER was the name stencilled on it—relic of Phillip's farming days—a hundred second-hand corn sacks bought at auction, during the pre-war depression. Bodger dead and turned to clay, to stop a hole to keep the wind away.

" 'BODGER of GREAT SNORING'. Genuine name, genuine place. I dub you Sir Bodger of Shep Cot, and declare this sack to be your territory." He transferred the dog to the sack, and lay on the floor beside it, arms round the little body. When Phillip got up, the dog returned to its corner.

So Phillip moved the sack there. Bodger left to eat bread-and-milk, thereafter returning to his sack. Again Phillip lay beside him, stroking him; then moved away slowly, as though he had forgotten the dog; who remained, on its new territory, its base, curled tightly upon itself.

"Here we are, a couple of crocks together, old Bodge," said Phillip, as the dog's eyes slanted upwards from head on paws, and a tail stump wagged once.

Comforted by the presence of Old Bodge, Phillip sat at the table, trying to free his mind of the smallholder Kedd, so that an idea might come—a theme—for the editorial of his first number of *The New Horizon*.

The idea came. He began writing.

THE LOST LEGIONS

'One morning, in the winter of 1919–20, I went into a Public Library in a suburb of London, and drew up a chair to a table whereon lay magazines and periodicals. The library, one of many founded on the generosity of a Scots-American millionaire, Andrew Carnegie, was a place where shabby old men and nondescript out-of-work ex-soldiers like myself went to rest and find interest away from drab pavements and street-movements outside, which had little or nothing to do with their lives.

'Usually in that place a magazine soon lost its attractiveness; indeed, it was likely to be soiled within a few hours, for most of the old men, I noticed, were preparing, while reading laboriously down a page, to turn it over, by rolling its lower corner between an occasionally licked finger and thumb. By the afternoon of the day of its first appearance a magazine or journal was in a repulsive state. To my critical self it was a detail of that state of unself-consciousness of which Somme and Passchendaele were the apotheosis.

'There was one weekly lying on the long oaken table that was usually clean, seldom if ever picked up : an old-fashioned sixpenny called *The Athenaeum*. I had heard the editor spoken of with reverence by a literary acquaintance, who declared that the finest literary critic in England wrote in it every week. So I sought it; and the first thing I read has remained in my mind ever since : an essay with the title of *The Lost Legions*, by John Middleton Murry.

'Fortunately I bought a copy of that number, which lies beside me on the table as I write. I quote :—

One day, we believe, a great book will be written, informed by the breath which moves the Spirits of Pity in Mr. Hardy's *Dynasts*. It will be a delicate, yet undeviating record of the spiritual awareness of the generation that perished in the war. It will be a work of genius, for the essence which must be captured within it is volatile beyond belief, almost beyond imagination. We know of its existence by signs hardly more material than a dream-memory of beating wings or an instinctive, yet all but inexplicable refusal of that which has been offered us in its stead. The autobiographer-novelists have been legion, yet we turn from them all with a slow shake of the head. "No, it was not that. Had we lost only that we could have forgotten. It was not that!"

No, it was the spirit that troubled, as in a dream, the waters of the pool, some influence which trembled between a silence and a sound, a precarious confidence, an unavowed quest, a wisdom that came not of years or experience, a dissatisfaction, a doubt, a devotion, some strange presentiment, it may have been, of the bitter years in store ... a visible seal on the forehead of a generation.

'The above passage is the beginning of a review of *The Letters of Charles Sorley*, who, a captain of 19 years, was killed on the Somme. Sorley had begun to write when at Marlborough. It was the breath of life to him, and with the oxygen of newly-discovered writers—Masefield, Hardy, Goethe, Jefferies—his mind shone with the brilliance of a magnesium ribbon in flare.

'It was about three years after that review in *The Athenaeum* that *The New Horizon* appeared on the London literary scene. I bought it eagerly: H. M. Tomlinson writing of a Devon estuary in prose that was the reality of the place itself—the haze of summer heat upon the sand-dunes and the level forsaken shore, the white crinkle of Atlantic rollers upon the sand-bars of the estuarial mouth, the North and South Tails, dreaded 'white water' of sailors; D. H. Lawrence, always a little wry, seldom serene, in his descriptions of elemental human nature and the life beyond his eyes; Wallington Christie, a scholar-critic whose 'gods' were Shakespeare and Hardy; Arnold Bennett, penetrating but urban in outlook; H. G. Wells, praising *Lady Into Fox*, by a young writer, as a great book; Middleton Murry, editor of *The Adelphi*, whose writings seemed to change after the death of his wife, Katherine Mansfield.

'I met one of those famous contributors during the recent war. Wallington Christie had instituted a community farm where nearly all the communiteers, as they called themselves, had conscientious objection to war—young men and women who went to work on the land within the Island Fortress, as Churchill called Britain in the early period of the war.

'Often I wondered how they were affected by the spirit of those dark days. Were they able to live the more serenely because of the expenditure of others? For some people of the first war had changed their ideas in middle-age, and recanted from the ideals of their own youth; some indeed in my presence declared with pride that in that war soldiers and civilians were in it together. The 8th British Army in Africa and the 14th in Burma must have been amused at that idea.

'During hostilities, and shortages everywhere, *The New Horizon* inevitably got thinner, but still kept its platform from which a man might proclaim his faith. And recently, after nearly quarter of a century since he brought it to being, Christie decided to 'bring it to a tidy end'. It so happened that I was with him just after the time of this decision, and hearing it, I begged him to let me carry it on.

'For what the lost legions of another generation died for must not be lost. They died, in all armies, for the brotherhood of Europe; for the true, the constructive resurgence of the European spirit. 'The grass grows green again on the battlefield; but on the scaffold, never'.'

Here the unfed editor's energy petered out. The doldrums of depression succeeded. I might be in Valerian Cottage all over again, the year nineteen twenty one, on the south coast of Devon, only cups of weak tea for breakfast. Yes, I am still the same pattern.

Bodger growled. At the same time Phillip heard the slop of horse-feet on the cobbled pattern outside the cottage, saw a shadow across the casement followed by a brown slouch hat and recognised Molly Bucentaur.

"How glad I am to see you!"

"I'm on my way to Lynmouth, and smelled your wood-smoke, and had to drop in to see how you were getting on. Do tell me to go away if I am disturbing you."

"Not at all! It was time to stop. Have you had lunch? I can offer you eggs, cheese, tomatoes—"

Two shirts, part buttonless and torn, hung inside the open hearth. He lifted them off their nails, and put them away.

"Do let me make you an omelette, Phillip. I don't eat lunch as a rule, but rules are meant to be broken. Thank you so much for your letter after our little party. Is this the little dog Miranda and Fred Riversmill told me about?"

"Yes. He belonged to a somewhat odd smallholder, who hangs out in the next coomb."

"That must be the odd creature I passed, with a half-load of dead salmon in a ricketty old butt. I asked him where you lived and he eyed me as though I was something out of *The News of the World*."

"He reads that in conjunction with the Old Testament, I expect."

"Is this the frying pan? How clean you keep it. Now leave things to me, my dear, and carry on with your writing. Would you prefer tea or coffee?"

"I've only got tea."

"Much better for you. Oh, before I forget it, 'Buster' asked me to lend you Hereward Birkin's book. He sends greetings, and you are to regard it as a review copy. That is, should you want to mention it, of course. Now you return to your table, and I'll make you an omelette."

Jubilantly Phillip returned to the table to read the preface.

This book is written by a man without a Party, as an offering to the new thought of Europe. Deliberately, I refrained from forming again a political movement in Great Britain; in order to serve a new European Idea. At this time, no other is in a position to state any real alternative to the present condition of Europe. The existing rulers of one country, because it has been heard before. The past has imposed stand on the graves of their opponents to confront the Communist power of their own creation. No alternative can come from the architects of chaos: all others have been silenced. So, I must give myself to this task. My life striving in the politics of Britain made known my name and character: my voice can now reach beyond the confines of the earth are responsible for this darkness of humanity; they the duty of the future: I must do this thing because no other can.

"It's just what I wanted for the magazine, Molly!", he cried. "I am so glad you brought me this book."

It was a most succulent cheese-omelette in the thick, cast-iron pan.

"I'm in touch with life again, Molly! No, I'll wash up. I know exactly where everything is."

"I'll be able to do some typing for you, if you bring it over. Come any time, we are nearly always there, and make yourself at

home if we're out, won't you? Oh, your shirts, my dear. Do let me
repair them for you. May I take them? I'll let you have them
back very soon."

And so saying, Molly rode away; and Phillip continued typing
his Editorial.

'I have just received for review a book by Sir Hereward Birkin,
called *The Alternative*. It was prepared during the war, while the
author was in prison, and written after his release in November,
1943. He was then held under house arrest. Sir Hereward and I
both served as young soldiers with the British Expeditionary
Force in Flanders in 1914, during the battle for Ypres and the
Channel ports

'One day it will be widely known that Birkin's political career
began with original thinking at least two generations before his
time. Some of my older readers may remember that he was the
youngest member of Parliament soon after the Great War ended;
that he left the Tory party because they represented the old order
of Europe which crumbled into war in 1914, and faced the post-
war period with the same ideas, and attitudes. So he joined the
Labour Party. Many perceptive men recognised him for a young
man of outstanding brilliance, industry, and courage. Now let the
author of this book speak for himself :—

> We were divided and we are conquered. That is the tragic epitaph
> of two war generations. That was the fate of my generation in 1914,
> and that was the doom of a new generation of young soldiers in 1939.
> The youth of Europe shed the blood of their own family, and the
> jackals of the world grew fat. Those who fought are in the position
> of the conquered, whatever their country. Those who did not fight,
> but merely profited, alone are victorious.

'There follows an analysis of failure, due to 'the split mind of
Europe'. Fascism failed because it deserved to fail; it was too
national. Its opponent of a financial democracy failed, too. It
could only frustrate those who would build a New Order. And
the New Order failed because of its own inherent weakness. The
author examines the odd behaviour of Hitler, when the British
Expeditionary Force was routed in May 1940, and nothing was
done, at the time, to follow up the victory by Germany.

> Why the first principle of the pursuit was not applied in these
> circumstances remained one of the mysteries of History. Now it

appears that it was not only not attempted but it was not even seriously contemplated ... Was it some extraordinary idea existed that all could be settled by political skill alone when passion had reached such a point? Was the illusion nurtured that the British mind in such circumstances would move as logically as the Continental mind, which knew something of military matters? If so, both the invincible courage and the yet more invincible ignorance of the English were profoundly underrated. Did some extraordinary sentimental consideration traverse the mind of German leadership to the destruction of every realistic consideration? It is almost unbelievable that any such feeling should have influenced so far: but it is one of the tear-laden paradoxes of History that the man, whom the mass of the English learned to regard as their greatest enemy, cherished a sentimental illusion toward a 'sister nation' which, in the eyes of historic realism, must border on the irrational, and, in the test of fact, was pregnant with the doom of all he loved ...

It is clear that in the German conduct of the war at this point every rule of real policy was broken ...

In all real things which concern the clash of body, mind and will the same eternal reality holds: when the big fellow staggers—attack——attack—attack—no other thought until it is done. If it was not contemplated that the attack on the French front in 1940 would succeed, it should never have been undertaken. If it was considered, as must have been the case, that it would succeed, the pursuit to the conclusion of the war, which could only mean the invasion of Britain, should have been prepared in advance by express and urgent instructions of political leadership. Nothing should ever be put into execution which has no chance of success; if success is won the opportunity which it presents should never be neglected, particularly if that opportunity is the chance of a final decision ...

What strange enchantment brought the long pause on the German side after the fall of France until they again violated every principle of real policy by turning their back on an undefeated enemy to advance upon Russia? They turned their back, too, on an enemy still resolute. He was mortally weak, it is true, but he had vast latent resources available to him for slow building into effective operation, and a long array of friends and relations—including the potentially strongest country in the world—who could gradually be cajoled and manoeuvred by a great traditional political skill, in alliance with the incessant intrigues of the Money Power, into a world coalition of overwhelming force. Did the tomb of Napolean, enshrined in the vast bitterness of that same, and then, ineluctable experience, never whisper again in the Paris of late 1940, "ask me anything but time".

The wounds of Europe must be healed before   ʳork of construction can begin. They are wounds of the spirit, .   hey are kept open by animosities and memories of atavistic sav·   . These old things have no interest to the creative mind, but they impede our work. That is why we ask Europe not to look back, but to stride forward. In these pages I have attempted to describe some possibilities which beckon us onward in the march of the European spirit. They are worth that effort of the living mind and will, which forgets the past and, thus, achieves the future. Division is death, but Union is life.'

At this point Phillip felt a return of exhaustion; his left eye was aching; and pulling himself upstairs, fell upon the bed. Soon there was the *tip-tip* of claws on wood, as Bodger walked up, to curl beside the bed-frame. The dog was shivering. Phillip took off his jacket and laid it over the dog so that only the nose was visible. And there the two lay curled, man on bed and dog on floor, while the room lost light and the moor beyond the window dissolved in mist.

Early in the morning he wandered down to the village to buy food for Bodger and himself. The appearance of a man fishing from the shore was somehow familiar: that sturdy frame, yellow-grey unbrushed hair, was surely of Osgood Nilsson, fellow Brother Barbarian? With an expert flick of a short steel rod he sent soaring a leaded silver spoon to fall into jostling white of waves breaking as though irritably away from the tide flowing fast up the Channel. Phillip had had a good breakfast of tinned herrings in tomato sauce, with brown bread-and-butter, and felt optimistic. He could see the glint on the metal spoon just before it went into the water. And the leap of a bass which had taken it, shaking head in air before falling back to dash seaward to the screeching of the reel-check.

"See that?" cried the fisherman, half turning his head. Yes, it was Osgood. How glad he was to see the dear old fellow!

After the fishing they went to the Rising Sun, an inn aptly named: its windows caught the first light of morning above the Severn sea. One had to watch old 'Goody', of course, and break away as conveniently as possible after he had pulled up one trouser to show a suppurating wound from the First War ... sign that he was about to go on the bottle.

Carrying a 4-pound bass, and some dried bay-leaves for seasoning, Phillip set off for home, knapsack filled. And as he was walking across the common to Shep Cot a mounted figure appeared on the skyline, an arm waved: horse and rider lost definition as they sunk the hill, until a white speck made it plain that the rider was Miranda, followed by her goat.

Phillip was surgingly happy; alarmed; querulous for the break-age in his writing. These contrary feelings left him void yet ele-vated; and pretending not to have seen her, he went into the cot and sat down at the table, picking up and strewing about various foolscap envelopes containing contributions.

"Lie down, Bodger. Quiet now!"

At last a knock on the door, which he had left half open. "Good afternoon, Cousin Phillip. Am I disturbing you? I've brought over one of your shirts."

"How kind of your mother to send you, Miranda. Let me tie your cob to the Silver Eagle, and so provide my worn-out old engine with more horse-power! Hullo, Capella! I see you know Bodger," as the animals touched noses.

"Cousin Phillip, what I'd like to say is that it would extend my education if you'd allow me to help you with your magazine. Addressing envelopes—anything at all. It's my half-term." She was nervous, she lost colour. He put an arm on her shoulder, and kissed her lightly on the forehead. "What a kind family you Bucentaurs are!"

"Well, you see—," she went on, her vitality returning, "I want to be a writer when I leave school. Meanwhile, if I can be of help to you, I shall be getting some idea about technique. I can more or less type, Cousin Phillip, would you mind if I answer letters for you on your portable Royal?"

"Well, I certainly need help, Miranda—someone to pick out the best of the contributions sent in. There's a score and more envelopes on this table, most of them unopened. The first number ought to be going to the printer—and I haven't yet found a printer!"

"Mr. Riversmill told me there's one in Minehead who has some good type faces which might suit you. So I got his trade card yesterday. Here it is. May I put it on the chimney shelf, for when you may want it?"

"Wonderful girl!" He wanted to kiss her. She knew this, and was a little disturbed.

"The printer said he might be able to get local advertisements, if they don't cost too much."

"Hurray! I've got a business manager, as well as an assistant editor! One other thing: Do you know how to cook a bass?"

"Well, as you haven't a grill, Cousin Phillip, it might be broiled in your crock, gently, with bay leaves, and fennel."

"I've got some bay-leaves. And potatoes. I'll do that, Miranda.

It would help more if you'd look through these contributions."

She drew up a stool beside the hearth, and began to read. Bodger and Capella curled side by side on the corn sack. Phillip, sitting at the table, glanced at the girl, so intently reading on the three-legged milking stool, which he had bought for half-a-crown from the farmer's wife across the common. Cinderella : all but one ear and tip of nose hidden by dark hanging hair.

He went on with his typing, adding to the quotation from *The Alternative* one short sentence.

'Well, there speaks the authentic voice of the' Lost Legions of 1914–1945.'

And had no further idea until Miranda showed her face to say, "Oh, Cousin Phillip, this is a beautiful poem I've been reading! It was written by James Farrar when he was sixteen, in the late summer of nineteen forty. There are other poems, too, and some prose sketches. It's beautiful and precise, like your own prose and that of Hereward Birkin!"

She put typescript pages before him, and went back to the stool. Phillip read; and exclaimed,

"This Battle of Britain poem has almost the mastery of Wilfred Owen, Miranda! We must get in touch with the writer at once. What is his name and address?"

The girl didn't reply. She seemed to have grown smaller as she sat huddled by the fire, arms drawn in, hands pressed to bosom, head bowed, eyes closed. He saw tear-drops on the tiled floor beside the dog-ear'd Notebook; and reading the letter sent with the poems, that the author was dead, resisted an impulse to comfort her; and went on typing.

'What poets fell in the continuation of the fratricidal European war which re-started in September, 1939? I know of one : James Farrar, a luminous youth who in a brief life wrote several lyrics in the English language which gave promise that here was a master.

'James Farrar's promise revealed itself when the tall, fair-faired boy was about sixteen years old. Imagine him wandering in the Surrey countryside one afternoon in the late summer of 1940, while the Battle of Britain was being fought twenty and thirty thousand feet over his head.'

SEPTEMBER 1940

I walk endlessly, no clock drips by the hours,
   The burnished hedgerows, clotted and high,
The still woods, the dead meadows, the closed flowers,
   Shrunken under that bright scarred sky.

A light-play, as of sun on August leaves,
   A height-soft moan, a wooden intermittent rattle,
And, as the scrollèd conflict eastward weaves,
   Feelers drooping darkly out of battle.

They come slowly, soft tap-roots questing down,
   At the groping tip of one glisters a bead of light:
I see them, as waterflies struggling not to drown,
   Soundlessly pass into earth, and meet night.

What is it that they are fallen?
   Sane men hold it to be just
That each, when dead feed the earth like pollen,
   Lies strewn in some broken field in a wrack of dust.

"Cousin Phillip, I like this poem also, *very* much!"

THE BELOVED

When I am in the fields she lies
Alone upon the hills, for she is Day
And I am Night, and brightest shine her eyes
When I must look away.
But briefly as in summer dawn we meet,
Her beauty in a flood
Burns vagrant through my blood.

And when the swift floats high
On molten tide of sunset, silently
Together in the meadows do we lie,
But never wed shall be:
For soon she sleeps in mist and I must rise,
And when the stars are grown
Must seek the hills alone.

"I must go now, cousin Phillip. Thank you for letting me see
the contributions. I hope the shirt is all right. May I bring over
the other tomorrow, if it's a fine day?"

       *   *   *

Lucy returning from the garden where she had gone, at Jonathan's imperious bidding, to see an owl.

"It sits on that old appletree every evening, watching for rats after the chicken food, Mum, and swivels its head right round to look down over its back! There! It's just flown away!"

The moon was shining. Lucy felt happy and relaxed, after taking old people in the Ford 8 to hospital, during the afternoon. There were letters to be opened. The first was from Phillip.

"He sends his love to you, Tim, and says he knows you'll succeed with your lathe work."

Tim was now regularly making boxes of ivory and sandal wood for a shop in Bond Street.

"Well, well, well," replied Tim—an expression of happy surprise.

Lucy made some tea, and then opened her other letters.

"Tim, do you remember Cousin Molly Bucentaur? She says she's got a new little place on Exmoor, and mentions the Rivers-mills—you know, he's the painter, he did a painting of one of Uncle George Abeline's hunters. Molly says if ever the little boys want a change, to send them down to her next summer, during the holidays." Lucy glowed with pleasure. "How very kind of her. I haven't seen or heard from her since she dropped in to see us at Flumen Monachorum, when Phillip was away with Ernest, he'd just bought Deepwater farm. She had a sweet little daughter with her called Miranda."

"Ah."

Tim Copleston still felt a little uneasy whenever he thought of Phillip; he felt again the humiliation at the failure of those ghastly Works he and his two brothers had built in the old garden at Down Close, in the 'twenties, and lost all their money. Phillip had come to help them.

To the simple-minded Tim, his brother-in-law had at times seemed to be mad. Once he had left a 'little note' for Phillip, putting it on top of a pile of County Court summonses, writs, judgment summonses and other beastly communications. Tim had written, *To abuse us is to bemuse us,* and Phillip had replied *What do you think you three babes-in-the-wood do to me?*

Tim felt extra happy that Phillip had sent his love. He was look-ing forward to a long and happy life, with Brenda and their small son, staying in Lulu's new house. It was almost like the old home at Down Close, he and Lulu together again!

There was plenty of room wherein Tim could feel himself to be his own master. There were four main bedrooms, and four smaller

ones, reached by three staircases: one central to the larger bedrooms; another to a wing; the third leading from the kitchen—
approached by a stone-flagged passage to the rear of the premises
—to what had once been servants' quarters. The main bedrooms
had heavy oak floors, laid down in the seventeenth century:
planks sawn in timber pits, top-sawyers and bottom-sawyers sweat-
ing it out with saws ten inches deep and seven feet long, seventy
hours and more a week. An oak-framed house, latticed windows,
dark beams and rafters, lath-and-plaster inner walls and ceilings.

"By Jove, Lulu, I simply love it here!"

"Yes, Timmo, so do I! And the children adore it. Jonny with
his secret passages, he and David playing hide-and-seek in the
attics. Hark! They're up there now!"

Thumping noises came through the oak-frame of the house. The
boys had climbed up through a trap-door to their hidey-hole
in the cavernous gloom under the slates of the roof.

A wonderful place for the children to explore!

"Mum and Uncle Tim," said Jonathan, coming into the kitchen, "I've written four pages in my note-book on the habits of
bats. They eat death-watch beetles, so they do some good!"

"Cor, I what-you-call like this house, 'bor," said David to
Uncle Tim.

"Ah."

In Devon Phillip, too, was happy.

"Cousin Phillip, I've brought over your other shirt."

Miranda again on the stool, checking Phillip's typescript against
the copy. "It's all so vivid, isn't it, Cousin Phillip? I know the
mag. will sell. Do you think readers would like to read how poets
acquire their style?"

"The good writer re-creates what he sees and hears. Robert
Graves writes somewhere that Keats often used the sense of taste.
'And lucent syrups tinct with cinnamon'—all lip-work. But clear-
seeing is the true writer's base—his eyes. A blind writer produces
an oddly colourless prose." And he thought, I mustn't work so
long by candlelight. My left eye feels as though it has a thorn in
it. Well, if I *do* go blind I'll still have colours in my brain-cells.

"It is awfully good of you to spare time for the magazine,
Miranda. *And* for bringing back my shirt. I suppose you're on
your way to Lynton?"

He hoped she would say no.

"I must go sometime today, Cousin Phillip, to see 'Buster'.

There's no particular hurry. How did the bass taste?"

"I gave what I couldn't eat, less the bones, to Bodger. Look at the result!"

A barrelline Bodger was lying, legs straight out, on the sack. But one eye was open, taking it all in.

"You didn't bring Capella with you this time."

"Mummie thought she should be kept in the paddock while she's in season."

"I suppose the Boniface herd is more or less of one blood, like the ancient Pharoahs?"

"So far as we know, Cousin Phillip. There's no stud book. Daddy's giving the goats to the Lynton Council when he comes home in the summer for the cricket. He wants the herd to remain all-white, and in one locality."

"To be uniform with cricket flannels, boots, and pads, no doubt!"

"Of course!" she laughed. Then, "May I help you today, or shall I be a nuisance?"

Bodger's eye closed. He had heard it all. She was staying, so was Phillip. He could go to sleep again.

"Read some of Farrar to me, will you, Miranda. Your voice is so soft and sensitive." I am courting her, I am seducing her spiritually—Miranda sitting on the stool—Cinderella with happy face—one hand slowly stroking the ear of Bodger, who had moved beside her. Then dog's head stretching up on neck, cocked ears directed towards door. Phillip saw two shadow-breaks in the light between door-skirt and threshold. "We've got an audience of two boots outside," he whispered.

"That smallholder?"

"How we think alike." To Bodger, "Calm down, those boots won't kick you again. Please read on, Miranda."

The girl hesitated. "Cousin Phillip, I'm afraid!"

"We'll soon settle that!"

He went to the door and pulled it open.

"Come to see how Bodger is getting on, Mr. Kedd?"

"Noomye! Now mind what you'm about wi' thaccy maid, midear! I've told ee!!" And turning round, the fellow shambled away.

"Poor chap, what a mess he's in", said Phillip, quietly. "I'll see you down to Barbrook when you have to go, Miranda. Can you spare the time to read a little more? Your voice is so clear, and I live what you're reading."

After giving an account of green plovers on an airfield getting in the way of an aircraft taking off, and being driven right through the leading edge into the wing of an Oxford, wedged into broken plywood, her voice stopped. Pretending not to notice her emotion, he said, "By hard objective writing the effect is greatest on the reader, Miranda. The writer feels the emotion, but transmits it calmly. Also the good writer knows the value of original detail— he was what a child once said I had—'gazing eyes'—he sees his own detail, in contrast with that used by most writers, out of somebody else's books or newspapers."

"Your eyes still do gaze," she said, looking up at him. "Sometimes a little disconcertingly. Oh, I'm sorry, Cousin Phillip, I didn't mean to be personal! Shall I go on reading?"

"Yes please."

" 'A few nights ago we had twenty degrees of frost at only fifteen thousand feet. One kite was at twenty-two in thirty-five degrees of frost. Facing backwards in the famous Beaufighter near-hatch draught, I lost my right hand fairly soon. I haven't been so cold since early in 1940 on the farm at Epping. When I was at last able to turn round and begin thawing out, a strange thing happened. First I held my gloved hand under the heater— only for a short time as I could feel the bursting sensation which indicates that external heat is not good when there's no circulation. Then I pulled off the leather gauntlet and the silk glove and rubbed my hand against the other glove. All things were now equal, though I didn't know it. My slight knowledge of physics supports it adequately, but at the same time I was slightly shaken to see greenish two-inch sparks coming from my finger tips when I began to push them into the silk glove again. Later I drew my full-gloved fingertips down the perspex and little bristly sparks, bright green, danced about them'."

"Excellent stuff! We'll include that, Coz. What fun it is you're here! Work is a pleasure!"

"I've chosen three more pieces, Cousin Phillip. Shall I read them? They're short."

"But if you're going to see 'Buster', oughtn't you to go now? I don't want you to be lost on The Chains in the dark."

"I can stay the night with Cousin Hugh. Please let me read just this one piece."

He nodded. She read, " 'First there is only the ghost. Far down in the black water, a ghost of light. It is a pallid thing, like the gleam on the side of some great fish that speeds through the depths. Very gradually it rises and gleams a drowned red, and then becomes brighter. And at last begins to writhe, and is a dreadful orange fan facing across the water with a mist of the same light about it.

" 'The blazing bomber sinks to embrace it. For a long moment, as if in a final agony, it holds off. But it droops. It begins to fly through a vaporous glow as the propeller-tips touch. Then the strength goes out of it, and four white ribbons sear across the face of the water, and very suddenly there is a great brow of spray flung forward, and a slowing surge, and the other bombers are going on alone while a flame dies into the sea behind them.' "

"Marvellous writing, Miranda! We'll print all your selections! Now I'll see you on your way to The Eyrie."

"I think I'll go straight home. I've just thought that Cousin Hugh may be in London."

When he had returned from seeing her as far as the Exe Plain, well beyond Aaron Kedd's cot down Horrock water, Phillip continued the typing of his editorial, again working by a single candle until the pain in his eye seemed to be about to burst the eyeball. He sat at the table, both eyes clenched tight.

While he was feeling his way upstairs, Molly in 'Goats Castle' (as local moorfolk called the combined cottages) was saying good-night to Miranda, who now had a small bedroom to herself.

"Darling, you've been weepy again."

"I know, Mummy. It is all so beautiful, and yet so sad."

"What is, my pet?"

"The poet we've been writing about, a boy called James Farrar who was killed flying with the Royal Air Force."

" 'We've been writing about', darling? Who is 'we'? Do you mean Cousin Phillip? I thought you were going to see Cousin Hugh this morning?"

"I was on my way there, but dropped in at Cousin Phillip's place, to leave the shirt you'd mended, but stayed to help. The time simply flew!"

"You were there all day, darling?"

"It was so interesting, Mummy, really it was. The extracts from the Notebook were so good, I simply had to stay and help finish them. I copied one out, *please* listen and understand, Mummy darling!"

AFTER NIGHT OFFENSIVE

Glowed through the violet petal of the sky
Like a death's-head the calm summer moon
And all the distance echoed with owl-cry.

Hissing the white waves of grass unsealed
Peer of moon on metal, hidden men,
As the wind foamed deeply through the field.

Rooted to soil, remote and faint as stars,
Looking to neither side, they lay all night
Sunken in the murmurous seas of grass.

No flare burned upwards : never sound was shed
But lulling cries of owls beyond the world
As wind and moon played softly with the dead.

Molly went downstairs thinking that Miranda was too young to
be emotionally disturbed : she must drop a hint to Phillip that
Anda, for all her apparent objectivity, was very temperamental,
and emotionally immature. She was at a difficult age. Why this
extraordinary obsession about the Great War? Well, it was the
age of anxiety, someone had written. War—war—war—would
there ever be an end to it?

The following day, when Phillip called to thank her for mending his shirts, and also for putting him on to a printer, Molly had
determined what line to take.

"I'm so glad Anda was able to be useful for your first number,
dear Phillip. Hugh Cloudesley did say something about a girl
friend in London who may be coming down to help you both in
your literary work—you two sharing her services. Until she comes,
I am most willing to help you in any way I can. I'm not clever
like Anda, but I may be of use in weeding out the wrong sort of
articles sent to you."

"What a kind family you are ! I must say I *do* feel a little
overwhelmed. By every post review copies of all kinds of books
arrive, ever since an advertisement I put in the 'Literary Supplement'. It's a good thing I've got the Silver Eagle to collect them
from the Post Office. Now I suppose I must go to London, while
the galleys of the first number are being set-up in type, to canvass
advertisements from publishers. It's no good merely expecting
them to send them in."

"Why not let Laura do that while she is in London?"

"She's a writer, too, Molly. I don't like to interrupt anyone who has a book on the stocks."

"The pearl in the oyster comes by irritation, my dear."

"So does many a human embryo, but when the mother's in labour she mustn't be disturbed! Oh yes, I wonder if I might leave Bodger here while I'm away in London?"

"Capella will simply adore to have a playmate, dear Coz."

He drove away east at a moderate speed, since petrol was still rationed, and he wanted to keep the reserve of six two-gallon tins brought from the farm.

Laura greeted him quietly: yes, she was writing her novel: no, she was sorry she couldn't possibly break off to canvass advertisements at the moment.

"Perhaps you should wait until Miranda leaves school."

He spent two days going the rounds of publishers. Thirty-two houses, some new-started by printers whose paper supplies were not rationed, promised to write to him . . . the usual polite dismissals. He telephoned Laura.

"Will you dine with me at the Medicean tonight? I'm going back tomorrow."

"I'm already dining there with someone else," a very quiet voice replied.

"I see. Well, goodbye."

"Good-bye."

Hitherto Phillip's letters to Laura had sustained the wilting bloom of imagined, or romantic, love in the little attic room in Old Compton Street. Not the flower of her life—that was her art, her dream, for, like Phillip, she had her being almost entirely in the imagination. Phillip was the sap rising to the flower of her spirit, the bloom by which she felt a glowing happiness, as she created an imaginary world by the art of words. But all blooming expends the resources of the plant. When sap ceases, blossom wilts. Then thoughts of death blight the being.

With each letter Laura was renewed—the force of sap was the force of love. Darling, darling Phillip! When her book was completed she would go to him in his cot. The morning might be dull and dead outside; Phillip was the sun, shining in her mind. Unlike 'Buster' he was not ruined to love, only alienated. His love would heal her, give the fulfilment she had always longed for. Those two had both had terrible experiences in their different wars.

Neither seemed able to forget. Would Phillip be free, even when he had written his war novels? O God, whenever he spoke of his war she felt a chill, as of fog over the face of the sun. Could she be good for him, if she resented even the look on his face whenever he thought about his friends of that faraway time?

Sometimes Laura saw herself as wholly selfish. I want his sperm and his essence for myself. I need him to companion my genius. I *know* I am a genius. Or is it self delusion? An evil genius, a Medusa, as some man I took to bed once told me? Medusa, with hissing snakes in her hair? No, no. I am Kundry, awaiting redemption from Parsifal. My writing is a search for the Holy Grail. If I did not believe that, I should want to drown myself, like Shelley's first wife, Harriet Westbrook. O, Phillip, darling sensitive Prospero, your Ariel is coming to you!

Many times she had imagined the two little rooms, in Phillip's words 'up over Timber Hill into Blanket Field', over the kitchen in Shep Cot; one room for her and her work—entirely private. Phillip in the other room.

Where would they sleep? Upon a heap of bracken on the kitchen floor—under blankets woven of local sheep's wool—before a log fire in the great open hearth. Like Sigmund and Sieglinde in Hunding's cottage! And the morning sun would blaze upon them lying together, utterly relaxed. And they would run out naked and lie in the stream below the coombe and let it take them down, down in its clear bubbled run. And through the eastern window at night the moon would slant on his face beside her while he stroked her hair, and she, with a finger, traced the outline of brow, cheek, chin before winding her arms snake-like around him while he held her in the safety of night glowing with darkness under the stars.

Chapter 12

FLOWERLESS LOVE

One thing had come of 'Buster' dining as Phillip's guest at the Barbarian Club during the London visit to publishers' offices : a house-parlourman for The Eyrie. The new man was, in 'Buster's' words, "an addition to the gaiety of nations." Mornington had been engaged on Phillip's recommendation, and he had turned out to be, 'Buster' told Molly on his return to Exmoor, a jewel : willing to turn his hand to anything—sawing logs, cooking, repairing roofs, gardening, an expert mechanic. He had been almost everything, according to himself—cowboy, gold miner, actor, opera singer, secret service agent, pearl-diver, barman, racing motor-driver, and night-porter at the Barbarian Club.

"And it appears to be true, that's the excellent part of Mornington! Phillip? I have an idea he didn't manage to persuade any publishers to take space, as they say, in his little magazine."

Later in the month, there was an outbreak of measles at Miranda's school, and those girls unaffected were sent home for a week. Miranda arrived much excited by a book someone had given her at school. Molly took the excitement to be a sign of possible infection, and put her daughter to bed and the book into a hot oven, just in case. It was called *A Cosmic Concept of a Fifth Gospel, received from the Unknown Soldier of the Great War,* and came out of the oven with brown edgings upon the leaves.

"It says that a revelation will come on Oldstone Down this summer by a message from the Seventh Plane. The book is by Major Piston, whose mother runs a boarding house in Lynmouth called Shelley's Cottage."

This was reassuring for Molly. The craze for poetry, etc., would soon pass.

"I must read it, Anda darling. But don't you think Major

Piston is just a little teeny-weeny bit bogus? Like that Caspar
Something at Oldstone Castle?"

"Oh, Mummy! I *know* Major Piston's sincere! He was blown
up on the Somme, and in hospital at Lynton the same time as
Cousin Phillip! His old mother is a very sweet person, and also
a medium. They are both spiritually based, and don't eat meat or
even fish, nor does anyone who stays at Shelley's Cottage."

"That doesn't mean that Major Piston isn't deceiving himself,
darling."

"William Blake wrote, 'What is now achieved was once only
imagined'. Major Piston says that the universe is based on an
expanding Idea. Why shouldn't the expanding Idea include
communication with other planets, or worlds? All things are
related."

"But he says his mother has ridden about in flying saucers—
as though they were taxis, darling."

"How do we know there aren't any? Mrs. Piston received a
message to await the coming of someone from the Seventh Plane
an hour before dawn on Oldstone Down last year. She was taken
up in a flying saucer and told that the coming of a stranger, who
will be an old soldier of the Great War, will reveal a way to heal
the world. I think I know already who it is."

"She was obviously meaning her son, darling."

Molly of course knew that her daughter had Phillip in mind.
She was greatly relieved that Anda's feelings for Phillip, like those
for that Piston creature, were no more than a green girl's imagin-
ings.

"Darling, I'm not doubting the sincerity of you or anyone else.
But most people do deceive themselves, you know. Perhaps not
philosophers, but then how many understand what they've
written. How hot your head is. Just a moment, my pet. I'll get a
thermometer."

She took her daughter's temperature. "It's normal, thank goodness."

"Then may I ride over to Shep Cot and see Cousin Phillip
tomorrow?"

"If you want to, darling. Ask him to come over and see us. I've
asked him several times, but he's only called in once, and then he
couldn't stop. You may be more successful. Tell him we can always
give him a bed. He'll have to take us, goats and all, as he finds
us. What will happen to the goats if your father doesn't come in
August hardly bears thinking. They eat everything, including

a cricket ball I gave them to play with. I simply daren't have any laundry drying outside."

The next day Miranda set off on her cob for The Chains, accompanied by Capella. She loved that sky-wide tract of land on the top of the moor. On fine days you could see the dull blue tors of Dartmoor humped along the southern horizon. There the air was seldom still, shaking white blossoms of cotton grass like wisps of wool straggled by the rains. And the Atlantic ocean lying distantly away to the west—a scatter of pale gleams below cumulus clouds billowing whitely in line above the unseen estuary of the Two Rivers.

She halted her cob beside a tumulus on the highest point of The Chains, and when she saw the sun-shafts pointing to the sea, she thought of Donkin drowned. Phillip had written that book, about his cousin Willie. Would he be writing if she called again? What had Mummy said to him—'not to let her be a nuisance?" She felt suddenly inadequate. Phillip was so clever, he knew everything; she knew only what she had learned at school, and read in books. It was terrible!

What could she do? She turned away from the west, and looked across the pale almost milky blue of the Severn Sea, calm with St. Luke's Little Summer. It was what 'Buster' called soaring weather: there was another squadron of clouds becalmed above the mountains of Wales. Then, looking east, she saw a glider rising in circles beyond Dunkery beacon. 'Buster'! She felt excitement, then optimism; and touching the cob with her heels, went in the direction of the unseen cot lying below the northern slopes of The Chains.

'Buster' Cloudesley had seen bubbles of warm air arising to colder levels above the Black Mountains, where they hung condensed as vapour. It was a rare, clear day: thermals would be ascending from the warmed vegetation covering the great sponge of the moor, to become clouds floating as on summer days, galleons in line astern, come to anchor.

With his new man beside him, he drove the Bentley down to the Porlock marshes, where a runway had been made behind the ridge of grey boulders above the line of high tide. There was not really sufficient length for a fool-proof take-off. Safety depended on the speed of towing over a limited runway: the acceleration of the $4\frac{1}{2}$-litre supercharged engine.

The wind was from the west: ideal. Mornington, on a trial

run, was splendidly efficient. The glider rose to six-hundred feet well before danger of the motorcar shunting: 'Buster' released the nylon tow-rope and was on his own. For some minutes he circled in wafts of westerly sea-airs, neither gaining nor losing height; then, chancing his arm, he went inland towards the wooded slopes covering rising ground, and rose on the uptrend. Over the trees he found warm air streaming up from the topmost leaves, and soon was circling well above those northern slopes of the moor covered by acres of warm heather. Up—up—four thousand feet on the altimeter, and still climbing. He thought of the Azores, of the far Falklands, of the deep, the green, the tiger-haunted mountain forests of Brazil. O, life was always wonderful, away from the inhibiting life of houses, the map-like earth so clean and orderly! He felt to be one with Laura, in the altitudes of mind. Theirs was indeed Shakespeare's 'marriage of true minds', without impediment.

No overcast to act as a wet blanket to *Falcon One*. Looking round and above him, he counted seven ravens crossing the sky; and heard, above the sibilance of air past sails and cockpit, the throaty croaks of joy of five young with their parents. The cockbird did a half-roll on black wings, recovering immediately. The flight-leader waggling his wings, signal to dive! He heard the throaty chuckles of joy, from cock to hen, when the young birds, as one flight, dived and rolled. By God, it was like his father's war! Now that Laura was coming, they really must get on with Manfred's biography. Thirty seven Hun aircraft shot down; eleven wounds; two books of verse published, and four gongs before he was twenty one . . . and while trying to fly home to his wife in Cornwall, from New York, falling into the drink. And two years later, 1932, his last message, in a bottle, rolled upon the shore near Lyonesse . . .

The ravens were playing in the blue halls of the wind. It was one of those days when Nature let down her hair. And now, by heck, the ravens were making for a flight of buzzards soaring in tiers on outheld wings, one hawk above the other, simply for the hell of it! If he could find a convolution of thermals he might— with luck (for it was always luck with gliding) reach 10,000 or even 15,000 feet! The real big stuff was done in thunderheads, with a possible 60–100 m.p.h. lift—and the risk of getting caught in an associated down draught, and hurtling down with a cracked frame, wings torn off as neatly as lesser kestrels, in thermals over the Bitter Lake, nipped off the wings of advance parties of locusts

migrating in their swarms. Paired-wings of locusts twirling down
like silver sycamore seeds.

The ravens were now in line astern, ignoring the buzzards;
probably making for a dead sheep somewhere on the moor,
thought 'Buster', climbing steadily in wide spirals. Now the buzzards were diving into the oak-woods they shared in mew-and-
snarl with carrion crows. He watched the crows flying up to harry
the hawks, for there was perpetual war between the two species
of predators. Harrying black anger pursued mewling mottled flap-
wings until evasive action was taken among the trees.

My Prospero!
    I love you, I love you; I will die with you in the sea like Shelley;
but I cannot live with you. Set your Ariel free, O my master! I am in
thrall to you all the time; I shall always love you; *but I must be free
of your image.*
                                        Laura.

Two days later, when Laura read Phillip's reply, together with
a poem on the drowning of Shelley which he had enclosed, she
fell into despair, from which she found relief only in the thought
that she must go to Exmoor before it was too late. The poem could
only mean that he, too, wanted to die. To drown himself! Oh no,
let it not be too late! She ran down the stairs and out of the house
to the post-office, and sent a telegram telling him the time of her
train's arrival at the junction; unaware of the fact that Phillip had
told them at the post-office to keep all letters and telegrams until
he called for them.

In the train she read an article in *The Saturday Evening Post*
by a sergeant of the U.S.A. Army, one of the hangmen at Nuremberg, who declared that he had been waiting months to get his
hands on Herman Göring, for the pleasure of watching his slow
death by strangulation. The print was so vivid that she felt she
could not breathe, and left the carriage to stand by an open corridor window. In her mind was printed the photograph of the
hangman : fat and revengeful as Göring had been in similar revengeful, self-righteous moments. An eye for an eye—O God,
when would it stop, blood calling to blood in revenge down the
ages—

She sought refuge in Phillip's letter, feeling strange beauty in
the poem he had enclosed. Darling Phillip, he was a medium,
truly in rapport with the dead. Was a wiser, older Shelley speak-

ing through him? She re-read the poem slowly; and then the
letter—

Shep Cot

Dear Laura,

I am no Prospero. My staff, or pen, has been lost long since.
Perhaps it was broken for ever, thirty two years ago tomorrow, under
the moon of Hallowe'en, 1914, on Messines ridge in Flanders, 'which
still doth haunt my dreams, a grim, unbidden visitant'.

Do you remember telling me of Jane Williams, the girl Shelley
called Miranda, to whom he lost his heart when he was living at
Lerici? Well, it seems that in 1812 he spent part of a summer at
Lynmouth. I think he found little there, for he refers only once to the
scenery. (Even today, Devon is known as the graveyard in the book
trade). Fanny Burney didn't care for Devon, nor did it make much
impression on Keats, or Hardy. But to me, it is home, where some
of my maternal forebears lived for centuries. Such things, I am sure,
pass on in the blood, which determines the personality—and its
immortality.

I almost believe in spiritualism, too—communication with stray
shades of the dead—the homeless ghosts of the Chinese. I believe,
too, in the continuing life of the spirit after the body's death.

In her last letter to Shelley, Jane Williams wrote: 'Why do you
talk of never enjoying moments like the past? Are you going to join
your friend Plato, or do you expect I shall soon? Buona Notte.'

The letter was dated July 6th; Shelley was drowned on the 8th;
and the poem is his imagined reply from another world.

The poem was psychic! Phillip was seeing his own death in
Shelley's! She stood by an open window in the corridor, imagining her hand opening the door—her body throwing itself out—

At last, at last, with a sick feeling, she arrived at the Junction,
to leave her hold-all outside the telephone box and telephone
The Eyrie. Supposing there was no answer? Everyone away, round
the coast, searching for Phillip's dead body? With a shock she
heard the voice of the late night-porter of the Barbarian Club,
while her heart boomed in her ears.

"I expect your hearing my voice down here is a bit of a surprise,
Miss. I left the Brotherly Barbarians a matter of a week ago, to
take up my new post with his Lordship."

"I'm so glad to hear your voice, Mr. Globe-Mornington!"

"Equally glad to hear your voice, miss."

"Is everyone all right?"

"Right as the weather, miss. His Lordship is out gliding, or should I say up gliding, though that sounds a bit silly doesn't it. You're coming here, I hope? Splendid news, miss!"

"Have you seen Mr. Maddison today?"

"No miss. He appears to have taken to the simple life like Leo Tolstoi."

"Has anything happened to him?"

"Tolstoi? Oh yes. World fame, miss. And to think he never even bought a railway ticket for his last journey on earth!"

"I mean Phillip Maddison! Is he dead?"

"Dead? Not him, or should I say he? No miss, I was referring to the late Count Leo Tolstoi. He seems not to have possessed the wherewithal for his fare, and didn't like to risk a platform ticket unlike that chap—"

"Cut!" cried Laura. "I must find out about buses!"

"You've got twenty minutes to get to the bus station at the Strand over the bridge before the next bus leaves, miss. Mr. Maddison's right as rain miss, so not to worry. Will you be staying here? We need someone to cheer us up. Anyway, I'll tell the temporary housekeeper, that's me, to have your room got ready. And would you like the groom, that's me too, to saddle-up the pony for you? I'm sorry I can't bring the Bentley to meet you, I'm standing by to collect his Lordship on his return to *terra firma*—"

"Is the turning off for Shep Cot at Barbrook?"

"That's right, miss. You go over the bridge there and follow your nose up the lane. I understand it climbs steeply and twists about but when you go through the last gate to the common you'll see Mr. Maddison's hide out. That's what you want, isn't it? You can't miss it."

"Only half-wits unable to communicate say 'you can't miss it'. I *can* miss it! I'm *always* missing it!"

"You've got bags of time, miss. Now you get the bus from the Strand and I'll bring the pony to Barbrook and meet you there. I need a walk to stir up the old phagocytes. As I said, I'll meet your bus at Barbrook, it leaves in fifteen minutes, and it's a quarter of a mile walk over the bridge to the Strand. At Barbrook you get off, see me, and I'll put you on the way to Captain Maddison's hermitage. Another poor fly in the spider's web. No offence, miss, I didn't make the world. Talking about flies, there's a friend of Mr. Maddison's down here called Major Piston whose mother saw one of those mysterious Unidentified Flying Objects above Oldstone Down the other day. It come down with a message from the spheres or stars, I forget which, anyway it took the old

lady up to the Seventh plane, about a book her son had written
to save the world from the atom bomb—"

"You're making it up!"

"I'll spit through my hand and may it choke me if I am, miss.
Major Piston said that the copyright belonged to Messrs. Jorrocks,
or whoever it is prints the Bible, anyway the old lady took up
a proof copy and our Lord gave it His blessing. It's all right,
you've got plenty of time for your bus."

"And Mr. Maddison is really all right?"

"Looks very thin, miss. Doesn't feed himself properly. So he
can't write, and it worries him. And others worry him, too, from
what I hear."

"What others?"

"Well, he's an object of curiosity, if I can put it like
that."

"What are you trying to say? Has he got someone staying with
him?"

"Not that I know of. I'll meet your bus at Barbrook, it's a lovely
day, you'll love riding up to the Hut Circles. There should be a
thermal rising off The Chains by then—all that cotton grass drying—All right, keep your hair on, miss. I was about to say that
if you look up you may see his Lordship going round and round
like a falcon waiting on, as bird-watchers say. Are you still there?
Hullo! Hullo! Oh, you've rung off, you bitch."

The war-time bus, a single-decker, was slow and old. Gears
grated, carden-shaft thumped, exhaust gases came through the
floor. It was market day. The bus was filled with smallholders'
wives, many with baskets on knees, and shaggy drovers with sticks.
What they said was unintelligible, weather-blurred speech
amidst laughter revealing teeth rotten from acid-soil water. The
man from Porlock who had stultified Samuel Taylor Coleridge
with the innocence of incomprehension. Small hopes for Shelley,
with his Declaration on Freedom, posted up in Lynton and Barn-
staple, before being prosecuted for blasphemy. His children taken
from him by law, driven to live abroad, to drown in the waters of
Spezzia—

Hardy in September 1920, writing *At Lulworth Cove a Century
Back,* where Keats had embarked for Italy in September, 1820—

"You see that Man?"
That man goes to Rome—to

death, despair;
And no one notes him now but you and I;
A hundred years, and the world will follow
him there,
And bend with reverence where his ashes
lie."

Francis Thompson, in his *Shelley essay*—

Keats, half-dying in the jaws of London
and spit dying on to Italy—posterity,
posterity! posterity which goes to Rome,
weeps large-sized tears, carves beautiful
inscriptions, over the tomb of Keats;
and the worm must wriggle her curtsey to
it all, since the dead boy, wherever he
be, has quite other gear to tend. Never
a bone the less dry for all the tears!

I am a puritanical harlot and my own posterity, I am weeping
large-size tears for my own bones—my unwritten novels. Where,
O where, am I going, and why? People are looking at me; looking away; back again. Two small boys on the cracked imitation-
leather of the seat opposite are staring at me like a pair of constipated little owls. Stuffed with gurk-making greasy Devonshire
pasties; staring like two forked-radish freaks with umbrellas and
bowler hats and F.R.Z.S. after their names on a Sunday morning
in Regent's Park.

She stared back at them until their gaze dropped; then she
said, "Do you like riddles? What is the difference between a
constipated owl and a poor marksman?" When there was no reply
she went on, "Don't you know? Then I'll tell you. I heard it on the
Children's Hour of the B.B.C. Well, speaking only for the poor
marksman, he can shoot, but can't hit."

The owls stared, waited unblinking.

"I'm too high-brow, perhaps? Well then, are you mechanically
minded? Yes? Then here's another question for your Brains Trust
—that's you. Tell me if the thumping under this bus is due to
a worn carden-shaft, or to a loose gear-box with chipped gears—
or both?"

The larger of the two boys continued to look unblinking at her,
then raising crooked elbows and shoulder-blades until the lobes
of his ears were touching the collar of his jacket, he spread his

hands in a slow gesture disclaiming all knowledge of what she was saying.

"They two boys be Frenchies, my dear!"

The over-weight farmwife across the gangway leaned sideways and said, while her bosom quivered with her words, "They boys be French boys, surenuff. Ay, they be. They'm on holiday like, come yurr vor learn our English." She quivered over a basket and pulled out an apple turnover.

"Goo on, my dear, you 'ave it! You'm looking 'ungry like, you come a long way? You'm pale, my dear, now don't ee deny your stummick, there be plenty more apples whoam!"

The food made her realise how hungry she was. The journey along winding valley lanes became pleasant, she was no longer isolated. Up and up the bus groaned and bumped its way, following the old coach road until it descended steeply to a village, with cottages on either side of a narrow road leading to the high moor. Grinding up in low gear, eye-smarting exhaust through the floor, steam from radiator. Her mind turning with the wheels, heaving them round—quicker, quicker—more and more desperately as the carbon-monoxide fumes polluted her bloodstream. Christ, let me get out, let me get out, and walk! Shoving herself past knees fat and knees nobbly, baskets and rush-bags, Laura jumped off and breathed deeply of sunlit air. And looking into the sky she saw 'Buster's' glider, in a serene circle at three thousand feet. Thank God, thank God he was safe! And if anything had happened to Phillip, 'Buster' wouldn't be gliding!

She got on the bus at the top, and sat happily looking through the window as it moved past a prospect of heathland, and afar, of azure sea and the distant coast of Wales below woolly clouds calling to mind Bards and Druids, and the magic of Merlin.

Then down, down, all the way down the valley of running waters, and there at the bend, where the bus stopped, was dear, dear Mornington holding the pony's head, saddlery polished and even the irons shining.

Miranda crossed the northern slope below The Chains with Capella in attendance. Seeing smoke above Shep Cot, she laid the reins on the cob's neck to direct it to the northern slope. Down, down a fairly steep descent, and so to a thread of water moving through swampy ground rough with clumps of purple moor grass and rush. Thus, unknowing, she crossed the West Lyn river at one of its sources.

The door of the cot was open. She found Phillip sitting by the open hearth whereon sappy oak logs hissed and fumed. He jumped up when he heard her, and took the reins to loop them through the rusty ring on the door post, saying gladly, "Do come in, dearest Coz! It's lovely to see you!" while wondering if he dare hug and kiss her.

"I've baked you a plum cake, cousin Phillip. Have you finished the first number of the magazine?"

"Yes, and it's gone to the Minehead printer. Sixty-four pages, to be sold at half-a-crown!"

He opened the parcel, to see a dark brown shrunken object that looked as if it had never seen a baking tin.

"My favourite cake! Do sit down."

"I love this little milking stool, and the polished fire-dogs Cousin Phillip."

"I'm going to rebuild the hearth, and bring the back forward four-fifths of the way up, and then sharply back, to limit the amount of cold air being drawn across the floor. You see, flames and smoke should enter the chimney proper through a narrow throat, like a pillar-box's opening for letters. There's room only for flame and smoke; no gate-crashing cold air."

"We've had to have a plate glass put up below the lintol in ours, to stop it smoking. Didn't you live like this when you first came to Devon?"

"Yes."

"You appear to have travelled in a circle."

"Yes, I'm now trying to round off my life."

"Have you started the novel series?"

"My little galaxy is still nebulous."

His eyes looked tired, so she said, "Surely a candle isn't enough to write by at night? I mean, doesn't it strain the eyes."

"It does, rather. I'm thinking of having a small propeller fixed to an old motorcar-dynamo on a pole, to charge my car battery for extra light."

"Cousin Hugh has an oil-engine to charge his batteries at The Eyrie. Have you seen his searchlight? It's wizard. He's got all sorts of gadgets."

She began to feel nervous, her mind quested for something to say. They both said together, "Do you like gliding?" and laughed. Animated now, she said, "Did you see 'Buster' going over? He may be over again now! Come and see!"

Child-like, she took his hand and led him outside. There the silent movement was, slowly involving itself in a wide circle on wings that seemed calmly indifferent to all life below. Then those long and narrow wings appeared to fore-shorten, to shrink, as it banked at the turn, to resume slow movement while appearing to be not so big.

"He's rising fast!"

"Let's go up to The Chains!"

Hand in hand they scrambled upwards, animals following, to reach, after nearly an hour, the crest; and there to see gossamers everywhere linking stalk and fluff of cotton-grass: myriads of silken lines from tiny spiders which had cast off into the warm airs of early afternoon. The sun's rays were everywhere in reflection along the threads, which in multiplication appeared as a golden tunnel ever receding before them.

"Why, they're little money spiders!" said Miranda.

Still holding her hand, he laid it for a moment against his cheek.

"Oh Miranda, if only I could write what I feel. I can see my father now, explaining that Linyphia, the money spider, releases gossamers from its spinnerets, which the wind bears up, taking the spider with it. Do you know where I last saw them, Miranda? And thought of my father, with all the love that I never had for him when I was a boy? It was in the chalk trenches of the Bird Cage, on the twentieth of March, nineteen eighteen, the day before the great German attack on a sixty mile front. It is all around me now!" he said, tremulously, his eyes strangely bright. "That morning of quiet sunshine, I sitting with 'Spectre' West, my Colonel, after an inspection of the Brigade battle-zone, which in a few hours was to be destroyed and overrun in the German assault. Their code name for it was *Michael*. I remember thinking,' he went on like a man possessed by the most innocent thoughts, "how your shadow went everywhere with you, it was always with you, it fore-shortened when you were asleep, it arose with you when you got up, but when you were dead it did not last long, but broke up with you. How strange I should remember it so—I feel it with almost a shock! I can remember exactly how my thought seemed to flow like poetry—it remained your shadow until leaving you it was given back to the earth of your genesis, and then your earth-bound self was drifting on like a gossamer, beyond the wooden crosses of the dead."

He walked away from her, possessed by happiness, feeling that soon the impulse would come, and he would bring back all, all to life; then, returning, he saw tears in her eyes, and heard her say, behind the visor of her long dark hair, "It is all so beautiful." She shook away the hair, and looking at him, said, "Darling Cousin Phillip, I'll help you—I'll do anything—so that you can write your novels!"

"Darling Miranda! You *do* help me, just by being you."

A thin white thread fell from the glider and broke into a green ball of light. A whiteness fluffed above the flare, opening into a miniature parachute. An arm waved far above, and the glider was going away to the south.

"It's a message, I'll get it!" she cried.

HALLOWE'EN PARTY EYRIE TONIGHT

BUSTER.

While they were going down to the common, they saw Laura on a horse outside the cot. When they came to her, Phillip gave her the little aluminium canister. "We've just collected a message for you from 'Buster', Laura."

"Are you sure it isn't another one from Shelley?"

"Well, it has just come down on this parachute. And there's the glider up there."

The kettle was simmering as it hung to the lapping crook. Laura refused a cup of tea. Miranda did not stay long; she was inwardly furious by the way Phillip was being treated. She mounted the cob, and saying, "See you both tonight at 'Buster's'," rode away, followed by Capella.

The air seemed colder.

"Have you had any food today, Laura?"

"Food! Who wants food!"

Just as in 1939, when she had bicycled forty miles to the farm. He filled the pot and poured a fresh cup for her. She pushed it away.

"I told you years ago you were a liar, and you *are* a liar!"

"What have I said?"

"It's what you wrote! That you were going 'to join your friend Plato'—your very words!"

"That poem was about *Shelley!* And it wasn't—"

"You sent it to worry me! You wanted me to think you were going to drown yourself! You did! I know you did! O Christ, why do you haunt me? If I see a man in the street with white hair I want to follow him. I never want to see you again!"

She ran outside. He stood so still that a robin flew into the kitchen and perched on one of two boiled eggs cupped together on a plate. The bird slipped on a white dome, fluttering; tried again, stood balancing until, feeling heat under its toes, it flew with stitter-cry to Phillip's shoulder. Laura watched through the window. Then she walked slowly to Phillip, holding out a finger to the bird. It flew out of the doorway. She put her arms round Phillip's chest, and hid her head against his jacket. He stroked the dark hair above the white nape of neck bowed as though for execution, before bending down to cherish so vulnerable, so entangled a girl. She sighed, thrusting her face under the jacket flaps as though seeking shelter there for ever. She inspired slowly; and then releasing a deep breath, looked up at him with tender mouth and eyes.

"You don't really love me, do you? Oh, I know the answer. No one can love me. I am a daughter of Chaos and Night. I shall send your poem to my half-brother Charon, down a tributary of the Styx." And folding the poem, which was on a separate quarto sheet of paper, into the shape of a paper boat, she led him by the hand to the head-water of the Lyn where it flowed small and clear out of the bog.

"Shelley used to sail paper-boats, didn't he? Perhaps I'll be drowned one day, then you'll be free to marry Melissa—or will it be Miranda? Or both?"

"You'll be the one to marry."

They went back to the cottage, where they ate the boiled eggs, followed by slices of whole-wheat bread with butter and honey.

"Oh Phillip, I am sorry. Why did you pretend you were going to drown yourself? I am sorry I was so awful to you. But when I was coming here, I lost the way, and found I was in another valley. I saw a cottage, which I thought might be yours, and went to knock at the door, leaving my horse's reins over the gate. There was an awful black sow in the garden, eating a dreadful sort of brown fish, very thin, and covered with yellow clusters like toadstools. Then a man came to the door, and pulled me in by an arm, and Phillip, he began to masturbate himself, while shouting out what he was going to do to me! I screamed 'Phillip!', and he ran out of a door at the back. I ran away, and just managed to get on my horse, and seeing two figures against the sky, I made for them, and so came to this place. Is he a murderer, that man? Do you know who he is?"

"He's called Aaron Kedd."

"He's sick, Phillip."

"Of course. We're all more or less sick."

"All this whole moor is haunted!"

They sat on the corn-sack, before a blazing fire. She undid the buttons of his shirt and found a way in to draw fingernails up and down his spine before giving sharp jags, as though to stir him to action. He thought of Kedd and his onanistic jags, and wished she would not try to force emotion; then he thought of Miranda, and was still within himself.

"I know what you're thinking of!" she complained, leaving him abruptly.

"I'm thinking that it's Allhallows Night, and wondering who will be there."

"What schoolgirls—or schoolgirl—you mean!"

She left him and went upstairs to her room. When after some minutes she didn't come down, he went up and saw her writing in her foolscap-size diary. He sat beside her on the bed. She closed the book, and was a rather sad, voiceless creature allowing him to put an arm round her shoulder.

As they lay upon the bed, momentarily at peace, through the casement window could be seen the eastern line of the moor gradually dissolving in a gold lustre; and in dissolution coming alive with a light now denied to those gossamers which, as the sun went down to its Atlantic grave, were mere containers of the cold light of day's end. And when Phillip had gone downstairs, Laura wrote words on a sheet of paper which she left on his bed in the next room.

This is a new beginning: the full moon is rising out of the east, to offer cold charity alike to your homeless ghosts of the living and my ruined saints of the dead; and from all these may we both be delivered, O Great Pan!

Chapter 13

HALLOWE'EN

Molly Bucentaur now felt happy that Miranda and Phillip were good friends. His coming had filled a gap in Anda's life. The girl was intellectually mature far beyond her years. She had never been keen to be with others of her age. She missed a father, the well-named Peregrine—wanderer indeed, living for himself, anything to distract him from inner emptiness: from big game hunting in Kenya to salmon fishing in Norway—polo, deer-stalking, fox-hunting, and cricket—the complete extrovert. Perry, living on what was left of the family capital, coming home once a year, regularly, for cricket in summer; and then away again.

So, Molly thought, Phillip was to Anda a sort of foster-father ... until the girl's return from Shep Cot that afternoon, and her announced intention of helping Phillip with his magazine and other literary work in a full-time job when she had left school.

"I don't want to go to University."

"Yes darling, I know how you feel. But at Oxford you will get a wide grounding on all sorts of authors."

"I'm getting that already, Mother."

"Darling, your father might not care for the idea of a young girl alone in a remote cottage, even with cousin Phillip."

"It's nothing to do with him."

"He is your legal guardian, as well as your father."

"He seldom sees me, he's probably forgotten my existence."

"He's very fond of you, darling."

"Then he should let me do what I want to do."

"He expects you to go to Oxford, you know."

"Well, if I must go, why can't Cousin Phillip live in a village not too far outside Oxford? Then I'll be able to bicycle there and help with reading contributions, and also see that he gets proper food."

"You and Cousin Phillip have talked it over, I presume?"

"He doesn't know about it yet. It's only my idea."

Molly was relieved. "What will Laura say to that, darling?"

"Laura is selfish, she can't help it I know, but she's no good for Cousin Phillip. It isn't fair, the way she behaves towards him. Oh, I know she needs constant reassurance herself, owing to an emotionally upset early life. So does Cousin Phillip, in another way. But not Laura's way. Those two are impossible together. She can't help sleeping with one man after another, and what good does it do her? It doesn't fill the gap of basic loneliness."

Molly tried again. "You should be a writer, with your penetration and sympathy."

"That is what Cousin Phillip says, Mother dear. He is a master, why can't I be his pupil?"

Towards midnight, when the party at The Eyrie was going well with distillation of grain, grape and grape-skin, and juniper berry, 'Buster' turned his searchlight into the trees of the wood growing steeply down to the rocks creamy with the surge of tidal waves. Smoke had been straying to the terrace, and 'Buster's' idea was to try and attract some of the witches of the coven known to be holding their first revel there since the end of the war.

"They build a fire, throw off their clothes and dance around it, going through all kinds of mumbojumbo," he said.

"But darling Hugh, wouldn't that be a bit *outré*? I mean, to expose them in your searchlight?"

"My dear Molly, I don't mean in the way of being a peeping Tom. But light attracts, and a fixed beam might bring them up to the terrace. I really would like to meet them. There's a sense of delightful other-worldliness about it all. This is no Saturnalia, since the naked body in gymnastic action sets free the horrific convolutions of the mind. On second thoughts I'm not so sure that Mornington would approve. He is a respecter of women—a respect derived from a holy fear of the young female, and an equally unholy fear of what he calls old faggots. What do you think, Laura?"

"I'm nearly an old faggot myself—here goes my last chance!", cried Laura, throwing off her clothes while uttering the high, sharp screams of a vixen calling a dog-fox.

Miranda was about to follow her, but Molly restrained her daughter.

"Why not, Mummie? Blake said that 'Everything that lives is holy'."

"I don't want you to catch a chill, darling. Also, some things are not always so holy as others."

"Well said!"cried Riversmill.

Laura went down among the trees, to introduce herself to the witches and wizards (of the evening) carrying out coven rites by their fire.

Mornington helped 'Buster' to bring boxes of magnesium flares for his master to touch-off among the shrubs and bushes of the garden, and on the terrace in front of the house. Laura came up through the woods and concealed herself behind a cypress tree on the terrace, to watch Phillip and Miranda, who were visible standing side by side in green-powdery light among slanting shadows.

Unknown to Laura, Kedd had been watching the revellers in the wood below the house; but on seeing the naked girl arrive, his stew of feelings had been directed to her. He had followed her nearly to the terrace, and behind a tree was awaiting an opportunity to expose himself before her with onanistic fascination.

Standing still, Laura could just hear what Phillip and Miranda were saying.

"Life is so beautiful when I am with you, Cousin Phillip."

"I feel the same, Miranda."

"Do *I* make you feel happy?"

"Your presence, yes. I feel we can be tremendous friends—we are both what is called spiritually based."

"It's such a lovely world when there are people in it like you, Cousin Phillip. You will begin to write again soon, won't you? I wish I could leave school this term. I'm wasting my time there. I no longer want to go up to Oxford."

"Oh, Oxford will be great fun. It will remain with you and affirm you all your life."

"Do you sometimes feel that life is a dream?"

"Many people have felt that, Miranda. The great poets and artists not only feel that, but they *are* that."

"You are so sweet! And after all you've been through, you're never bitter. 'Buster' says when the commandos shot you on your farm, and he was sent to apologize to you in hospital, you were simply terrific, saying it was all your fault because on the Western Front no one in khaki ever fired at you and so you didn't know any better! Did you really feel like that?"

"At first I was in a rage, and did know better than to walk into their fire. Probably a little bit suicidal, too."

"You won't let yourself ever feel like that again, will you? I won't let you," and she took his arm.

Not far away a second man was concealed behind a tree. He, too, was watching Laura. When he moved, a twig cracked; and Miranda looked towards the noise without moving her head. She whispered to Phillip, "It's Brigadier Tarr. Mummy says he leaps on anyone. I hate him because he calls you 'the fasciste!' He thinks women are only waiting to go off with him."

From the terrace came the shrill scream of a vixen. At once the sturdy figure of the Brigadier moved uphill. They watched while he walked, crouching a little, towards the cypress tree. They heard him saying, "Your dog-fox is ready at stand, pretty girl." There was a white movement of withdrawal before a multi-shadow'd figure with arms held before it like a Japanese wrestler in position for karate blow. Gravel rasped as it shifted position to bar escape.

They heard the Brig's voice saying, "Come on, no more bitchiness darling" as the Brig went up to Laura, intending to put an arm round her waist and the other hand ready to grope.

The hand was seized, twisted, jerked : Brigadier Tarr was falling, bottom uppermost, over Laura's shoulder, and then she was gone among the trees, where a voice yelled, "I see'd 'ee! Sodom and Gomorra lot, all of 'ee be! Yew wait, midears, you'll zee what be comin' tew ee!"

"Sounded like poor old Kedd" said Phillip.

Now some younger members of the party, having thrown off all but basic garments, began to whoop and leap around the apparition of the Wissilcraft turning cartwheels before resting, like a female Nijinski, pallid and self-possesed, against the trunk of a tree. After this exhibition Molly and 'Buster' claimed Miranda, so Phillip wandered off alone through the wavering light of flares rising, hovering, floating down under little parachutes upon Noman's land from wan dusk to gangrenous dawn, the great livid wound of the Western Front lying across Europe from North Sea to the Alps.

In the magnesium lights on the terrace, Laura's lips were livid under eyes that were blue Valkyrie glints.

"What is Miranda to you?"

"A good friend."

"Have you had her?"

"Do you ever think of anything else?"

"No!"

*   *   *

The old Western Front was pale under the same moon. Were there now foxes in the country about the Somme river? Trees grown high again to cluster together as woods above the Ancre stream, haunt of wildfowl which had never heeded the flashes of guns in the valley below Thiepval and the Schwaben redoubt.

Now only the moon. The last flare had spluttered to a dull blob, the searchlight swept its last inquiring look at the racing tides of Severn Sea. Coven gone, vixen too, it seemed. Tiny flashes of lighthouse along Welsh coast, stars cold. Then his hand was taken and there beside him on the terrace was Laura, clothed, the others inside drinking tea to take away taste and clug of grain alcohol.

"Oh Phillip, never leave me. Please never leave me," as he sheltered her with his arms. "I am so afraid—like you."

"I am not afraid when you are yourself."

"But how can you love me?"

"We are really brother and sister."

She drew away. "Damn that! Is there anything between you and Miranda? Is there?"

"Kinship of ideas—that is all."

"Yes, it *is* all." She sighed. "Phillip, please tell me truthfully— Do I inhibit you? I know my manner does some people."

"It's not you Laura, it's I who am inhibited—or inhabited."

"Inhabited by the 'enlarged and numerous senses' which William Blake said were the requisite of the poet."

"Or, as Conrad wrote ironically of such gifts in Turgenev, 'There's enough to ruin any man'."

"But ruin is the basis and material of art."

"It's the past that makes us. If we are kind to the past, we get clear of our prejudices and fears, I think. You must *write*, Laura. So must I."

"We'll always be 'with' one another, as we are now, won't we? Even though our bodies don't 'fit'?" She clung to him. "I love you when I don't feel sexy."

" 'Love has its tidal moments, lapses and flows due to a metrical rule of the interior heart'. Francis Thompson quotes that, of Alice Meynell, in his tremendous essay on Shelley."

"Phillip, I now realise that the poem you sent me was prophetic of my own death in the sea. As I wrote to you, I will die with you, but I cannot live with you. And that poem was so beautiful—

'Ariel to Miranda :– hear

This good-night the sea-winds bear;

And let thine unacquainted ear

Take grief for their interpreter'—No, don't talk, Phillip. Let me finish. I think drowning is the best death. It's the cleanest, and it's over soon, and no-one sees your body. I have a horror of that; I mean, lying on some slab, when it isn't you any more. But I don't want to die now. I am so happy! I feel, at last, that I am on Prospero's isle, and I am your Ariel. Let's go to Corfu, and write there! Come and ask Molly about it, she's been to Corfu."

"Before the first war a woman would have said, 'Please take me in'. But the revolution started when women began to work in munition factories, then to clip tram tickets. I remember—"

Laura's eyes widened. "You know what you can do with your old tram-tickets! God, you old sweats are either all nostalgia or all cock, like Brigadier Tarbaby!"

Dreading a scene, he said, "Let's find out about Corfu. Molly will be able to tell us."

He took her arm, they went in together. Just inside the room the Brig was giving advice to Molly. "You want to keep an eye on Miranda," Phillip heard him saying. And Molly's reply,

"I don't understand you, Brig."

"You know what the Americans say, don't you?"

"They say a lot of things, no doubt."

"They say, 'When you're big enough you're old enough, and when you're old enough you're big enough'."

"What exactly do you mean by that?"

"The *fasciste* is trying to seduce your decoy."

"*My* decoy?" she replied, distinctly.

"Come, don't beat about the bush. You visit him don't you? And send your girl over—"

Molly said slowly, "Which character is it in one of Oscar Wilde's plays who says, 'Never ascribe to your neighbour motives meaner than your own'?" She turned her back on the Brig and said to Laura, "Did I hear the word 'Corfu'? I spent my honeymoon with Peregrine there. The very place for writers. Truly a magic isle, my dear. One can live there very cheaply." She put an arm through Phillip's, the other through Laura's, and led them to the terrace. "Take your Ariel to Shakespeare's 'magic isle' dearest Phillip. One can go quite cheaply by tramp steamer, and see the dolphins that Byron watched from his yacht."

"Two tramps on a tramp, what?" said the Brig, who still stuck to them.

"Oo-er, I do believe you've been listening to the Light Pro-

gramme of the B.B.C., Brigadier Caliban!" said a mock-demure
Laura.

Phillip's room was next to Laura's. Hardly had he arranged
the pillow, having switched off the light, when Laura hopped into
his bed. There followed a new experience for him : some sort of
hobby-horse release of the neurotic or erotic female imagination
achieved—to her apparent satisfaction but not to his—after which
he lay awake wondering if the rôles of male and female, due to
some evolutionary switch, were about to be restored to their
original status. Was it unknown in law for a woman to rape a man,
to use him as a vehicle of onanism, before discarding him, and
incidentally pinching all the bedclothes?

He shook with silent laughter, while faint little snores came
regularly from Laura. He punched her gently in the back. When
she sat up he hauled some of the blankets to his side of the bed;
but with a turning cocoon movement she managed to draw to
herself even the strip of sheet and corner of eiderdown he had
held on to before.

He got off the bed and looked out of the window. An owl, one
feather upstanding over each eye, uttered a single note from a tree
outside. It called again, *Who*.

"Me," said Phillip.

"Who're you talking to?"

"A long-eared owl, almost a rare bird. I thought you were
asleep."

"What, after you've rolled me into a Swiss roll?"

"You cocoon'd yourself."

"You forced me to, otherwise I'd've lain here starko."

"That wouldn't have been an entirely new experience."

"You talk like one of your old tram-tickets."

From below the window came the high triple bark-scream of
a vixen. Life half-ripped across. At once Laura was beside him.

"Poor darling," she whispered. "I hope he'll be kind to her."

They got back into bed. He held her, and while stroking the
back of her head, there came the remote clang of a dustbin. "That's
the dog-fox," he said. "The town foxes are a different lot from
those on the moor. They live out of dustbins. He'll bring her bacon
rind, or a mouldy chop bone."

They remade the bed and snuggled up for warmth. "Go to
sleep, you're tired. You need a long rest."

Someone was blowing a hunting horn out of a window. "It's

the Brig, Phillip. He blows it sometimes when we're gliding. He's so happy in the air."

They lay still, nearer to being real friends after the shared fun of the night. But lay not at peace. Shortly Laura left him to visit 'Buster' down the passage, a night-light burning by the bed-head; little boy lost—to whom all tenderness—

On the bedroom wall hung a portrait in oils of his father, Major Manfred: a youth in the 'maternity jacket' of the Royal Flying Corps, a khaki jacket fastened at the neck by invisible button, then diagonally to the waist. Across the left breast his 'gongs'—including the Victoria Cross. On another wall, most dim in the little candle-gleam, a portrait of 'Buster's' grandfather, the canvas torn where the lead pellets of a 12-bore gun, fired by Manfred, had passed through it.

"Laura," said 'Buster', "we really must start work on my un-happy father's biography. Come New Year's Day, which is in two months' time, he will have been drowned in the North Atlantic, on a Great Circle course, twenty three years ago. A strange man. While the history of the Peerage is full of odds and sods, I think he must be the only one who fired a twelve-bore Purdey gun at the portrait of his dead father." He reflected, while she gently caressed his forehead with little kisses. "Indeed he was a strange man. After the Treaty of Versailles he took the sins of the British upon himself, particularly the lies of that upstart Mr. George, the Prime Minister who can be excused, in part perhaps, because he had no idea of manners. Be it as it may, my father returned his 'gongs' to the War House, and later virtually committed suicide by attempt-ing to fly from New York to Cornwall, where we lived then, in a monoplane with one engine. Years later a bottle was washed up on the Cornish coast, near Lyonesse, with his last letter to me. I've got both bottle and letter in the bookcase in my study. Remind me to show them to you, will you?"

From Laura came a little snore. Then others. Gently he took her in his arms, she turned over and settled to sleep; while he lay still and desolate as Phillip in another room.

Chapter 14

WINTER ON THE MOOR

The long journey eastwards across Exmoor in the Silver Eagle, Laura wearing Phillip's black leather flying-coat, helmet, goggles, fur gloves, plaid rug around knees. Windscreen down against frost patterns on glass. Through Taunton and the winding road to Wincanton; on to Wiltshire and the Great Plain at a modest, a steady forty miles and hour ... then the crisis, Laura, silent for miles, suddenly screaming, trying to throw herself out. Whimper of worn tyres, car slewing, sliding to standstill. Engine switched off. Silence. Flask of hot coffee refused. Likewise luncheon at Mere. Thence mute to London, drab traffic on Great West Road, second-gear crawl amidst fog-thickened diesel fumes. Fanless radiator boiling. At last Old Compton Street, the silent packing of tin-plate perforated names and addresses of subscribers; card indexes; piles of Mss. and stamped, addressed envelopes. Returning down the stairs, Phillip to Barbarian Club.

"I'll call for you in an hour's time, Laura."

Dinner at the Medicean : Laura running out half way through the meal. Having paid the bill, he followed. Driving in silence to Old Compton Street.

"Do tell me what's the matter, Laura."

"You know very well what's the matter!"

"I do *not* know."

"Good-night then—Buona Notte!"

Then she was running down the stairs, imploring him to come back and sleep in her room.

Both lying still in the single bed. Laura withdrawing, to lie on the floor. What a life! Alarm clock ticking like death-watch beetle, set for 7.30 a.m. Boat train leaving 9.30. The polar night's huge boulder hath rolled this my heart, my Sisyphus, in the abyss ... Edith Sitwell a great poet.

Breakfast. "You're naturally upset by the change, Laura, but

161

you'll settle down in Corfu. Shouldn't you eat something? It's a long journey to Brindisi . . ."

No reply.

"Laura, please do try and help me—and yourself."

And then, "It's time to leave, Laura."

Victoria Station. Her silence maintained while waiting in queue. Shuffling movement, barrier open, tickets please, leaving her to show hers while he dashed, carrying suitcase, to platform-ticket machine. Buy fruit—Canadian apples, oranges, bananas, grapes. Then up and down the long train to find her. 9.25. Where was she? Ah! Behind that window, face turned away.

"Here's your case. Sorry I forgot about the platform ticket. I'm always terribly nervous, too, before I start a book, Laura. When the first draft of my novel is finished, I'll join you in Corfu, Laura. And we'll walk, and swim, and live in the brilliant sunlight of an Ionian spring."

"Charming!"

"At last the oracle! Have some fruit. Almost like pre-war!"

"That must cheer you up. What're the new tram tickets like? The nineteen fourteen ones?"

"Yes! How did you guess?"

Blue leaden eyes upon him. "Why are you trying to get rid of me?"

"Now be fair. Corfu was *your* idea!"

The guard was standing on the platform, green flag under arm. Phillip went to the end of the coach to say at the open door, "How much longer before the train leaves?"

"Two minutes, sir."

"Laura, I must say good-bye now. 'All partings are a little death'. I wonder who said that."

"You did!"

"Tactless of me."

"Oh *no*. You *don't* say!"

Reversion to the semi-peasant girl from 'silly Suffolk'. Guard taking watch-on-chain from fob. "Well, au revoir. Let us part kindly, Laura."

No reply. 'Silly' Suffolk or saintly Suffolk, this was Medusa he thought, leaving the coach.

Guard closing door behind him, whistle to mouth . . . door flung open, recoiling against strap-hinge, Laura leaping to platform, Medusa snake-arms round his neck, "Oh Phillip, why are you sending me away from you? I love, love you. Promise you'll look after yourself?", unwinding arms to look into his face.

"Come on, miss! Take your seat, please!"

He almost said *Buona Notte* but changed to "Au revoir".

Guard blowing on-your-way whistle, Laura hanging out of window-space, "I am with you always!", palms of hands pressed against his narrowed face. He had to break her hold, push her back into the coach as the train drew smoothly away.

A last cry—"Don't forget me!", and he was standing there waving, waving—the train smaller and smaller round the curve.

Station Buffet. 10 a.m. Phillip sat by a cup of weak coffee growing colder on the table beside him, as he wrote in his journal. Before going to the warm room he had stood for some time on the empty platform, imagining the long train on its way to Dover— Paris—Rome—Brindisi—the rusty ferryboat over the wine-dark sea to Corfu.

"Is that your black open motorcar on the taxi waiting-place, sir?"

"Oh yes, I think it must be."

"If you could take it away, sir."

"Of course, officer! At once!"

London. Emptiness, pain; but—one must hold on.

The grass grows green upon the battlefields.

"Well, how very nice to see you!" said Lucy, blushing.

"Yes, by Jove, Phil, I can't tell you how good it is to see you!"

"Things going well, Tim?"

"Oh, one mustn't grumble."

"How's Brenda and the boy?"

"Oh, well, quite happy, I'm glad to say."

"It's half-term for Peter," said Lucy. "He *will* be pleased! Rosamund's due home tonight for three days, too."

"Is this the baby? Heavens, how she's grown. May I take her?"

"Of course, my dear! Do you know, Sarah is just like you! Same eyes, same nose, very energetic, and sees everything! I *am* so pleased. There now, isn't she a darling?"

"What long narrow feet."

"Just like yours, Pip. She'll make a good horsewoman, too, with those long legs."

"Another throw-back in the family—what bad luck for you."

"Not at all, my dear, not *one little bit* at all!"

Lucy flushed again, conscious of her boldness in thus contradicting Phillip. "Have you had any food? Well then, how about a cup of tea?"

"By Jove yes, Lulu, just the thing before I go to the station to collect Rosamund!"

Tim had an old Morris car, for which he had paid £30 at the end of the war. Now it was worth £130, a thought that constantly gave him pleasure.

"Would you like me to put the Eagle in the garage, Phil? And if you're not going to use it, I suggest you let me drain the water from the lowest point. There's a sharp wind-frost most nights now."

"Thanks, Tim. I must be getting back to Exmoor fairly soon—"

The open hearth burned well. His deep leather saddlebag-chair. Heavy, split oak logs from the farm. Upstairs room with the lattice casements and polished corn-merchant's double desk—why not edit the magazine from there? And write his own stuff at Shep Cot? All his books in the two tall cases. No trouble about food. £22 in bank; he could write his monthly article for the *Evening Telegram*, arranged that morning at 25 guineas a time. Then, in March, to Corfu: novel finished, magazine established—

"I've promised to stay at Molly's during her children's half-term, Lucy."

Miranda had written, *Mummie asks me to say come over and stay as long as you like, dearest coz. We do so want to help with New Horizon. I can sort out the articles, and send the others back with a letter of thanks, to soften the blow of rejection. Please do not lose my address: the school's back at Cheltenham. Please write soon. Always your loving Miranda.*

P.S. Bodger is happy, Mummie says, but he seems to be waiting all the time for you and listening to motor engines.

"Well, stay a day or two if you feel like it, Pip. I'm sure Cousin Molly will understand. Why not telephone?"

"You mean from the public call-box down the street?"

"Oh no! We've had the telephone connected. It's useful for Tim, about orders for his trinket boxes. You see, it saves him going to London to ask the little man in the Bond Street shop."

Lucy and Tim's 'little men' of that Dorset backwater of twenty years ago—

"Yes, I might be able to work up quite a good connexion, Phil. For a year or two, anyway, while the sellers' market lasts. It all depends on that, and Lucy, of course, how long I stay here."

You might include me in the list of credits, thought Phillip. After all, I've made it all possible.

"You see, Phil, it's very hard to get a cottage now, all the Service people being demobbed, and I could get one of course, but that would mean working as a labourer on the land, and I certainly don't intend to do that."

"Ah."

Phillip played with Sarah on the sofa. No staring in face, or making forced noises. He looked away, to give her leisure to assess him, while making between his front teeth a curlew's bubbling call as it floats, wings downheld as though in sheltering position for its imagined young in the rushes of The Chains, five hundred feet below. The bird in joy imagining its young.

Sarah liked what she heard and saw, and worked her legs to jump, frog-like. He pressed a thumb under each big toe, so that she could grip them.

"*Homo Sapiens* is a scandent mammal. The tree-grip is security. Isn't it, little growing-up baby?"

She held up her arms, he held her on his shoulder, one hand for the grip of feet. She smiled and smiled; her face puckered when he put her down. He whistled, the hoarse-sweet cry of a male curlew. All was well again.

"How is my elder daughter?" Rosamund was now adolescent.

"She's *such* a great help, Pip."

"Mum, may I cook the supper?" asked Roz. "You have a rest by the fire. I've learned to cook at school."

Peter came into the sitting room.

"Good evening, sir. I mean Father. Dad."

"Good evening, young sir. I mean Peter. Son."

Peter, a school prefect, with the assured gentleness of a good leader. His face had thin white scars where the dark and passionate Roz had, in fury of his slowness, clawed at his eyes because he had not understood what she, a small child, had failed to make clear to him. Now the budding girl had protective love for brother Peter.

"What do you want to do when you leave school?"

Faint colouring rising in cheeks. Hesitation. Then, "Oh, the Royal Air Force, I suppose, Dad."

"David?"

"Royal Air Force, chooky."

"Jonny?"

"Same, I suppose."

Here was human warmth, a home; books in the library rising on shelves to the ceiling. A leather armchair, table, open fireplace; but it was not the wilderness. Wind rattled the leaded panes of the otherwise bare room in the south wing of the old house. Specks of sleet entered through the loose glass of one casement, with faint cries of wind, scarcely more than sighs. I must go before the snow comes, and snow-drifts lie beech-hedge high on roads of the moor. I must write; or perish. There might be a letter from Laura ! No : I don't want her to write to me—

The weather report on the B.B.C. that evening was alarming, if he was to get back to Shep Cot.

"The wireless says it's beginning to freeze all over Europe, Tim. 'A long sweep of Siberian air is beginning to move across the continent from the East'. That's an entry I made this morning in my diary. I must leave first thing tomorrow, Lucy."

"Well, if you must, my dear. But you're perfectly welcome to stay here, you know."

"By Jove, yes, Phil, do stay as long as you like."

"Thank you, both. But I should go. I really must begin my novel series." He sighed. "Just fancy. I conceived the idea in nineteen nineteen, intended to start in nineteen twenty-nine, and now it is nearly nineteen forty seven. Almost thirty years—"

He was staring in a strange way at the floor, and Lucy knew it was no good trying to stop him going. Then she remembered to ask about the magazine.

"Oh, we printed five thousand copies, and subscribers number about three hundred. Molly is going to use the metal stencil cards to address the wrappers. I arranged in London with the railway bookstalls to take four thousand on sale or return. That leaves five hundred which I hope to get booksellers in Devon and Somerset to take, also on sale or return. Though they'll want a whacking discount, I suppose, sixty per cent or more."

"You haven't any with you, I suppose?" asked Tim, modestly. "I could have a display in the wide window of my machine room, which looks on to the main road through the village."

"I'll send up a hundred copies by rail, Tim. Thanks for your co-operation."

"Not at all, not at all" murmured Tim.

The grey north-east was blowing, day after day, over the moor; but there was warmth within Shep Cot. Phillip had raised the hearth by three courses of brick. Simply laid them there end to end—no mortar—and this had limited the area by which gate-crashing cold air could pass over the floor and up the chimney. Also the diminished flame-space caused blue skeins of smoke to creep up close to the blackened back-wall; to slide, with occasional farewell hesitations and waverings, up into the hollow chimney square.

There were two tons—twelve loads brought in the box-body of the Silver Eagle—of five-foot long oak poles standing against the outside walls of the cottage.

Safe until Christmas. Now he must write his second Editorial for *The New Horizon*.

He walked about, picking up odd objects—sea-shells, an acorn, smooth red half-brick from the sea-shore, a stag's-horn . . . waiting for an idea to drift, seed-like under parachute, from his mind.

Upon plain wooden shelves fixed to the kitchen wall stood lines of books, pick of his library of the 1914-18 war—British, German, French records, memoirs, personal accounts—together with a file of letters from the ghosts of that time—Desmond Neville, Lily Cornford, his parents, Grandfather Thomas Turney, 'Spectre' West and others of the Regiment; and his own letters from the Front, which Elizabeth had allowed him to take away after Father's death, together with his trench maps: large-scale sheets red-threaded, like veins in the human body, with German trench-lines and serrated obstacles; simple blue lines, without particulars, for the British front positions. The Germans built to hold; the British to push forward from. Germany blockaded: Great Britain ruled the waves. Only a question of time—

Map sheets backed by linen, stained by rain, dog-eared, marked with indelible pencil for particular objectives—behind them the transport routes, locations of canvas horse-watering troughs, ration dumps of tools, wire, and ammunition; drinking water points where petrol-cans were filled; first-aid posts.

Ordnance Survey sheets of the 1916 battlefield of the Somme giving way to more Ordnance Survey sheets with trench-free, green and brown contours—virgin land—chalk downlands happily reached after the German retreat to the *Siegfried Stellung* in March 1917, all the muck and the shell-holes and the dead left behind and forgotten . . . until the Spring battles—Arras and Bullecourt, Monchy-le-Preux. And in June all the heavy stuff, the howitzers and great railway guns going north to Flanders. Map of battle objectives—green, red, blue, yellow lines, July 31st opening battle,

Pilckem Ridge—the rain, rain, rain, all August, dry in September, the swamps of October in the Salient . . . that wonderful walk with 'Spectre' West up the duckboards past the Steenbeke and the line of 18-pounder field-guns sinking into the mud, to Kansas Cross and on up to the Gravenstafel ridge hidden from the German observation posts on the higher Passchendaele ridge. Then to the Roulers railway embankment, to find themselves through a gap in the German lines and the way open to the Passchendaele ridge! Then 'Spectre' was hit, and he had to make the return journey alone with a message for G.H.Q. as darkness came on. The exhilaration of four thousand British, French and German guns firing all together, the battlefield one vast cauldron of light, making you feel you were floating on sound-light forever and ever lost to the old pre-war world. And more by luck than judgment he found the way to the Menin Road and so down to Ypres.

Phillip, lying in bed, began to toss and turn, to mutter, and curse!—himself : shocked by his own weak conduct, as the mind-cells revealed visual-oral pictures of Hell. Self-hate, self-pity no good. The *artist* must rule in life. If he died the life of his days would never be re-created, for now the Salient was all farm-land again—

19 July, 1919. Versailles. *La Revanche.* Clemenceau and the slogan, *Germany is a lemon which must be squeezed until the pips squeaked.* The blockade of starvation still on, German bread half-sawdust. French colonial troops in the Rhineland, rape of little Hans and Gretchen, child prostitutes asking for—soap. Civilians pushed from pavements, hats knocked off. Poles with a few hundred roubles coming from the ghettoes of Warsaw, becoming mark-millionaires almost overnight.

Phillip, wet with sweat, shouting, "And the pips squeaked! Reparations took all the lemon juice! The victors loaned money to be repaid as further reparation! The pips screamed in *halle* and *platz* and *burgerkeller* and over the radio, and it all blew up again for lack of green-grass thoughts!" For God had not been allowed to come down from the scaffold to lay a healing touch upon the self-enslaved spirit of Western Man.

It was as though a blackthorn spine had pierced his left eye. So sharp was the pain that when he half-rose he upset the table. This was much worse than any former pain. Had the retina become clouded by the burst of a blood vessel? He tried to open his eye but it was held in stabbing pain. I am done for. While he sat there the dog's cold nose touched his hand. It was reassuring; dear, dear Bodger!

He bathed the eye, after much flinching from raising the lid, in an eye-bath holding glycerine and rose-water. He could just see his way upstairs. But sleep was broken by perilous thoughts, so he got up; and having connected a long lead from the car battery to a 12-volt bulb suspended from the ceiling, began to scribble rapidly.

If there be any young writer, survivor of the Second World War, who aspires to write a *War and Peace* for this age, to him I send my thoughts this frozen January night.

Will you, eager writer of genius, with nothing to sustain you but the wings of your own spirit, to whom these thoughts go out this night, in your vision unimpeded and unimpaired by contemporary massed emotions, show truly the luminous personality of Adolf Hitler in a room with those who believe in him, who have faith that his clear commonsense will avoid a war which they know, and he knows, the Fatherland cannot sustain? And will you show this Lucifer, this light-bringer, in a scene of Tolstoyan scope and sweep, as one in those early years of the 'thirties possessed harmoniously by the highest spiritual force, gentle and magnanimous, yet also the man of cool calculation, of immense patience and understanding of all problems when he is talking with a young Englishwoman whose sensibility matches her physical grace, who is clear in the sense that, like Shelley, she saw him plain?

Will you relate this trait of feminine sensibility in Lucifer, making him vulnerable outside the artists' world, to the moods which arose from a weak or diffident inner-core, so dangerous to itself and to others, whence arose those terrible ragings and cries of contempt and hate that mortified the feelings of those who loved him so that they were as pillars of salt while he was so possessed, since in those moods all hopes seemed purposeless and void, as a black polar wind blasts all life?

If you write justly, that is, truly, you will reveal that the rare quality which accompanies genius has its fatal defect or weakness: you will bring upon your pages the spirit that believed with all the passion of a levitated being in the glories of the freed soul of man at peace in the resurgent Western world, inspired by the spirit of Hellas, and show also this same vehicle being swept in contortion more and more by forces beyond self-control to effects which were the antithesis of all he believed, as evil is the antithesis of good, and fear the absence of love.

To write with divination and truth, without admiration or con-tempt, and above all *without moral judgment*, of the causes and effects of the tragic split in the mind of European man, from which arose this war, will require in a writer, besides the gift of seeing with paradise-clearness, an immense patience and sustaining power.

Let me illustrate this with a mechanical analogy. In theory the perfect racing-car carries in its engine and chassis not a gramme of metal that does not work to win the race, to break the record, to surpass the old with the new. In theory it is built to endure until the chequered flag is passed, when, completely used in every gramme of metal it carries, and all its power expended, it disintegrates. All is used by the spirit of the design to achieve what lesser men declare to be impossible: a new form. The car has broken a record, but also its engine: its bearings clank, it is smoking as it stands in a pool of oil, its tyres are stripped of their rubber treads, its driver is quiescent, trembling, his face blackened around the white patches where his goggles have been pushed back.

Likewise the creator of a work of art which will reveal the truth of this age—holding in balance the forces and counter-forces which led to the disintegration of the West—must with devotion to such an immense task willingly, unwillingly, see himself as one born to lose his natural happiness of life, even life itself, in the fulfilment of his task.

All the poet can do today is to roam in spirit the world's seas, viewing men in open boats bowed over oars they are too weak to pull, sustained by less than the blood of the albatross; to lie prostrate beside them on rafts awash with the grey nihilism of waves; with them he drowns in the blue twilight of submarine death.

Above the piled majesty of cumulus, in the clear infinity of space, under the metallic blue of the troposphere, he streams with vapour trails through the skies; and falls without curiosity or emotion that he has had it at last; and as the earth comes larger and recognisable, so does the moment of truth, and in curious detachment he wonders if he will hear himself screaming in the black-billowing and impenetrable bright flames.

From the heat that breaks as with phoenix-claws the small clearness of self from the charred diminished body, the poet moves instantly to the sleet of the steppes, to lie with limbs gangrenous in frost and eyelids crusted with pus, the army in dissolution; and what are his thoughts of his Führer: are they no more than, in the slogan of youthful days, 'We are born to die for Germany?'

Thence to the stars shining sightlessly in the bitter North African night, to men of his own kin lying prostrate under winds that rave with the dust and sand of the desert, while the sky leaps alight, and what are his thoughts before the barrage: are they as of those on the battlefields of Somme and Ypres—or is it clearer this war? And do men die the easier because they have an ideal beyond themselves, beyond the 'little ego'? And are the thoughts of lost men the thoughts of children betrayed?

From simple soldiers to the good generals and the tired generals; from the inner hopes of the Light-bringer distorted by power to the inner hopes of the Jew purified by powerlessness.

Of the identity of fear and frenzy, of love and hate, and how nearly related are they in the same man. Did not the ancient Iranian poet believe that God had two sons—both sons of genius—Eosphoros the brilliant illuminator in the darkness of men's minds; and Kristos the compassionate?

The mind of the poet must traverse without sentiment or bias but always with detachment and clarity, assessing a fatal magnanimous gesture towards an admired 'sister nation' when the life of that nation hung by a thread in the early summer of 1940 (and the thread was not cut) thus exposing the West to a greater ruin from the East, but not altering the fate of the world; even as it assessed the dismissal, eleven months later, of a messenger of peace, by a leader with four centuries of calculated power-balance in British history behind his judgments: and how far thereby was endorsed the further decline of the West?

The artist must know why an Englishman, expressing the character of the nation in fear, did not express the feelings of that nation freed of fear. And what shall be written of the soul of Britain? That it had no soul, since it was not a race of men but a mixture of many races, of many 'little egos'—of Gaul, Teuton, Celt, Anglo-Saxon, Phoenician, Roman, Jew, Dane and Viking—so for soul it has only a disruptive determination, arising from its insular position as a land of coal and iron, and because of that position and wealth from trading, its policy for four hundred years has been to rule by Money, thus keeping in division the continent of Europe, as Winston Churchill has written in an early autobiography. And will history decide that this European of great talent and emotion felt it to be his crowning purpose in life to baulk and destroy a fellow European of genius—who could build only because he had forced out Money for money's sake?

And that Great Britain and the Empire fell from a supreme position because the majority failed to perceive that another survivor of the battlefields of 1914-18 had a vision to build, but was denied by Money in the hands of those who could only frustrate.

The thorn in the eye seemed to have withdrawn itself during sleep. Could the cause, after all, be nervous strain? Result of psychological depression? At times he could focus with clear definition.

Bodger rejoiced with him, running in circles and occasionally barking when they walked to the village to post to the printer the 'copy' for the Spring number of the magazine.

The next job was to clean Shep Cot. The bookshelves were collecting dust as befitted the hush of an age gone by. Dear Walter de la Mare. There was the book of poems, found in a shell-hole by cousin Willie, and brought home; later to be handed over by Uncle John with others of the books of drowned Willie. Rows and rows of Wilfred Owen's Greater Love War. I must leave my country books to Jonnie. He will be the writer in the family if it be my fate to die soon.

East wind blowing; little sudden moans across chimney tun; timid retreat of smoke into room by day; sharp stars by night, wheeling past window. Little gentle crystals of sleet greeting his face peering at the open door, in hopeless hope that someone might be coming . . .

Chapter 15

PRINCESS EIRĒNĒ

By day all the landscape looked pinched, seeming lifeless. Icicles under waterfalls, green sponge-moss all frozen tears, amber water running silent under ice-plates whereon skittered vacuous sleet. Wild red deer gone down into warmer oakwood coombes. Once, through the small casement upper window, a quartet of hinds looking up at his face before galloping away.

In the tattered shed, between wooden walls of 18-inch oak logs, stood Silver Eagle, water drained from radiator, engine block *and* that yellow-metal pipe connecting both from below their bases. No more local boils and cracked cylinder block! O God what a bloody awful life I am leading. Will there be a letter from Corfu today? How can I earn, replace the hundred pounds I gave Laura, to last her until March, when I am to join her in Corfu : she with her book finished by then, I with first volume completed—my series conceived nearly thirty years ago, carried in the womb of my time ever since; and now powerless to be born? I am too old, my time has run out. He went to see Molly to tell her that he would have to work steadily for a period, and so would not be able to see them all at half-term.

"Well, do come over, and stay, whenever you feel like a change, won't you, dear Phillip?"

Every day he walked down to the village, staff in hand, army valise on back, guarded by skirmishing Bodger. One morning he met Osgood Nilsson, fellow member of the Barbarian Club, with his rosy-faced wife. When her husband had gone into the Lyndale hotel bar, she remained outside with Phillip.

"I hear you're writing a book, Phillip—may I call you Phillip? Do come and see us whenever you feel free to do so—we live up in the woods near that odd recluse, Lord Cloudesley. Seems stiff and stilted to me. Oh, you know him, do you? What's he really like? And that girl, with the rather fey look, what's she doing

173

there, d'you know, besides helping him to write a biography of his father, Osgood was telling me. He flew the Atlantic, didn't he, and was never seen again."

"I met the present Lord Cloudesley briefly, when I was farming, in East Anglia. Well, I must get back before it snows. Au revoir!"

It was too cold for snow, bitter frost-wind was still pouring down the glen. Thank God his old Army pack—'valise' of those days, had carried back enough tinned off-the-ration provisions for a week, and a 7-lb bag of puppy biscuit-meal. This had to be soaked (for Bodger had half-decayed teeth). What had seemed to be little more than a puppy had turned out to be an old dog— eleven years of age. Yet Bodger was still lively, due to exceptional intelligence : an innocent, ageless manner that often went with high perception. Whom the gods love remain young.

If the snow came and drifts blocked all the lanes, at least he had his pair of skis. So far, no sign of snow : but wait : it was in the air. At night the stars burned bright in a sky of dark ice. From frozen horizon to frozen horizon was the 1916/1917 battle-field of the Somme : an area as wide as Exmoor iron-hard between lip-to-lip shell-craters brittle-white with ice powdered by moon-light. How everyone was apprehensive of high explosive shells bursting on impact, splinters flying! That.would catch the files of donks going up the line nightly, with rations and ammunition, it was said. But, strangely, the German shelling was desultory. It ceased. Hard ground gave the old Hun his chance to pull out his heavy stuff north to Arras, to meet the British and Canadian push known to be coming in the spring. And in March the old Hun went back to his new immensely powerful line built twenty miles away by two-hundred thousand Russian prisoners during the past six months. So the Somme was left behind, forgotten as the battle of Waterloo : except for little gangs of international de-serters, who waged war it was said for gold in the teeth of skulls— among themselves in the underground catacombs. Distant hand-grenades bursting at night—competitive civilisation starting up in the wilderness . . .

The east wind faltered. The chimney smoke veered to the south-west. Now for snow, if it went round to the north-east! But the dragging ocean-clouds fell as rain until water was running every-where upon the moor.

One morning he thought to call on Piston—that dark, furtive clown of 1916 at the Lynton Convalescent Home—Mad

Piston and his perforated fire-pail filled with driftwood from the boulders of the shore. Wig of sea-weed on head, simpleton playing with children; adopting Aunt Dora as 'Auntie'—Piston working his ticket, and getting his discharge and a disability pension, the sprucer!

A white-haired figure, with gentle face, welcomed him with, "Well, Masson old boy, how goes it? 'Auntie' told me you were here. I was going to look you up—pay the old call—but Mamma and I have been rather busy. Come and meet my mother—you'll like her—she's almost completely etherialised. Lives entirely on the Seventh Plane. She's also a vegetarian, like me and 'Auntie'. Mamma, this is Phillip, my old chum, author of *The Water Wanderer.*"

Phillip saw a small alert woman with shrivelled skin of face and neck. She had the dark eyes and look of a Romany gipsy. If her son seemed softly foolish, she had a shrewd look. The eyes were intelligent.

"That's a dear little dog you've got," she said, while the animal looked up and gave one wag of its stump. She knelt to pat it. "I see he's been badly treated," as she felt the lumpy ribs.

"I know where he came from," said Piston. "I know that smallholder, Aaron Kedd."

"Seems to be a distracted man."

"He's a local preacher, of the hell-fire sort."

"Poor man, he's obsessed by carnal sin," said Mrs Piston, gently. "He must be prone to ruined hopes, without self-knowledge."

"We all reveal ourselves by our fixed ideas, Mrs. Piston."

"Yes," she replied, softly. The eyes were now reflective, she looked young when she smiled up at him. "Your *Water Wanderer* is clairvoyant, Mr. Maddison. I think the elemental spirits of the moor helped you to write it."

There was bone beauty in the small face. Phillip saw a resemblance to his own mother: true, sensitive, child-like in a hard world. He liked Mrs. Piston, felt warm towards her. Piston too. Perhaps it was for his mother, he the only child, that he had swung the lead in the Casualty Clearing Station below Albert, pretending to be shell-shocked, and rushing about after imaginary Germans. Anyhow, he'd worked his ticket.

"Sit you down, Masson old lad. Mamma will bring some coffee. 'Auntie' told me you haven't been to see her, you naughty man. The poor old gel lives all alone, you know. Remarkable old lady —great Greek scholar, too, into the bargain." His voice dropped.

"Between ourselves, we're on the verge of an entirely new dimension. Mamma has great psychic forces coming through her. She helps people in Oldstone Castle to become clear about themselves, and their blockages. What stops them from being clear and happy, Masson. She's also in touch with the dead. I mean the dead persons or person in every living man or woman. Shelley probably lives again in you. I feel it. This place is full of his aura. You must, if you're interested, come to one of our séances. You're a good man, Masson." Tears formed in his eyes. "I knew that when I read that book about Lutra, your otter. It's got elemental life in it, it reveals the unseen world, too. I can feel it coming through the printed page. You did, too, I reckon, when it was writing itself. Do you know what I mean?"

"I certainly do. It wrote itself at times."

"All good books seep through from the unseen world, Masson. This cottage is saturated with Shelley's personality. He lived here all one season, you know. Yes, the place is alive with him. He used to sail paper boats in the river outside, when it was low in summer. A true mystic."

"The whole of the Universe is run by God, which is one vast Imagination, struggling against the almost irresistible brute forces of the cosmos."

"Yes! And that's why this cottage is full of it. Scientists are only at the beginning. Look at radio waves. Simple, you say. Well, they were there before scientists uncovered them. The rocks glow with power, I've felt the power. But science has gone wrong, as Caspar Schwenkfelder says, you know the one who teaches at Oldstone Castle. He got his ideas originally from Richard Jefferies' *Story of my Heart*. We've got to begin again from the beginning, or we're done for. Look at the atom bomb—a terrible discovery, or uncovery. But you know all about that."

"Do you believe the dead help the living?"

"Of course they do. We're all part of the dead. The dead live in our blood—that's obvious, it's a simple law of heredity. As for the dead haunting a particular place, it's only a hangover of inharmonious vibrations which have impregnated the furniture, part of the walls, or other matter. Science is able to get personality on to celluloid by means of vibrations, and celluloid's only matter, after all."

"Piston, may I ask a very personal question?"

"Anything you like, Masson my dear."

"You know when the Lynton convalescent home went up in

flames in August, nineteen-sixteen. Did you start the fire? You
always had a fire-bucket, and collected driftwood, didn't you?"

"I don't know, Masson. I was ill in those days. My mind was
haunted. By what I'd been. As a child, I was always terrified of a
steel engraving we had in my father's house, Wellington greeting
Blücher at Waterloo. The dead and wounded, Masson. Then the
war came, and well—you know the rest. I was a coward, I was
driven to get out of the Somme, and the war, I simply could not
face the *idea* of battle. I was a sort of lead-swinger, I suppose, and
then I wasn't. I was the lead itself, old boy. Gone phut. Dead.
Heavy. My body like lead, killed inside me. Beyond despair. All
my blokes killed in no-man's-land in the first minute after Zero
Hour. Didn't know what I was doing. Not altogether. Was *aware*
of myself, mark you. But had no reciprocity with or for others. I
was mad. I felt life screaming through me, and my picture of myself was lying dead just by the horses of Wellington and Blücher. I
must have been killed at Waterloo."

He looked like a sad little boy, appealing for help to Phillip as
he went on, "I let my men down. I pretended I was knocked out
by a shell, and lay doggo in no-man's-land. Then I didn't know
if I had been shell-shocked or not. The next phase was a sort of
madness I couldn't control, I saw myself rushing about the ward,
which was deep like the Jerry first line, you may remember."

"You were obviously shocked." Were Piston's theories but a
sublimation of shock?

"When I was invalided out, I got a job with Munitions, bowler
hat and umbrella, bogus retired temporary officer and temporary
gent—acting captain, then major. All very bogus, like making the
manager of the Great Eastern Railway a temporary major-general,
Sir Guy Somebody or other, in the war. To give some sort of
authority among civilians. Lloyd George's idea, I believe. Any
more questions, old lad?"

"No, Piston," and Phillip put an arm round the trembling man.

"People think I'm part of a motorcar," went on Piston, suddenly
happy. "They forget that just as shrapnel was invented by a
Major Shrapnel of the Gunners, so the piston was invented by a
bloke called Piston. Oh, I know I used to say my name came
from Pistor, some old Roman god, but that was camouflage,
Masson. All nature is more or less camouflaged, ever thought of
that?"

"Your mind is full of baffles, like a new silencer of a motorcar.
I suppose we all baffle ourselves, one way or another, old chum."

"Caspar Schwenkfelder removed all mine, Masson. I'm now clarified. I can let myself go right out of the body into the ether, laddie! Like a yogi. My mother's been up to the Seventh Plane. The transference took place on Oldstone Down." Piston's voice was low. "I thought she was dead. She did die, I think. She had a message to go up there, so we went up in the car. She stood up in the heather, on a little mound she said was the remains of a Roman fort. Archeologists say the Romans never got so far west of Exeter. But Mummy saw them, the Romans, she was quite close to them. She could almost touch them, her hands were bound, she was terrified they were going to kill her. It was a wooden fort, a look-out place above the sea, to look out for Welsh raiders on their shipping going up the Channel. Mark my words, Masson, one day they'll dig there and find Roman remains, pottery, perhaps coins. You'll see, I'm right!"

"I did hear about some sort of flying saucer."

"A ring of pure light, Masson. Saul saw it on the way to Damascus. Mummy was 'out', her heart scarcely beating, for over an hour. When she came back, her face was young and beautiful." Piston breathed deeply. He had gone pale, he spoke in a low voice. "She had seen Jesus. She took my book with her. Not the actual paper and binding—that's of the letter of reality—but the spirit of my words. What's so strange about that? They can send pictures through space, by television, can't they? Mummy saw Jesus—" His eyes ran tears again. He took Phillip's hand. "Masson, old boy, she says you are one of the chosen ones. She does, honestly. She says you have an aura about you, only it's dim at the moment. You've not come properly through yet."

"I've been through, but come back—to nothing."

"We all do, old boy."

"Tell me about Schwenkfelder."

"He's a pioneer. He started as a psychologist, but found fault with Freud's findings. Then he saw it was a growing racket— psychiatry, I mean. So he started at the beginning. Reading Blake, who saw an angel on a tree. A true poet, Masson, he sees like Jefferies, into the unseen world, which is the true world. Schwenk, as we call him, fought in the late war, as an airman. He had a little cash, and bought Oldstone, where his pupils come and learn the procedures of Ideopraxitism. That's Greek for— well, ideas. Ideas are cart-horses; it's what's in the cart that matters. Then he changed the name to Diaphany. It means Light. I'd like you come to one of Ma's séances, and see for yourself."

"I'd like to very much."

"You do that, Masson. 'Auntie' wants to come too. And Mrs. Bucentaur, who's a cousin of 'Buster' Cloudesley—you know, the bloke who lives in the woods up there, and does a lot of gliding. He was a stout fellow—badly hit after the Rhine crossing. Quite a decent bloke, Guardee-commando type. You must meet him."

"I have met him."

"His father tried to fly the Atlantic solo, and went down somewhere west of Ireland in the early 'thirties. His old soldier-servant, a chap called Corney, has a pub on the moor, *The Marksman*. A real old sweat, very regimental and keeps his place in good order. He's psychic, too."

Phillip thought, this will interest Laura, collaborating with 'Buster' on his father's biography—if and when she returns from Prospero's supposed home, Corfu, to get away from her supposed Prospero. Oh, I must begin my novel of my parents' youth, and their secret marriage—

"Now be a good lad, Masson, and go and cheer up 'Auntie'. You know what my mother calls her? Princess Eirēnē. She is, too. Reincarnation of the Greek goddess of peace. We're all reincarnations, old boy. We live again and again, death is only a rest for the poor old body we muck about so."

Followed by Bodger, Phillip went down the street overlooking the river rushing noisily around boulders of all weights up to twenty tons, he supposed : all smoothed by constant degradation through the centuries, water-quarried from the gorge below the dark trees and moving gradually down to the sea, never for a moment free of the friction and abrasion of time. Rocks : a building up by fire; destruction to detritus by water : both elemental gods of the cave-men!

He knocked at the door of Ionian Cottage. Its paint was cracked, blistered, faded. Again the friction of unoiled bolts, squeaking key chain rattle.

"Hullo, Aunt Dora. I'm Phillip."

What had been a ghost in lamplight was now an Edwardian-clothed skeleton with protruding teeth, *pince-nez* spectacles covering life-averted eyes.

"Pray come in, Phillip."

There followed an elaborate reassembly of bolts, chain, lock-tongue at war with rust.

A kitchen-table, floor space taken up by cardboard cartons

filled with empty tins. Bread-board with dry curled slices of whole-meal loaf.

"I am fasting," the voice piped remotely. "This is my thirty-ninth day. One of the evils of the past has been that the classes have all eaten too much, while the masses of working people have starved."

She went on as to herself, "I am trying to cure my migraine by prayer and fasting."

Bodger, who had been summing-up street-dog society, was now anxiously scratching at the front door.

"My dog is outside, Aunt Dora."

"By all means let him come in."

Bolts, lock, chain.

"Sit, Bodger! Good boy. He's a cross between foxhound dam, and terrier sire."

"I'm afraid I haven't a bone for the little fellow."

"Bodger's got no teeth now for bones, Aunt Dora."

"Have you heard from your sister Elizabeth? She is supposed to have come some weeks ago, to make her home with me."

She sat at the other end of the table, supporting brow on hand. Thin fingers of a poet shading weak eyes. "No one in the family told me of my brother Dickie's death. I heard it only from my bank manager." She went on as though speaking to someone invisible, "It is all to be expected. My old home, Fawley, is gone. I suppose when my brother John died, the house died with him. Hilary is gone, too."

"As I expect you know, Aunt Dora, Uncle Hilary sold the land to the War Department before the war." When there was no reply he went on, "I bought land in East Anglia, and we farmed there during the war."

She said tremulously. "Billy was killed, I am told by Elizabeth. Such a dear little boy. I was at his christening, when his baby brother was baptised with him. Lucy—" She took a deep breath, sighing inaudibly. "Divorce—no, no. It is not like the Phillip I knew."

"We are not divorced, Aunt Dora. We are still friends."

It was his turn to shield eyes with hand on forehead. Now she was able to look at him, to listen.

"Lucy is most magnanimous. I have made over all I have to a trust, for her and the family. I am down here only to write— while my eyesight lasts. I may go blind."

"Then you must fast, Boy. Fasting will cure all ills."

The air was cold. A feeling of Time suspended. He walked home. Home! Everything would be the same when he got there. It was the same—kettle cold and fire dead, bed unmade, candle in dented Cromwellian brass stick, a late moth embalmed in the little crater out of which stood a bent black wick marking the grave of the mite who had mistaken its light for love.

And in the morning he awoke into a curious pallor. Through the casement all was white.

Snow fell with quiet resolution, drifting down gently, all that day; but in the afternoon programmes on the B.B.C. were interrupted with warning to shipping in Irish Sea, Rockall, Malin Head, Lundy, the Fastnetts, Dover and North Sea. A Force Eight wind was imminent. Long, high waves were rolling before waves of air streaking the dark sea. The six o'clock weather forecast, preceding the news, gave a special warning that in places the gale would increase to Force Ten. At eight o'clock programmes again interrupted by an announcement that a Force Twelve wind, of hurricane violence, was screaming its way from the North Cape, filling the darkness with foam and spray above a completely white sea. All coastal shipping was advised to make for roads and harbours.

At midnight the wind of the Furies was upon the moor—the Erinyes of Aunt Dora, who once had told him that the euphemism of the Eumenides, the kindly ones, was a placatory term, like a dog lying on its back before a snarling aggressor.

From Padstow Point to Harty Light is a watery grave by day and by night. Phillip lying in bed thought the casement would burst, chimney tun crash through ceiling, so he went downstairs, away from the low fire and its embers scattering, at particular buffets, over the lime-ash floor—constellations of dying dwarf-stars brightening in the draught under the door. But each spark, at its brightest, flashed out.

A sleepless, an exhilarating night. Towards dawn the wind-thunder had passed; and at first light he saw drifts six feet and more deep where the wind had eddied, leaving snow quietly to lie.

All Europe was covered by snow, announced the eight o'clock news, from Northern France to the Pyrenees. Passes in the Massif Central were now impassable; trains run to standstill, aircraft grounded; Alpine towns and villages cut off. By six o'clock the hurricane had run itself out; and a long drift of cold air crossing all Europe to the Iberian peninsula.

Was there snow along the Mediterranean shore, and Prospero's Isle stricken?

On the moor, small birds were dying, of cold and starvation. Phillip put on his skis and climbed to the southern sky, but the hummocks of The Chains were impassable. He returned, and made a way down the lane to Barbrook, but it was easier to walk, drifts varying with icy patches of shillet. The tarmac road running above the wooded gorge, following the course and descent of the river, gave good runs until the road steepened sharply to a drop of one-in-four, where he unclipped the goatskin thongs, and leaving sticks and skis over the low stone wall, went niminy-piminy, holding, stooping, sliding, down to the village. Men with shovels were digging away six-foot drifts in the main street of Lynmouth. They had not got so far as Ionian Cottage; so trudging, with difficulty to the post-office, he bought one tin of soup—all that was allowed—and began the slow, bleak return to nearly nine hundred feet above the sea. Bodger, left in the kitchen, was shivering on the sack when he returned. The dog did not move; only one eye was watching. Phillip gave him his supper, made up a great fire, and fried eggs and bacon for himself. Afterwards he danced to gramophone music, while Bodger pranced around.

Theodora Maddison lying on her bed in her day clothes covered only by a travelling rug, thin and discoloured, more than half-a-century old. She lay on her back, hands folded across her chest, legs crossed at ankles. She had ceased to inspire deeply, to as slowly respire. Even that effort exhausted her. She was beyond despair; she accepted, as she had accepted for years, that human life, and her life particularly, was fore-doomed to failure. She remembered how, six months ago, her sister Victoria had come to see her, ostensibly to take care of her, but had stayed only one day after learning that the Will left all to Phillip. *You should not let the family capital, restored by Hilary, pass out of the family, dear Dora. It is your duty to leave your estate to my daughter, your niece Adele, after my tenancy-for-life.*

The Will in Phillip's favour had been dated September 1916. Dora had, off and on during the Hitlerian war, been disturbed by her nephew's behaviour, as told to her by her niece, Elizabeth. So after Viccy's abrupt departure she had written to Elizabeth, saying that if she would come and look after her—"It will not be for long, dear child"—she would make a new will leaving all to her niece. Elizabeth had replied by telegram that she would come very shortly, after she had disposed of her cottage and furniture in Dorset.

So Dora had made another Will.

Elizabeth had not come. Only her nephew Phillip had come. She had not been kind at his coming, and shown it, perhaps. That was inexcusable on her part. What ulterior motive had Boy for coming to see her? Indeed, he had had none! Poor, dear Boy: he was permantly exhausted by the First War. And she had rejected him—and on the word of that very stupid woman, Victoria. Poor Phillip, he had been the unhappiest small boy she had ever encountered. And despite that, he had made good and used his talent wisely. *The Water Wanderer* and *The Blind Trout* were already small classics. O, she had made a sad mistake! She must write to the Trustee Department at the Bank in Exeter, and revoke the will leaving all to Elizabeth. Boy must have, too, all the family papers on her mother's side, the von Föhres of Württemburg. If Boy wished to write novels with a family background, as Thomas Mann had done in *Buddenbrooks,* he would require every help. Thus, with happier thoughts, Theodora Wilhelmina Maddison, spinster, aged seventy three— Eirēnē, goddess of peace to Mrs. Piston and her associates— arranged the travelling rug around her body before drawing up her knees for warmth; and with one arm around her neck, as though in a caress of love she had found with a married man, only to renounce that love of one who had died in the South African War, she lay quiescent; and with thoughts of Aeschylus, Socrates, and Euripides she passed through the valley of the Erinyes, the Furies, and went down, down to her beloved Shelley in the glooms of the halls of Pluto.

Phillip want to the cottage on his next visit on skis to the village, and when there was no answer to his knocking, decided that Aunt Dora had gone away. He called again a week later; no reply. She must have gone away, perhaps to visit her sister Victoria in Bournemouth.

The bleak weather continued until early March, when the thaw came. The Lyn ran high with snow water. Salmon appeared in the tidal pool, but none faced the run up through cold and turbulent waters. One morning when he went for his mail, the postman said there were several parcels for Miss Maddison, did he know when she was returning?

The following day he agreed with the village constable that

a window should be forced. On going upstairs, the wasted body was seen to be lying under an old travelling rug.

An official of the Trustee Department of the Bank arrived from Exeter when death had been certified by the doctor as due to natural causes. The name of the deceased, an aunt of Phillip Maddison, author of *The Water Wanderer*, was published briefly in the Press.

Chapter 16

BOY ON A BICYCLE

Jonathan, in his hidey hole under the rafters of Birdy House saw, through a nesting hole made by a starling, the Silver Eagle draw up on the edge of the cobbled sidewalk below in the village street. He worked himself back from the pegged slates and stepping from joist to joist reached the trap-door and lowered himself on his rope; to slide down two rows of banisters and, reaching the ground floor, dash into the kitchen and cry, "Dad's come! Cor, the starlings are what-you-call tisky!"

Jonathan spent many hours, when not at school, in the attic. The spaces under the eaves were now a-rustle, for the swifts had returned from Africa to their nests.

The starlings waged territorial war with them. Frightful cruelties went on behind the small entrance-exit holes. Thin high screams of swifts, flutterings, harsh cursings of starlings. Sometimes a narrow white egg dropped from under the guttering, the shell hole'd by thrust of starling-beak. Never a larger starling-egg, azure as clear summer sky between dawn and sunrise—a colour which should have belonged to the swift, thought Jonathan, since these mysterious birds, each a thin crescent of black, never left the sky at night to roost under the eaves.

"You mean they sleep on the wing, 'bor?" asked David, imitating the east anglian vocal lilt, and inevitable diminutive of neighbour.

"That's right, 'bor."

"Cor, that's what-you-call funny, 'bor!"

"Ah, 'bor."

Early one morning, before the sun had risen, Jonathan looked from his bedroom window and saw many black specks coming down out of the sky like a lot of gnats. He heard the swifts' thin high whistles before he made out their scimitar wings. A flight peeled off from the main flock, and wheeled around the church

185

steeple half a mile away, where he had seen swifts entering through
ventilation slats above the belfry.

"Perhaps they go up so high to sleep above the pull of gravity,"
suggested David, seriously. He was a reader of little grey-paper
books about flying saucers, space-ships from Mars, and other
imaginative post-war literature generally regarded with amused
tolerance by most adults.

But Phillip, enjoying a meal with his children at home for
Whitsun half-term, didn't regard such stories as laughable. "What
is now achieved, was once only imagined," he quoted William
Blake. "Also, the Germans had blue-prints of rockets which could
reach airless space so high that the pull of gravity doesn't exist.
Where men in special clothing and oxygen masks would walk in
space, and erect platforms to support great curved mirrors which
would be able to concentrate sunshine on parts of the earth, to
work steam turbines for generating electricity."

"Cor," said David, listening with mouth open.

"Also, Hitler wanted to build a great barrage across the straits
of Gibraltar, and use the tides for electricity for the top half of
Africa."

Jonathan listened with a remote look in his eyes. He wanted to
tell what he had discovered about the swifts. "Dad," he said,
when his father had finished, "do you mind if I tell you something? Well, you see, the starlings are attacking the swifts. Before
you came, I was lying down by the little slits of light, watching
a starling pull a hen swift off her two white eggs. The starling
had hold of one of the swift's pinion feathers, and it tugged and
tugged the swift through that hole under the eaves. When I went
down I looked in the road outside our house, and found the
mother swift lying on the ground, unable to get up. She was oar-
ing herself along with her wings. I threw her up, but she
spun down again, because one of her main flight quills was missing. Also, I found the two white eggs the starling had chucked
out. Now the starling intends to lay her first egg in the swift's
nest."

"What did you do with the swift?"

"It was crawling with lice, so I put flea powder on it, but it
died of fear in my hand. So I brushed it and gave it to Eric our
cat, who wouldn't eat it. So I buried it under the pear tree with
the old dried-up black pears still hanging on, for compost."

The blossom on the gnarled pear-tree in the garden had fallen
to form new fruit, nourished by Lucy's hens in the orchard. Small

boys in the village were now at their annual rite of tearing-out nests in hedges, copses, and spinneys of level farmlands. Jonathan saw one boy with a long-tailed tit's nest, moulded of grey lichen covering mosses, horse-hair, sere grasses and lined with hundreds of hen's feathers—each feather borne cross-wise in a tiny beak against the winds of uncertain English weather. Jonathan told the boy that the birds would be grieving. The boy, with pale-faced inhibited desperation, punched him and made his nose bleed and Jonathan went home feeling sad and ashamed because he could never fight for himself.

"You will be interested to hear," said Tim to Phillip, "that the prisoner-of-war camp is now empty, awaiting demolition. The Ukrainian soldiers have gone, some I think, to Australia. The Prussian doctor, who was on von Rundstedt's staff, called to say good-bye with the English nurse, the other evening. Both asked me to thank you personally, on their behalf."

"They were so glad to find somewhere to sit and talk together, the poor dears," said Lucy. "Well, and how are you getting on? Have you made many friends, other than the Riversmills and Molly and her little family, I mean?"

"Oh yes. There's 'the Mad Major', as some call old Piston, who was with me in the nursing home in nineteen-sixteen, and his mother. They're both a bit cranky, but otherwise quite pleasant people. There's an American writer, Osgood Nilsson, and his wife —he belongs to the Barbarian Club, I've had a slight acquaintance with him there for some years. And Molly's cousin, 'Buster' Cloudesley, who you met at the farm. He's an awful nice man— so balanced. Well, I must be off now, I suppose. I hope to call in and see Piers Tofield on the way back."

Phillip had come to draw the family's holiday caravan to the moor. Laura had written that she was returning from Corfu, and the idea was that she would live in the caravan, and there work on the biography of 'Buster's' father, until the family came down at the end of July. Then she would return with her script to The Eyrie. No scriptual servitude, as she called it, during Saturday and Sunday. Then she and Phillip would explore the countryside, sandy shores and rocky headlands—even tramp across Dartmoor! This time, all was to be as regular as clockwork.

"You know my aunt Dora died, I suppose, Lucy?"

"Yes, my dear, we did. Poor darling; and how sad it must have been for you. What an awful winter it has been for everyone." Lucy didn't like to ask if Phillip was proposing to live in the cottage. "Where was the funeral, at Lynton?"

"She asked in her will to be cremated, and her ashes taken out to sea. I was the only mourner, for Elizabeth couldn't come, but she got someone from the Trustee Department of the Bank to represent her, and her interests. Aunt Dora left everything to her."

"Oh."

"She made another will just before she died, it appears. The Bank official practically ignored me. He took away all the family papers, including her German mother's pedigree, grandfather Maddison's diaries, her own diaries and letters, family photographic albums—in fact everything, before he locked the door and left."

"I suppose Elizabeth was the sole beneficiary?"

"Yes. Doris was left out, as well as me. Anyway, she died in the winter, too. God, it's like a Greek play—one is destroyed by a fault in one's character. There was a post-mortem to determine cause of death, and apparently she died from iodine poisoning. She went from doctor to doctor until she got one to give her iodine injections to cure a non-existent goitre."

"Poor Doris! She was always so stubborn, wasn't she?"

"I saw how her obstinate streak built up when my father beat her for threatening him—she was then about four years old—'With a big knife', for making Mother cry. She wouldn't say she was sorry, but continued to defy Father. He beat her again and again, but she would not give in. She was lost to life, or that part which is love, from that moment."

"What will happen to her two boys?"

"Doris had her share in Grandfather Turney's trust, when Mother died, and I suppose there's her pension, it may be commuted to a lump sum. I don't really know. I only knew about her death when Elizabeth wrote to me and told me that it was my duty, as head of the family, to provide for them."

"Why can't Elizabeth help? She's got enough money, surely, from Father's death, and now Aunt Dora's?"

Tim had tested the towing bar of the Silver Eagle, and the automatic brakes of the caravan. Pumped up the tyres, greased points etc., while Lucy cleaned the interior, equipped with two beds, cooking stove (oil) and oil-lamps. Plates, cups, table things —blankets—all in order for when Phillip should come to take it down to Devon.

"Would you like Peter, David, and Jonathan to come down

and help you in the summer holidays, my dear? They could bicycle down by easy stages, avoiding main roads wherever practicable. It should take four days."

"If you could fit up the boys with a button'd hip-pocket, each could take three pounds. That should see them through."

"I'll see that the pockets are in order, and that they have the money. Well, if you must go now, you must, I suppose. Can't you stay another day, and rest? You look so tired, my dear. Come for a walk with us in the park. It's so lovely there, now. The old dwarf oaks are said to have been standing there since Plantagenet times."

He hesitated; then said he must go.

"Well, we'll try and see you in the summer then, may we, the boys and Sarah and I?" She hesitated, while her cheeks coloured. "I rather think that Melissa wants to study at a place on Exmoor, where there's a school for a new kind of spiritual healing. Perhaps you've heard of it—I think he's a naturalised German, who lives at Oldstone Castle, I think she said."

"I've just heard of it. Well, thank you for all your kindness. How good the caravan now looks!"

So while Tim got on with his precise lathe-work, turning ivory, ebony, and lingum vitae wood into little round boxes for dressing-table trinkets, Lucy and her sister-in-law wheeled their perambulators in the deserted park enclosed by the tall fences of barbed wire which had been the prisoners-of-war camp.

"I'm so glad for Phillip that he has made some friends down there, Brenda. He deserves a quiet and peaceful time after all he's done. When I drove back to Banyards the other day, to see Mrs. Valiant, who used to work for me in the farmhouse, do you know what she said to me? 'Pity the Captain didn't have a thousand acres, and proper help. He looked after his men and his land well, everyone says that now in the village'."

"He's less nervy than he was, isn't he, Lucy? He loves Baby Sarah doesn't he? And she likes him. Isn't she strong, and always laughing when she sees her father?"

"She's got his long legs and feet, and his quickness, too. I expect she'll grow up to be the friend Dad has always wanted—won't you, Sarah darling?"

"Dad-dad!" cried the baby, struggling against straps to sit up, to find the father who had left while she was asleep.

Phillip on roads almost empty across the flats of the Brecklands, passing abandoned R.A.F. stations of the concrete aircraft-carrier lying off the coast of a to-be United Europe as urged by Hereward Birkin. The little boys will be bicycling through this heathland soon, I should be with them, O my three-speed, monthly-payment Swift of long ago!

June 1914

I am the summer night upon the downs,
The rosy streamers of the rising sun,
And long tree-shadows reaching to far copses,
Where nightingales are weary of all dream.

O sun, thou hast freed me from the wraiths of the night!
Riding down steep Biggin Hill, I am borne on
                                          the air of morning,
One with the spectrum-glinting grasses
On the meadow by the lakes of Squerryes.

Where is that boy on a bicycle
In the sun of noon resting
Where wind the shadow-leafy lanes of Kent?
Afar the cuckoo calls, and nearer the quail cries
Anxious within the corn. The turtle dove
Flies to the brilliant flint-dust on the road,
And my life is for ever and ever.

I think the first volume of my novels should start before I was born, in the late 'nineties, in North-west Kent, now a brick-suffocated suburb of London, otherwise The Smoke. All the prototypes but one are dead—my parents, uncles, aunts—their photographic exteriors guarded by my dear godmother-aunt Victoria Adele Frederika Lemon, who looked at my Donkin novels years ago and said to her brother Hilary, *Oh so dull and dreary.* You of course are right, dearest godmother; I am beyond you, my name is Ishmael. There are two securities for man : poetry and money. Poets have risen from their near-strangled selves : Pluto, or Pluton, your unappreciated sister Theodora told me, was at first a surname of Hades, god of the lower world; Pluton the God of money, deprived of sight by Zeus, therefore Pluton gives his gifts blindly, indifferent to merit. A man based on money alone is a man distorted. Poor dead Dora, all were indifferent to your merits, except perhaps me. I told you a lie, that I was going blind.

Or was that prevision?—a little boy otherwise distorted, telling Blakian lies, angels in no-man's-land among dead Europeans? Why are the trees of the avenue before me blurred? That telegraph post looks queer. Could frost have split it, so that it appears to be oval? But the next one is concave—my liver, perhaps—the beer I drank last night with Tim to celebrate our getting on so well together? I had four pints; yes, it may be liver, I must drive carefully.

My sight must not blind me to what my fellow mortals see, or I shall find myself in Luthany, the region Elenore.

Here is Heathmarket, where I, a tall bony subaltern back from Flanders, found myself with the untried, the static Edwardian spirit of good form, within the presence of Rupert Brooke's poetry, it was the summer of 1915. Bertram Baldersby, of Baldersby Towers, Berkshire, the senior subaltern who said I was an outsider, as I was, indeed.

Racehorses are still being exercised on grass, walking in file. They look to be thin, perhaps from rationing? Yet others are swelled, like those pictures of refugee children of Europe seen in newspapers, thin limbs and distended bellies. I am never really happy, something in me is pining, all the time. Poor Laura, too— she lives in the hell of childhood strangulation. We all put our hells on to others, she with a bewitching look. Cleopatra: I am dying, Egypt, dying. I have immortal longings for thee. Shakespeare was an angel of light, to divine the soul of woman.

Did poor, silly Bertram Baldersby suffer? He was killed later on the Western Front. He was rather like Brigadier Tarr—a lost child, seeking rest from torment, peace in the body of any young woman. Bald-headed, stumpy, pushing his middle parts of fortune against padded fork after fork: fashioned public school drink-jag'd lecher, feeling female breast with circular movement of hand and grinning, "Ring me up sometime, I'll come hard on your call". Wishful thinking, out of a torment of self-ruin? No communication with the feelings of others. He must suffer greatly— even a bird of prey tastes grief. Or are there some who enjoy killing for self-righteousness' sake? Who say, The only good German is a dead German.

What say you, Wilfred Owen? Are you still haunting the Western Front, on guard, lest it happen again?

Wretched are they, and mean

> With paucity that never was simplicity.
> By choice they made themselves immune
> To pity and whatever mourns in man
> Before the last sea and the hapless stars;
> Whatever mourns when many leave these shores;
> Whatever shares
> The eternal reciprocity of tears.

Oh hell, I can't see through the orbs of my own eyes, I have gone too far south, stupidly, unthinkingly, I have taken the road across the Great Plain. No, not Rockhurst; never more those hills of the morning, and the beaten-gold shimmer of the Longpond. For there I was defeated; and my dead have not yet buried the dead. Uncle Hilary, where are you now?

Suddenly exhausted, he drove on to the turf, to misspend the night by the monoliths of Stonehenge, huddled in his war-time flea-bag: an enlarged chrysalis, torn by the furies of its own failures.

Vapours of the night-brain were scattered by a dawn of great stillness and beauty, despite the lack of larksong, for all the ploughed acres of the Plain, sown to corn, had recently been sprayed by yellow D.N.C. weed-killing compound, to which sulphate of ammonia had been added by the scientists to justify their customers'—the fertiliser merchants—claim that the yellow chemicals increased harvest yields of grain. It did—by the addition of sulphate of ammonia—which caused the death of several men driving tractors pulling spraying machines whence issued noxious gases.

Phillip, after breakfast cooked on the paraffin-oil stove, wondered whether to go south and call on Aunt Victoria; or to continue on to the West Country. Should he ask her if she had referred to him as 'the black sheep of the family' when Father died? She wasn't at his funeral, although it was at Bournemouth where she lived. He decided to stand up for himself for once and ask her that straight question.

"Well Phillip, this is a surprise. What brings you here?"

"I am wondering, Aunt Victoria, if it was my presence that kept you, firstly, from my father's funeral, and then again, from Aunt Dora's."

"Why should you think that, Phillip?" the old woman replied, as her face became more pale.

"I thought that perhaps you regarded me as a waster, for I heard from my sister Elizabeth that I was the black sheep of the family, in the eyes of one of my father's sisters."

"What gave you that impression? Surely nothing of that kind was said by me when you were here last?"

"It was said to me before I came here, Aunt Viccy."

"By whom, may one enquire?"

"My sister Elizabeth."

"I am not responsible for what your sister may, or may not say, Phillip."

"I see. Perhaps I did not hear correctly."

"I should *say* that you were once the odd one out of the family. But that was some time ago, surely? Since then you have worked hard on your own land in East Anglia, and increased your capital into the bargain. *You* are not one, I should say, who waits for dead men's shoes. Or should I say *contrives* that the shoes come a *certain* way?" She looked at Phillip with pale eyes. "While doing nothing to help take off the shoes of the dying."

"On two occasions, Aunt Viccy?"

"On two occasions, Phillip."

The old girl seemed to be cheering up, for she said, "I'm going to make some coffee. Will you join me?"

"Thank you, a good idea!"

"Have you had breakfast?"

"Yes, thank you. I am making for Dorchester, to lunch with a friend there. Then I'm going down to Queensbridge to see a doctor, who is a good eye man."

Here I am, back in my boyhood, telling lies. I'm going north to Colham, to see if Piers Tofield is at his home, Field Place.

"If you want a really good man, go to Endicott here in Bournemouth. He still charges two guineas, as before the war."

Over coffee and wheaten biscuits she said, "Did you know—has your sister Elizabeth told you—that I offered to name her in my will as the sole beneficiary of my estate, after the tenancy for life of Adele, my daughter and your cousin? And do you know what your sister replied, Phillip? She said to me, 'But I am older than cousin Adele, and she isn't likely to die before me'. Those were her very words, Phillip. I should tell you that my offer to her included the use, rent free, of one half of this house, also I would pay all bills of housekeeping, including food, fuel, electric light, and rates. If Elizabeth became ill, I could look after her, and vice versa. But no! Elizabeth proposed that *she* be left a tenancy-for-life, the capital in due course to go to *my* daughter! That proposal was not acceptable, I told her. From me she went directly to my sister Theodora, and tried it on her. With success, this time. I'm telling you all this in confidence, mind!"

"Of course, Aunt Viccy. Still, I suppose there are other kinds of black sheep who aren't interested in other people's money? I am not Pluto, caring only for money. I don't know who the god of poetry is, Apollo I suppose. He's my sort."

"But isn't Pluto the god of the nether-world, Phillip?"

"Also of money—the same thing, Aunt Victoria. Zeus made him a blind giver of wealth, thus men were destroyed. And women too, I suppose."

When Phillip left, he gave his aunt a kiss, much to her surprise, and it seemed, approval. "Do come in whenever you are this way again, and do not fail to let me know what Endicott says."

Dr. Endicott. Light beam of opthalmoscope into left eye, then right.

"This eye is a lazy eye. The muscles are partly atrophied. Now the left eye again. H'm. You seem tense. Tell me about yourself."

Dr. Endicott listened.

"I see. Well, hypertension, due to chronic frustration, can be one of the causes of opacity in the crystalline humour, tension of the globe, and possible deterioration of vision, due to a fibrous tissue behind the lens of the eye. You were temporarily blind in both eyes from mustard gas in 1918, you say. That could well be a contributory, if not altogether an initial cause of renticular fibroplasis."

"I may go blind, doctor?"

"Have you anyone with you?"

"I live alone on Exmoor."

"You are not staying with Mrs. Lemon?"

"I am on my way home. Shall I be able to drive?"

"If you proceed carefully. Now put your hand over your lazy eye and read the letters on that card on the wall. What do you see?"

"All the letters seem to be bent, and there is a darkish blur about each one as I try to focus on it."

"I would welcome another opinion; and will give you a letter to a retired colleague of mine who lives at Minehead. He's also something of a naturalist like yourself, and a particular authority of wild life on the moor. Yes, I shall welcome another opinion."

North for Cranborne Chase; over the high downs and onto Colham. Would Piers be at home? Passing the lodge, he saw neat cords of sawn wood in the park. And driving on, was startled to see a small dark-red house where Field Place had stood. Orderly piles of stone came into focus. Of course! Piers had said the shell was being sold to a building firm, together with doors, window frames, lintols, oak flooring—everything had a value in a time of acute shortages. 'Money for old rope', they said.

Evidently the Palladian structure had been built around the original house, a small Jacobean affair of brick and tile baked from local clay. He went through the postern gate to the court-yard, which remained. It was swept and tidy. He knocked at the kitchen door. A young girl, looking to be about seventeen, opened it wide.

"I'm Phillip Maddison, a friend of Sir Piers," he said, taking her for a kitchen maid.

"Do come in," she replied, in a calm voice. "Piers is working in the walled garden, he spends all his time there. He's often spoken of you." She took off an apron, revealing a slightly bulbous front. "I'm Beth. You know Laura Wissilcraft, don't you? I heard from her only this morning, she's back from Greece. Let's go and find Piers, shall we?"

Beth? Beth? Ah yes, the girl with the sadistic husband, aborting her every time she was pregnant; murderer of a prostitute, hanged about the same time as the Nuremberg 'war criminals' Laura saying, *She looks like sixteen but is twenty-eight*. Must be a strong character.

"Piers, you've done wonders! Look at everything! Marvellous vegetables—fruit trees pruned—"

"I've got a good man, I take orders from him. Well how are you, Phil? Tell me about Lucy and the children—"

"They're very happy. Boys at school, also Roz. Baby Sarah has a great sense of fun."

"Well done. You must bring her down sometimes to play with ours when it appears. You're writing hard, I hope."

"I've done nearly a hundred thousand words—all synopses of scenes for my novel series, since I went to Shep Cot."

"Good for you."

"I also walk a lot on the high ground of the moor."

"Nothing like it. You look lithe and fit. How's 'Buster'?"

"I see him now and again."

"Archie Plugge called here the other day. He's public relations to a sort of Ouspensky revival down your way, at Oldstone." He laid a heavy split section of beech-trunk on the hearth.

"I'm glad you've kept the kitchen, Piers. And opened up that hearth."

"Nothing like a wood fire. We cook on it—the old lapping crook, crock, cast-iron frying pan. Suits me."

"Just like my hearth in Shep Cot."

The young woman put a small table beside Phillip's chair, and covered it with a table-napkin. Soon a plate with omelette, deliciously cooked. Mug of tea.

"I've got an old friend down your way, Phillip, go and see her and give her my love—Molly Gildart that was, she married someone called Peregrine Bucentaur, who writes articles on big game hunting in Kenya for Country Life."

"I have met her—not him. Molly is a splendid friend."

"She always was. You'll stay, won't you," Piers went on. "Plenty of room. Thank God those bloody hens are gone. What sadists they were, pecking and treading one another."

"May I stay the night, and go on tomorrow?"

"Stay as long as you like."

"Will you mind if I leave you," said Beth. "I'm painting one of the bedrooms at the back."

"May I help you? I've done painting before."

"All aid welcome" said Piers.

The surfaces had been prepared—cleaned, pumice-stone'd, dried. She gave Phillip a door to paint.

"Laura had a bad time as a child, Phillip."

"She told me."

"Nursing was very good for her. 'My therapy', she called it."

"I suppose I'm a border-line case in a way. No-man's-land, where miracles can happen—"

"But a place to be wary of, generally speaking, didn't you find?"

The dialogue continued while both went on painting.

"I had a brilliant husband. Half-angel, half-devil."

"Usual mixture when among women," said Piers, coming in to borrow the wall-scraper.

"I suppose all men are potentially that?"

"Women too," said Piers, going out.

"We're all mixtures of fear, and the loyalty called love, Beth."

Work continued, while she asked him if he had anyone to help him in his cottage. "So you 'do' for yourself altogether. Piers did,

for a period. Did he tell you how I came here? Well, it was rather
funny, I suppose. He was taking me home in a taxi, after we'd
been to the Medicean Club. He wanted to have me in the taxi
but I wouldn't. I liked him, you see, and wasn't going to be
regarded merely as a fourpenny touch. When he cried, I suggested
he take me home with him, meaning the next day. 'Right', he
said. We went back to the Medicean and he got some beer bottles,
whisky, glasses, and a lot of sandwiches. Then to my room, where
I packed some clothes. That's how we came here, by taxi."

"All through the night?"

"We stopped now and again for a drink and a sandwich. The
taxi driver was a sport. Piers gave him double fare, including the
return. So here I am, pregnant to my satisfaction."

"Congratulations."

"Thank you."

She went on painting.

"How long have you known Laura?"

"Ever since we began nursing during the war. There were three
of us, the other being Melissa Wilby. You know her, don't
you?"

"I did once, long ago. She and Lucy are coming down to
Exmoor in the summer, by car."

"Do tell them to call here. We can put them up for the night,
and I know Piers would love to see them again."

Phillip telephoned the retired eye-specialist at Minehead before
going to see him.

"Ah, at last I have met 'the water wanderer'!" he said, with
gentle satisfaction. "You'll be pleased to hear that we have under
observation a blackcock's nest on Winslow Hill," as he brought
forward the opthalmoscope. "You've been burning the midnight
oil to excess, I expect." He peered. "Ah, there is a blood vessel on
the retina of this eye, which appears to have broken. Yes, the
grey hen brought off her brood, despite the attacks of crows. The
bleeding may stop, and heal. You'll also be glad to know that
two corncrakes have hatched off a clutch of seven eggs. They're
getting rather rare. Some of the trout-fly-tying johnnies will pay
two pounds for a skin. You must rest from your labours. Another
book on the stocks? What is to be this time? Well, have a rest;
ideas will come the easier, then. Come and see me again. Don't
read too much. Get in the open air. It is possible that blood vessels
may leave scar tissue, which will be in the direct line of vision,

and prevent both reading and writing with direct focus. No fee, my dear boy. But if you care to send me a copy of your next book—"

James Joyce went blind. How did he manage to finish Ulysses? Large BBB pencil? Helped by Samuel Beckett? His style all private notes, conglomerated. Delius wrote music when he had gone blind, squired by Eric Fenby. Perhaps Miranda—

He would never ask her.

From first light to the sun rolling away half his gift of day, curlews were crying their linked bell-notes in the upper airs of the moor. No longer were they afraid of the man and dog walking among the tussocks, often two-feet and more across, beside which their young were crouching, obedient to warnings from above. For the carrion crows quartered The Chains, an inherited right, seeking nests of large blotched eggs, and later the speckled young below. The crows hunted from a height of from six to seven hundred feet; they knew the habits of curlew, knew that a standing hen nervously regarding them was near her nest. And the cock-bird circling above them, with urgent thrusts of wings, calling with sharp and ringing alarm when directly over the young birds, pointed the objective to be assaulted. So one crow would flap down, as though lazily, a decoy to draw the cock curlew in tumbling flight after him. *Car-car-car!* Signal for crow's mate to flop rather than fly down and make open-mouthed cursing dash at hen curlew.

Phillip could tell what was happening by the cries of the birds. He could discern aerial movement, but no definition. Bodger waited with quivering stump.

"Goo' boy, Bodger!"

And off the mongrel would go upwind, leaping over long wind-stroked grasses arisen from the tussocks : to stand where the female curlew had arisen, with ringing scrape of melody, to fly wildly about the sky. Bodger on guard, looking up at crows sloping away with muttered curses.

Phillip walking over to Bodger. "Good old boy, Bodger!"

Sometimes in those sunny days of early June he would play a game with the little dog, while, unseen by him, two gliders soared overhead. 'Buster' now had his war-time comrade with him, Brigadier Tarr, to train new pilots. Laura was his first pupil. She was all air-minded, finding fulfilment by identifying herself as an Icarian spirit, seeing the earth below as the pantheon of the

gods of Hellas. For Greece, and particularly an experience in
Corfu, leading to a temporary liaison with another visitor there,
was now shaping in her mind for a novel.

Phillip would be a Prospero-figure, she thought, as she saw
him and the little dog below, and wondered what he was thinking.
Sometimes he lay down upon the long green grasses, resilient and
soft upon the clumps, and stared into the sky; she waved, but
he took no notice.

For Phillip had not seen the gliders overhead. His idea was to
lose Bodger, away hunting on some scent, mouse or straying rabbit,
so that the dog would be able to find him should he ever lose
himself. So Phillip was lying hidden, waiting for the dog, upwind,
to find him. Would the genes of a foxhound mother—emblazoned
on Bodger's coat in patches of lemon, tan and black—come to
his aid? Raising his head a little, he could just discern Bodger
standing still, facing east, staring for any movement. Seeing no
movement, Bodger changed position to stare south. No scent; for
Phillip was downwind from the dog's nostrils.

Dog faced north; stared awhile; then west. No sight, no scent,
of master.

So Bodger set off to find Phillip. He ran down wind for half
a mile, to stop on the crest of The Chains, casting. He crossed
the wind, until he got his master's scent. Then upwind, tossing
scent on black nose, until he came straight to warmer scent of
master lying face-up in a green bed of softness.

And looking up to spy around, Phillip discovered Bodger sitting, composed and now looking elsewhere, less than a yard away
from him, downwind.

One morning Laura walked to Shep Cot. She was seen by
Aaron Kedd, the smallholder whose eyes watched with covetous
disapproval the length of her naked legs : for she wore a bathing
dress with short linen jacket belonging to 'Buster'. She found
Phillip lying in the heather outside his open door, and came to
the point at once.

"Why are you avoiding me? I waved to you as I passed over
this morning, but you took no notice !"

"I'm afraid I must have been in what used to be called a brown
study. How high were you?"

"A thousand feet only. And don't try to avoid what I'm saying !
You *did* see me ! You looked at me and when I waved you deliberately looked away. I suppose it's all Miranda now?"

"I seldom see her."

"That's her handwriting!" She pointed to a letter beside him. "Postmark Cheltenham!"

"I've only just got it from the post office, and haven't opened it yet."

Laura walked away. She returned. "Phillip I'm sorry. Please be kind to me. Why are you keeping yourself away? Even 'Buster' feels you've dropped him. Are you writing?"

"I'm making notes. How goes your stuff?"

"My *stuff*, as you call it, is being composed all the time—in my head."

"So is mine. How's the gliding?"

"You *are* keeping something from me! I was quite frank with you about the composer in Corfu. He said he wouldn't ask for children, and would let me go on with my writing while he wrote his music. But I kept thinking of you, and how you were getting on, with no one to look after you."

"I'm no good for you. You know that. Oh, listen to the curlews. There's pure prose for you."

She sat beside him, and stroked his chest and neck with a crow's feather.

"Darling, you are a curlew, you are Prospero, who understands his Ariel. If I come and live with you, you won't mind me having other men sometimes, will you? I can't help it, Phillip, it's my nature. I'm very passionate, but I can't bear the idea of having children. My life is my writing." Then she said, "O, it's so lovely by the harbour now! Do let's go down and swim!"

Aaron Kedd watched them crossing the common to the lane. Thaccy scarlet woman had bestways no right to paint her lips, and go whoring after men! He grunted when Phillip called out, "How's the root crop? Any fly on the turnips?", considering this idle remark to be a jeer, because he hadn't yet drilled the seed.

Reaching the village, Phillip and Laura went into a shop for coffee. Visitors were now numerous in Lynmouth. An occasional young American voice was heard, in connexion with words like *doctorate, skedule, comparative literature.* Shelley's cottage had a board beside *Bed and Breakfast,* saying *Full Up.*

"Phillip, I am fascinated by gliding. It's as near to heaven as one can get. And to fall, fall, fall as Icarus!"

"Do you know Francis Thompson's lines from *The Mistress of Vision?*

" 'O dismay!
I, a wingless mortal, sporting
With the tresses of the sun?
I, that dare my hand to lay
On the thunder in its snorting?
Ere begun,
Falls my singed song down the sky, even
the old Icarian way.' "

"Thank you! That's *most* reassuring!"

"Apologies for taking your fancy literally. How's the biography of Manfred Cloudesley going?"

"It's been stopped for the time being, by a local irritation, calling itself Osgood Nilsson. He keeps asking 'Buster' for details, including 'any of his father's letters he happens to have by him'. The man has the hide of a rhinoceros! By the way, 'Buster' doesn't want him to know that we're writing his father's biography. He doesn't want any publicity, in case someone like Nilsson rushes something out first. 'Buster' worries about it, you see, and so can't concentrate on the book." She added, "He has to take sedative drugs, his spine never ceases to ache."

"He's a very brave man. Also, a grand man. He never 'blows black smoke in other people's faces'."

"He's wizard when in the air. So am I! We're both Icarians in this wonderful weather of thermals!"

"Including your instructor, the full-rigged and tarred Brig?"

"Phillip, he's quite different in the air! He's like a boy again, before his father was killed in nineteen seventeen, after his mother had bolted with someone else."

She appealed to him with limpid eyes. "Phillip, I know you will understand. He had a bad time in his war, you know. He was blown up on a land-mine, and it affected his brain. You won't tell anyone, will you? I know you won't, but he's been in the loony-bin, his brain is still hurt—" Her voice was almost inaudible, she was nearly crying.

She recovered; and asked him if he would be going to Oldstone Down for the Midsummer Eve Festival of the Eirēnēan Society.

"You know Piston, don't you, Phillip? Some people laugh at him, but I don't. Oldstone Down is one of those charged mountains, like the Hartz mountains in the Black Forest, where people see the Brocken. You do believe in the unseen world, don't you?"

"I believe in Blake, who said, 'Everything that lives is holy'. He didn't mean that all living acts are holy—but the potential for holiness is there. Bodger lying there is holy. Aren't you, Bodger? His tail says 'Yes'. Laura—did you ever read W. H. Hudson's story of two dogs on the pampas of Argentina remaining with the master who had fallen off a horse and broken a leg? When the vultures came and sat near him, the dogs remained on guard until their tongues were dry with heat, and thirst. Water was near, but whenever they began to slink away to it, the movement of the birds towards the man brought them back to defend him. Hudson says he does not like dogs, they are stupid he says : and goes on to say that, otherwise, one would have gone to drink while the other remained on guard. So dogs are not really to be admired. It is so strange that Hudson seemed blind to their selfless courage, and saw in it only stupidity. I've heard young men, not born when my war was being fought on the Western Front, declaring that all who remained there to die were a lot of bloody fools. Do you mind if I read you something I've just written?" He took out his note-book and had got so far as saying, "This is about an incident at Passchendaele—", when Laura got up and left the café.

Returning up the street, Phillip saw smoke coming out of a chimney on Ionian cottage. Osgood Nilsson's old jalopy was parked by the gate. Standing behind it, he heard voices. Mrs. Nilsson was talking at the open door, beside his sister Elizabeth. Had she come to live in Lynmouth? He felt thin and anxious; and turning back, returned home by way of Mars Hill, desperately forcing himself up the narrow, twisting lane.

Chapter 17

A VISIT FROM ROSALIE

Mrs. Osgood Nilsson, like her husband, was an odd mixture. Her mother was of Irish lineage, being a daughter of The O'Croglin of O'Croglin, head man of a hill tribe of Celts in County Galway. Her father had been a British actor who also wrote ghoulish *extravaganzas* under the *nom-de-plume* of D. Raquller.

Osgood Nilsson never mentioned this aspect of his father-in-law's authorship, lest the fact somewhat tarnish the connection with The O'Croglin of O'Croglin, and also diminish his status with his own soldier grandfather.

But when Nilsson thought of his own father, he backed away from the image in his mind. All his need for assurance came from the disastrous memory when a small boy of finding his father shot, by his own hand, one morning.

The ghost walked from his mind when his blood-stream was polluted by excess of alcohol, and unknowingly he tried to transfer the ghost to others... Unknowingly, yes; for Nilsson at heart was a warm and generous man. Self-knowledge, in relation to the defects of others, was denied him; so he remained a second-rate, or superficial writer.

Otherwise, he was an amiable man. His wife was a generous woman, impelled by this trait to interest herself in the lives of others. Some people, who did not fully, that is intuitively, realise the chronic anxiety under which Rosalie Nilsson lived—never knowing when Osgood might fall under a stroke, or be killed while driving his motorcar—considered that she was merely a gossip, a retailer of the peccadilloes of others—in confidence, of course. Never tell Rosalie anything, these members of the *haute bourgeoisie* told one another, unless you wish everyone to know it...

Mrs. Nilsson was by now much interested in how Phillip was getting on, and what he was doing. Elizabeth's account of her brother's faults, from his earliest years, had surprised her; the poor woman obviously had a 'thing' about him; even so, there was much that intrigued her. The fact that he had been a 'bad' little boy meant nothing; and since his sister was obviously a neurotic character, much could be discounted. But other facts—if indeed they were facts—were surprising. Phillip had won the D.S.O., but relinquished it before going to prison in Wormwood scrubs, for arson! And he'd had an illegitimate son, and tried to get Lucy his wife, who'd had a child at the same time, to register both infants as her twins! And Elizabeth declared that he was always trying to get money from his relations, after *refusing* an inheritance of twelve hundred acres from his uncle, Hilary Maddison! There was something rather odd there—surely he could have sold the land after his uncle's death, were he so keen on money?

These statements, taken into consideration with stories about him from other sources—mainly about his womanising in Shep Cot—Molly Bucentaur *and* her 'teen-age daughter Miranda—and other young women, including that girl with an odd name—one of the pseudo-literary world. The stories excited Rosalie Nilsson, so she decided to have a look at his ménage one afternoon. She could, sincerely, tell him how much she thought of his work; and invited him to have a meal with Osgood and herself.

She drove her car through the steep and narrow lane as far as the open moor, and walked across the heather, to find the door open, and no-one at home.

Then she saw him with his little dog, outlined against the steep heather slopes leading up to The Chains; but just in case someone was in the cot, she called out, "Hullo there! Anyone at home? Mr. Maddison, are you there?" A robin flew out of the doorway, and thus encouraged, Mrs. Nilsson walked over the threshold.

"Anybody at home?"

No answer. She entered and looked around before advancing to call up the stairs. "Are you all right?" She said, just in case someone was up there, "I'm Rosalie Nilsson, Osgood's wife. This is a call, I suppose!"

Still no reply, so she returned outside. The common was empty for a quarter of a mile around. Thereupon she returned to the kitchen and quizzed first the bookshelves, then the papers on the table. There were two small piles of typed sheets: one on yellow paper, the other on white. After cautiously going up the stairs, to be sure no-one was there, she went down again and picking up the yellow sheets began to read.

That these last three days spent with P. have been perhaps the best time we have had together I cannot deny. But fundamentally there are the same doubts, and I find myself grieving because I know I cannot ever hope to really share myself, my life with him. There is a general sapping away of my spirit and thereby my creative reservoir gets clogged up; P.M. tries so sweetly to give me everything that I may need—but I cannot help feeling myself ever so often in some terrifying Faustian situation...

This was exciting. Rosalie turned over to the next page—no signature. Who could it be?

I want to help him—to restore his belief in himself, but it all seems beyond my capacity. I think the fact that he has not become my *real* lover accounts for a lot—for the desolate moments. There is a great tenderness between us and I feel now that I could not bear for us to make love in any way—

The visitant examined the typing; it was done by a typewriter different from that on the table. Could the writer be Miranda, of whose infatuation for Phillip she had heard at a cocktail party in Lynton? "My dear, old enough to be her *grandfather!*" A ridiculous remark—for Phillip was, according to *Who's Who,* fifty one. He would have to have been very precocious to be a father at seventeen, and his son also a father at the same age, to be Miranda's grandfather! 'Buster's' secretary, perhaps? That was nearer the mark : the girl, Laura someone—very odd name—had a withdrawn look about her, eyes anywhere but on the faces of people in the street when she had seen her in Lynmouth...

I want above all to be a good, true lasting friend BUT I think P. hopes and longs for more. What am I to do? I am filled with such anguish at times for him, my own inability to *love* him completely, enough to say I shall be with you always we will make a life together. I know, *feel,* that there can be no change.

I think Melissa must have suffered the same feelings—though she was wiser (?!) in being objective from the first. The age difference is there and cannot be dismissed; M. knew and understood this from the first. I tried to believe otherwise (that essence between two people is the main bond.) But it has to be sum total of what we are from what we have been.

How can I free myself from P. without bringing him more anguish—how can I make him realise that I cannot be/feel as the image of a woman he has imprinted on his heart all these years: his young wife, the first one, who died when she was nineteen, his ideal companion? When with him there are some very lyrical moments, at the same time there is an aspect of life—a part of me—that seems to be cut off. I try to forget this, but it is there confronting me round every corner. It is I think a certain possessiveness of P's side that weighs me down; and any lightness of spirit/thought by this almost obsessive demanding nature that P. has—even his way of leaving me, giving me freedom is something *he is giving* and not something that happens as a mutual recognition and sympathy that two people should have when with each other—

Yes, it must be that odd girl, Laura Wissilcraft. What a curious name! Transferring her own attitudes to Phillip, from what I have heard . . . very much so. That young woman had a flashing temper at times! It was said that 'Buster' had felt it on more than one occasion; but kept his feelings hidden, literally, under his mask. Osgood had a theory that he had something to hide about his own father, when the real reason of the poor man's reticence was due to his incapacity—like the hero in Hemingway's first novel, *The Sun Also Rises,* in hopeless love with Brett, the girl 'built like a yacht'—

Hence the headache that is with me today, for I fail to find a good solution to all this. I could not write a line while in Corfu.

So it *was* Laura, after all!

Time alone—but meanwhile? Oh dear God, help P.! Give him a little understanding of my situation. Give him strength and grace to go on alone and not delude himself and others any more. My heart is heavy. My spirit in splinters. No one has ever had this effect on me. Is it love? A love of the spirit that can in a sense be almost destruction, dangerous in its absorbing power?

In a way, therefore, I hope he is able to make love to Miranda, who goes to see him whenever she can from her school, which she is soon to leave, I hear. An old stallion with a young mare produces the liveliest foal, they say.

Poor Laura, what a mix-up. She is quite right, this situation isn't any good for her. Obviously it has no true base. I'd like to talk to her, if I could do so without appearing to be interfering . . .

Mrs. Nilsson took up the differently typed sheets. These were obviously Phillip's work.

31 July 1917

The barrage fills a world pallid-black before dawn. The sky bubbles with light, the very earth is trembling. What tempests of fire! What upheavings and shakings! Tens of thousands of tons of brown earth going up every few moments, a slow advancing barrage in six lines of fire from more than a thousand guns of all calibres: six rolling walls of fire moving east in flame and smoke, concentrated on a 12-mile front, lifting 25 yards every minute: waves of infantry advancing 50-100 yards behind those curtains of flame, smoke, and all-obliterating noise. One is stunned, lifted out of body, struggling over torn clay of a dream-nightmare world, half-choked by fumes, crawling up pits of broken, smoking earth, seeing nothing except blackened clay and broken sandbags and twisted buried wire this side of an inferno of bursting shells.

The Great Push has begun. Third Ypres. The sky is a dragging grey, moving over from the south-west, the Atlantic. Will it rain? The battlefield is below sea-level, contained behind the dykes of Nieuport and Dunkerque.

I awoke this morning, as usual, with a feeling of deep depression; but managed to hack out the above words.

My problems, as L. would call them, appear insuperable. They *are* insuperable, the handicap is too great, one cannot win this race unless one travels alone. Perhaps no one can win this earthly race. Even Tolstoi, at the end, was defeated—hiding on a railway station from the anguish of a possessed wife.

Of those hundreds of thousands, those millions who died, young, between 1914-18, and again 1939-45, the poet Laurence Housman wrote,

> They shall grow not old, as we that are left grow old. Age shall not weary them, or the years condemn ...

I could no longer type in bed on the tea-tray, I got up and built the fire, rather than lie still in bed like a dying man, with diminishing consciousness: Death the Antic sitting between chest and belly, my life fading out like a film that is switched off. The images linger a moment, they diminish, the light is gone. And that is how one dies, I am sure. Consciousness lessens, recedes from 'little body'—lying below one—while one thinks 'that is not me, that is poor little body lying down there'. One is suspended above, looking down, in a strange calm unemotional bliss-azure feeling.

Later, I typed by the fire, warm tea inside me, a sandwich of Molly's whole-wheat bread with butter and honey. Gone is my dismal grave-shroud mood of 5 a.m.; vanished those phantoms of despair waiting, like heirs in silence around my bed.

10 p.m. Laura and I were going to a beach on the north-west coast, (I have taught her to drive). I also wanted to write. "Take the car"

I said. "It is yours". She said she'd be back at six. She arrived at ten.
She showed me shells, glass pebbles—some lovely aquamarine blue
of 1880 bottles.

"Aren't they beautiful?" She set them out. A rare sunset shell ...

"So that's where you've been. On cousin Willie's beach, that he
called Shelley Cove."

"Yes," she replied, looking at me steadily. "Would you like me to
leave tomorrow?"

"No, of course not. I'm sorry I was bleak when you came back a
little late." She was four hours late, she said she'd be back for tea. I'd
eaten little, she was to buy and bring back food. "Sea-shells, Sabrina
Fair—how alike we are."

"You make me feel guilty!" she cried. "I *won't* feel guilty!"

Out she stormed, banging the door, and leaving me talking to
myself.

I begin to see shape, and depth, for my novel. It will be several
volumes. *The Flying Dutchman* theme—alienated first from my
mother when 4 or 5 years of age; the wound healed by Barley; opened
by her death. Yes, *The Flying Dutchman* theme. *They're all dead*
sings the chorus of girls after waiting in vain for the sailors from the
dark ship to come to the wedding. A ghost ship indeed. The chorus
is sung so lightly, lyrically, softly withal, like maiden girls tossing
flowers. *They're all dead*, both spring-song and requiem. Threnos.
For those sailors are of all human life and death, they could be
emanations from the Western Front, unreal, pursuing a dream, caught
up in a dream of fair women, on the very margin of death. They live
inside ruined bodies, each man with a figment of beauty and calm
and intelligence always to be by his side, and he by her side.

I walked about the room, talking aloud to my Doppelgänger,
"I am, as Marcel Proust was, all locked up inside, I cannot share my
personality at this time. I need months of calm, with someone like
Melissa to wean me from this shadow, or death-wish. My courage-
fear death-wish!"

Laura, who apparently had been listening, at this point pushed the
door open and cried "You cannot forgive yourself because all your
friends were killed and you were not!" Then she said, "You are
Christ's boy, you want to go back in Time and be crucified!
To lie in crater-zones, to join your German and English brothers!
You are dead, dead! Like your Lucifer, your Hitler who stopped the
advance on Dunkerque and let three hundred thousand British troops
get off more or less scot free! 'Buster' told me that! Hitler stopped
his tanks! And you told 'Buster' that Rundstedt's doctor told you the
Generals implored him to end the war by leaving no one to return to
England. Hitler is like you. It was all a dream, like yours, a 'Revolution to Destruction', as one of his Ex-Nazis who became a sensible
refugee wrote in nineteen thirty-eight, in one of 'Buster's' books

which was prophetic! So for God's sake, cease *your* horrific convolution to destruction! You, 'Buster', the Brig, are all the same, you're all dead, all dead, like the sailors in Wagner's Flying Dutchman. Forget your cousin Willie's 'dream of fair women', or rather his nightmare of disembodied, onanistic love. You're strangling me, and my hopes of happiness with you! My talent is suborned, destroyed by a parasite. Not you, my poor friend, but your *ideas*. Wagner has done it all, once and for all! What do you want now, a *Götterdämmerung?* Like 'Buster'—playing over his Bayreuth records half the night. Listening with eyes closed to all else but his own noble death in a Great Cause? To rescue that poor sad creature who flew to England and fell among thieves? What would Hess do without his dreams, withered as his own body, if he and 'poor little body' were set free? He'd be lost, without his torment! He's lived in hell so long he's become an angel, knowing no other condition of life! Can't you see the truth of what I am trying to tell you? For you're killing me! I am Mother Earth, as you once said, I am Proserpine, but what are you? Shall I tell you? The Flying Dutchman!'

The door slammed again, she was gone. I felt like a fly bitten by the poison-fang of a spider. I was paralysed, appalled, and afraid. Frozen. It was the same when we were in London. She was rude, bad-mannered the night before she left for Corfu and we were in the Medicean Club. She got half-way through dinner and left abruptly. It was more than humiliating, it was shattering.

She has never understood what it has meant to have gone through two wars and be left with a sense of failure in all things. Or has she understood, with her terrifying clairvoyance? It is her manner which inhibits me. I have heard that the German Generals were often inhibited, in Hitler's presence, by his bad manners. They were not used to being shouted at. Yet who am I to judge? Haven't I, in the past, shouted at Lucy? Before the silent children? Good Generals use their heads, not their emotions. The German officers were trained to politeness, and could not cope with bad manners. As Lucy could not cope with mine, and for the same reasons: my cursed drive to perfection, which is the artist's problem, and one not to be shared with others, unless they are to be destroyed. At least I know, and knew it. I don't think Laura does know it, of herself; for she also is in her writing, is dedicated to perfection. And I stand in the way. We are two people trying to occupy the same place: Siamese twins each struggling to be supreme. For she, too, is all inside herself, appearing insensitive, *in action*, to the feelings of another, in her turn. She is, as I said, all inside herself, shut off: a subjective writer. And she damns me for being that: I, who am striving to get outside my subject, which is no less than the dilemma of Western man, viewed from all aspects, with sympathy and precision.

For the Great War was the epitome of lovelessness in Western

Civilisation. That is the theme that has long possessed me. And Laura, with her eyes haunted and compassionate, sweet girl, longs to seduce me from this death-work, seeing herself as Persephone leading me back to life from the gentian-blue halls of Dis, into which poor D. H. Lawrence entered when he died at Vence by the Mediterranean Sea in 1930.

Laura carries within herself the main lament of Eve, of Erda the earth-Mother; of Persephone dedicated to bring back the dead to life, that the phoenix may accept its failure and become whole again, so that it shall cherish the turtle dove waiting to build her raft-nest in the hawthorn bush, thereon to lay her two eggs—innocent and white, without camouflage, visible to every pillaging crow and magpie.

I was a loveless boy, unit of a loveless Europe sending Youth to the Western Front, and again, after two decades, another generation to the Steppes of Russia and the shambles of Europe, followed by its scape-goats to the gallows and the crematoria. But on my Western Front there were little candles throwing far their gleams in a naughty world . . . Christmas tree candles on German parapets of front-line trenches, to welcome the *Engländer Kameraden*. What shall I do? I said to myself, helplessly. Then the door opened, and in she came again, putting down a yellow paper in the table, while saying quietly to me, "Read that, please. You will find the answer to your question there."

She has gone, I feel, this time, for ever. I do not know what to do. It is too late to think of writing my novels now. How wise was James Joyce to give up everything in time, to begin and carry on and finish his work while yet his sight remained.

I must now go with my dog and walk on The Chains and try to sleep in the sun.

What a good thing I came along, said Mrs. Nilsson to herself outside the cot. She hesitated. Could she manage to get so far as the crest of the moor? For while she had been an athletic type at school on the South Downs near Brighton, where she was captain of hockey, swimming, and cricket, sturdy athletism had taken or added its toll in later life, while in no wise diminishing her jollity. She was as innocent as a seal, itself a warm-blooded creature and covered by plenty of fat.

While she was trying to make up her mind, she was being watched by the smallholder, Aaron Kedd. Another woman come whorin', all rinnin' after he, and one a witch! And they high-go-glee goin's on at thaccy Lord's house 'mongst the trees to Lynton!

Mrs. Nilsson decided to go on up. She was soon puffing, but she persevered, and at last, wondering if her heart might give up at any beat, she came to the top of the hill, and walking south, came to a sea of deep, soft grasses growing from clumps more than knee-high; and there she saw a little dog looking at her, and Phillip lying beside Miranda, arms under heads and staring at the sky. Some distance away was Miranda's pony, cropping the shorter grasses of a tumulus, beside a white goat.

Seeing her, the two got to their feet.

"I called at your cot, and screwed up my courage to enter, finding the door open, Phillip. May I call you Phillip? Osgood has long wanted to ask you to come and see us, but hearing you were immersed in a book, I forebore. How is it going? I saw some typed sheets on the table."

"I've been preparing some scenes, Mrs. Nilsson, so far. Winter is the time for writing."

"Osgood also finds it difficult to concentrate when the sun is shining. As it does sometimes even in Devon," she went on cheerfully.

"What a wonderful view, Miranda! No wonder you two come here!"

Far in the sky a glider was making a slow turn.

"I expect that's 'Buster' up there,' she said. "He's always at it. You know him, of course, Miranda?"

"Yes, Mrs. Nilsson."

"Weren't you both at the Hallowe'en party last autumn? I hear it was quite a party!"

Miranda smiled.

"I hear he's writing a biography of his father, helped by a researcher from London, a Miss-, Miss-, some odd name, it just escapes me."

"Wissilcraft," said Phillip.

"Of course! Do come and see us, Phillip. Osgood gets so depressed at times, it's his leg you know, he won't have it off. It's been like that ever since he crashed in Egypt while training with the R.F.C. in the first war. He'd have been much happier without it, but I suppose vanity makes him cling to it."

"A wounded man feels inferior, I fancy."

"Yes, of course. You've known that odd creature, Major Piston, for some time, I'm told. Weren't you two together on the Somme?"

"Yes. He lost all his men, so did I, in the first few minutes."

"How do you mean, lost? Through inexperience?"

"Scythed down by machine guns."

"Oh yes, of course, it was terrible, wasn't it? I had just left school, and went to nurse in Mrs. Hall-Walker's home in Regent's Park. She was a great tennis hostess, that's how we met before the war, although I was never in the top flight. Do you play tennis, Phillip?"

"I used to, Mrs. Nilsson."

"*Do* call me Rosalie! And *do* bring Miranda with you to have a knock-up on our daisy and dandelion patch sometime. Osgood and I don't like to think of you existing all alone in your cot. Any afternoon, take us as you find us." She looked at a merlin circling above, watching for skylarks. "I must tell Osgood about that! He's keen on wild birds. Our garden is a sanctuary. Gold-finches are already flocking to our dandelion heads, with their young. What a dear little terrier that is. What do you call him?"

"Bodger, named after a sack he sleeps on."

"How interesting. That must be the sack I saw in your sitting room. Bodger of Great Snoring. A joke, I suppose?"

"There was a Bodger who farmed at Great Snoring in North Norfolk, Rosalie."

"Sounds like something out of 'Itma', doesn't it? Look at him, he's seen something!" Bodger was growling; he had got the scent of his former master and tormentor.

"Maybe he's got the scent of a fox, Rosalie. Foxes come here for frogs, so do otters."

"How interesting! I must tell Osgood. Well, I must be going. I hope I haven't unduly disturbed you, Phillip."

They walked together to the common. The glider was now high in the sky, almost out of sight. "Ten thousand feet, would you say, Phillip?"

"Nearer fifteen, I should say. It has a good wing-span, more than most German aircraft in my war. They usually came over at about ten thousand, the observation planes I mean."

"So you call it your war, do you." She stopped. "Phillip, I've a confession to make. I took a casual peek at what was on your typewriter roller, and was fascinated by your description of Third Ypres. No mere mud and blood stuff, but all exact reporting, as Osgood would say. But do you think there is any interest left in the Great War? I seem to remember a spate of angry young men all writing books in the 'twenties. Oh, I don't mean that your sketch is part of the spate! But, please don't be angry, I read on for a bit, and saw how you link it all psychologically with the second war. I suppose its logical? I never thought of Hitler's war as stemming from the first. But I suppose it did?"

"Directly, in my view."

"Then you should write it, my dear. Your writing fascinates me! It is so understanding and compassionate! I nearly wept, really I did. I could see it was a sort of précis sketch of a modern heroine, battles, et cetera, and as I said, I found it fascinating. How you imagine it *all* like that, completely baffles me!"

Phillip, not taken in by this pretence, replied, "Oh, a bit here, a bit there, out of life."

"I shall be fascinated to read the whole book when it appears, Phillip. You'll have rave notices, I'm certain of that. So you *do* use 'real' people?"

"Not as a transcript. All should be transmuted through the Imagination "

"For fear of libel, you mean?"

"Not altogether. Transcripts are never real to others."

"Yes, that's what Osgood says. His god is Turgenev. But then he was in Russia during the revolution. He thinks the Russians are streets ahead of all European novelists. Particularly Dostoieffsky."

"Yes, Dostoieffsky sees through people, but always with compassion."

Her motorcar stood by the gate leading to the common. "Now do come, my dear, any time, any day. Take us as you find us. Too much being alone leads to all sorts of mental fixations, I find. It does with Osgood. You've seen him when he's not himself, poor man. His leg gives him hell; but he's the sweetest old dear when he's off the hard liquor, so don't be put off, will you, Phillip? He has a lot to contend with, I do assure you. Yes, do come!" To Miranda she said, "I hear your father is coming for the cricket, and also to hand over the Boniface herd of goats to the town council. Well, if we don't meet again, we'll foregather in the Valley of Goats, you'll be there, of course, won't you? Do you write, too?"

"I help Cousin Phillip with the magazine, sorting out articles."

"How's the magazine going Phillip?"

"None too well, I'm afraid. Most of the subscribers won't renew, and the railway newspaper stalls have sold practically none, all on sale or return of course."

"I did hear you were just a little controversial in your Editorial, quoting passages from a book by Birkin. You must be careful, my dear, the war is still a very sore point with most people. Those concentration camps, surely you don't justify them?"

"Did you see a copy of the magazine, Rosalie?"

"Unfortunately I didn't, Phillip. I must send you a subscription. What is it?"

"Ten shillings a year, four issues post free."

"Well, I think we can run to that. Make it a nature magazine, why not? I am sure it would then go like hot cakes. What a jolly old caravan you have got. I suppose you're going to let it for the summer?"

"I thought Lucy and the children might prefer to camp out beside the Lyn, on Green Meadow, just below Barbrook, with the baby—"

"Oh, there's a baby, is there? What a remarkable man you are, to be sure."

"*She's* remarkable for a child only a year old!"

"What fun for you to have your family with you again. I suppose you'll keep your *pied-à-terre* to yourself, now you're writing again, after the years of farming. Well, I have so enjoyed my visit, dear boy. Do bring your wife over, won't you? *And* Miranda. Anytime—come for a meal—we keep open house. Osgood has food parcels sent over by his American publisher, so we always have plenty of Spam."

Mrs Nilsson got into her car and drove away, eager to tell Osgood her latest news.

"My dear, that affair between Phillip Maddison and that strange girl with the odd name has evidently not gone well. Apparently he prefers other company to hers. One can quite see how attractive he would be to any romantic young girl. I wonder how Miranda will feel now that his wife is coming down?"

"Molly you mean, don't you? She's been using her daughter as a decoy."

"How exciting! I do love a bit of gossip!"

Part Three

SUMMER IN ANOTHER LAND

Chapter 18

OSGOOD NILSSON INVESTIGATES

Osgood Nilsson was, among other literary activities, a roving correspondent for a New York newspaper. He had proposed to his editor that he write a series of articles for the Magazine of the Sunday issue of the paper. The theme had suggested the overall title—*Living under the Harrow;* Churchill's Island Fortress since termination of the war in Europe, particularly the growth of 'the lunatic fringe of religions and breakaway groupings stemming from the rising generation's rejections of pre-war sexual restraints, customs, mores, and accepted ideals which had produced the British Empire'.

Nilsson set about getting the low-down, for his first article, on the College of Diaphany established in a Victorian castle on the coast of Devon. It was run by an American calling himself Caspar Schwenkfelder, who had come to Britain with the U.S.A. Army Air Force, married an Englishwoman, and settled there.

Doctor Schwenkfelder claimed, in a brochure sent through the mails, the distinction of a Doctorate awarded to him by the Faculty of Therapeutic Medicine Hat Ethical and Philosophical Society.

Nilsson had gone to the Castle posing as a student requiring a course of instruction. Asked to wait in a room, the first thing he saw was an Abraham's Box. Here was something! A fad of the 'thirties, which, by electrical currents, revealed what the patient should or should not eat and drink, and what hidden diseases you suffered from, such as cancer. A fortune had been made in Park Avenue and Harley Street by the Abraham's Box racket!

Looking around the shelves of a bookcase in the waiting-room he came upon a volume entitled *Assorted Articles,* by D. H. Lawrence, published in 1930. In one article, a reprint from a London Sunday newspaper of November 1928, called *Sex versus Loveliness,* he found heavily marked passages.

Sex and beauty are inseparable, like life and consciousness. And the intelligence which goes with sex and beauty, and arises out of sex and beauty, is intuition. The great disaster of our civilisation is the morbid hatred of sex. *What, for example, could show a more poisoned hatred of sex than Freudian psycho-analysis?*—which carries with it a morbid fear of beauty, 'alive' beauty, and which causes the atrophy of our intuitive faculty and our intuitive self.

The deep psychic disease of modern men and women is the diseased, atrophied condition of the intuitive faculties. There is a whole world of life that we might know and enjoy by intuition alone. This is denied us, because we deny sex and beauty, the source of the intuitive life and of the insouciance which is so lovely in free animals and plants.

... Whereas, what a lot of dead ash there is in life now.

Nilsson slipped the book into a large inner pocket, lined with water-proof material, made for holding trout while wading in water. He picked out another book, *The Story of my Heart* by Richard Jefferies. This also had heavily marked passages.

1. In the march of time there fell away from my mind, as the leaves from the trees in autumn, the last traces and relics of superstitions and traditions acquired compulsorily in childhood. Always feebly adhering, they finally disappeared.

There fell away, too, personal bias and prejudices, enabling me to see clearer and with wider sympathies. The glamour of modern sciences and discoveries faded away, for I found them no more than the first potter's wheel. Erasure and reception proceeded together; the past accumulations of casuistry were erased, and my thought widened to receive the ideas of something beyond all previous ideas. With disbelief, belief increased. The aspiration and hope, the prayer, was the same as that which I felt years before on the hills, only now it was broadened.

2. All the experience of the greatest city in the world could not withold me. I rejected it wholly. I stood bare-headed in the sun, in the presence of earth and air, in the presences of the immense forces of the universe. I demand that which will make me more perfect now, this hour.

One midsummer I went out of the road into the fields, and sat down on the grass between the yellowing wheat and the green hawthorn bushes. The sun burned in the sky, the wheat was full of a luxurious sense of growth, the grass high, the earth giving its vigour to leaf and tree, the heaven blue. The vigour and growth, the warmth and light, the beauty and richness of it entered into me; an ecstasy of soul accompanied the delicate excitement of the senses: the soul rose with the body. Rapt in the fulness of the moment, I prayed there with all

that expansion of mind and frame; no words, no definition, inexpressible desire for physical life, of soul-life, equal to and beyond the
highest imagining of the heart.

The Story of my Heart joined *Assorted Articles* in his fish-
pocket. He was looking around when a fat man with a round face
prominently set with dark horn-rimmed spectacles, came into the
room and with confidential *bonhomie* (as Nilsson wrote later)
told him that Doctor Caspar Schwenkfelder was in London for a
conference. How could he help Mr. Nilsson, whose books he had
read and enjoyed?

Nilsson was about to ask him which books he had read when
the fat man said, "My name is Archibald Plugge, I'm public
relations. I was a major with the Army of Occupation for my sins,
and you, of course, served with distinction in the Royal Flying
Corps, as it was then, in War One. Your *Sinner's Way* is terrific,
if I may say so. How very glad I am, sir, to make your acquaintance at long last! You'll have a drink, won't you. I'll lead the
way. When will Doctor Schwenkfelder be back? I wish I knew,
my dear sir! He is going on to Paris from London, to lecture on
the philosophy and practice of Diaphany."

Having said that, the speaker burst out laughing. "My Welsh
upbringing still clings in tags and tatters, sir! Now what will you
drink?"

When glasses were filled he said, "By the way, don't we have
a mutual friend, Phillip Maddison? You know the story, I expect,
of the members of the National Free Trade Club being allowed
into the Barbarian Club when their premises were blown up by
a flying bomb. Well, as you know, sir, the Free Trade Club is
mainly political, and most of its members wear what is known as
Black Foreign Office hats? Phil came into the club one night
and saw a double row of such hats monopolising two whole rows
of pegs, and proceeded to turn them into what later, when
apologising to the Committee, he called a Cuneiform shape, by
pressing each hat into a narrow wedge, a—well—you know the
Latin derivation, of course—*cuneus*. He explained that he did it
to help restore the *morale* of the Free Traders, sir, ha-ha-ha!"

When a bottle of Plugge's 'gin' was a dead man, Nilsson left
to cable his New York office, suggesting research into the Doctor's
campus background. The cabled reply said there was no Doctor
Caspar Schwenkfelder in the records of Medicine Hat Ethical
and Philosophical Society.

In the meantime Rosalie Nilsson, who had been a journalist in her youth, had been doing some research for her husband into the background of Major Archibald Plugge, and discovered that he had been dismissed the Service. This information she got from a certain Brigadier Tarr (retired) living at Minehead.

She had also found out, by the simple act of looking in an encyclopaedia, that someone called Caspar Schwenkfelder had been a member of a Protestant sect founded in Silesia in the 16th century. Mr. Schwenkfelder had died in 1561, in his 70th year.

With this information, Nilsson paid a second visit to the Castle, where a number of serious young men and women, paying students, he guessed, were about to sit down in the Great Hall to a vegetarian lunch. He was invited to join them by a blonde young woman who said she was "the châtelaine".

"Major Plugge asks me to give you his compliments, sir, with his apologies for absence. He is composing his weekly Report to the Doctor."

"Then you know where Doctor Schwenkfelder is?"

"He is now with an order of Radamanthine Friars in Kent, meditating, sir."

"Meditating on what? His Abraham's Box? Or his birth in Silesia four centuries ago?"

"I'm afraid I don't understand you, sir. The Abraham's Box was left here by the British Secret Service, who requisitioned the Castle during the war for alien detainees, sir. Major Plugge will in due course be able to answer all your questions, I am sure. Ah, here he is! I'll leave you two gentlemen to it."

Late the next afternoon, after recovering from another bottle of gin shared with the hospitable Plugge, Nilsson went to the local club, and asked some of the members at the bar about the origins of the Castle, who built it, etc. This investigation absorbed two-thirds of a bottle of whisky, and his wife had to fetch him. On the way home he called on Plugge. In haggard mood next morning —for Plugge's 'gin' was 100 per cent surgical spirit—Nilsson began his story.

After describing the set-up at the Castle, he reported that he had been unable to get 'Doctor Caspar Schwenkfelder' to face an interview.

Your Correspondent was fobbed off with a handout, a laborious effected statement by the self-styled Public Relations Officer at the

Castle. This man, Major Archibald Plugge, late of the British Air Force—photo enclosed—gave me the following statement.

Doctor Caspar Schwenkfelder claims that most if not all of the disorders of the Western World including the United States of America stem from the malpractices of Freudian and other psychiatrists and theorists of the false science of activated druggery by words, chemical soil-poisons and the atom bomb.

Major Archibald Plugge was obviously affected by alcohol when he gave me this statement. Your Correspondent has ascertained, and checked, that he has been a liaison officer between the British Army of Occupation and the Civil Administration of Enemy Territory. He held down this appointment exactly for one week before being dismissed the Service by order of a General Court Martial, the charges being fraternisation, drunkenness, and looting.

With this information I paid a third visit to the hostess, or self-styled châtelaine of Oldstone Castle. I read my list of proposed questions.

'Would you say your 'Doctor' Casper Schwenkfelder is a spiritualistic manifestation, appearing through the mechanics, if any, of Abraham's Box, of Caspar Schwenkfelder who died in 1561, in his 70th year?'

'All things are possible in heaven on earth, our Founder declares.'

'Does your Founder claim that he is the original Caspar Schwenkfelder? If so, would that make him easily the oldest living man in the world of our time and age?'

Ex-major Plugge, looking like a pickled owl, at this point burst out laughing.

My next question, when silence was restored, was 'Does this 'Doctor' Casper Schwenkfelder exist in this world? Or does he inhabit the unseen one? Have you seen him yourself?'

'I certainly have seen him right here, in the Castle, many times', declared the châtelaine, coming to the rescue of ex-Major Plugge, who was beaming happily, as though it were all part of a spoof.

'Then is he descended from his old ancestor in Silesia in the sixteenth century?'

'I have no idea who his father was.'

'If his ancestor is the original Casper Schwenkfelder, a Protestant, does this present set-up tie-in with Protestantism?'

'Doctor Schwenkfelder is not a Protestant or member of any established religious caste.'

Your Correspondent then told her that research revealed no existence of records of any Medicine Hat Theosophical Society or of any 'Doctor Casper Schwenkfelder.'

*   *   *

The article was duly published in the Sunday Magazine Section of the New York newspaper; and one Fleet Street picture paper followed up with 'Amazing revelation—Spoof Doctor or Spy Ring?' The more sober *Daily Trident* declared ' 'Doctor' Schwenkfelder was not at home when our reporter called at the Castle, but the P.R.O., ex-major Archibald Plugge read 'an emended Statement', because, he claimed, he had been misquoted by an American writer of garbled fiction called journalism'.

'All pioneers, from Socrates to Louis Pasteur and the late great peacemaker Henry Ford, have been condemned by the massed mediocrities of all the arts, professions, and vested interests.

'The world has also suffered from such institutionalised so-called savants, and the present time in no wise excludes their malpractices.

'Caspar Schwenkfelder, founder of Diaphany, has disassociated himself from all institutionalised groupings of a moribund civilisation due soon to vent its psychological disturbances upon Asia solely owing to greed for the dollar and sterling.

'Caspar Schwenkfelder furthermore declares that by and large Science has done immeasurable harm to mankind and to humanity in general by issuing drugs which are mere palliatives of psychosomatic disorders, based on theories which are harmful in the long run and fruitful only of increasing mental illness. Science has discovered soil-sprays and poisons disastrously affecting the farm-dirts of the world by which all mankind must live; and to crown all with darkness, Science has prostituted the genius of Einstein by inventing the atom bomb which speaks for itself in that mankind now has the potential to entirely destroy all the races of the world, without discrimination of colour and notwithstanding the true progress of the soul, which Science denies.

'For these reasons therefore the Founder of Diaphany has abjured all titles and nomenclatures and declares his irrevocable wish and will therefore be known in future as plain Cas Field.'

For a couple of days after his efforts Nilsson remained on the drink. His lush voice was to be heard every evening in the bar of a local club. From encountering Fred Riversmill, the painter, there, he got the substance of his second article : the decadence of the arts, due to the war and 'Churchill's England' still under rationing of food, gasoline, housing and other shortages.

This second article was easy to do : Nilsson had been in London off and on during the war, and knew how to shape his subject after years as a foreign correspondent.

It was while lying in bed one morning, looking idly at an old volume of *Who was Who,* while chain smoking and drinking pints of tea, that Nilsson got an idea for his third article. He shouted for his wife.

"Now give your mind to this, Rosalie. How comes it that the father of 'Buster' Cloudesley—Manfred, twenty second Baron Cloudesley—survived so long as a fighter pilot—from 1915 until 1918—without becoming a casualty? He must have survived through cunning : one, by never taking on any missions but safe ones; two, by concentrating for his kills on cold-meat artillery-observation buses, slow two-seater camera jobs; and three, by always keeping well up in the sun, so that the Heiney crates he took on never had a chance to attempt evasive action. A matter of cold-hearted calculation for the acquisition of gongs. Six enemy aircraft got you a British Military Cross; six more, and you put up the riband of the Distinguished Service Order. D'you hear what I'm saying? Well, another dozen, and you sewed on a silver rosette denoting a bar each to M.C. and D.S.O. What then? Well, easy. The 'Knight of the Air', as the British quaintly called their noble ace, had a conscience under the usual British phlegm of the upper classes. He was a show-off. It says here his last act was due to bravado, which was awarded the Victoria Cross. This is down here, printed just as I said. The editor of Who's Who must have known something, I guess. And I'm going to find out just what it was."

At this point Nilsson became depressed. His thoughts hovered around his own secret, sheered away from further probing : it touched a damaged nerve-cell of his own need to keep going against an unforgettable, unforgotten memory of drunken father bullying mother until—darkness absolute—his father shot himself while pretending to clean his gun.

He was about to go downstairs for the whisky bottle when Rosalie said, "The peal are running, they tell me! You'll go fishing now, if I know my good Os!"

Phillip and Laura, out for a walk, saw Nilsson spinning for sea-trout at the harbour mouth beyond the harbour, where the Lyn merged with sea-waves of the lapsing tide. Nilsson had had no strikes for more than an hour, and was about to chuck it, having decided the fish didn't like a mixture of salt and fresh water : they wanted to run straight through to the fresh, and would do so when the tide turned.

He reeled-in his line and waved to Phillip before picking a way over slimy pebbles exposed by the low-tide. Despite rope-soled shoes he made slow progress; and when, on reaching easier shingle, he continued to move towards them with a limp, the cause was visible. A yellow-red unhealed wound several inches long beside the bone of one leg. When he observed that Phillip had seen his wound, Nilsson stopped, looked down at the leg and said to the girl beside Phillip, "I got that flying on S.E.5a in Egypt during the first war with your Royal Flying Corps. I guess I crashed while training, so never saw combat action. And let me tell you—this is interesting—I've tried nearly every doctor in the U.S. and Europe for a cure, from penicillin to serum from seal-bite, but the wound won't heal." He put the leg further forward so that they could examine it.

"I guess that's a record. So hows about a drink? Come help me move my trailer to park it beside the East Lyn, then we'll sit down and talk, like Isaak Walton and Cotton. You've written a mighty fine book, Phillip, in *The Blind Trout*. You know something? I took a two-pounder on a dry-fly in the alder pool last summer— he was pretty black—how's that for a record in a stream that holds three-ounce average trout?" Anticipating glow came upon the broad face. "And I'd like to hear your views on Exmoor becoming a Nature Reserve under State control, like our Yellowstone Park way back home."

Having sat herself beside the driver, Laura turned to Phillip entering the back and said, "This is rather fun!" He felt happy, and began to laugh.

"What's so funny?" asked Nilsson.

"Oh, I'm so pleased to be driven by someone!" He felt like saying that Nilsson's car should be under State control, as being the only fully-stocked lepidopterous nature reserve driven by petrol north of the Equator.

For the worn corduroy upholstery was a breeding, feeding and cocoon-cradling ground almost entirely given over to little drab moths and their crawling offspring. The lower spaces below the seat were also a repository, or depository, of ancient newspapers, many still in their wrappers with foreign postmarks and stamps upon them. Some were in process of conglomeration almost geo- logical, being several strata deep, pressed firmer by the muddy

boots of what appeared to be innumerable workers on wet land;
but were the results of wading while fishing, and being driven
home asleep in the back of the car by his good wife.

Not all the lepidoptera, however, had their origins in nature.
Some were works of art. A passenger was liable to leave his temporary seat impaled by a No. 12 sneck-bend steel hook, fantas-
tically dressed as for some miniature fancy-dress dance in feather,
bristle, silk, varnish, and wire. The gut of silkworms, drawn out
and gone brittle, trailed after the minute barbed hook, which
impaled itself usually in trouser seat or jacket sleeve. Osgood
Nilsson's tweed hats, jackets, and often trousers trailed these relics
of deception : he was journalistically famous as a fisherman, sometimes guilty of poaching, in waters salt, acid, and alkaline, in lake
and river of nearly all those places of the world which he had
covered for his assignments. Now his travelling days were over. He
lived and wrote and enjoyed himself—with periods of black depression—by the sea-coast of Devon : a sort of Jekyll and Hyde
life, swaying between the two sides of an uneasy and egocentric
nature.

Laura, sitting in the front seat, was affected by the condition
of the upholstery. She felt the state of the car to be the condition
of Nilsson himself—upholstery dilapidated; glass of one headlamp
shattered, the other lamp still retaining the tar-marks of blackout days—tyres worn to the canvas—blue smoke issuing from a
perforated exhaust box. Fumes came through the rusted holes
in the floor. Suddenly she felt she couldn't breathe : she must get
out! She sat there while the automobile ground slowly up a long
winding, narrow lane, rising above red cliffs, leading to the northern escarpment of the moor.

Phillip saw that the driver was holding steering wheel with
both hands at twelve o'clock. What if one of the front tyres burst?
And now—O my God!—Nilsson had removed a hand to search
for a cigarette! Again, for his lighter . . . while the trailer-caravan
slewed sideways, the rear wheels of the motorcar spun . . . and
there was only a narrow grassy bank between road-edge and precipitous descent to tiny white wave marks on the rocks far below.

"Your accelerator pedal seems to have stuck," he said, over
Nilsson's shoulder. "You ought to switch off."

"Nuts!"

Phillip prepared to seize the wheel, to control an inevitable
wobble should the steering wheel spin out of Nilsson's hands.
What a fool he was to have come! He had been wary of Nilsson

from the first meeting in the bar of the Barbarian Club—wet smiling lips vague blue eyes, alcoholic *bonhomie,* exhibitionism of festering leg—

"Stop, stop!" screamed Laura.

Nilsson turned his head and began to say something in his fatty voice when Phillip seized the steering wheel and said quietly, "Would you like me to drive, Nilsson, then you could talk in comfort."

"Think I can't drive?"

"No, I don't. But your car can't respond."

The rusty springs were loose in the shackle-bolts. Moths, stimulated by the vibration, were flitting and crawling about.

"There's a dog-fight going on in the back here, clothes-moths versus earwigs."

"Earwigs can't fly."

"Yours can, anyway."

"They're not mine, you zyme. They're British earwigs. You think I can't drive, is that it? Well, what'd'you know!" He trod hard on the accelerator, and kept his foot down. The vehicle bumped and lurched, and made skidding progress up through pot-holes revealing red ironstone metalling under broken tarmac.

- "Stop!" Laura cried again. "I'll walk!" She struggled to turn the door handle.

"Won't open," Nilsson said, laughing.

The bank was now higher, they were nearing the crest. In silence they arrived at the Marksman, a pub standing in a lower valley. It had a thatched roof partly covered by corrugated iron rusting beside sodden clots of thick green moss. No repairs had been done since long before the war.

Within was a long farmhouse table, and benches made by some hedgerow carpenter, both deep brown from tabacco smoke and spilled ale. The lime-washed ceiling was yellow-brown and flaky. Above the bar hung an oil-lamp with a reflecting cowl like a dustbin lid. Nilsson greeted the landlord with "Corney, you old hero", and invited a white-haired figure with reflective eyes who had stooped under the low lintel of the barrel room to drink with him.

Nilsson became mellow after several glasses of whisky, his voice bland as a slice of fresh-cut ham as he began to talk about himself —fifth generation of middle-west Swedish emigrant, his Osgood grandfather a general of Confederate forces, his grandmother who had danced with the President at the White House—evidence of

which he exhibited by bringing from a breast pocket an old photograph of a man with whiskers and drooping moustache wearing
a sort of frenchified uniform jacket with kepi, sword, scabbard,
and shapeless trousers.

Phillip had observed, more than once, the exhibition, or fetish,
of the Confederate general. It usually led to Nilsson declaring to
his listener, "You haven't got a general on your pedigree! You're
a man of no family! You're nothing but a zyme."

One of his scapegoats was Piston, who was foolish enough,
when he met Nilsson in one or other of the village pubs, to bear
with his tormentor. Piston invariably took it meekly, hoping that
nothing worse would follow : how he had swung the lead, pretending to be shell-shocked after the Somme, and got out of the
army with a disability pension—confidences that the foolish fellow
had once entrusted to the alcoholic Middle Westerner.

"Now tell me, Mr. Corney. Come here, come on, come nearer,
come on, and drink up. Fill the glasses—never mind those two
beer-drinkers—they're nothing—they're zymes—now give me the
low-down, Corney. I've heard that Manfred deserted his wife
when she was going to have a baby—to follow a young German
girl to my country—is that so, Mr. Corney? Tell me what happened."

Phillip, who had remained quiet so far, suddenly shouted, "I'll
tell you what happened! In the words of the poet Barry Cornwall
writing of Thomas Lovell Beddoes!—'He's dead; he died young :
as the great will die; as summer dies, by drought and its own
fevers burned to death'." Then getting up, he went out.

"He's a zyme", said Nilsson. "Now tell me about Manfred and
the Fräulein, Mr. Corney"

"Well sir, you know that people talk wildly when they don't
know what's true."

"Then he didn't go after the Fräulein?"

"She was gone back to Germany before he sailed for New York,
sir."

"I've checked with his Manhattan publisher—Homer, the President of World Books, is still alive. Manfred sailed in the early
'thirties, didn't he? I was interviewing Gandhi then, I guess, in
India."

"Yes sir?"

"Were you with him when he sent back his decorations to
King George the Fifth at Buckingham Palace?"

"I posted them myself, in a box, to the *War Office,* sir."

"Why was that, Mr. Corney?"

"He told me he wasn't entitled to them."

"Ah! Ah!" cried Nilsson, like a crow, "That's it! I knew it! You mean he faked his combat reports?"

"No, sir. Too many green huns was cold meat. My gentleman said it was robbing an incubator."

"Were you with him when he commanded Sixty Squadron?"

"No sir, it wasn't Sixty. That was Bishop's little lot. But all young Jerries from 'seventeen onwards was easy meat, so to speak. So was our own green huns. Up with the rocket and down with the stick, sir. Flamers most of'm. Seventeen and eighteen-year old, they was."

"So his conscience at last drove him to take on his equals, was that it?"

"You've got it, sir. He wanted to test himself on 'is own and hedge-hopped over Jerry's lines to Mossy Face Wood and shot up two of the Richthofen's little lot as they was taking off. Then he climbed and taunted the others to come up. It was a proper dog-fight, sir. My bloke was hit in the left arm, then in the leg, and again in the shoulder. He kept firin' burst after burst until the blood was in 'is eyes, sir. They reckon he'd got seven when Göring put paid to 'im with a bullet through 'is engine, and my bloke crashed. Seven he got—nine counting the two cold meat ones—over Mossy Face that day. He got the Cross for that."

"Victoria Cross?"

"That's right, sir."

"Mr. Nilsson, you can check this with the official records," said Laura. "I am no longer content to listen to your sadistic shriving of conscience upon a dead man!", and she got up to follow Phillip out of the room.

"Hold your horses!" cried Nilsson. "Fill the glasses, Mr. Corney! Now tell me, Mr. Corney, did you see anything on the night he went down in the sea, on his way back solo from New York and Gander?"

Laura returned. Mr. Corney stood at attention, while looking straightly at Nilsson. "As true as I'm standing behind this bar, I saw his Lordship's black greyhound that he had put down a couple of years before he went to America! I saw the dog standing in the kitchen as clear as I see you now as when I was sitting by the hot-water boiler." He looked at Nilsson and then at Laura. "I saw him as plain as I see you gentleman and lady standing there before me!" He began to tremble as he faced Nilsson again. "I swear my oath on it, sir! I was in the kitchen, by the boiler, and all doors shut. Then the black greyhound come through the wall, ears up, lookin' for 'is master. Then it was gone." He stopped, wiping eyes with back of hand. "That dog, sir, was put down before my master went to America! God A'mighty, may I die now if I speak the untruth! I knew then—I know now —he was gone down. I'd been listening to the wireless—he'd been seen by the *Empress of Britain,* flyin' back to her Ladyship." With piteous face, he appealed to Laura. "Every word is true, miss!"

"Were you on the bottle?" asked Nilsson.

The man did not reply at once. Then he said, "I'd had a nip or two. It was the strain of waiting by the wireless, sir. We was all standing by, to hear anything special."

"Including Lady Cloudesley?"

"No, sir. Lady Ann was dead of a haemorrhage, at five o'clock that morning. And my gentleman come home just before dawn the next morning. It was then I saw the black greyhound, sir."

"Tell me what else you saw, Corney. Have another drink first."

"Not at the moment, thank you, sir. Well, sir, my lady's old nurse, what was living with us, come down from upstairs and she was shaking so she could hardly hold the candlestick in her hand. She said her lady, what had died in childbirth that afternoon, and 'adn't bin laid out then, was standin' by the window, lookin' at a big white star rising up over the hill."

"The nurse said that?"

"Yes, sir. It was the morning star. I saw it myself. I was shivering with cold, so I went back by the coke boiler. Then Nanny, that was the old nurse, sir, was being called by little Hugh—he what is now his Lordship—and when she went into the night-nursery again the candles was burning blue in her Ladyship's room as though in a draught, she said, but all the windows was closed." He poured himself a drink. "If anyone ever saw ghosts, they were seen in our house that night."

Laura shouted, "You're not to say any more, Mr. Corney!" She turned to Nilsson. "You ought to know better than to pry into other people's private worlds! Especially when you were told some time ago that 'Buster' is writing the biography of his father! I suppose *you* want to cash in first—everything is dollars with you Americans!"

"Hold your horses," he replied, in a voice now lush. "In a democracy all news is for free." He wagged a finger. "Don't think I don't know all about the plot to rescue Rudolf Hess from

Spandau prison outside Berlin! You won't get away with it!
The Commies will see to that!"

Nilsson remained at The Marksman until an hour after closing
time, talking at the landlord, who gave a remarkable imper-
sonation of a man listening while sleeping upright with eyes open.
At last Mrs. Nilsson arrived in the taxicab which was hired half-
a-dozen times a month to fetch her husband home from some inn
or hotel. Paying off the taxi, she took Osgood home in his pre-
war sedan smelling of goats and journalism. He was clutching
the photograph of his Osgood grandfather late of the Confederate
Army in the war between the Deep South and the Yankee North.

The next evening Nilsson was in high feather in what he called
the 'Zymes Club' as he sat apart from those around the bar—a
sprinkling of doctors, solicitors, and business worthies, some of
them ex-officers of the late war recently admitted to what, before
1939, had unofficially been known as the Gentlemen's Club—
landowners, retired regular officers of the two Services, including those originally seconded to the R.F.C. and later transferred
to the R.A.F., together with parsons, doctors and solicitors who
had, generally speaking, served their interests.

Nilsson was tolerated as a 'character' in his 'Zymes Club'; he
felt himself to be several cuts above them—he, a writer of international reputation : author of books on travel, in which were
described his meetings with prominent politicians, writers, artists
thrown in with a measure of international financiers and crooks
and a king or two. In fact, the books were a rehash of ephemeral
journalism spiced by fishing and shooting experiences (some in
poached preserves) in various parts of the world.

In drink, Nilsson was ready to enlarge on those experiences and
to give opinions on world topics; but this evening, among the bar
habituées who foregathered there after the days' work, Nilsson
remained silent; an odd bird in lush plumage, preening himself
that he was on to a good thing in his new series of articles. He
considered : what had the son of the late Manfred Lord Cloudesley
to be so reticent about? What family skeleton was he keeping
hidden? Why hadn't the family, long ago, permitted an official
biography to be put out? Could it be for the same reason that
no biography of Colonel Lawrence of Arabia had been allowed
by the trustees of that mysterious 'hero'?

The Club was in a little house off the High Street. When the time approached for the steadier members to go home to dinner, Nilsson was still simmering happily alone, occasionally addressing, in his hammy voice, inconsequential, semi-inaudible remarks to one or another of the members gathered there to relax and hear the latest local gossip. To them, so far, old Osgood had remained comparatively quiet; but suddenly, throwing down the local paper with its announcement of Lynton's forthcoming Festival of the Arts Week, when the Amateur Dramatic Society would produce *Yeomen of the Guard,* he fired the first rocket of the evening.

"It was Shakespeare who said, 'Pistol's cock is up, and flashing fire will follow'. Don't mistake me, you Zymes nattering away over there! I'm not referring to your bogus Major Piston, who's got a little-end loose."

"How d'you know that, Nilsson?" said one of the topers, an articled clerk who was hoping to become a solicitor. "Is your own little-end loose, or is it a big-end, old boy?"

"Your Amateur Dramatic Society couldn't even get stuck into 'The Thirteenth Chair', let alone 'Yeoman of the Guard'. Your country of Devon is known in the publishing world as 'the graveyard'."

"Since you've come here, you mean, Mr. Nilsson?" asked the articled clerk.

"Piss off" said Nilsson.

"Is that what your New York editor advised you to do?"

After these fatuities, heads returned to the bar; but turned round once more at a cry from Nilsson, "You there! You're a no-good man! You haven't got anyone like this in your family!" as he felt in his breast pocket.

"Now it's coming" murmured the articled clerk. For they were by now familiar with the daguerrotype of Nilsson's grandfather.

"Ha, your respected grandfather was an actor, I see, sir!" said the articled clerk. "He's wearing one of the uniforms sent to us by a London theatrical costumier as you will have read in our local paper."

"This rag," cried Nilsson, picking up the paper in order to throw it down again, "is a permanent all-time low! It's just about what it calls itself, 'The Lynton Lantern'!" He picked it up once more. "See the splash on page one! Half a dozen old goats to be turned loose to replace a similar lot of upholstered old hat racks standing about in the Valley of Rocks until they were eaten by you peasants during the war! I quote :– 'Colonel Peregrine

Bucentaur has graciously offered to present to the Devon County Council his famous Brockholes St. Boniface herd of wild white goats, whose pedigree is said to go back in direct line to Caractacus, the Welsh partisan in the fight against the Romans in the reign of the Emperor Claudius, 54 B.C.' You call that bumph, news? It stinks, like the goats!", and Nilsson tore up *The Lynton Lantern*.

Ignoring the tipsy American, the articled clerk, who had been born in Somerset, told his cronies at the bar how Colonel Bucentaur once had a private golf course in his park.

"The goats used to wait for the balls, and run off with them, sometimes chasing the crows who pinched them first! An old fox used to join in sometimes, playing with the crows and the goats! Honestly, I'm not making it up! There was a tennis court above a haha, to keep out deer, and later, cattle in the park, but the goats got up all the same. Some used to leap over the net! They were used to playing with the family children, you see. When the Abbey was sold, Flash Billy, the Plymouth circus proprietor, tried to buy the goats for his circus, but Colonel Bucentaur wouldn't sell."

"You're a zyme!" called out Nilsson. "I'll tell you somep'n! Your British Empire was founded by a lot of old goats glued together by cricket! I speak straight from the shoulder!"

"Your trouble is that there isn't any shoulder," retorted the aspirant solicitor. "All you can do is to emulate Balaam's ass."

This put Nilsson in a rage. He stood and pulled up the trouser of his left leg. "That's what I got, fighting for you half-krauts!"

"Ah, Exhibit Number Two. We wondered when another inquest was due."

"Right now, you bogus attorney, right now! You British like to keep your 'heroes' on ice, else they melt away to nothing if exposed to the light of day. Your 'Lawrence of Arabia' was one, and Manfred Lord Cloudesley was another. How did you manage to win both wars? Shall I tell you zymes? You fake history, it's as simple as that. We Americans won both Kraut wars for you! We gave of our dollars and our blood, which is thicker than your beer. You want to know what Dwight Eisenhower said when he got his first taste of British beer? He said, 'Put it back in the horse'."

"That beer had been kept waiting for him three years, midear, that's why it had gone flat!"

On that the zymes went home, leaving Nilsson addressing an impassive club steward behind the mahogany counter.

Chapter 19

FROM THE VASTY DEEP

Piston was awaiting the guests to his mother's séance. That afternoon Mrs. Nilsson had called to ask if her husband might attend 'as an observer'. His mother had said yes. Piston was anxious, a little unnerved at the thought of Nilsson. However Phillip was coming. Piston felt safe with him now. Also 'Buster' and Laura were O.K. Of Brigadier Tarr he had a real fear. The Brig at any moment was liable to become bloody-minded. As for Nilsson—

A curious thing sometimes happened when he thought of Nilsson : he felt to be almost outside his body, seeing it just beside him : everything seemed a little unreal. Piston believed that Nilsson's evil side was trying to take charge of him. And he feared a collapse.

Soon after the 1914–18 war Piston had been subject to epileptic fits. To fall down before others was to a him a wounding disgrace.

He began to walk about the room, to plead with Nilsson for understanding.

"Please don't come, old boy. Honestly, the vibrations have to be right on the beam, otherwise no reception. It's all part of the natural world, you know. You were damned unfair to Caspar Schwenkfelder, you know. He put me right with myself. He could put you right with yourself, if only you would give up your defences, otherwise blockages."

No one was in the room with Piston. He was addressing the detachable and hurtful image of the American writer.

Those present that June evening at Shelley's Cottage were Molly Bucentaur and her daughter Miranda, 'Buster' and Laura, Brigadier Tarr, Phillip, and surprisingly, an old acquaintance last seen many years ago—Archibald Plugge, a little fatter, curly hair greying and recessive, owl-eyes behind thick concave glasses beaming benevolently as in the old days of the B.B.C. at Savoy Hill.

"My dear Phil, how good to see you again, looking just the same as ever! Have you heard any news of Piers Tofield? The last time I saw him he was, well—not at his best," he laughed. "He told me you were coming down this way."

"He's recovered, Archie. How are you?"

"My dear old boy, I can't tell you how what you say delights me. Oh, I'm not so bad, old boy, not so bad at all. You probably know I'm public relations at Oldstone Castle?" His voice dropped. "I suppose you saw all the stuff in the papers? It's the same story of the B.B.C. and the gramophone companies over again. You may remember how they objected to their records being played over 2 L.O., thinking it would ruin their sales?" He moved away from the others. "We are simply overwhelmed by volunteer students applying to attend our courses of Diaphany."

"What exactly is Diaphany?"

"The literal meaning of the word is the power to transmit light. I'm not familiar with all the processes, but the idea, roughly, is that most people are self-frustrated by some concealed fear, or shame, which, if not cleared, that is released, causes depression and finally, serious illness."

"There's something in that. Does it cost very much to be a student?"

"Well, we aren't out to make a profit; but at the same time food, light, housing and other services have to be paid for."

"Students come for idealistic reasons, I suppose."

"Yes. At the same time, the courses are pretty strenuous."

"Do you apply electric treatment, or drugs?"

"No. We regard such practices as destructive, while not removing the causes of blockages."

"Who started Diaphany?"

"Jesus Christ, Goethe, William Blake, D. H. Lawrence, Richard Jefferies, Father Teilhard de Chardin—the main object is to try to release the essence of poetry in people."

"I'd like to meet your friend. Will he be coming tonight?"

"I'm afraid not. He's in London, old boy, arranging details of the new centre in Hampshire, to take the overflow. We've got a friend of yours coming here shortly, by the way—Melissa Watt-Wilby. Now, before I forget, old boy, I can give you several whole-page advertisements for your *New Horizon*, if you like. And an article, free, about our Founder. What's your circulation?"

"Not much, I'm afraid. Half the five hundred subscribers wrote to cancel their subscriptions when Christie gave it up. And my first number gave offence to others. Chiefly because I quoted some of Birkin's post-war writings."

"You did rather ram Birkin down their throats, old boy, didn't you? But seriously, we could help you, if only you'd do the same thing for us. Not that we need publicity. But no prophet likes to be dishonoured. Would you like some backing? I fancy my boss would take to the idea of a quarterly house-journal. The name is in line with our teachings, too."

"What does he teach—in a sentence if you can?"

"That we must go to the creative side of the mind, which when sick is the cause of all illness. Put the mind right and few will be ill. Psychiatry is superceded." His voice fell to a whisper. "I hear you knew our host Piston in the first war? Was he in the Army?"

"Well, he'd just come out of July the First on the Somme, badly shaken."

"People down here say he wasn't in the war at all."

"Of course he was! I saw him in the Casualty Clearing Station at Heilly, on July the First. He was as mad as a whirligig beetle waltzing about on a pond after a mate."

Plugge laughed so much that his coffee spilled into the saucer.

Just before the séance began Mrs. Nilsson arrived alone. "You know how Osgood gets sometimes. Oh," she said cheerfully to Mrs. Piston, "Don't misunderstand me, my dear, it's not his leg that's worrying him this time, but his deadline for the New York paper." Turning to Phillip. "Is your sister Elizabeth coming? I thought perhaps you might be bringing her," she went on untruthfully, for Elizabeth had responded to her caller's friendliness, and told her a surprising lot of things about her brother, about whom she obviously had a 'thing', Rosalie had told others.

"We had such an interesting talk, Phillip."

He felt himself becoming feeble.

The french windows looked out upon the lawn, beyond which an aspen stood, its leaves shivering in the warm airs ascending. Beyond came the noises of rapid water in the Glen.

Piston now brought the two halves of the window together, almost closing them. He put on a gramophone record of Holst's *Planet Suite*; music flowed serenely, as from the deep calm of re-mote starry space. They sat round a table, curtains drawn across windows. Two candles on a sideboard. When the music ended Mrs. Piston, who had been an actress, asked them to hold hands, and rest them on the round table. Then, after a silence, she began to recite, speaking in a soft voice that made the words seem to be floating through from beyond the french windows.

" 'The summer night waneth the morning light slips

Faint and grey twixt the leaves of the aspen, betwixt the cloud bars.

Far out in the meadow above the young corn

The heavy elms wait.' "

She drew a deep breath and as though helplessly waved a hand before closed eyes. Through light-streaked edges of the curtains came the call of a cuckoo in the Glen, with intermittent rushing sounds of water deflected under the leaves of the aspen on the lawn, shivering, shivering.

The medium, her eyes still closed, continued with occasional shrill overtones.

"I see a comely young woman looking out over water. There are white houses at the edge of the sea. The sky is blue, but the waves look agitated. There has been a tempest, the sirocco has been blowing from North Africa to Italy ... I see a mirage." She stopped and sighed, bent her head, wiped her eyes with a small handkerchief. Drew a long breath, respired as slowly, went on in a tired voice,

"Paper boats, paper boats—rather than weep away the hours I see you sailing paper boats under the leaf-shadows of the Glen —you have come back, your hair is matted with salt water—you are forever seeking her whom you called Miranda."

Molly Bucentaur's fingers moved to cover her daughter's hand, while the medium uttered a sound between sigh and groan, her hand passing several times over her face.

"I see a letter—it is being written by the woman who was standing on the shore—among the white houses—I see the words—the date is not clear but the month is July—the letter is borne on a little paper boat—the letter is the boat—it is folded—a message. The woman writes to the youth sailing paper boats, hour after hour, as he lies beside the waterfall in the Glen—she asks him why he is always talking of never enjoying moments like the past —she wonders if he has second sight—if he will shortly join his friend Plato—or does he expect her to do so soon—she signs her name—and then adds two words—*Buona Notte*—then in English she says, *Good night*."

Plugge was staring at the tears falling down the old woman's face. A genuine communication, he thought. Laura looked fixedly at Phillip. Her eyes narrowed. Phillip knew what she was thinking, and dreading an outburst, kept his gaze on the table. In a faint, strangled voice the medium whispered, "I see the face of Shelley—he is trying to come through—he is struggling in water —he is trying to speak to the young woman across water, on the sea-shore, by the white houses." The medium spread her hands, moved them as though helplessly. "He is replying from another world—

"Ariel to Miranda : hear
This good-night the sea-winds bear;
And let thine unacquainted ear
Take grief for their interpreter.
Good-night; I have risen so high
Into slumber's rarity,
Not a dream can beat its feather
Through the unsustaining ether.
Let the sea-winds make avouch
How thunder summoned me to couch,
Tempest curtained me about
And turned the sun with his own hand out :
And though I toss upon my bed
My dream is not disquieted;
Nay, deep I sleep upon the deep,
And my eyes are wet, but I do not weep;
And I fell to sleep so suddenly
That my lips are moist yet—could'st thou see—
With the good-night draught I have drunk to thee.
Thou can'st not wipe them; for it was Death
Damped my lips that have dried my breath.
A little while—it is not long—
The salt shall dry on them like the song . . ."

The medium appeared to be fighting for breath. In a choking voice, thin and strained, she went on,
"Now know'st thou, that voice desolate
Mourning ruined joy's estate
Reached thee through a closing gate."

The voice became shrill.

" 'Go'st thou to Plato?' Ah, girl no !
It is to Pluto that I go."

"A most moving performance," said 'Buster' to Archie Plugge, while they were having drinks at The Eyrie.

"I was most impressed, sir."

"Bloody rubbish, if you ask me!" declared Brigadier Tarr.

Laura, who had been unusually silent after the séance, now turned to vent on Phillip her suppressed feelings.

"*You* wrote that poem! You emotional blackmailer! Playing now on that schoolgirl's feelings! You fixed it all to deceive that poor old woman!"

"No," said 'Buster'. "The poem came by water. A drowned paper boat. Piston showed it to me some time ago. I must add that I did wonder if it were a practical joke on someone's part to copy out Francis Thompson's poem, and sail it down the Lyn. It was almost illegible, the writing, but I managed to decipher it for her. She really believes it was put there by Shelley's ghost. Don't disillusion her. She lives almost entirely on a spiritual plane, as did Phillip's lady Aunt. The material means—what are they after all? The actor—is he only pretending? The painter with his box of colours, and jar of brushes, is part of the evolutionary impulse to create beauty out of what—chaos?—spiritual forces? They are of the unseen world all about us. Even Osgood Nilsson, with his debunking mind and manner, is only trying to get straight, or clear, with himself. At the same time, I'm not sorry he didn't turn up tonight."

"Dear 'Buster'," said Laura. "Dear, dear 'Buster'." She took Phillip's hand and kissed it. "I'm sorry, darling, truly I'm sorry."

"We'll all meet again for the Midsummer Festival on Oldstone Down," said Buster as the guests departed later that night.

The following week Osgood Nilsson told the story, with trimmings, in the Zymes Club, including in his account how Molly Bucentaur had to take her weeping daughter away from the Piston séance. A dark horse, indeed yes, Phillip Maddison he said, beaming blandly, his mouth loose and wet with the present amiabilities of whisky. He went on to recount all his wife had told him concerning Phillip : his seducing his fifteen-year-old cousin when he returned from running away during the battle of Messines in 1914; trying to join the Navvies Battalion to avoid going back to the front; pushing his baby sister in the fire when she was sixteen months old, and going to prison after the first war for arson, after failing to convince the police that the fire was started by his best friend, and not himself. Then his admiration for Hitler, having given his wife a baby two days before he gave one to a girl-friend, and then trying to get the two registered as twins; and other stories which held the attention of the drinkers at the bar, who wondered how far he would go, being an American with apparently little knowledge of the British laws of slander and defamation.

"He's a no-good man!" concluded Nilsson. "He's a man of no family. His wife has the money. Look!", and he pulled forth the photograph of the Confederate General—his talisman, his reassurance.

Oldstone Down between the lights of midsummer. The form of a motor-coach visible beside motorcars on heather growing beside the narrow coastal road. Far below, tidal currents of the Severn Sea were enscrollings of reflected sky. A lone gull called, spirit of blind ocean.

An all-night journey from London had brought fifty to sixty members of the Eirēnēan Society. They had left the coach and were standing upon the stone-scattered site of a prehistoric barrow.

Mrs. Piston, facing east, was holding up her arms, palms to the sky. The semi-circle of young people—with a few adults—stood behind her also holding out their arms.

"Princess Eirēnē," intoned the old woman, "we, your sisters and brothers greet you. We ask for your blessing for our prayers—to help restore to the world the spiritual values you taught us here below. We believe that the true basis of life in the visible world lies within the unseen forces all about us."

"Amen" intoned the semi-circle of aspirants.

At that moment, across the Severn Sea, a scintillant white flame shot up into darkness from the direction of the Welsh Mountains. Its reflection dilated upon the clouds.

Unseen by the watchers on Oldstone Down, showers of sparks were raining down on cobbled streets and slate roofs of mining cottages. These people lived in a world of fire from the Bessemer Steel converters. Balanced on iron trunnions, high above but well apart from the rows of cottages, the great iron "eggs" had been slowly inverted, to pour molten steel, in dazzling streams, into ingot moulds below. Each square mould effervesced in a white rain of ferric oxide—the metal burning away to hissing points, and to specks of bluish light. The oxygen was released, and the main molten mass still within the converters, now fully inverted, poured down with a great roaring noise and the tongue of that fire, seen across the sea, cast its light upon the mountains.

"They're blowing the vessels," said Piston.

"Let us keep our inward eyes upon the heavens," said his mother. "There are young stars in the halo of the Milky Way above us of unmatched brilliance, could we but see them with mortal eyes. They are the Blue Galaxies, evidence of a cataclysmic universe which pulsates in a finite, closed system. The first light waves caused by the explosion have stretched through a trillion light-years—"

"Now let us stand 'all Danäe to the stars', in the words of the poet Tennyson. Let us, by breathing deeply, float from our bodies, and absorb the power of the Great Spirit flowing from our hands. Thus we receive the Spirit of Life."

The old woman's arms began to shake. Piston and another moved to support her. One on either side, they lowered her upon a mat.

"She's in a trance," said Piston. "Her spirit may now be travelling to a higher sphere."

He whispered to Phillip and Laura, "She may be seeing Jesus, whose whole being is turned to love, originating from the planet Venus. It says so in the Bible. We believe that God cannot be limited, least of all by man. William Blake was despondent, I think, when he wrote 'all human deities reside in the human breast'."

Phillip said, "Blake was thinking of the clerics who take the New Testament literally, instead of taking it poetically; for the potential of deity resides in the human consciousness."

The eastern sky became a vast flock of flamingoes above a sea enscrolled in gold. Larks were rising up to sing. All life seemed happy around the barrow, for it was being renewed.

Weariness set in with the risen sun. The congregation went down the wooded valley to Lynton, where a breakfast was prepared in a café. Afterwards Laura said to Phillip.

"Do let's go for a walk. Take me to the Burrows of 'Cousin Willie'."

She was thinking, If I can exorcise the ghost of 'Cousin Willie', and Phillip's guilt that he was not also killed in that old war, then he may be re-born, and able to see Shelley plain—and me, as I want to be with him.

It is well known how atmospheric variations affect all terrestrial life which includes fish and insects. Above the moor detached clouds of cumulus were dissolving as he glanced into the blue sky, his heart lifting with the colours of moor sedge, bell heather, and yellow flowers of furze.

They left the Silver Eagle in the village, and walked beside the Lyn, where waterflies were swimming up as nymphs, to split their pellicles and rise as winged creatures into what must seem to be paradise, he said to Laura.

"Their mouths are sealed, they need neither food nor drink, their year of underwater life is over. Now all is for love, a flight into the sky in the afternoon, followed by a sunset dropping of eggs on the shining surface of the river."

They sat down on a bank among wood violets. "Tell me about them, Phillip." She wanted to use the scene for her book.

"Well, as the atmospheric pressure lightens, what we call a rising glass, the nymphs are hatching on the surface of the stream. The trout are rising, too, for fish with their swim-bladders are most sensitive to air pressures. In close thundery air, which affects you and me, trout lie torpid, as though suffering, on the bed of a river. When the air clears, up rise nymphs of Olive Dun and Pale Watery; and whether one is a fisherman or not, one shares in the general lifting of the air, for the pressures upon the body always effect the mind."

He went on to tell her how larks arise, the chaffinch sings in the hawthorn, turtle doves send their throbbing notes under the trees. "Oh, my heart lifts with the sun, and the vapours, actual and psychical, are gone! And suddenly what Jefferies described as 'the blue-stained air' is without flaw. What's the matter, Laura?"

She was looking around, as though expecting to see someone looking at her.

"It's so gloomy and out of the sun here. Take me to the sea, to the sands! I love the sea, even if it did drown 'Cousin Willie'! That's what you're thinking, isn't it? Why can't you emulate Jesus, and let the dead bury the dead. Or are *you* the more dead, because you're still alive?"

She got up and walked back along the path they had followed. Bodger whined, and looked at Phillip. "Let her go." But she came back, all gentleness, saying "I'm sorry," to be greeted by Bodger rolling on his back.

"We go at once to the Santon Burrows."

Bodger pranced, and led the way to the Silver Eagle.

They drove inland, to avoid the main roads and holiday traffic, and were soon lost in a maze of narrow sunken lanes which led past farmhouses and cots of slate or thatch; and driving by the sun, which was high in the south, came at last to what had been, before the war, a little moor of furze and heather, but now was all cornland or grass. And after some turning and reversing, came suddenly to a view of river estuary widening to a miniature Arabian desert, and the sea beside a long dark-blue headland. The headland, he told her, was called Hercules Promontory by the Romans, who knew the power of ocean waves rolling wooden galleys to wreckage upon the bouldered shores and pinnacle'd rocks of its twelve-mile 'arm'.

And there, this side of Hercules Promontory, lay the Atlantic, open to far Labrador. They breathed the sea-air, stood absorbing the azure of ocean fuzed with the sky.

And turning south, saw the hills of Dartmoor, a darker blue rising under the sky forty miles distant as the falcon glides.

"In my young days, three of us walked from the South Coast across Dartmoor to the fishing village over there, built round that conical hill. That's Appledore, where the salmon fishermen live. It was a haunt of mine in pre-war days, with Piers Tofield and his first wife. Do you see the dark ridge, half-covered by the tide, in the estuary, by the lighthouse? It's called the Shrarshook, after a sailor who was washed off it and drowned, called Charles Hook."

"God! Can't you get away from death?" she cried, and ran down the hill.

How still it was, how vacant now upon the hill. A wood lark singing somewhere on a stone wall below. Afar the slow murmur of the sea.

When she did not return, he walked on with his dog, making for the Burrows, or what was left of them. For during the war the churning tracks of American tanks, practicing for the invasion of Europe, had done some damage there.

East of the Burrows lay the Pans, an area holding brackish water where grew the first vegetation of the land proper. Worthless to the farmer, the Pans remained in their primeval state. Here were mosses, rushes, the pink bog-pimpernel, and the dwarf willow ... onwards to a no-man's-land where every species of wildflower known to grow in England had its home.

A haunted land for Phillip: here had walked Willie with Mary

Ogilvie, in that tragic summer before his death; here, too, had followed himself with the ghost of Willie between him and Lucy Copleston—days long past, recalled with sudden stillness of the heart, for that they were of Time lost, yet waiting to be brought back from ancient sunlight—

Now before him lay slopes of sand, wreckage of former hillocks once crested with marram grasses like great, green-quilled porcupines; but here military manoeuvres with live shell and other explosives had taken place on and through what, in 1940, had been wired, mined, tank-trapped and set with poles against enemy airborne landings.

And yet, how trivial it all had been, when seen against the eternal war of the elements! Sand originally of rock and sea-shell smashed by sea-wave, harried by air when washed upon the land, to be dried in summer and sent spinning in vacuous ropes by the screaming gales of ocean. How are the mighty fallen! Vast rocks from the Promontory of Hercules himself, rolled by tides along the foreland until they rested awhile as smooth pebbles; but always trituration by wind and wave, from quarrels by Fire and Water, brother ousting sister upon the faces of land and sea—until the bastion rocks were no more than dry skeins of sand faintly hissing, piling drift on drift until the hills were formed, and bound by marram grasses.

Phillip dropped down, to lie on his back, face to the sun, feeling himself slowly to be consuming within.

Laura crossed one valley after another amidst the rust and bleach of army litter until she felt to be lost. Above her arose a pyramid of sand which appeared to have escaped disintegration. Up she struggled, to look around from on high, with views of the sea whose cool airs were drifting past. No sight of Phillip. She sat down, she tried to think what she could do. Thought, or rumination, led to incipient turmoil, so she ran down the northern slope amidst the bleached bones of rabbits and a large kind of snail-shell, perhaps one brought by the Romans?

My feet are purring in the hot sand, and is it fancy, do I hear a rising and falling music—? Is it the hot grains of sand slipping down, their sounds multiplied—Is it *really* music—the music of this magic place? The glare of the sand is eye-tightening under the sun; but a sun in declension, alas, for soon it will move out of Leo into Virgo, which for all the good this relationship is might as well be me.

I am alone in a hollow where four plants of the Great Sea Stock grow. And over there is a Sea Holly, whose spiny leaves are as formidible to my naked foot as they are beautiful. Glaucus may be the word to describe their hue. If it is a wrong word I do not care, I do not bother about words while I am in this still and hanging air. And, O Great Pan, there *is* a strange, remote music!

She listened, and a line of poetry came to mind—her own line —*the dunes were dulcimers*—

Is Ariel come again? Those eyes of melting blue, the gentle lips of Phillip, why do I still whisper the name Prospero? This dull ache within—But all life is a dream. There it is again—one note seeming to descend an octave before rising again into the sky.

Does he see only footprints of Willie leading to the wind's oblivion? I must ask the sea, I must let myself drift, drift, for on such a day as this the ocean's pulse is all gentleness. Each wave rises thin, and its leading edge falls gently, to tinkle its white drops upon my face and back. I have miles of sand to myself and only the ring-plovers and shore-larks to see my naked body. I am the wave, the sea-shell, I am known to Botticelli and Milton—

And sitting naked among little waves, she murmured to herself,

Sabrina fair,
Listen where thou are sitting
Under the glassie, cool, translucent wave,
In twisted braids of lilies knitting
The loose train of thy amber-dropping hair.
Listen for dear honour's sake,
Goddess of the silver lake,
Listen and save—

Now the sun had gone down below the smouldering rim of ocean, night was coming to the earth. Then as she wandered along the tideline she saw flames on the beach half a mile away.

There Phillip was kneeling, feeding drift-wood to the fire, thinking of the beacon built by Julian Warbeck in the night of the recovery of Willie's body from the sea.

"Find Laura, Bodger! Goo' boy—find Laura!"

He sat under the peering stars, the drift-wood fire burning yellow with salt in the wood, and was about to search for more fuel when he saw a dark form coming towards him, and he was comforted a little by Bodger's cold nose touching his hand.

Chapter 20

TO THE WEST

Miranda brought to her mother in the kitchen a letter with a Suffolk postmark. "Who do you know who lives in Bussdall?"

"Oh, it will be from cousin Lucy, I expect, to say when she's coming down with Melissa."

"Who's Melissa?"

"Lucy's cousin, as well as mine, darling." Molly always tore open envelopes. "They're coming down with the baby the second week of August. Oh dear, just when we'll be preparing for the cricketers." She read on. "That's better! Cousin Lucy and the three boys are going to camp out in tents and caravan. I do hope it won't rain. August is usually a wet one on the moor, I'm afraid."

Miranda looked to be downcast. "Penny for them, Anda."

"Oh nothing." The girl's lips quivered. She was liable to tears, this 'green girl', for that was all she was, after all—"Darling, we all felt what you are feeling now, when we were your age. It will pass—"

"I don't want it to pass! I want to go on helping Cousin Phillip, don't you see?"

"Darling, we'll be able to see him just the same. But I don't think it advisable for you to go over by yourself any more."

"But he needs help! And why doesn't his wife live with him?"

"He's a little difficult, I suppose."

"That could easily apply to me. You know I don't get on with anyone at school, except some of the mistresses, who are all older than I."

" 'Older than me' surely, darling."

"Older than *I* am old, Mother."

"Darling, you have a fine mind, we all recognise that."

"Then why can't I help Cousin Phillip? I *know* he wants me to."

"Well, you have helped him quite a lot, haven't you? But it's more than that, Anda."

"What do you mean?"

"Darling, you mustn't become indispensable, so that Cousin Phillip will be unhappy when you have to do other things with your life."

"What other things?"

"You may fall in love, and want to get married."

"I shan't want to get married. I love Phillip."

"Of course you do, darling, we all love Cousin Phillip. But there are other things than affection and admiration, you know."

"You mean that Cousin Phillip may be wounded like 'Buster' was?"

"That was never in my mind. Now tell me, what made you say that?"

"Well, one of the reasons why Laura isn't always happy is because she loves 'Buster', and he's practically a cripple. Well, Cousin Phillip isn't."

"Darling, I wonder if you know what you're saying."

"I know that Cousin Phillip doesn't want Laura in his bed with him, because she's frightened him off."

"I wonder if you know what you're talking about, Anda."

"I know that she discourages him spiritually. And spirit and sex are the same things basically."

"D. H. Lawrence—," began Molly.

"I don't agree with his theories. Most of the time he was fighting his wife because she wasn't his mother."

"Wherever do you get all these extraordinary ideas?"

"I read in the school library. Anyway, Lawrence's theory about the sexes needing to fight is unsound. Laura says he used sex to get rid of his childhood repressions, because she does exactly that —when she can. She can't with 'Buster', and Cousin Phillip doesn't want her, so she's in a mess most of the time."

"A woman must be loved, you know Anda, to be happy. Physical love is ever so important to a woman, darling."

"Age does not affect affinity, Mummie. And affinity is not infirmity. And I *know* Cousin Phillip is normal."

"Miranda, have you let him make love to you?"

"Not yet."

"That's frank anyway, darling."

"Dear Mother, you're so sweet and understanding that I can tell you almost anything."

Molly resisted asking what was being held back. "Darling, you will be careful, won't you? There's Cousin Phillip to think of, you know, as well as yourself." She kissed an unresponsive daughter. "Of course we all love dear Phillip. He's so gentle and understanding. But he belongs to an older generation. So we must both think of him, mustn't we, and not let anything interfere with his writing, don't you think?"

"But the point is, he and his writing *are* interfered with, all the time."

"Then we must all leave him alone to get on with his work, surely?"

"It's not you or me, I've told you—it's Laura!"

"Well, as you said, he is not able to return her love."

"I don't wonder at it! She *cows* him, deprives him of spirit, so he simply daren't start his novel series! The other day he took her to the coast, the Burrows of Santon, and what did she do? Just because he had many memories of the place, where Willie was drowned years ago—his cousin, you know, the one whom the Ogilvie girl, Mary, wasn't it, was going to marry, only he was drowned. Phillip took Cousin Lucy there before he married her. Well, the point is, just because it is a special place for him, a sort of pilgrimage place, Laura leaves him flat, and goes off on her own, so that he was looking along the coast half the night, and finally lit a fire. Then she turned up."

"Did Phillip tell you this?"

"No. I heard it from Cousin Hugh's man, Mornington. She didn't get home until after four o'clock in the morning."

"Perhaps they enjoyed themselves by the fire, darling."

"Then she never spoke a word to Phillip when he said goodnight. She's paying him out for what her father did to her when she was young."

"Miranda, what are you saying?"

"She tells everyone that her father raped her when she was small."

"That was hardly her fault."

"That's not the point! And anyway, I don't believe any father would do such a thing to his child. The point is that Phillip needs to feel that there are months and months ahead of him in the clear, before he *dare* begin his life's work! He had a terrible time in the first war, he wasn't cut out to be a soldier, but a dreamer, like Shelley and Francis Thompson. Even so, he forced himself to be a good soldier. Then in the last war they didn't treat him well where he had a farm. They thought he was a spy—someone on whom to vent their own deprived feelings. Some workmen beat him up on the quay at Crabbe, and if that wasn't enough, Brigadier Tarr sent some commandos to fire live ammunition on his meadows without permission, and wounded him!"

"Yes darling, I heard all about it from Cousin Hugh. That sort of thing happens to many people in wartime."

"Can't you see how he felt when his first wife died when she was only nineteen? He's never loved anyone since! Then his son, the child of that love marriage, was killed in the last week of the war! And now Phillip is like the Unknown Soldier, shut up in a tomb! And will remain so until he is rescued by true love, and can get back to the sun again, like Persephone from the dark blue halls of Dis!"

Miranda hid her face in her hair, and ran upstairs.

Molly was alarmed, she had never seen her daughter so distressed. She found her lying on the bed, in calm aloofness.

"You are a good girl, darling. A very good girl. I know you'll be a good, steady friend to Cousin Phillip. Be his chum, but nothing more. Then, when you are older, perhaps—"

"Why are mothers afraid to let their grown children love?"

"They don't want their children to be unhappy, I suppose. Or to make others unhappy. Cousin Phillip is so vulnerable. And as I've told you, he isn't a boy, darling. He's a mature man. He's fifty."

"Fifty-two. What does age matter if, as I said, there's affinity? And what is affinity but attraction? Look at Daddy! Women still think he's wizard."

"He's a butterfly, darling."

"What's wrong with that? Anyway, I suppose I take after him. I wish I could see more of him. Not only for a couple of weeks in summer and a few days at Christmas *if* he isn't in Africa shooting big game. What went wrong between you two? Was it his women?"

"Not altogether, Miranda."

"Then tell me. I want to know."

"His father came home a cripple from the first war, and when he died, lots of death duties had to be paid. Then the second war meant higher rates and taxes, forcing Daddy to sell Brockholes to the Somerset Asylums Board."

This was a reference to Brockholes St. Boniface Abbey, seat of the Bucentaur family since the Tudors.

"You see, Anda, Daddy thought, at least in the Second War,

that he was fighting for his home, as Churchill said, and not merely for the tax collector."

"Well, someone has to pay for the Cads' War."

"Wherever did you pick up that expression, darling?"

Miranda had heard it from Phillip, but she said, "Someone told me it was used by Lord Hankey when we started bombing civilians in Germany."

"Well, to come back to your father. He's never really settled down, and after the war he simply couldn't face living in this poky little shack, as he called it."

"I think it's a wizard home, Mum. Even with the goats on top of us. I wonder why they smell more at night? The pong in my room is fairly strong sometimes."

"They'll all be gone, thank goodness, when Daddy hands them over to the Council."

"May I keep Capella?"

"That's for your Father to say, darling. He'll be here with his Eleven fairly soon. I suppose we ought to be thinking about camp beds and tents for them."

"Would you like me to see about it?"

"It would be such a help it you would, darling. I'm going into Minehead to shop this afternoon."

The girl got off the bed. "Mummie, would you mind very much if I first rode over to see Cousin Phillip?"

"Of course not, darling. Do ask him to come over in his wonderful old motor, it will be so useful for collecting tents and things."

"You won't talk to him about me, will you?"

"There's nothing really to talk about now, is there, darling? I'm so glad we had this out, it's cleared the air, hasn't it?"

"Well, sort of."

"At your age, one takes one's fancies so seriously, Miranda darling."

"Like you did, mother dear, when you were seventeen?"

"Things were simpler then, darling."

"Did you elope?"

"It wasn't necessary. My papa gave his consent."

"And if he hadn't given it?"

"Well, until one is twenty-one, one's father is the one to say, you know."

"Say what, Mother darling?"

"If a child should want to marry before coming of age, when the law regards her or him as an infant, the father can withold his consent."

"If Daddy ever did that, I'd use my switch plan."

"And what is that, darling?"

"As you said, Mother, we must think of Phillip."

One day, as Phillip sat at the open door, mending a willow log-basket, the behaviour of some crows over by the farmhouse across the common—the constant cawing, black ragged shapes flapping up and dropping again—made him hasten over the heather to the gate. Four birds were flying down, and rising up again from a particular place on the opposite side of the hedge. Like all the moorland hedges, it was a raised bank of earth and stone, topped by beech, thorn, ash, bramble and furze. The bank was tunnelled by rabbits. Aaron Kedd, the smallholder who lived down the coomb, set his traps along the hedge.

Opening the gate, glancing down the bank, Phillip saw a lean crow hanging by a foot, head downwards. On seeing him, it flapped about. The leg was held by a gin-trap on a pegged chain. It was a thin, scared-looking bird, with comic eyes; and the other crows were its nestling brethren, which still flew about with their parents. It looked pathetic, and was too frightened to peck the human hand taking it out of the trap.

Phillip stroked its poll, while it gasped with open beak, and its three companions circled in the air above, cawing. He threw up the bird, which uttered a gawping cry and flew down the coomb, followed by its companions. Then Phillip saw the two old birds, flying high in the sky above their agitated young. After watching them away in the direction their young had flown, he went back to the gate, where Aaron Kedd was waiting for him.

"Thaccy be my bliddy craw you took out of my gin, and I'll hev 'ee to Town for thievin', you zee if I don't !"

"Let me pay for it. Here's a shilling."

Kedd took the coin, and said in a less disturbed voice, "They bliddy craws, they'm all flamin' thieves! My Gor', wan last year found a yaw (ewe) of mine on her back, and before you could say knife, her pots (intestines) was pulled out yards and yards. Bliddy craws, they'm worse than thievin' bliddy rats or magpies! And I'll tell 'ee another thing! Thaccy young leddy what rides over vor zee 'ee, what do 'er want vor bring a goat wi' her allus? The bliddy thing snatched at my flat-poll, ah I scatt 'er wi' a long stick, di'n I tho! They gentry riding about think they can

do what they'm a vancy for, but not likely! What for do 'er
come yurr, I know why, and you can't deny it, grabbin'. seaweed,
that be your game! Us zees lots like 'er about in summer—"

He was left complaining to the wind, for Phillip was walking
away. Back at the table, he wrote in his journal.

> In spring and early summer my neighbour's voice is to be heard on
> the wind as he works his allotment of five acres with a shaggy moorland
> pony, either harrowing with deep-tined cultivating harrows, or scuffling
> cabbages ('flat polls') and roots between the rows. The pony pulls
> strongly, eager to snatch at the oats growing at one end of the rows:
> then I hear the hoarse cries of the smallholder, hanging on to stilts
> of the wheeled hoe. "You booger, you! You flamin' bliddy rogue, I'll
> trim ee! Gr-r-r-t you! Come up you, aaa-aaa-ah!" But there is no call
> for an R.S.P.C.A. inspector, for he is all bark and no bite. Bitter years
> are behind him, he is lonely, his only reading is the *Old Testament*
> and *The News of the World* by candle-light in his thatched two-
> room cot.
> A human hedgehog—a small man with no war to light his back-
> ground, staring at life with sunken uneasy eyes under ferny eyebrows;
> the near-tortured face, the dyspepsia, the inefficient would-be market
> gardener who rents odd splatts or parcels of land and grows in rotation,
> year after year, without muck from bullock, sheep, or pig, potatoes,
> potatoes, potatoes—his idea of the rotation of crops. There is an acre
> of ground on the common of which the humus was fully one foot deep.
> Thereon he has grown potatoes year after year, using only chemical
> fertiliser, until an exhausted soil suddenly gave up yielding. Even
> thistles do not grow today out of the sour, gritty, iron-stone subsoil,
> the fertility of which has become a box of coins under his bed—for
> he is the kind who distrusts all banks.
> Undernourished and undeveloped, tortured by and from what he
> lacks—or lacked as a child, how can Aaron Kedd ever be made whole?
> The sleepless hours of darkness for him are 'black monarchs which
> rule by torture'.

On the second day of the summer holidays, at the beginning
of the fourth week of July, the three brothers—Peter, now seventeen years old, and still on the small, thin size; David, thirteen and
not yet come to puberty; Jonathan, eleven, small and dark, spiritually aware with sharp sight and sympathy connected directly
with insight—were strung out in a line of fifty yards, and pedalling, with heads bowed, on the left of the road, into a strong
south-west wind. All three were thinly clad, the two smaller boys
in reach-me-down, threadbare suits.

They were now in the fifth day of their journey. Owing to wind blowing from the south-west into their faces, they had so far covered little more than two hundred miles. At times the wind was so strong that they had to stand on the pedals to make progress.

It began to rain again, so they stopped under an oak-tree beside the road.

"Cor, I'm what-you-call tired," said David.

"Ah, 'bor," agreed Jonathan.

"How long before we reach Father?"

"Well, if the wind changes direction, we might get there to-morrow night, Jonny."

"Cor, that will mean we'll do a hundred miles in one day!"

"*If* the wind blows from little old Birdy House," said David.

"We'll have some fish-and-chips as soon as we get somewhere," Peter promised.

Money was low. David had lost his £3, and Peter had spent thirty shillings on a new chain and sprocket. Peter hadn't liked to ask his mother for more, and his father had little money, too, he thought.

The rain fell through the oak-tree, so they pedal'd on. There was no fish-and-chip shop in the next village, so they bought three kippers. Coming to a wood beside the road, they made a fire and each boy grilled a flattened corpse impaled on the sharpened end of a green stick. The kippers tasted of tar. They ate them in their fingers, glad that the rain had stopped, but not the wind, and went slowly on their cape-flapping journey.

"Cor, I hope we won't be late for what-you-call seeing the Brockholes goats scrapping out of the horse van, chookies!"

"Ah, 'bor. Don't forget the cricket, too. I hope it won't rain all the whole time."

"Wet weather in Devon clears up suddenly," said Peter, as rain fell again.

The caravan was damp, so was the cot, what with all the rain, so Phillip had arranged for the boys to spend the night of arrival at Shelley's Cottage where, he had written to Lucy, Mrs. Piston would welcome them.

"No charge, Masson, for troops coming out of the line into billets," said Piston. "After all this rain, your young soldiers will be pretty well out, old lad."

Phillip was anxious. The boys were overdue. He was worrying, too, because of the presence of his sister Elizabeth at Ionian cottage. Aunt Dora's will had been proved : Elizabeth, after death duties, had inherited £11,000. He bore no resentment that he had been left nothing; he was nervous at the thought of her in what he regarded as his territory. Her presence always had diminished him.

So he avoided walking down the main street above the river by climbing up the lane which, descending along a path through the slopes of the woods to the quay, brought him to the harbour mouth. There he hung about, hoping to find the boys, for surely the first thing they would make for was the sea.

Osgood Nilsson was fishing. He called to Phillip, "Hullo, there! The school peal are running !", and fumbling in his inner pocket, he held up two small sea-trout seemingly linked together. "I've just taken this one, pound and a half, I guess."

Puzzling : alarming : for now beside Osgood was another figure like him—Siamese twins standing in a twin-waved sea below the duplicated pebble ridge on the east side of the channel marked by tall poles, each one topped by a herring gull. While he stared, a gull flew to a pole and alighted on the back of a gull already perching there. He felt faint, his heart thudded in his ears. Am I losing reason as well as sight?

"Hullo, Dad," said the voice of Peter beside him. "We thought we'd find you here, somehow," and coming towards him were two blurred figures with elongated heads, which settled into the recognisable outlines of David and Jonathan.

"Cor, look at that gull up there, sitting on another one's back!" cried Jonnie.

"There *are* two gulls, then?"

"Why yes, Dad !"

Peter was looking at him anxiously. Phillip could see his son's face clearly now. He felt suddenly happy. He could see Nilsson clear and undivided. He felt a rush of affection for Peter. "How long have you been here?"

"About half an hour, Dad. Mr. Osgood saw us and asked if we belonged to you, and when we said yes he took us into a cafe and gave us coffee and doughnuts !"

"Cor, we were what you call hungry," said David.

"We hitched the last fifty miles by coach," went on Peter.

"The driver gave us a lift, and put our bikes in the back with the luggage," added David.

"We didn't have any lamps, you see," explained Jonathan. "It was ever so dark until the moon rose up behind us."

"You travelled at night without lights?"

"We thought we'd be late for the ceremony of the white goats," said David. "Peter said we shouldn't bike in the darkness, but we felt so cold trying to sleep beside a haystack we decided to get warm pedalling."

Peter explained that they had seen the headlights of the coach a long way behind. "We got beside the hedge to let it pass, but it stopped. The driver said he recognised us two days back, in the rain, this side of Salisbury."

"We went to look at the Cathedral, and stopped there to get warm, Father," said Peter, a little afraid.

The emotion passed, yielding to affection when Phillip said, "My poor children, why didn't you go to a Cyclists Touring Club lodging, as I suggested?"

"We didn't have enough money for lodgings as well as food, Dad."

Peter explained that a pound had to last either for four nights with no food except breakfast, or if with supper they must sleep out.

"Oh God, what an awful father I am!"

"You're not!" cried David. "Any way, we loved coming, didn't we, chookies?"

He yawned, he was pale and drawn.

"Well, you three tough guys are to sleep at Major Piston's cottage tonight. He's an old friend of mine from the first war. Go to bed early, you'll sleep the clock round. By the way, don't forget to thank Mrs. Piston when you leave tomorrow, and also write her a letter, Peter."

"Very good, Dad. Is this your little dog?"

"Yes, that's Bodger."

He left them with the dog, saying he'd have a word with Osgood Nilsson, and then they'd all go up to see 'Buster'.

"Have you got a chain and padlock for your bikes? Good. By the way, you should address our host as 'Lord Cloudesley' and not 'Buster'."

"Of course, Dad," said Peter. "Mr. Osgood gave us a canoe, he said he was too big for it now."

"Well, you must never go out to sea in it, any of you."

"We thought we'd only go in it in the harbour, when the tide is coming in," said Peter.

"You can all swim?"

"Yes, Dad!"

After Phillip had thanked Osgood for his kindness, they all went up the lift to Lynton, and down a path to The Eyrie. There they had poached eggs on toast with baked beans, their favourite food.

"Sir—I mean Lord—is that right, Father?—"

"My name is 'Buster', Peter. It helps me to feel not so old. What were you saying, David?"

"Do you believe in flying saucers, sir? I mean Cousin 'Buster'."

"Unidentified flying objects have certainly been seen by accredited witnesses, pilots flying over the Atlantic, for example, David. But some may well be due to ice-dust layers, which can diminish and so give an illusion of moving away from orthodox aircraft at a considerable rate of knots. They are similar, in my view, to what my father, in one of his letters here,"—he held up a bundle tied by faded ribbon—"speaks of as 'the queer circular rainbow' in front of his scout 'plane—or fighter aircraft as you would have called them in the recent war. The rainbow, or rain-circle, is visible in certain lights and atmospheric conditions, due to the refraction of light into the colours of the spectrum. What do you think, Brig?"

"Possibly, 'Buster', possibly."

Brigadier Tarr turned to Peter. "I want to apologise to your father's eldest surviving son for my bloody-mindedness towards him during the war. I was arrogant, and somewhat shaken after I came back from Narvik. It was I who told the troops on your farm in Norfolk to shoot first and ask questions afterwards. I thought all German sympathisers were—well—not my cup of tea. I learned differently in Holland, after the drop at Arnhem—" He raised a shaking glass and shouted into the air, "Where Eisenhower left us alone to be cut to bloody ribands!" He drank, then said quietly. 'Yes, I was bloody-minded then. I'm fairly humble now. Lost me arrogance, thanks be to God." He emptied the glass. He stared into space.

"All my men went west at Arnhem, while we"—banging his fist three times on the table—"waited—waited—waited for American help!" He glared at nothing and yelled, "In my opinion ˋEisenhower ought to be shot!" A glisten of sweat broke on his bald pink pate. Bodger crept under Phillip's chair.

"I understand, sir" replied Peter. "My father was very upset at the time. In fact, sir, he shouted, too!"

The Brig. went to Phillip, patted his shoulder, and left the room.

"Well," said 'Buster', "it's a rising glass, I think I'll go gliding Do bring your boys to see me again before cricket week, won't you," to Phillip.

At Shelley Cottage, when their father had gone, Jonathan said, "Cor, I what-you-call like this place, Chooky."

"Yar right, 'bor."

"It's the best holiday I ever had," said Peter.

The rising glass hovered, then fell. Rain beat upon the common. The boys passed the time in the caravan, leaving Dad to his writing. Soon Peter had taken over the house-keeping—such as it was. Daily on their bikes the brothers went down to Lynton, returning with what they could get off the ration—usually kippers, as sold at that time throughout Britain—black oily split fish which had been dipped in creosote to give the appearance of having been smoked above a dull smouldering of oak saw-dust.

Chalk was still an 'additive'—scientific jargon word—in bread.

"Blast, I wish we had some of our own wheaten scones" said Peter, who looked thin and pale.

"And Mum's honey" said Jonathan.

"Don't forget our own butter," added David.

"What about some rabbits? Let's take sticks, and Bodger to hunt them!"

"He's too old to run fast" said Peter.

"I know! Let's watch the buzzards, and when one drops, send Bodger arter'm!" suggested Jonathan.

So the boys went down Horrock water, where rabbits lived. They were not so common as before the war, and the great dusky-winged hawks were fewer, in that country of the sea-winds. Before the war as many as a dozen were to be seen at once, sailing in tiers above the hills; somtimes plunging down the invisible precipices of the wind, crying their plaintive cries, and on up-tilted wings sweeping up again; or, falling away in the east, to the oakwoods where they nested, each bird growing smaller and smaller until but a tawny speck showed at the turn, from dun undersides of out-stretched wings.

The boys surprised one of the great hawks on the ground holding a rabbit in its claws, and flapping. They killed the rabbit and in triumph bore it back to the cot.

*   *   *

Now the cot was 'home', Phillip began to view the past happily. He told them how, on opening the door during the past winter, he had seen the constellation of the Plough lying above the eastern end of a beech clump, near the end of the lane across the common, and pointing to Polaris, the constant star of the North. In frosty weather, after the blizzard, and at the turn of the year, he had heard owls on his roof-ridge calling with a throbbing softness. They seemed to be following one another from hunting-perch to perch, to be playing in the quiet of the night, their cries gentle with pleasure. And now, when the rain had stopped, and the nights were quiet under the stars, the owls seemed to be playing again.

"Perhaps they are the young owls of this year" said Jonathan.

It was a warm and gentle night. Four of the Maddison family dining in the caravan by candle-light on rabbit which for three hours had simmered in the crock hanging from the chimney bar. With the rabbit were potatoes, carrots, onions, and half a bottle of O.K. sauce.

"Very tasty" said David. "Good old Peter!"

Phillip felt a little guilty that he had left all the cooking to Peter, that loyal and uncomplaining aristocrat among the children. Soon they would be leaving; their mother was coming down with the baby, to camp in tents and caravan beside the West Lyn below Barbrook, going to sleep to the gentle music of water playing on stone beside them.

Phillip felt already an underlying poignancy that the boys would soon be leaving him. Still, they would be happier in the caravan beside the Lyn, on the Green Meadow camping site, with their mother. Also, he must carry on with his notes for the novels.

Yes, the family would be happier in the caravan on Green Meadow. They had got so wet walking through the heather, day after day of rain, that he had told them to give up wearing shoes and stockings, and walk bare-footed. And those poisonous kippers! White bread and margarine, and a tiny ration of cheese—poor diet, with an occasional orange and apple. The main diet was soup of potatoes and cabbages boiled in the cast-iron crock.

They felt contentment after the rabbit stew. The three boys and their father were sitting in the yellow haze of candlelight when a wood owl hooted almost with flute-like quality on the roof of the cot, forty yards away. It was the bubbling, quavering call, a little uncertain, of a young bird which had lost its parents and was seeking hopefully for an answer to its feelings. Phillip replied with a short, clear note, the call of a male bird. After awhile the quaver came again; and upon being called once more, the bird flew nearer. The conditions for mimicry, or art, were perfect : the upright, solitary candle-flame : the immobility of the boys, their alert faces : the windless night wherein sounds travelled afar— they could hear an owl crying in the valley leading down beside the Lyn a mile away. No cloud over The Chains, only stars. There had been no rain for three days; gossamers strewed the heather, mushrooms were appearing in the enclosures behind stone-walls topped by furze and bramble. The voice of the young female owl seemed to become more tender as it cried again through the darkness.

"She has almost forgotten the owl far away in the valley. She is entranced. She has heard the perfect hoot. She dreams of wonderful eyes, of the tenderest beak preening her feathers."

There was now complete silence within the caravan, the door open wide to the night. Then with a slight bump on the painted canvas roof they knew the owl had arrived. They dared hardly to breathe : the quavering came again, startlingly near : they could hear the sighing away of the frail and tremulous note.

A soft answer from the caravan. Far away across the common, the other owl was calling. They hardly dared to raise their eyes from the plates before them. Then the owl fluted again; hopefully, thrillingly, trustingly. Was she awaiting her bird of paradise to fly forth from the cavern below?

The candle flame began to quiver. Jonathan, who was dark and Celtic, was silently a-giggle. Whereupon David, thirteen, blue-eyed and Germanic, assumed a clown-face, and stared at his brother, his own face owl-like. Hush, their father whispered, don't disillusion the bird. What could they do? How get out of it? *Oo-oo-woo-loo-woo*, came the soft throbbing above their heads, as the egg-shaped swelling in the bird's throat subsided. The owl in the valley had ceased to call. They began to shake with silent laughter.

Then David gave an imitation of a cuckoo. After awhile there was a reply from the owl on the roof; but a note of doubt was in the fore-shortened reply. *Cuck-oo* cried David again.

They waited. A less hopeful, a half-sad, melancholy note in the bird's voice now. David let out another mellow *Cuck-oo*. Their laughter broke. Then they were sorry for the owl, until later there came a bubbling and wauling and baying across the common, where beech trees stood.

"Cor, I'm what-you-call glad to hear that, 'bor!" said David to Jonathan. "I reckon they'll pair for life after that hullaballoo!"

They decided to sleep in the Cot that night, to be together. When the boys were in bed, David's voice said, "This place is haunted, d'you know why? Dad's got our grandfather's bones, or the bits that aren't all burnt up—you know, they burn up some people who prefer to be buried that way, first I mean, because they don't like the idea of worms eating them up underground, I suppose."

Phillip heard this talk as he sat by the hearth, there was no door to the bedrooms. He went upstairs with a copy of a book, and said to Peter, who was sleeping on the floor, "Read this passage aloud, please. I'll put the candle on the floor beside you."

Peter read slowly,

"The supernatural miscalled, the natural in truth, is the real. To me everything is supernatural. How strange the condition of mind which cannot accept anything but the earth, the sea, the tangible universe! Without the misnamed supernatural these to me seem incomplete, unfinished ... As I move about in the sunshine I feel in the midst of the supernatural: in the midst of immortal things ... as commonly understood, a 'miracle' is a mere nothing. I can conceive soul-works done by simple will or thought a thousand times greater. I marvel that they do not happen at this moment. The air, the sunlight, the night, all that surrounds me seems crowded with inexpressible powers, with the influence of Souls, or existences, so that I walk in the midst of immortal things. I am myself a living witness of it. Sometimes I have concentrated myself, and driven away by continued will all sense of outward appearances, looking straight with the full power of my mind inwards on myself. I find 'I' am there; an 'I' I do not wholly understand, or know—something there is distinct from earth and timber, from flesh and bones. Recognising it, I feel on the margin of a life unknown, very near, almost touching it: on the verge of powers which if I could grasp would give me an immense breadth of existence, an ability to execute what I now only conceive; most probably of far more than that. To see the 'I' is to know that I am surrounded by immortal things. If, when I die, that 'I' also dies, and becomes extinct, still even then I shall have had the exaltation of these ideas.

"How many words it has taken to describe so briefly the feelings and the thoughts that came to me by the tumulus; thoughts that swept past and were gone, and were succeeded by others while yet the shadow of the mound had not moved from one thyme-flower to another, not the breadth of a grass blade. Softly breathed the sweet south wind, gently the yellow corn waves beneath; the ancient, ancient sun shone on the fresh grass and the flower, my heart opened wide as the broad, broad earth. I spread my arms out, laying them on the sward, seizing the grass, to take the fulness of the days.

"Could I have my own way after death I would be burned on a pyre of pine-wood, open to the air, and placed on the summit of the hills. Then let my ashes be scattered abroad—not collected in an urn —freely sown wide and broadcast. That is the natural interment of man—of man whose Thought at least has been among the immortals; interment in the elements. Burial is not enough, it does not give sufficient solution into the elements speedily; a furnace is confined. The high open air of the topmost hill, there let the tawny flame lick up the fragment called the body; there cast the ashes into the space it longed for while living. Such a luxury of interment is only for the wealthy; I fear I shall not be able to afford it. Else the smoke of my resolution into the elements should certainly arise in time on the hill-top."

"Thank you, Peter. It means that everything you see about you is something that was first only imagined. A clock—this candle —this room—the blankets and pillows, were imagined before they could be made real."

"Sort of invented, Dad" said David.

"Exactly! And trees and grass were invented, and animals and birds."

"You mean 'evolved', sir?" asked Peter.

"Yes. They didn't come about suddenly, but gradually. Their evolution, or change, took place under a plan, a haphazard plan if you like, but the Idea was there first, or, as Keats the poet wrote, the Imagination. Love was evolved, too—the love of a cat for her kittens, a bird for its eggs, the cockbird for the hen he has married —married by the Imagination. So love is a great force in the world, and as for men, we are social animals, like some birds and animals in flocks all over the earth and in the sky. Richard Jefferies, who wrote what you've just read to us, loved the air and the countryside so much he couldn't bear the idea of being buried when his turn came to die, and longed to be burned on a hilltop, his ashes scattered. And your grandfather, who had to work in London year after year, also loved the country. So I thought we'd have a pyre on The Chains, and cast his ashes into the flames. Do you think it's a good idea?"

"Yes, Dad!" they cried together.

"We'll build the funeral pyre when Mother comes down."

Lucy and Melissa started west from Suffolk one morning at five o'clock, to journey upon empty roads with the sun behind them, and to have the cool of the morning. For weeks rain had been falling every day. Now the weather had changed. The day had risen with the sun to be one of great heat: a windless shining upon field after field of laid corn.

Melissa had spent the past four months undergoing a rebuilding of the flesh of part of her face, and a course of Diaphany in a Surrey country house. This course had been arduous; not only all the terms used in an entirely new idiom, almost a language in itself, but the approaches to questioning patients was as original as the language, which was a conglomeration of new—some critics said fanciful—theories expounded by an adaptation—the critics declared mongrelisation—of Greek and Latin words. At best it was jargon, they declared.

The founder answered these objections simply. "All technical terms are jargon. The ordinary human mind is cluttered with jargon. We unclutter it. We help it to see plain."

To Melissa, all was plain: Faith, Hope, and—*Clarity*.

The vapours of the night, which had gathered upon the sodden fields, were risen by noon to be high cloudlets, like a scatter of pale breast feathers of some slain heavenly bird thought Melissa, as she sat beside Lucy driving the little Ford 8 saloon car.

The baby was asleep in her cot secured upon the back seat. It was nearly noon when, in the distance, the tall spire of a cathedral came into view, as they ran down the road from the downs, crossed the river, and followed the road between water-meadows to Salisbury.

There Lucy drove to the car-park, and sat with Melissa, quietly resting for a few minutes, both windows open under a high sun.

"Shall we drive on and see Piers?" said Lucy, "or would you like to eat our sandwiches here?"

"I'm happy to do anything you like, Lucy."

"Well, Phillip did write and say Piers would be glad to see us, so perhaps we should drop in."

Phillip's letter had said also that it was delightfully informal at Field Place, "Just as it was years ago at Down Close when I first knew you, and you were living there so happily with Pa and the Boys."

"Do you think it might make our arrival at Molly's too late for you to go on to your family?"

Lucy began to have doubts. Perhaps Mel had some reason for not wanting to see Piers? How silly of her : of course it must be the scars down her cheeks, where she had been slashed by a demented Indian soldier-patient in a Calcutta hospital during the war. The scars were still noticeable, despite the skin-grafting. Why hadn't she thought of it before !

While she hesitated, Melissa, who had divined Lucy's thoughts, said, "I'm not unduly sensitive about my appearance, Lucy. Really, I'd love to see Piers again."

"Perhaps we can have a picnic on the way there? It's so lovely on top of the downs."

As she drove up to the Great Plain it was to Lucy almost a home-coming. Far away to the south lay the heights of the Chace, with its dissolved blue shimmering of tree and drove. Somewhere below lay her old home of Down Close; while, to the north, under other downs, was Skirr farmhouse to which she had gone as a bride, Phillip driving his motor-bicycle, she in the sidecar with little Billy. Twenty one years ago! Now it was all part of the summer day—a happy summer day—for since Lucy had been on her own, she had seen her relationship with Phillip, and particularly her own shortcomings, in perspective. Phillip to her now was one who had had always far too much to do, while insisting on doing his very best in all he undertook, at the same time never being able to say no to anyone in trouble. So he was almost always in a muddle, she considered, in her simplifying way. She hoped he was happy at last, able to write without too many human disturbances. And O, if he needed her, she would be always by his side !

There was communication between them, for Lucy said, "Phillip deserves peace and happiness, if anyone does."

Melissa said, turning bright blue eyes upon her cousin, "I am so happy to be with you again, Lucy! And to be back in this lovely country. Nothing has changed, really! You look just the same, and I begin to feel that I am *me,* once more."

Other contours of the Plain were ahead; they stopped on the crest of the down to sit by a tumulus. Harebells azure as the sky moved with the warm airs arising from cornfields spreading away and below them.

"The whole Plain has been ploughed up, Lucy !"

Wheatears were gravely watching them from the old grey sward of the tumulus before abruptly breaking away in flight as though in search of a lost world.

The baby awakened. Melissa took her in her arms, but the baby wanted to walk, she struggled to be free of gentle lip-to-cheek kisses. She pulled off her woollen socks, and standing still, put one foot forward, but when she tried to move the other foot to beside the first, she had to sit down. Then, between the two women, little hands held by larger hands, Sarah was borne lightly across to the tumulus to climb up, up, up to where blue hill-butterflies and wild bees were at the honey of thyme and hawkbit.

They rested for half an hour; then on across the westward slopes of the Great Plain spreading away and below; another sea of adolescent corn lately pressed flat by the wet waves of the wind. And down a familiar road descending in curves before the right-handed turn to the Colham road, and so to Field Place. Whatever had happened to the house?

The grey Palladian circumstructure had gone, and among its ruins stood a small Jacobean farmhouse.

"Of course, Phillip said it had been pulled down. What a relief it must be to Piers!"

The walled garden still stood, and as they drove nearer they saw Piers with a gardener pushing a hand-cart filled with lawn cuttings to add to a compost heap outside a gate leading to the high-walled kitchen garden. Beyond was the gardener's cottage, by which small children were playing.

Piers greeted them warmly, and took them to see his work in the walled garden. The fountain was in play, greenhouses had been re-glassed. The stable clock struck eleven; it was half past two; but it was going. "Must adjust that," said Piers. He was lean and sun-burned, his eye clear as they walked along weeded paths to a postern gate leading to mown but still mossy lawns, divided by clumps of rhododendrons and a cedar tree before the modest remains of what had grown to be a mansion but now had returned to a seventeenth-century barton.

While they sat on the grass, a black rabbit ran to Piers and got up on its hind-legs.

"Inky's begging for bread and butter. He doesn't like finding the cupboard bare, so watch out!"

Hardly had he said that when Inky lolloped forward and was about to bite Piers' trousers. Then another animal which had been lying, throat to grass, a dozen yards off, crept up, body held low, towards the rabbit. It looked like a fox, but was slightly larger, with darker coat.

"Father a fox, mother a spaniel," Piers explained. "Inky, a cringer if ever there was one, is inclined to get rid of his inferiority complex by attacking passive objects like young chickens and children."

Sarah was crawling on the grass. The rabbit lolloped to the child. "Manners, Inky!" said Piers, sharply. The dog put itself between Inky and Sarah. "On guard, Foxy!" Whereupon the fox-dog put its head under the rabbit, tossed it aside, and lay flat, yellow eyes fixed on the rabbit. "Foxy is our Chief of Secret Police. Foxy thinks, don't you Foxy? When wild rabbits invade the lawn he starts rolling, getting nearer and nearer to one before springing up and catching it. No, he doesn't kill it, but takes it to the courtyard pond and drops it in. Does the same with Inky, usually, when he tries to bite. On guard, Foxy!", for Inky was again lolloping towards the baby. "Now watch!"

With steady fast movement Foxy moved in. Inky made a feint movement, changed direction and leapt over its opponent's head. Equally quick, Foxy swung round and at a cry of "Banish Inky!" took the rabbit by the scruff and trotted away with it round the house.

"Don't worry," said Piers. "It's a game they play. Come and see the end of it."

They walked together through open double-doors at the end of a croquet lawn, and came to the kitchen door, followed by a bedraggled Inky. "He always has potato crisps with yeast after a ducking. Naughty Inky!", addressing the rabbit. "You only bite my trousers in order to get flung in the pond and get extra food, don't you, naughty Inky?" The kitchen door opened, a young woman came out.

"Beth!"

"Melissa!"

Surprise. Smiling faces. Happiness.

"When did you leave India?"

Explanations. "It's a small world after all, isn't it? Mel and Laura and I nursed together in Calcutta during the war, Lucy."

Inky was striking the floor with hind-feet. "He's angry because I haven't added Bovril to his crisps," she said.

"Gets away with it every time," said Piers. "Well trained, aren't you Inky," as the rabbit went to bite his trousers. "Manners, Inky!", whereupon Inky tried another way : he sat up and begged. A teaspoon of Bovril was flipped over the crisps, and the rabbit settled down to nibble.

"Foxy brought him in one morning, when he was small. I think Foxy knew we liked curiosities. Inky's remained here ever since. He chases away ordinary grey rabbits, being a bit of a race-purist, I fancy."

He put the kettle on the crook.

"How is Phillip? And the other children? Sit down, and tell me all the latest. How is Laura, is she happy with 'Buster'?"

"Why not go out and sit by the cedar tree?" suggested Beth. "I'll bring out the tea-trolley. No help needed, thanks, I can manage."

And sitting in the shade of the cedar's dark horizontal branches, while ring-doves coo'd among distant oaks and beeches, they enjoyed a tomato lettuce salad, with herb omelettes, radishes, and spring onions on tender green stalks. Then a plum cake, and farmhouse pot of tea in West Country style.

When Lucy and Beth went inside the house with the baby, Piers said to Melissa, "I suppose you'll see Phil while you're down there?"

"I hope to see Laura, too. I hear she's learning to glide, with 'Buster' as tutor. But my first objective is to finish my advanced course of Diaphany, under Caspar Field."

"Archie Plugge was here the other day. Apparently his boss sacked him. Archie had all sorts of tales about the place, some of which, when drunk I suppose, he 'leaked' to the reporters. I know nothing about Caspar Schwenkfelder, or Field as he now apparently wants to be called."

When she did not speak, Piers went on, "Archie said something about Phil's sister, now living at Lynmouth, but refusing to see Phil, or was it the other way about. I couldn't really understand what Archie was saying, he was economising on his usual tipple, surgical spirit. Asked if he could stay here. I'm afraid we hadn't a room ready."

"Is Phillip writing?"

"I gathered not. Archie had a story of some local complications, but then again I couldn't quite make out the details."

Lucy had told Melissa that there had always been trouble between Phillip and Elizabeth. With complete belief in Diaphany, she decided to ask Lucy, later, to take her with her when she went to see her sister-in-law.

When they were on the road again, Lucy said, "Piers is all right at last, thank goodness," as she thought contentedly that she would soon be seeing the boys; and on the following day, meeting

Rosamund at Minehead, from her school in Berkshire.

Meanwhile, the idea was that she and Melissa should stop the night at Molly's, and go on the next day to Shep Cot, leaving Melissa on the way at Oldstone Castle.

Melissa believed that Diaphany was the only way to free the spirit, to bring light to the darkness of a torn and revengeful post-war world filled with neuroses and despair.

And while they moved east across the moor she was thinking. If only Phillip will believe that Diaphany is in line with all he has written—a means to free the spirit! Dear, dear Phillip, you have revealed to others the true way, but cannot heal yourself—without my help.

Melissa in her bedroom at Oldstone Castle: late afternoon shadows slanting to the east: the open window of the bedroom looking upon small sloping fields divided by stone banks: open moor beyond, rising to the sky.

At first, she had felt a great loneliness coming from the moor, which had drawn her to walk on the lower slopes where heather, ling, and dwarf furze with its dark yellow flowers were hot in the sun. The only living things she saw were rock-pipits, drab little birds of the wilderness: nothing else, no moving distant figure of man or dog.

Upon returning, she felt mournful, and went upstairs to lie down in her bedroom. There, upon her bed, she read Phillip's editorial in *The New Horizon*, and thought that among those lost legions were her two brothers, killed in the Second World War. And lying there, she became aware of the scent of honey. Nigel had kept hives: could it be—Bees were passing the window. She got up to watch them. The air held a ground-swell of almost imaginary vibration: probably a secondary honey-flow to the hives within the walled garden. Molly had said that the July rains, followed by sunshine, had brought new blossom to the ling and the bell-heather.

While she stood there, a shadow moved across one of the distant small fields, then over another, silently sweeping across stone-walling, to be lost in dark brown heather of the incult moor. Looking up, she saw a glider about to bank for a turn.

The sail-plane seemed to pause in flight before going towards the sun. High in the sky above it, hung a fleece of grey cloudlets reminding her of the dapple on her nursery rocking horse. In her mind she saw her brothers, Giles and Nigel, wagering with bullseye sweets, who could move Dobbin on his stand around the nursery floor without upsetting. The picture dissolved; giving way to lines of a poem by Walter de la Mare.

> And, like clouds in the height of the sky
> Our hearts stood still
> In the hush of an age gone by

Nigel. British War Cemetery, Bayeux. Three years since he was left with most of his platoon in the long grass of a Normandy *bocage* during the breakout at Falaise. She read again the last part of *The Lost Legions*, printed in the magazine lent to her by Miranda.

A light-play, as of sun on August leaves,
A height-soft moan, wooden intermittent rattle,
And, as the scrollèd conflict eastward weaves
Feelers drooping darkly out of battle.

Giles. R.A.F. Cemetery. Runnymede. Battle of Britain, September 1940, Biggin Hill.

Laura, now some miles away in Falcon One, was dazzled by reflected sunlight splayed upon the sea to the west. She was moving fast, at nearly a hundred miles an hour. Soon the glider was over the Atlantic. She saw diving birds sitting on the wrinkled sea far below, as she approached Lundy. A feeling of quiet sadness possessed her. It is always so, she thought, for those who reflect. The sun-god is going down to his grave. The genes of innumerable forebears speak through the poets.

> Comrade look not on the west :
> 'Twill have the heart out of your breast;
> 'Twill take your thoughts and sink them far,
> Leagues beyond the sunset bar.
>
> Oh lad, I fear that yon's the sea
> Where they'll fish for you and me,
> And there from whence we both are ta'en,
> You and I shall drown again.
>
> When you and I are spilt on air
> Long we shall be strangers there;
> Friends of blood and bone are best,
> Comrade, look not on the west.

"I shall look on the west, old Father Housman!" she shouted as the mercury fell.

It had been a day when her thoughts had turned perpetually from the visible to the unseen world—to the cosmos perceived from within, that world wherein the Imagination works to create the visible.

"O God," she said aloud. "What am I doing here, in this contrived image of a bird! I am not a bird, I am a woman. I must be loved or I don't want to live!" She became hysterical. "Blood of my blood, bone of my bone, where are you? Where are you, my bloody, bony comrade? The bed of blood and bone is best, you tell us; but what sort of a bed did *you* lie upon, old Father Housman? Your thoughts gnawing the image of that undergraduate love-of-your-life who went into the Indian Army and left you alone on the banks of the Cam? Is there ease for you, where you now lie, wearing the turning globe, my Shropshire Lad that never was?"

It is best to be beyond the sunset bar, she thought, as she turned back. But where could she go, when she returned?

Far below, gulls assembled on the sands were seed-pearls. As she watched, the pearls were scattered by a running speck; pearls sprouted wings and were flying low over waves to their roosts upon cliff-ledges of the two rocky arms enclosing the bay. The speck-like dog then raced, apparently, to its master, walking on the sands. Could it be Phillip? Could she land on the sands beside him? How was the tide?

A cohort of black swifts moved, screaming, past the glider. The birds began to ring above her, she could just hear their whistling above the hiss of air flowing over her own aluminium sails. She thought of the poem in Phillip's magazine by the dead pilot. O, she could have loved that boy!

> And when the swift floats high
> On molten tide of sunset, silently
> Together in the meadows do we lie
> But never wed shall be . . .

A longing to see Melissa came upon her. Lucy with her children had come out of the water-lift ascending the steep rocky face to Lynton that morning, and they had had coffee together. Lucy told her that Melissa was at Oldstone Castle. And so that afternoon, having climbed on a thermal from Porlock marshes,

Laura had sailed over the castle on a flight to the sea, into the setting sun.

Now she was set for the return—eager to see Melissa, to drink ale together in the Sun Inn. The altimeter registered five thousand feet. If she met with no disturbances she would be able to reach the launching meadow in one gradual descent.

A slight wind was now moving from land to sea, by which she gained another five hundred feet in a series of spirals before putting down the nose five degrees for a straight course. Thus it was that Melissa, a little over twelve minutes later—for Laura now had an air-speed of nearly seventy miles an hour—saw a head looking over the edge of the cockpit of the glider and a hand waving. She waved back. Molly had told her who the pilot was; and both girls felt an inner warmth that they had something to look forward to.

It is such a beautiful day, Phillip said to himself, as they walked through the wood on the path beside the East Lyn river. Sunshine glinted above the branches of trees, whose leaves echoed dreamily the sounds, varied and gentle, of water and rock. The smooth contented gliding over stones deep bedded below the surface, nothing to disturb the water-flow : little quarrels under roots, water returning in eddy, unable to leave a query, a question, a quarrel over rights—water must move on, oak-root must stay, bubble, bubble, toil and trouble : reinforcements come in freshets down from The Chains, but no change, the talking went on as before during days of low summer level. Froth gathered, slowly revolving; water had no patience, although in time water always wore away every stone, shifted every rock, undermining every dam and weir and tree that stood in its way.

But generally in summer much of this wilfulness of being never at rest is abated. Yet water is ever on duty; it dies when it does not move, dying without the bubbles of turbulence from which it absorbs oxygen to nourish all life under its surfaces, from plant and shrimp and limpet to small fish and thence all the way up the aqueous scale to the lordly salmon born in nearly all the three score headwaters of the Lyn. There the alevin is hatched—right up under The Chains, there it poises itself with head upstream while yet its yolk-sac is hardly absorbed, watching, watching water ahead . . . growing to be a parr, with brown trout markings; and in May of the second year of its life it changes to a coat of silver scales for its journey down to the sea, no longer than a man's hand: to return after a year or two of rich ocean feeding, the length of a man's arm.

For if salt ocean is the Great Mother from whom all life has sprung, fresh water is the Nurse entrusted to nourish life within her wanderings and around her wave-lapped margins.

I am so happy, said Lucy to herself as the family wandered along the path above the East Lyn, on the way to Watersmeet, where a lesser stream joined the river, both hurrying to the sea. They were exploring. Lucy, Laura and Melissa walked together; while Peter, Rosamund, David and Jonathan were way ahead with the delightful new cousins, Miranda, Imogen and Roger, looking at all this wonderful new country with bright eyes, eager faces, and laughter.

Behind the three women walked Phillip, carrying an old army valise on his back, in which, like a papoose, baby Sarah was standing up, supported under her arms by straps out of which she tried continually to jump, in order to join the boys and girls far away under the beechen trees whose green leaves glittered at the top. He divined her feelings, and called a halt, to release a little white occasional quadruped.

They rested in the dappled light-shadows by the meeting of waters, Phillip saying to Miranda, "Here Shelley may have sat, and sailed paper boats down on the surface, with messages of hope."

"Did Harriet, his first wife, drown herself when he left her for Mary Woolstoncroft, Cousin Phillip?"

"I don't really know, Miranda. Both were very young, little more than children."

She sat unspeaking until he rose saying, "It is a wonderful picnic, Lucy, thank you all for such a lovely time. I must get back now and work, you do understand, don't you?"

"Of course, my dear!" exclaimed Lucy. "You must do just what you want to do."

Rosamund said, *"Do* stay, Dad!"; David said, "We do want you to stay, honestly, Dad, don't we, chooky?", to Jonathan who replied, "If he wants to write, he must go!"

Baby Sarah cried when he walked off; Miranda seemed not to have noticed his going as she knelt on the bank and peered down to see her own dark eyes staring up at her.

Chapter 21

ENTER PEREGRINE

The three Bucentaur children Miranda, Imogen, and Roger were having a final romp with the goats, which soon were to leave for a wide and open valley west of Lynton as a gift from their father. The animals were tethered on a long picket line, while the children played a variant of the game known as French Cricket; King Billy, patriarch of the herd, had a picket to himself; he was liable to act ferociously when free, being at what Molly declared to be the dangerous age. The old goat was frustrated; he wanted to join in the game, but his nylon tether had proved uneatable. An additional irritant was the free presence of Capella, who was attempting to run off with the red leather ball in her mouth.

In past days, all goats had been free to join in the children's games, which then became a sort of mad circus. Capella was the best ball-snatcher, bearing it away in her mouth, pursued by goats and children. The game caused so much laughter that Miranda had to bend down again and again, gasping while she spread fingers over her face at the sight of King Billy jumping about in a rage.

Watching the fun from her bedroom window, Molly told herself that Anda was still only a child, and that there was nothing serious between her and Phillip, who was surely only a substitute for paternal admiration and affection which every young girl needed for a balance of her emotions. Yes, Anda was still a child. Molly felt happy; not only were Lucy and Melissa arriving that afternoon, but Perry as well.

Miranda was excited : at dinner she was to wear the Edwardian ball gown in which Fred Riversmill had painted her portrait in the early summer. Yes, when the girl's father was home again, all would be well ! It was going to be a wonderful Festival week, like the happy summers before the war.

The play had been vigorous for Miranda, after the strain of

school examinations; now she was feeling the reaction. What would Daddy think of her? What would he say? Would he be pleased with the portrait? Supposing he wouldn't allow her to keep Capella? And then the arrival of her father, driving his vintage Hispano-Suiza motorcar, caused her to bloom with happiness. She had, of course, the sense not to make any demands upon him until the right moment—

"Daddy" she called to him, as she was dressing for dinner, "may I have a word with you? I want to ask a favour. Please don't be angry."

"Why should I be angry with you, darling" he replied, going into her room, where she sat in an Edwardian chemise before the looking glass. "My word, you are a beauty!", as she continued slowly to brush her long hair.

He knelt down beside his daughter, putting his arms around her to kiss, lightly and rapidly, the forehead, eyebrows, bone of each cheek, and side of the neck; thence to the base where little curling hairs grew out of a soft skin so tender and exciting, before a final communication with the lips while the hand, slowly caressing, went between silk and collar bone to the flesh on one breast, while he whispered, "You're a beauty! I adore you, my sweet darling."

Miranda, a little confused and trepidant, found herself uttering words she had meant to reserve for a future moment. "Daddy may I keep Capella? She will be terribly miserable without us all here, I know she will."

"We'll see, darling, shall we?"

It was not long before Molly was wondering about her errant husband's attitude towards Miranda. She now had her own bedroom converted from a box room; and when late that night Peregrine went upstairs to kiss her good-night he remained so long that Molly trotted up to join them—to come upon him kissing the child's breasts like a lover, while her head was turned away. So she waited in her own bedroom, behind the open door, listening.

When Peregrine returned downstairs Molly went into the box room, to find Miranda lying quietly in bed, crying.

"Darling, what is the matter?"

"Daddy says he has promised *the whole herd* to the Council, and a gentleman can't break his word."

Incest in some landed families was not altogether unknown in former days of isolation in remote country houses almost feudal in their self-containment preceding the Great War. Papa stern and distant, Mama amiable but remote and punctilious; both frigid in the accepted moral code based on a strict Protestant religion and the law of entail. These conditions sometimes led to irregularities among the older female children of a large family still in the schoolroom, and sent, in long white frocks and white gloves, under big hats, always chaperoned by a French governess, to sedate parties in other houses in a waggonet in summer days, or the family coach at Christmas time with cockaded coachman and footman beside him, through narrow lanes and up slow winding hills to other houses lit up for festival.

In particular, Molly remembered the case of a housekeeper, long in service with Peregrine's Uncle Rollo—who boasted, among other exploits, that he had eaten a stone of bullock steak a week —but who nevertheless, could not face up to the housekeeper and dismiss her because she had found, and kept, not only *billets-douces,* but a pair of his monogrammed pyjamas left in the bed of a young married sister.

The inclination to incest, as an escape from Victorian inhibition, seemed to run in some suffocating families. And the next morning, when Lucy went on to Shep Cot, Molly decided to send Miranda to 'Buster'.

"We'll need every available square inch for the cricketers' wives, darling," she explained to her daughter. "In addition we'll require at least three bell tents for the unmarrieds, with camp-beds and blankets, and also a marquee, with trestle tables, and forms to sit on. We'll be twenty three in all. Goodness knows what they'll do for baths. They'll need them, the place reeks of goats."

Molly, Miranda, and Melissa drove into Minehead to hire the camping requisites for Cricket Week.

"As I said, we'll need every bed in the house for the married couples, so I propose to put the bachelors—there will be six of them—two to a tent in the ponies' paddock. The goats will be gone by then. That leaves five married couples, including your father and me, in the house. Goodness knows how we'll all be able to fit in."

"Why can't Imogen and I sleep in a tent, too?"

"The ponies might get entangled in the ropes, darling."

"But what about the ropes of the cricketers' tents, if they're in the paddock?"

"The ponies don't know them, Anda. Supposing Bruno barged

into a tent for a lump of sugar in the middle on the night?"

"Bruno wouldn't. He'd come to my tent."

"Perhaps you could have your tent on the lawn. Goodness knows," Molly went on inconsequentially, disturbed by a vision of Peregrine creeping down in the middle of the night, "how we'll manage about baths."

"They can bathe in the sea."

"But the men can't shave in the sea, darling. The water is so sticky."

"Well, there's the swimming bath. That's fresh water."

"It's against the bye-laws to shave in a public swimming bath, surely?"

"They'll want latrines dug, too, Mummy."

"Darling, who will want them dug?"

"The bell-tent bachelors, of course."

"Very well, write down posts and hessian screens."

"In the Great War they used shell-holes. The ideal was to find one dry, fresh shell-hole, it was the only true life a tommy could get, Phillip told me, until he was either killed or wounded. Even then, at Passchendaele he would lie out alone, and die a lonely death—" She hid her face in her hands.

She is in love with Phillip, thought Melissa as she put her arm round the girl. Molly stopped the motor, a large black Daimler known as The Hearse.

"What odd things you two have discussed, darling."

"The realities, mother dear, which are the basis of true history. It was the only privacy a soldier in the line could get, to be alone with the sky."

"I can sympathise with that, Anda."

They went on down to Minehead. There, when Miranda had gone to buy a stamp at the post office, Molly said "Of the three children, Anda is the one who needs *shape*, if you understand. She's very intelligent and impressionable, and has too much to lose. The older she gets, the more complicated she appears to be. Usually gels grow out of their green sickness, but Anda—" She sighed.

Melissa wondered if Molly's reticence was a cloak to hide Phillip. For Miranda had talked, talked, talked to her about him: what he hoped to write—how he might begin—what form the novel should take—all autobiography to be transmuted by what Keats called The Imagination—

Miranda returned with the stamp. "I must have left my letter on my dressing table! I can't find it in my bag!" They searched in the car: no letter. Later, when Molly had gone to the dentist, Miranda said to Melissa, "Do you mind if I speak about Cousin Phillip?"

"Do, my dear."

"The letter was to Cousin Phillip, asking him if I had done anything to offend him. You see, he needs help."

"In his work, you mean?"

"Yes, Cousin Melissa. He's read to me all his war diaries which he kept while at the front, and wants to use for his novels. He's got whole rows of Great War books at Shep Cot—German and French as well as English, including official histories of all the belligerents, for he says his novels must be wider and deeper in scope than his own very limited experiences. I've never heard or read anything like the battle scenes, and also those behind the line, Cousin Melissa. Only, you see, he daren't start writing until he can see his way clear ahead for several years. I did so want to help him, as soon as I left school, but lately he has shut himself away, and during the last term he didn't write at all except only once, saying I must concentrate on my exams."

She turned away her head, then turned again to look into the older woman's face. "Are you sure you don't mind my unburdening myself to you like this, Cousin Melissa? I hope it isn't 'blowing back smoke in other peoples' faces', as Grannie would say."

"No, of course not, Miranda. I *do* understand, and I'm interested in all you feel you can confide in me."

"Phillip sees good in everyone, Cousin Melissa. He's not competitive, like most men are. That's a defect in life, he says, but a quality necessary in an artist. Fred Riversmill says he's like Turgenev, seeing all sides of a question, so that some people think he's not quite all there. Others think he is a fool, who refuses to see any evil in fascism. Of course he does, and did, but many opponents of fascism were just as bad in other ways during the war. And before the war, the self-righteousness of 'the intellectuals', Fred Riversmill says, led them to neglect the frightful social conditions at home, all the slums and unemployed people and starving little children—"

Miranda bowed her head, hiding her face in her hair.

"Molly! Why has my elder daughter gone to stay with 'Buster' as soon as I arrive?"

"To make a little more room for the cricketers, my dear."

"But the other children are remaining here."

"They won't take up any room. They can share a tent on the lawn."

"I asked particularly because, while in the Lynton club, I heard someone who looked like a boiled owl in spectacles, and obviously didn't know who I was, talking about a writer to whom Miranda as well as other women, pay regular visits."

"Didn't 'the someone' tell you that I also 'pay regular visits' to Phillip Maddison—a connexion of ours—he married my Cousin Lucy Copleston? Cousin Phillip is as honest, and as clear, as the day."

"I didn't get that impression from Humbert Tarr, who came in later. When I asked him who this chap Maddison was, he told me he was a fascist with none too savoury a reputation."

"The Brig is the last person to talk about that!"

"Anyway, I wouldn't trust any man with Miranda."

"But Phillip is *not* 'any man'. If anything, he's a little too ascetic."

"They're usually the dark horses."

"Anda has nothing to fear from Phillip. She's got plenty of sense—more than you think perhaps."

"What exactly does that mean?"

He took an envelope from his pocket. "Read this! I happened to find it lying on the stairs and considered it my duty to open it."

Molly read the letter, and put it in her handbag.

"Anda's generation is different from ours, Perry. They are much more serious, for one thing."

"Miranda is hardly a 'generation'. She hasn't come out yet, she's still in the schoolroom. And I will not have my daughter talked about! Certainly not in that club as it is today. Anyway, where there's smoke there's fire. People only want to know others for what they can get from them. She mustn't see that chap again. Will you support me in this?"

"Very well. Now I must get on with my work, if we're to be ready for your Crimson Ramblers."

Peregrine went down to be among his own sort at the Polo Club. It was empty. England has gone to pot, he told himself; and went on to 'Buster's' to give his daughter a talking-to.

Breaking away from the partly maintained social façade of the 'twenties, Molly Gildart, *débutante*, had 'kicked over the traces' with others of her young London friends, to the distress of the pre-1914 *regime*. Peregrine Bucentaur had shared in the post-war dissolution of those who had been just too young in 1918 to take part in the Great War. Based on escapist excitation, the Bucentaur-Gildart marriage had not been a success. Inevitably Peregrine had gone his own way. His absences, while regretted by Molly, were a relief to her. Perry had a limited imagination; while she was musical, 'adoring', as 'too, too wonderful', both opera and ballet. She had her being in the works of Mozart, Wagner, Beethoven, de Falla and the Russians—all lumped together by Peregrine as 'a ghastly din'.

Peregrine was the elder of two sons. This absence of any feeling for the poetry of the human spirit was in-born; it simply wasn't in his blood. He took after his father, a double reason for his mother's dislike. So from the early years the mother had disliked her first-born. She had tried to avoid this dislike, but never succeeded in overcoming an aversion for the child. It had an instinctive origin. She had submitted to her husband, who had exercised his marital rights, or rites, without any attempt at courtship, even of a lascivious kind, during the honeymoon. The nearest he got to any kind of communication with his bride was when, to end a period of boredom during the honeymoon when the Casino at Monte Carlo was shut one Sunday evening, he said, "How about coming upstairs and attending to the needs of nature, what?"

It was that invitation that had preceded the conception of Peregrine—the traditional name of the heir to the manor of Brockholes St. Boniface. This property had been acquired by the Crown, otherwise Henry the Eighth, during liquidation of the monasteries with the help of a lawyer called Thomas Cromwell. One of Cromwell's myrmidons, an adventurer from Venice who was not above murder, had been awarded the manor in 1540. The arriviste Bucentaur had practised flattery at Court : praised the Royal musical compositions : paid tribute with a coachload of looted paintings by foreign masters—thus an honourable exchange among greater thief and lesser thief.

There was, however, a covenant with the copyhold : a score of pickled and smoked brock hams payable annually to the Court; these to be stuck with cloves and roasted under a baste of sugar. The hams of brocks, or badgers were an especial delicacy obtained from the 'antient holes or holts' tunnelled into the hillside wood known as Grete Bere.

If Peregrine's mother had disliked him, while showing a marked preference for her younger son, his father made no bones about the misfortune to himself in having to put up with such an heir : one who was, in fact, exactly like himself. So the unwanted elder son had been forced to excel at games and all field sports : as it were to turn himself inside out—an extravert as the saying in the 'twenties ran—by fully entering upon an outside world wherein he had been capped for cricket (being an outstandingly good bowler) and on the football (soccer) field, a half-back who could be relied upon to break-up an advancing line of forwards by a technique of hacks, trips, and bargings. Further, in another direction, he had exploited the admiration of small boys for their usefulness in *le vice anglais:* an unnatural twist due to the selfish stupidity of his male parent.

Peregrine—the once heir to great possessions—and a beautiful wife. The first blow had fallen when his father died within the five-year span required for the abrogation of death-duties. All the quarrels following the making-over of the estate to Peregrine—dissensions over points of estate management (for the old man never truly abdicated his place as head of both estate and family) had been in vain. Death duties required that two thirds of the land be sold. And it was a time when land values were the lowest for one and a half centuries.

To recoup, Peregrine tried farming some of what was left in hand of the Brockholes property. He lost money, for corn did not pay, nor did stock-raising, nor the ewe flocks traditionally used to restore fertility to the malting-barley lands of North Somerset.

Farming in the 'thirties was a mug's game, so Peregrine didn't so much get out as drop out. He tried to restore his fortunes by odd schemes, such as selling apple-trees by advertising in newspapers—'Get health and wealth by growing apples which Pomona Ltd. will buy from you at market value'. There was no market value for such apples : Peregrine knew that before he advertised his wares. He tried the same idea with mushrooms to be grown in suburban cellars. *Edible Fungi Ltd.* advertised for sale mushroom spawn mixed with dehydrated horse manure 'to be delivered in plain sacks'. A few months later, it was pointed out in the Bankruptcy Court that 'Edible Fungi' was hardly an attractive style and title for trading purposes.

By this time Peregrine was a marked man. A suave gentleman with pomaded hair persuaded him to buy a disused cannery in Cornwall (the pilchard shoals having declined) combined with a slaughterhouse where DOG? CAT? FOOD Ltd. could can portions of fish with those of old cows for suburban pets. (It was later, following disclosures in the Bankruptcy Court, that a scandalous weekly called *Keyhole* declared that Colonel Peregrine Bucentaur was like all professional soldiers, an addict of 'sado-masochistic-necrophilic practices, a hopeless worshipper of dead, dying, and miscarried small industrial concerns'. Anyway, the food-canning venture was doomed to failure before it started : no one, continued *Keyhole*, knew which tins were for dogs and what were for cats. 'The ex-squire of Brockholes St. Boniface Abbey in Somerset had gone bust on his little fanciful habits of tinned death-worship.'

Whereupon Peregrine riposted by buying up *Keyhole* and closing it down after one issue's blasting of the former proprietors, a trio of young writers. "That's put paid to that clap, anyway," he told his cronies at the bar of his St James' Street Club.

Peregrine's final bid to recoup was by hair pomade. Oddly, the idea had come from the first appearance of the gent who had been responsible for *Dog? Cat? Food Ltd:* to restore the illusion of youth to deciduous human scalps by a mixture of olive oil, honey and eau-de-cologne. He tried to get his Curzon Street hairdresser, Van Tromp, to stock it, without success. For *Fertility Pomard* attracted the wrong sort of hair, *viz* the bristles of flies, wasps and even bees crawling in summer upon senescent male skulls, the eyes in which stared wistfully at young women lying on the post-war sward of St. James' Park.

Thereafter, a soldier of misfortune, Peregrine lived up to his name—the Wanderer.

Lucy said to Melissa, "The trouble lies with Elizabeth, I think. She has always been a cause of unhappiness to Phillip."

"May I come with you when you go to see her?"

So Lucy took Melissa with her to Ionian Cottage. Half a dozen staring toy Pomeranian dogs scattered, fluffy jig-saw pieces, about the floors of kitchen and sitting room, barking with excitement for something new in their herded lives. Among them Elizabeth, also with staring eyes and pent-up spirit.

"Phillip let Aunt Dora die! She was lying frozen on her bed for weeks, and he never went to see her! He thought the will she had made, in his favour, still stood, you see! He wanted the money, and allowed her to die. He didn't know she had made a new will in my favour, otherwise he would have gone to see her."

Melissa saw a distracted woman.

"Aunt Victoria, his god-mother, refused to go to our father's funeral, well-knowing his ways. She called him 'the black sheep of the family'. He is ashamed of us. He hates me, he pushed me in the nursery fire when I was a toddler, because he did not want me, the second child, to replace him in our Mother's love!"

Lucy said, "It can be so difficult for the first-born, when another baby appears. The damage can be done in the first glance of a new baby in the mother's arms. Mothers didn't know, poor dears, in those days, what we know now."

"Oh, I don't believe in that Freudian Theory!" declared Elizabeth. "There is, after all, such a thing as heredity! Our father used to say that Phillip was a throw-back." Her voice became distraught. "He was a little coward when he was young, and always got Peter Wallace to fight his battles for him. Worse still, he used to *pick* quarrels with boys, and to get Peter to hold the boy's head under one arm and then to punch his face with his fist! He did it to a poetic boy, who used to come to see me, only to talk to me, and when he was found out, he told Father I had been lying in the long grass of the Backfield with him. from that day Father turned against me. It's true, every word of it! You ask, and see what he says! Who's that?", for the little dogs were yapping at the kitchen door.

"It is I," said the voice of Phillip, when the clamour of tongues had ceased. "My dog Bodger won't hurt your Poms. May I come in?", as he walked to the open door of the sitting room, and standing there, said, "What Elizabeth has just said is true about my early days."

"Not only the early days, but *now!*" cried Elizabeth. "The excuse you wrote to me for not going to see Aunt Dora—I have kept your letter! was that all the roads were blocked after the blizzard. They were at first, until they were cleared. You never went to see if she was all right, did you? Had I known, I would have come down to be with her! I meant to, but we were snowed up in Dorset, the weather was simply awful, the electricity was cut off for days, the lines were down in the village. Then electricity was rationed, and I had to buy candles, but the shop rationed them, and soon they were all gone!" She turned to Lucy. "Look at him, staring at me like that! He knows it's the truth! And he has been seen lying with a schoolgirl in the long

grasses on Exmoor! Somebody saw them there, and told me!
Get out of here! He's only come to make trouble! He'll kill me!"
she appealed to Lucy. "You tried to divorce him, you know what
he is!"

When Phillip had gone away, and the excited dogs were
gathered about her, she said, "He upset you, didn't he, my darl-
ings?" Then to Melissa, "That one's Fawley Prince. He's
blind. That's why he stares so, he finds out what's going on by
smell and hearing. The neighbours said I should send him to the
vet., because he's too old to use at stud now, but I won't have
you put down, will I, Fawley Prince? There, he knows what I'm
saying! He always barks when I tell him that," and she gave the
old dog a rusk. "He's lost nearly all his teeth, but he'll suck it
until it turns to pap in his little mouth, won't you, Fawley Prince?"

The old dog growled when a bitch lowered her head and
moved towards the rusk. "He's too old, you see, and cares only for
food!", laughed Elizabeth, a little shrilly. "In the old days Fawley
Prince would let Fawley Princess have the bikky, wouldn't you,
darling?"

'Bikky'—*Bikky*—biscuit—enchanted word first issuing from her
father's bearded, smiling lips when life was warm for ever and
for ever.

Chapter 22

THE SUN IN VIRGO

And now that to which the children and their new cousins had so eagerly looked forward to was about to take place. Events of the Lynton Festival of the Arts included a tennis tournament; bowls; pony races; dressage on hunters; swimming races; cricket matches; and on the meadow across the river, a Parade to choose a Beauty Queen.

In addition, for the cultured—a minority which Osgood Nilsson declared to be non-existent—there was an afternoon lecture on 'Lynmouth in Song and Story' in the Town Hall, and six evening performances, in the same place, of *Yeomen of the Guard*. The articled clerk had sent a letter to Mr. Osgood Nilsson inviting him to appear among the chorus in his maternal grandfather's Confederate General's uniform; but no written reply was expected.

For the small and immature, a Magician had been hired to produce, among other novelties, strings of flags out of an ear and a rabbit from a top hat.

The local inhabitants were not forgotten. There was Ye Olde Englishe Fayre, where prizes were offered for Guessing the Weight of a Fat Lamb, Climbing the Greasy Pole, and tugs-of-war between the regulars of various cider and beer houses. The Festival was to conclude with the Presentation Ceremony of the Brockholes St. Boniface Abbey herd of White Goats to the Lynton Urban District Council, followed by a cricket match between the home team, North Devon Savages, and Lt.-Col. Peregrine Bucentaur's Crimson Ramblers.

A Grand Festival Ball was to take place on this final night at the principal hotel, whither the entrants for the title of Beauty Queen were to be drawn, standing up in carts, by members of the Boys' Brigade. At 11.30 p.m. fireworks would officially end Festival Week; but many were looking forward to an unofficial Saturnalia afterwards which, generally speaking, would take place on the beaches, in motorcars, and under trees.

Lucy was in the caravan on the meadow below Barbrook, beside
the gently tumbling West Lyn, smiling happily to herself as she
glanced up from the pages of *Bevis* to watch Phillip playing with
Sarah, unaware that he was trying to focus his sight upon the
child's face, willing himself to be happy, to resist any weak
impulse to tell Lucy his fears. Bringing the child to her,
he said, "Well, I suppose I must go back to the Cot and
do some work. Au revoir, I'll see you tomorrow. Come on,
Bodger!"
The old dog, which had been tied to a tree lest it go too near
Sarah, leapt around and gave a joyous bark. It had developed
a habit of scraping its behind on the grass. Phillip, on taking it
to the vet. had been told that the cause was not worms; but a
developing cancer of the anus.

Melissa in her room at Oldstone Castle, was thinking, If I can
win his sister Elizabeth's confidence, she might agree to be
processed; and so bring to the foreground of her mind the
suppurating thoughts of a lost child, longing for a father-love
that at adolescence had been withdrawn; and progressing from
being clear to find herself able to accept objectively that it was
a common human fault to transfer one's own guilty feelings to
the image of another.
She must see Elizabeth the next day : it was imperative that
the blockage be cleared : and thereby, Phillip freed of self-
mortification.

Laura looking at the Brig, feeling tenderness for him, seeing him
as a little boy lost as she kissed his bald head as though he were
her baby. He was crying; he, who had never surrendered in war,
yielding all his life to her care as he thought weakly from the back
of his mind. My little girl loves me, O God, my little girl loves me!

'Buster' Cloudesley in The Eyrie taking the Message bottle,
dropped into the North Atlantic by his father before he was
drowned, from a corner cupboard wherein it was kept with rep-
licas of the Victoria Cross, Distinguished Service Order with two
bars, Military Cross, and two French decorations, the Legion
d'honneur and the Medaille Militaire.
There were times when, feeling wan, he put the bottle on the

table beside him, and read the only letter he had received from either of his parents.

To the Honourable Hugh Carew-Fiennes-Manfred, c/o Messrs. Elkington and Elkington, Solicitors, Lincoln's Inn, London; from Manfred Lord Cloudesley, his father, now derelict in the North Atlantic, the sun setting on the second Day of January, in the thirty sixth and last year of his life. Whosoever finds this bottle, please deliver as addressed.

Engine breakdown, just before dawn this day, at 2,400 r.p.m. having just corrected course by S.S. *Empress of Britain*. The throttle control jammed or broke. I did my best to come to your mother and to you. I was working hard in New York, for all our sakes and thinking of the future. Now the future may be for you alone.

'Buster' closed his eyes, and breathed deeply. After resting in thought, he read on, although he knew the words by heart.

If my desire could be fulfilled, then believe that I am always your friend, even as you will be the friend of your dear children. One thing I would have you believe, if so you may with truth to yourself, and that thing I do know to be true in this the probably last phase of my life:

Fight neither in deed nor in thought, be calm within thyself, act only to balance mind with body, see thyself as the sun to the flesh. In hope and in trust of the sun I bid you farewell, and through you all the friends of this the earth; and in farewell I do but greet you, yet impersonally, in the laughter of the sun, the servant of the Father of Man beyond time and space.

'Buster' never quite knew what these words meant, but he had a rough idea what his father was driving at. He had meant well, anyway, although perhaps he hadn't been the best of husbands to his mother. But by God he'd had guts, not only physical guts, but to fight against his own weakness.

Old friends of Manfred Cloudesley had told 'Buster' that he had seemed too frail for the touch life of a Guardsman on the Western Front, never quite hitting it off with the other officers in the Regiment. Not much good as a footslogger; but in the air, after a period of caution, and avoiding all possible flamboyance, he had made the grade. He had been a Guest of Honour, his host being Herman Göring at the Richthofen Club, Berlin, after the war.

"When would you care for supper, my lord? A cold collation is in the dining room."

"Thank you Mornington. Where are the others?"

"Lying down in their rooms my lord, resting."

"I'll wait for them to come down. Do go out and see the sights, if you care to."

"I thought of going to see the amateurs in the Town Hall, my lord. I had a season with the D'Oyly Carte company at the Savoy, in the old days. It will be interesting to see what the locals make of it. I understand the orchestra consists of one piano, one drum, one fiddle, and what looks to be what Thomas Hardy called a serpent, borrowed from the local museum."

"We may join you later."

"If I may say so, as a spectacle it should have its moments, my lord."

'Buster' put the bottle back in the cupboard, and went on the terrace, to look up at the sky like the breast-feathers of a slain flamingo. "He hath outsoar'd the shadow of our night" he said to himself imagining Shelley writing his threnody *Adonais* on the death of Keats. *Buona Notte* : Francis Thompson conjuring up from the vasty deep the dying voice of Shelley. But what written tribute have I paid to you, my father?

'Buster' was still sitting by the cypress tree on the terrace when he felt an electric chill passing down his neck to his spine. He touched the stone coping of the terrace, it was still warm. No leaves moved on the trees. He wetted a finger, held it up to determine the direction of any moving air. A normal slight loss of temperature all round the finger. No wandering night breeze. The air over land had the same temperature as that over the sea.

The spinal shiver was as though lifting the short hairs above the neck. Was that someone standing in front of him, a dim etching of Byron? My father, he thought, my father : the portrait by Orpen shows you to be on the small side, with Byronic shape of head, and something of Robert Burns in your face. O God, I wish I could remember my father. It all went from me when I bought that packet in the Reichswald . . .

'Buster' breathed deeply, respiring as slowly, to control emotion, to keep his mind calm as he went inside to switch on the B.B.C. news and weather report.

"A ridge of high pressure remains stationary over the North Atlantic east of the Azores, extending across Europe, and is likely to maintain itself for the next forty-eight hours . . ."

The image of his father persisted. He tried to rationalize the idea of the essence of personal survival. There was Hoyle and his theory of a self-regenerating universe; even a falling raindrop created electrical energy by friction : an ion of life which might help to create a portion of flower or flesh.

According to Caspar, the electric encephalograph could record the brain's pulses and recessions of energy; the mind was part of the physical tides of the salt, estranging sea. The instrument revealed harmony, dissonance, repulsion. The mind's despair when a deep-seated nervous inhibition was approached was indicated in a zigzagging graph, of cerebral cells grinding through temporary obfuscated memory; brain-cells in disconnection through fatigue following stress. The extremity of despair bordered on insanity : settled despair due to chronic lovelessness; stalagmites hanging upon the sick mind, with its four miles of veins erratically carrying turbid blood to the millions of cells . . . an entire universe in miniature was built-in with every wretched little animal created on the planet, to be held together only by love—Mahler's *Das Lied von der Erde*.

What a way to die! The stricken Mahler, warned of imminent death, sitting down to compose his swan-song—the lyrical joy of nature, the enduring love of Earth Mother! Mahler went out, not with a bang, not with a whimper, but in high faith and gratitude!

The icy feeling returned behind his neck : the psychic shiver. Had Father come to him, from the salt estranging sea? A falcon, each flight feather set with barbs, barbules, and barbicells, could find its way by *feeling* across hundreds of miles of alien land and sea and land, drawn in spirit by love to its native eyrie, its home, its base of life. My father and I are one, he said to himself, and going to the gramophone, put on *Four Last Songs* by Richard Strauss, and sat in his armchair, eyes closed; imagining the composer to be making his adieux to the golden threads of his life, calling up the spirit of Wagner among them. He sat still while the record ran off the last grooves and getting up, tears dripped from his closed eyes. I must rescue Hess, old flier on the Western Front, and your friend, Father.

Peter paddling in his canoe around the small harbour, taking first Jonny then David as crew. When they had learned balance, not to shift their weight, Phillip let them go by themselves; but

only when the tide was coming in. "You have a go, Dad" said
Peter.

So Phillip went out by himself, sending joyfully the light canvas-
and wood craft through the water with alternate thrusts of a
two-bladed paddle.

Why hadn't he returned to the sun before?

The sea lay azure smooth under solar brilliance. Upon the high
moor cotton-grass was in flower, as though in pattern with the
cirrus cloudlets remaining unmoving in the height of the sky.
Lucy was happier than she had been for years. She was living as
in the summers of peace she had known when she was a girl, and
in the early years of her marriage to Phillip. Dear Phillip, he had
done splendidly for them all.

Of the children, Jonathan was particularly happy. His father
had given him for his birthday his 7-foot, 2-ounce fly-rod, with
a box of dry flies—Blue Olive, Palmer, Red Spinner, and other
whisked-and-feather-winged Beauties, as Jonathan thought, gloat-
ing over them when he was not making his way up the Lyn, to
cast horizontally and thus to avoid branches overhead, and to
drop his fly lightly on run or eddy, watching that the fly did not
drag on the enamelled silk line greased so that it should float.
Fishing with dry fly in rapid, gloomy water needed a quick eye
and wrist, for the Lyn, like all rivers large or small, flowing fast
or gliding through level lands, was a confluence of many currents
moving at varying speeds.

A fly floating with wings cocked aided by a delicate touch of
grease, must resemble a living fly tremulous after a noon surface
hatching, following its swim up as a nymph and now riding down
upon the water-flow in a new and strange element of air. Let the
line but drag its fly askew, even under water, and no trout would
remain within its subaqueous stance, but dart downstream as
from menace. And so with the adult fly in early evening—its life-
span being but one day—when dropping her eggs just clear of
the surface—the angler, with his tapered gut cast, must send her
likeness to drop lightly, as though spent after love—when *snap!*
the fish has leapt to take the lure.

Jonathan cast his fly so that it touched the surface, and rode
down rocking lightly on the midstream current of his choice; or
perhaps he cast over to the farther bank, holding high the rod
point against drag . . . staring cat-like, he saw a dark neb appear
momentarily in no more than a petty rocking of water under the
shadow-dark Glen . . . with a wrist-flick he drove home the hook,

to wind-in swiftly to keep the pull on his line steady. The trout dashed downstream, the boy let-out line to be carried swiftly in a loop below the fish, which, feeling the pull from behind, went upstream. Now to reel-in the slack, keeping gentle pressure by the curved split-cane, and it was wound in, the net slipped forward from behind, as Dad had told him, and there was his first trout!

"Mother, I've caught my first trout! Look, it pulls down to that notch just below the quarter-pound—to five ounces!" Jonathan held it up on the spring balance. "Put it on a plate in the larder at once, before a fly smells it. The box larder under the caravan I mean, where no flies can get in through the gauze. Cor, I what-you-call like this place! I'll get some more for supper!"

Jonathan caught four more on that fly, and proudly gave them to Lucy.

That evening Lucy had a caller, announcing herself as a friend of Phillip. "I'm Rosalie, the wife of Osgood Nilsson. How happy you all look! Is that your little girl by the stream? She won't fall in and be swept away, will she?"

"I don't think so," replied Lucy, colouring. "Jonathan has tethered her to a peg in the ground."

"I can't see any rope."

"Oh, it's green nylon cord, one can't see it very clearly. It's well short of the river bank."

"What a good idea, my dear. Do you ever go down bathing on the beach?"

"It's a little difficult, with the steep hill. My little car won't take it, I'm afraid."

"I'd be only too pleased to take you down, Lucy. May I call you Lucy? I'm afraid I can never be formal for more than a minute! Yes, do let me take you down, my dear—"

Lucy and the children (with Melissa, who had walked down) spent the following afternoon on the grey bouldered beach of Lynmouth. They looked in on Elizabeth, who seemed surprised that anyone should want to see her. She kept looking at Sarah, and was delighted when the child wanted to climb on her lap, attracted by a cameo brooch on her blouse—one of Dora's Victorian relics. Once upon the lap, the baby wanted the brooch.

"So that's what you came for, is it?" said Elizabeth, the softness gone from her voice.

"All children are acquisitive—and inquisitive," said Lucy. "You should have seen Rosamund when she was that age."

"Yes, I suppose so," replied Elizabeth, looking dejected. She wanted to be liked for herself.

The boys played with the little dogs. "May we take them for a walk, Aunt Elizabeth?"

Again, hesitation : they wanted the dogs, not her.

"Won't you join us on the beach?" Lucy suggested.

At the end of an afternoon in the sun, by a gentle sea, Elizabeth felt herself to be happy again. How foolish she had been to think she might fall down in a fit if Phillip came near : that he had been telling people all about her past life! What nice children they were, so well-mannered, addressing her as Aunt Elizabeth and talking as though they had known her all their lives.

And what a pleasant young woman Melissa was! She took such interest in her little dogs, asking how they had been fed during the war, if she exhibited them, and where. Happy in sunshine, Elizabeth felt that if Phillip appeared suddenly, she wouldn't mind in the least. Phillip, when he wanted to, could be a pleasant companion. However, he didn't turn up, and in a way Elizabeth felt slight disappointment.

"Come home, all of you, to my cottage and have tea! We can buy some cakes on the way!" Fortunately there were sugar'd buns, with currants, too, in the shop, although both these things were still rationed. Lucy had a pot of honey, one of several dozen she had brought from the farm, and with margarine, the split buns tasted delicious.

After tea the closet was an object of speculation between David and Jonathan, as to where the contents in the pan went when you pulled the plug.

"I reckon it goes straight into the river, with all those old motor-tyres, pots and pans and criggely old bikes. It's polluted, like Dad's river was, on the farm! So you oughtn't to try for sea-trout," declared David.

"Why should anyone want to pollute the river when there's a sewer pipe set in concrete going right down to the sea the other side of the Rhenish Tower on the quay?"

"It looks very old and rusty, and may be cracked."

"But Mr. Nilsson fishes for sea-trout, he ought to know."

"I won't eat any fish out of this estuary, 'bor!"

"But it's only compost, and salt will kill any germs."

"Not typhoid, not likely!"

The argument continued until a compromise was made. Jonathan declared he would buy a bottle of red ink, pour it into the pan, pull the plug and see if any tell-tale stain showed in the river. They borrowed some red ink from Aunt Elizabeth, pulled the plug, and running outside, peered into the rapid flow of water past the mossy boulders.

"There you are, no sign of red ink anywhere!"

"It may still be inside the pipe, so let's follow it down and see if it comes out of any cracks."

The pipe went into the wall of the quay, and reappeared on the beach. The tide was low, they slithered over slimy boulders.

"Ugh, it's pretty foul," declared David.

"It's only algae, you fool!"

David cried with a laugh, "Algae met a bear. The bear met Algae. The bear had a bulge. The bulge wasn't Algae, but crap!" He staggered about acting the clown as he leapt from one boulder to another, pretending to save himself from falling by tottering on to the rusty pipe, while screeching. "It will crack, it will crack!" Then he found an old broken umbrella amidst other village rubbish, and opening its ribs and tatters, did a balancing act on the pipe, to the amusement of children hastening down the beach to watch.

"Blast, we're having what you call some sport!" said Jonathan. Then they were all looking up to watch two gliders passing in straight flight three thousand feet overhead to the Porlock marshes.

Later, at supper, 'Buster' told Melissa that Laura, with Brigadier Tarr as passenger, had reached 18,000 ft., according to the sealed barograph.

That evening, on the way back to the Castle, Melissa called in to say good-night to Elizabeth, who greeted her with smiles.

"How nice to see you, Melissa!" said Elizabeth. "Come and have some coffee." Later, she said, "Why don't you stay the night? You'd be most welcome! I've got a spare bedroom, if you don't mind sleeping in the one my aunt died in, during that awful winter. She was frozen to death, you know. And Phillip never bothered to go to see her!"

Melissa listened for over an hour to the poor woman's complaints. The condition of Elizabeth was frontally adverse: attributing motives to Phillip which were her own motives. The weight of a deep-seated insecurity was the cause of an imbalance of lovelessness. It would take some time to approach the block which had estranged her, as all growth denied under a glacier.

When Elizabeth is free, Phillip will be free, she thought as she lay in her small room, hearing the sounds of flowing water, and the wind in the trees outside the open french windows. Water and air were playing on stone and leaf and branch in the wan light of a moon fretting above high cirrus clouds. She could not sleep, she floated in a reverie of the past, seeing a lean, dark-haired Phillip with the soft voice and delicate profile of one born in full harmony with life and its creative purpose : a gracious presence which, when his unbandaged eyes had looked at her in her grand-mother's hospital for wounded officers for the first time, she had felt to be the nicest man she had ever seen. And that feeling had remained with her ever since, with what frustration and sadness only a woman, who had always longed to have children by a man she loved, would ever know.

She lit the candle by the bed-head, and read over a letter she had received that morning at Oldstone Castle. She read half-way, and paused, sighed, and read no more; but took up her diary wherein she had copied from an old book a poem which she had altered in places to fit her own thoughts.

> When will my May come, that I may embrace thee :
> When will the hour be of my soul's joying?
> If I may come and dwell with thee at home,
> Thy shepcote shall be strowed with new green rushes;
> We'll haunt the trembling prickets as they roam
> About the fields, and beechen hedges;
> You have a skewbald cur to hunt the coney
> So we will live and love most bonny.
>
> But if thou wilt not pitie my complaint,
> My tear, no vowes, nor oaths made to my lost Beautie :
> What shall I do, but languish, faint, and die,
> Since thou seeth not my teares, and my soule's dutie;
> And teares contemned, all vowes and oaths must fail
> For when tears cannot, nothing can prevaile.

From subjective feelings, her mind moved to Phillip's vision, as revealed in his books, its confluence with Birkin's thought—both streams of thought flowing with Diaphany—the firm belief in the positive, creative evolution of man : service not *in vacuo*, as priests in their devotions, but an amalgam of creative science with the Christendom of tomorrow, which would fulfil and fortify Man's deepest aspirations. Eugenics must raise the general level of intelligence to a higher empathy, or Man would meet his doom through malevolent application of the strayed 'wonders' of science.

She blew out the candle, and lay in darkness, before moving the camp-bed on to the balcony beyond the french-window. She was now over the river, listening for the undertones of the stream below. Ripple-echoes were fading out, but to return : a fast flowing succeeded by a sudden lull, an individual gushing of water, subsiding to a quietness of following streams preparing to gather strength again as though to assault that certain large boulder immediately beneath the window, to push it seawards : a hollow pause of water breaking back in bubbles on a large mid-river rock.

Or were the splashing noises made by salmon, or large sea-trout, which had come into fresh water with the tide : the slashing tail-swirls of vigorous, clove-spotted silvery fish eager for spawning in the little waters of their moorland birth?

Perhaps the origins of the water-noises were deceptive, being echoes pulsing over the surface of the stream, and combining, as nodes of musical vibrations, to a sudden loudness? Water noises were coming direct from many echoing places—from boulders, from hollows of banks, washed-down tree-roots, leaf-masses, caught up on a particular stone in the shallows?

To these night echoes within the room, she listened. The river in its broken flowings and gushings upon its bed of shillet and boulder had a rhythm or recurrence of water-pulses. Every so often the water swilled surging into some miniature bay or backwater, and made a hollow, chuckling noise; and the same pulse of the river, a temporary gathering of the many streams, sent a wave of water lapping over a part-submerged boulder, causing an equal back-wash which in daylight had sometimes looked, to the boys and herself peering over the wall of the river, like the swirl of a large square tail—the familiar tail of salmon or its cousin the sea-trout.

Noises of water on stone flowed past her, and then through her, as the short hours of darkness ebbed away. She could not sleep. Had Phillip's Aunt Theodora listened in the same way, so that the vibrations of her *feelings* were recorded in the walls and ceilings of the cottage : the vibrations that were the spirit of a place, of human thoughts—the spirit of life, invisible and unheard, lying behind all movement, all friction which were of the forces of creation, of all terrestrial life?

Inevitably all came back to Phillip. Could she but bring Elizabeth and him together, it would release in him forces of creation, so that he would no longer feel frustration, but become whole again, and live in happiness, and serenity.

And lying there, Melissa felt a surety moving upon her ... and awakened into the light of day, feeling herself to be strangely remote, and not unhappy.

Early next morning she walked up to the Castle, to continue the interviewing of aspirants who wanted to take the first course of Diaphany. Caspar Field, the Principal, was wary of accepting an aspirant except for a trial period. It was not always easy to detect hysteria emanating, possibly, from some deepest block which, unrecognised, could upset other novices. Like the black witch of pre-radio villages, a psychopath could communicate a spiritual malaise to members of a community unaware of its origin.

Melissa was an esteemed disciple of Caspar Field. That morning, during the coffee break, he saw that she was a little *distraite*. They had known one another for almost a year, and shared a mutual esteem. Caspar was happily married, with four children, to a wife whose face, many said, seemed to shine.

"Problems?" he asked. Melissa looked at him; he knew she was hesitating lest she impinge on his work. "Come into my room, and have some coffee."

"I'm wondering if it's a case with me of 'Physician, heal thyself'," she began. "Can one be of real use to others when one is worried continually by a personal problem?"

"The poet wrote that he 'learned in suffering, what he taught in song', Melissa. At the some time, to do one's work properly, one must be clear. A surgeon—and surgery is necessary sometimes—with problems is liable to slip—"

"May I tell you my problem, or rather, dilemma? I don't think I can resolve it by myself. It's of long standing, or deep-seated : what one would call a block."

When she had told him he replied, "I think I know to whom you refer. I've seen him occasionally; and of late he has appeared to be not so much preoccupied, as a writer is by nature of his work, but withdrawn."

A flight of fighter-bomber aircraft thundered over the castle. When they had passed away he said, "Soon the whole of mankind will be beset by material vibrations kyanizing the entire psychic force of this planet. The next few decades will be critical. The services of all writers, poets, musicians, and spiritual leaders of all races and creeds must come together in the services of Diaphany, the power of transmitting Light."

The weather being so fine that evening, such a sky of the Field of a Cloth of Gold, Melissa decided to walk up the lane and across the common to Shep Cot. She arrived as the colours of the sky reminded her of Turner's *Fighting Temeraire*.

Phillip was trying to build up a fire from the smallest beginning of one match, with which to enliven one spark on charcoal, then to blow it gently to a yellow, gem-like star; and having placed a second pennyweight of charcoal in the star-like flame, to add a wisp of dry grass, a leaf—and finally a pinch of broken larch twigs from a dead tree fallen in the plantation above Barbrook. The exquisite scent of larch smoke, redolent of boyhood summers and the chaffinch singing... Such child-like play with fire within a hide of little sticks would entrance him, sometimes for hours, adding stick to stick while staring into tiger-bright flames. Every fire must start with one match only—otherwise he would never be able to begin his novel-series.

Fire to Phillip was a friend: companion of frozen nights in a Flanders wood in 1914, by which he avoided frost-bite, while reliving days as a Boy Scout in Kent, always with his lone and familiar little fire, heating water in his billy-can or frying sausages in an old Boer-war collapsible pan.

Through the open casement Melissa saw the white-headed figure kneeling before the hearth. She tapped on the glass, the figure arose and came to the open door, saying, "Good evening!"

She thought that her face must be repugnant to him; he had not looked at her directly.

Divining her feelings, he kissed gently the scars on her cheeks. "That's what I know you by—the stigmata of a saint."

All she could think of saying was, "Are you sure I shan't disturb your work?"

"Oh, I'm not working. I suppose I've got what Freud called a complex and your man calls a block."

"Caspar Field is on the right track, Phillip. His philosophy is based on Blake and Jefferies."

"Yes, Laura told me about him. Also about your accident in India. You could not act otherwise than with magnanimity."

He put more sticks on the fire. Being dry, they soon flared. She sat on the sack before the hearth, saying "How good to see

BODGER OF GREAT SNORING is still with you! This sack, I mean. I saw it last seven years ago, in your Banyards cottage. You lit a fire in your room, and were anxious because there was no blackout curtain across your new wide window. Is this your dog?"

"Yes, called after the sack. Bodger didn't growl when you tapped on the pane. He knows what a person is at once. You have the stigmata of a saint," he repeated, touching the scars on one cheek. "You didn't wash your hands of that ruined Indian soldier."

He stroked her cheek with the back of his hand; instinctively, for a moment, she held the hand to her cheek.

"I'll make some tea."

He poured boiling water from the cast-iron kettle hanging from the lapping crook, into the teapot; and put three large logs on the fire. In flame-light he felt comfort; he sensed in her the same calm self-possession as of old; and taking her hand, laid it against his cheek-bone, holding it there while she turned to him, and said, with an unguarded smile hovering as though helpless upon him, "I love you."

These words made him feel estranged. He said, "I wish I didn't feel always so isolated, Melissa. I suppose all feeling is sublimated in me."

"That is how all artists feel, surely, when they are in the flow of creation?"

"When one is not writing regularly, the spiritual flow rots in one."

The tea warmed them.

"Phillip, I want to help you. May I ask questions?"

"Of course!"

"What is stopping you writing?"

"I suppose a general sense of loneliness and failure."

"Haven't you felt like that nearly all your life?"

"I started very young to draw away and live in my own world."

"From your parents?"

"Yes, and my two sisters."

"That's unusual. An elder, big brother—"

"They used to laugh at my feelings. In childhood my eyes easily brimmed with tears—"

"They do now!"

"May I give my reasons, even if they are camouflage?"

"Of course."

"I remember one reason, or rather cause. When the swallows were about to fly away one autumn, I felt it was summer's end, and I was desolate. I told them this while we were having breakfast. My younger sister pointed at my eyes and said 'Cry-baby, cry-baby!' She was, of course, merely imitating our father, for my being unmanly. In his Victorian eyes I was creepy-crawly, namby-pamby. My consequent evasiveness was a mark of degeneracy in his eyes."

"You resented your sisters' attitude to your tears?"

"Yes."

"But not your mother, who was gentle and sensitive, you once told me."

"I became offset from all at home, and lived in my own private world, giving my affection to wild birds. I was so happy, too, in the countryside, alone with my bicycle. Yet self-knowledge, as your Diaphanetic 'processing' reveals, cannot help, by itself, to replace what is lost—a natural spontaniety in love. I can love, in my head, any girl who attracts me, but I am stopped still, unlike most men, when, I suppose, I am expected to go further."

"Because you are afraid of being, in your father's word, 'unmanly'?"

"Not when I was adolescent. I could be 'manly' by allowing myself to feel triumphant towards a girl, if she were acquiescent. To pay her out, even to make her pregnant. That was a fine feeling!" He saw that she was biting her lower lip, and said lightly, "Proceed, O Diaphanetician."

"Do you still enjoy being cruel?"

"You asked me that eight years ago, on your twenty-first birthday, when you were having a bath at your old home. In fact you told me, then, that I was a sadist."

"Did I? So young? I must have heard the word somewhere, probably on my father's lips. You haven't answered the question."

" 'Am I cruel?' I don't think so. I have perhaps self-knowledge, and so remain as it were *in vacuo,* with a more or less chronically aching heart. Now have I 'processed' myself, as the much-derided Caspar would say? As though I were a breakfast food."

" 'Processed' means 'a method of scientific research', among other things. I wonder if I may ask you something rather personal?"

" 'Very well."

"You told me once you used to set fire to dry grass in summer, and then run away in terror, when you were a small boy. But why did you set fire to a wooden building soon after the Great War, and go to prison for it?"

"So that's what Elizabeth told you," he replied. "And did she tell you, also, that I tried to shoot myself, after returning from prison? Well then, you know all about me. Oh yes—I ran away in the light of the blazing windmill on Messines Ridge, during the battle on Hallowe'en, nineteen fourteen."

"I've tired you, Phillip, I'd better go." She took his hand. "I expect you want to rest."

"Must you go?"

"Do you want me to stay?"

"Of course I do."

"Oh darling, I do so want to help you! I knew why you weren't writing. I knew also that people wouldn't leave you alone up here. I guessed you were in thrall to Miranda. She is a sweet girl. And I knew, too, that while you remained alone you would never be able to sustain any prolonged imaginative work. The creative man, or woman, surely needs reassurance all the time, at least until one regains confidence by working, and discovering, so that one surprises oneself by what comes, and how it grows and builds itself up, to fulfilment, because one is increasing with true life. A creative writer gives so much out, yet he *gains* when he feels it is good, when it returns with compound interest, an increasing interest in what he is living in, and by. I learned a lot in India from the *gurus* I used to talk to."

"True-true-true," he said.

She cooked the herrings she had brought with her, for supper. They sat by the fire, talking with concealed restraint; and towards midnight, she dared to say, "It's rather late, may I sleep here?"

"Of course. I'll take you up some washing water from the kettle on the hearth." And leaving the can outside her door, said good-night, and went into his room, to sit on the bed for several minutes before beginning to undress. After lying uneasily in bed for some minutes, he felt that she was expecting him; and with a divided mind he got into bed beside her, feeling blank, devoid of desire; and fear, when she put an arm across his ribs.

He must do something, he told himself : be 'manly' (O God!) so he turned over and held her in both arms : but with no life flowing from him to her.

After an uneasy interval she said, "I must leave you for a while. Have you an electric torch?"

He felt under the bed and switched it on. While she was

going down the stairs he went to his own bed, to lie as though asleep when he heard her coming up the stairs; and remained still when she shone the torch for a moment upon him, before she went into the other room.

In the morning, when he took up a mug of tea she said "You were very tired last night, going off the moment your head touched the pillow, and snoring loudly!"

"Yes, I returned to my bed, otherwise you'd have had no sleep." He added, "I'm ashamed of my snoring."

"Everyone snores at times."

He sat on the bed; she drew him to her as he lay beside her, aware of her tenderness, her clarity, her simplicity—but feeling nothing more.

The day was already open and shining, though not yet six o'clock.

"I must go back to Ionian Cottage, Phillip. I'm staying with Elizabeth, she'll be wondering if I've fallen in the water last night, for I sleep on the balcony over the river." She touched his face, and said, "Why don't you look at me? Is my face simply awful?"

"It's my eye, Melissa. It can hurt suddenly, as though a vein or an artery in the ball somewhere gets swelled. You know how it feels when you get an eyelash sticking in a corner? Or as it used to feel, to me, when I *had* eyelashes. Mine got burnt out at the roots when mustard splashed my face. If you look closely, you'll see the scars on my cheeks—the skin came up in huge blisters—"

With shut eyes he yielded to her scrutiny, feeling again her tenderness as with finger-tip she traced the bones of his cheek and brow; followed by touch of lips upon one cheek; and seeing his smile, as gently took his head upon her breast, holding him thus until it seemed he was asleep. Then, withdrawing herself from the bed, slowly, making no sound, she dressed, and crept down the stairs, watched by Bodger on his sack before the hearth, one eye opened above folded paws. She stopped to pat him, and then, still watched by the eye, unlatched the door and entered the shine of the sun above the eastern line of the moor.

Phillip had not been asleep. When she was gone he lay blankly still, until into his mind arose the image of Miranda, dark hair covering a face downheld before him, while he started to take her with sensations of selfishness and triumph.

*   *   *

Melissa walking across the common. Why did he *have* to pretend that he had fallen asleep, when I looked into his room last night as I came up the stairs? Why is he still covering up before me? Or is it really very simple: he is in love with that girl Miranda with the large brown eyes? That would explain why he keeps his distance.

At her table in the Castle, awaiting her first aspirant, she wrote in her diary.

> How much I love him he will never know, for he has the kind of lonely pride which consists in relentless self accusation. And he holds *so* closely to himself: generous to all but to me—wholly selfish. So it seems I must for ever hide myself, and pretend less than I do feel for myself--but bleed as quietly as possible—and so give the least trouble to others.

When she saw Caspar again, he asked her how the auditing was progressing. She gave him her report.

> His sister when young was a dark girl with large, dreamy brown eyes. She was very fond of him until an act of his caused her father to reject her when she was twelve. She and a boy had a poetical rendezvous in a field of grass near their home. The self-righteous Philip, unconsciously in the pattern of his father, got a bigger boy, who used to fight his battles for him, to thrash the boy with whom she was once seen lying beside in long grass. The father was puritanically Victorian, and told her he no longer loved her. She ran away and was found late at night weeping alone on a hill.
>
> Long before this, Phillip, the first-born, had pushed her into the fire of the day nursery, an instinctive, atavistic act stemming from feelings that she had replaced him in his mother's arms.
>
> Elizabeth has never married, and Phillip is a failure with women. His love appears to be all in the head, a romantic or unnatural love. He forced himself to be brave in the 1914–18 war, and did well; but was lost after the Armistice, the world had gone, in which he had stood up for himself. He took refuge in writing an idyllic story, reliving his early chaotic life nearer to the heart's desire.
>
> As for his sister, she had heard stories of his supposedly bohemian life in the West Country, and dreads that anyone will find out the relationship between them.

"A hydra-headed stigma," remarked Caspar, putting down the written report. "Phillip's obsession with fire comes from guilt as yet only superficially recognised by him. From guilt stems his fear-hate of her image, and consequent transference to a Faustian

imprint of that young girl with the dark hair and brown eyes of
his lost mother."

Later, he left a note for Melissa.

> The long periods spent lying before his hearth giving himself the
> labour of a minimum Sisyphus might be due to weakness from lack
> of proper food, inducing masochism from guilt that he is escaping
> from a task which will need a steadfast and prolonged dedication
> to the wearying solitude of writing down what scenes and actions
> from lost Time are being relived by the power of the Imagination.

Piers Tofield and Beth drove in an open green sports-car along
the Somerset coast-road to Lynmouth; on their way up the steep
winding valley road they met Peter, David, and Jonathan, who
told them where they were camping.

So Piers drove to the Green Meadow where, under the canopy
of trees, the echoes of cascade and waterfall floated up from the
glen.

After greetings, Lucy explained that Phillip was at work in his
cot. "We thought it best to come down here, to let him get on
with his writing."

"It's good news he's started again, at long last, Lucy. How
many years since he published a book? Six, I fancy. Still, writers
mustn't be too happy, or they won't siphon off energy into imaginary worlds."

Lucy thought how trim and easy Piers looked. She liked Beth.
The two were staying in Lynton.

"England," went on Piers, "is once again a stone set in a
silver sea. Indeed, on the way down the tarmac was so hot that
it blistered in places. One could hardly bear one's hands on the
bonnet after stopping for a couple of minutes by the wayside."

The boys were admiring the low, holly-green Aston-Martin,
with its two chromium-plated flexes covering exhaust pipes issuing serpent-like through the side of the bonnet. "Is it the same
one you shot with your tommy gun?" asked Jonathan.

"No, of course it wasn't shot!" cried David, frowning at his
young brother to shut-up.

Piers said, "Quite right, Jonny. The engine needed a jerk put
into it. Runs ever so much better now. I had the block welded.
Being cast-iron, it had to be heat-treated first. That meant that
the engine had to be entirely rebuilt. Goes like a bomb now. Well
Lucy, I think perhaps we'd better not go to see Phil at the moment,

but do give him my love when you see him. We're only here on a flying visit. I must go back on Saturday to see my garden. What wonderful weather." He looked into the sky.

Cloudlets of high cirrus—mares' tails—in the height of the sky, appearing never to move. Only their colours changed: deep red in the pallor before dawn, they turned pink before the sun arose out of the far reaches of the Severn Sea. As the solar rim appeared they were drained of colour, becoming streamers, vacant and pale: mere wisps, lying inert above bright day.

"If you go back on Saturday you'll miss the great cricket match and the fireworks, Sir Piers," said Rosamund.

"What are the teams?" he asked, aware of her budding beauty.

Peter said, "Colonel Bucentaur's Crimson Ramblers are playing the North Devon Savages, sir".

"I must see Molly again. Beth, will it be all right for you to go back on Sunday?" He turned round. "Why, here's old Phil! My dear Phil, how glad I am to see you!"

Peter offered them his canoe; the two old friends paddled half a mile out to sea, and on return went to drink beer in the Rising Sun, feeling as they had felt in the old days.

Phillip in Shep Cot reading, with the aid of a magnifying glass, an official account of the anxieties of the German Main Head-quarters Great General Staff at Douai, on 15th June, 1916, and the discussion.

'Since the attack on the Somme front by the British Fourth Army shows signs of materialising, the British forces should be let through to create a large salient, and there be encircled by attacks driven into both flanks of the Fourth Army exhausted after their advance, with guns and transport, over the barren and upheaved crater-zone made by their own bombardments.'

The long light of evening lay gently over the moor, the sun burning away the west, fusing the moor to its own brightness: star and planet conjoined in an illusion of eternity.

Now he must start the engine of the Silver Eagle on the handle, to keep charged the battery.

Eight gallons of petrol, in four cans, lay on the wooden floor of the box-body, under a load of six hundredweight of oak-poles, topped by half-a-dozen faggots. The load was corded, ready to be driven to the crest of The Chains at night, with his father's ashes, for the funeral pyre.

PART FOUR

ST. ELMO'S FIRE

'Tout paysage est un état d'âme.'

Chapter 23

CLOVEN HOOF

Matches had been arranged to take place during Festival Week
between the Crimson Ramblers and various West Country teams,
on their home grounds. The first fixture was with the Barum
Barbarians. Their ground, immediately above the medieval
bridge, lay upon what once was the Seven Pilgrims Marsh; an
area of tidal swamp land rented from a local squire at a pepper-
corn rent for the purpose of dumping there the contents of Barum's
dustbins. Where burgesses of lesser sensibility might have run-up
factories etc., based upon a decade's deposition of urban garbage,
flattened motorcars, bones and skulls of slain sheep and oxen, and
other repulsive debris of *homo sapiens*, the local councillors had
created a pleasaunce of shrubs, trees, flowers and lawns amidst
sparkling fountains and abstract stone effigies of local worthies,
among them Bloody Judge Jeffrys (who once had slept in the
town) and Hartland's hero, the pirate Cruel Coppinger.

Now upon this beautified area stood a theatre, concert hall,
ballroom, squash court and swimming pools built around a
magnificent sports arena which included the cricket ground of
the Barbarians.

Having played against this team and won, the Crimson
Ramblers took on the Porlock Eccentrics, and were victorious.
Next the Bideford Barnacles, who lived up to their name, boring
into the bowling only to be scraped away by Peregrine's bowling,
which reduced a number of them by verdicts of l.b.w. There
followed a session with the Plymouth Corsairs (known locally as
the Plymouth Gin-tlemen); and, penultimately, the Instow
Inquilines.

As already announced, the final match was to take place after
the Presentation of Goats in the Valley of Rocks at Lynton:
Crimson Ramblers *v.* North Devon Savages.

Lt-Col. Bucentaur's eleven was composed exclusively of ex-
commandos and paratroopers who had served with Brigadier

Tarr and one of his war-time lieutenant-colonels, Lord Cloudesley;
a fact which, since Osgood Nilsson's article in his New York
paper's Sunday Magazine, had not been missed by a certain Fleet
Street editor.

Eight children were to have helped to pull the great roller
across the cricket field in the Valley of Rocks on the morning of
the match, but Miranda had not appeared. Her sister wasn't
very well, said Imogen. Soon she and Rosamund had paired off,
while David and Jonathan became a team of buddies with Giles
Bucentaur. What fun it was, to discover such jolly cousins! Only
Peter felt a little apart from the younger ones. He wanted to go
up to watch the meet of the staghounds on Summer House Hill
above Lynmouth; but, being the eldest of the rolling party, he
knew he should stay and look after the younger children.

"Look at the gulls!", he said to his mother, when Lucy arrived
at the field with Melissa and Molly, bringing a basket of food
for the children's lunch. "They're flying like swallows, soaring
and then flapping their wings to check suddenly. I wonder what
they are after?"

"They birds be arter antses'," said the groundsman, "that's
what they birds be arter. Tes the queen antses, they flee up and
the stag-antses go arter 'm. 'Tes the nature of the queen-antses
to fly up high to lure the stag-antses, and when the stag-antses
hev trod the queen antses they drop dead. The queen-antses flee
down agen to lay eggs in a noo nestie." He pointed across the
cricket ground. "They mounds you can zee over there be antses
nesties."

"I bet some antsies be falling in the Lyn, and trout are jumping at them," said Jonathan.

"Aiy, you'm right, midear!"

Peter said, "Mother, the stag-hounds are meeting on Summer
House Hill, I'd like to go and see them."

"Who told 'ee thaccy, midear?" asked Jonathan.

"Mr. Riversmill. He's gone to paint them."

"What colour, 'bor?"

"All colours, of course, like any other picture."

"I thought you said he was going to paint the hounds, 'bor." At
this the groundsman threw back his head and laughed. Jonathan's
face went red, then pale; he thought he was being laughed at,
and walked away, while anguish consumed his spirit. Peter went
after him, to assure him that the groundsman was laughing at

his joke, which was a very funny joke. But Jonathan, once stricken, took time to recover. So Peter led him among the rocks rising steeply above the bowl of the valley, and down to the path along the edge of the cliffs, where he said good-bye to Jonny, saying he was going on to the meet of stag-hounds on Summer House Hill.

Miranda was lying in her bed in 'Buster's' house, suffering from migraine, and what was presumably an exceptional period of menstruation; but Melissa, who had visited her in the morning, believed that her state was due to acute emotional disturbance. Miranda had told her that Phillip was deliberately avoiding her: that it was all Daddy's fault, for calling him a trespasser. She had repeated this again and again, with renewed waves of stress. "Daddy imagines that cousin Phillip is just like himself, which isn't true! And he only *pretended* to have forgotten that he had promised to give me Capella!"

Renewed hysteria.

"It isn't true what Daddy accused Cousin Phillip of!" and she hid her face in the pillow.

Melissa had to go on to Oldstone, but she promised to return before the presentation of goats, which was to take place at 2.30 p.m.

The girl lay mournfully in bed. It was not so much what her father had done, but the poetic feelings of the mind, her true or unbodily self, which had been hurt. Perhaps Phillip would now not want to have anything more to do with her, after what Daddy had done to her—

She must go and see Cousin Melissa, and tell her the truth about her father, in strict confidence. Perhaps she would explain all, one day, to Phillip . . . but at the thought of it, she broke anew into tears.

But Miranda must follow an idea once it had come to her. She felt the headache going as she put on breeches and jumper. Soon she was going downstairs to find Mr. Mornington, who was working in the garden.

"Your cob, miss? Certainly! He's in the loose-box. I was just going to give him a feed of crushed oats and bran, with some chopped carrots."

Voices approached. "My goodness, miss, here's his Lordship back with a party—I'll see to the cob in a jiffy."

The gardener, quick-change artist into parlourman in black

trousers and striped linen jacket, put a tray of drinks on the table.

'Buster,' the Brig, and Laura were in high feather, having returned from a ceiling of nearly ten thousand feet; 'Buster' flying solo, the others in the two-seater. They had come down to a thousand feet above the Valley of Rocks to make a 6-degree descent to the Porlock marshes. There they had fitted oxygen bottles, and new batteries for the 2-way radio in each sailplane, ready for another attempt on the height record that afternoon.

Then, collecting Peregrine at the Polo Club, they diced—Hispano-Suiza versus supercharged Bentley—up the narrow Porlock hill with its 1-in-3 left-hand turn, roaring along the road winding through a heather-grown escarpment to the descent at Countisbury, with its view of a grey bouldered shore divided by the Lyn flowing into the sea. Down to nought feet; and up, up again to The Eyrie, happy as birds in preened summer plumage as ice clinked in tumblers.

Miranda saw the Hispano-Suiza on the drive. Unobtrusively she came into the room. How was the headache?

"Oh, better, thank you. I think I'll hack up to Oldstone to see Cousin Melissa."

"If you're not fit enough to do a job of work on the cricket pitch, you're not fit to ride, surely?" replied Peregrine.

Miranda's eyes opened wide as she said, "I particularly wish to see Cousin Melissa at Oldstone."

"Are you sure it isn't someone else?"

In the silence which followed, 'Buster' said to the Brig, "Did I ever show you my father's last letter, or rather testimony, which arrived on the Cornish coast some time after he crashed into the Atlantic?"

"I'd very much like to see it."

'Buster' went to a corner cupboard, and returned with a bottle encrusted by small white shells, which he put on the table before carefully withdrawing a scroll of paper.

"I was a small boy then—" he began; but observing the upward glance of the girl's eyes, which were full of unshed tears, he hesitated. "One day someone of your generation must write his biography. Laura and I have tried, but I've no gift whatsoever." He hesitated. "Perhaps it would be better if you saw the message later on—"

He returned the bottle to the corner cupboard, aware of Laura's darkening thoughts.

"You'll one day write a fine novel around gliding, Laura. You're on the way to being a first-class pilot. Don't you agree, Brig? We must enter competitions. There's a young woman, who ferried Spits during the war, organising trials in Surrey. We must foregather there one day." He thought of twenty, thirty, fifty gliders one moonless night descending near the red-brick prison at Spandau—

He felt weary. He was worried lest Osgood Nilsson had written about his father on the lines of the Caspar Field article. Why was the good soldier always decried? The tyranny of the common man's mental fixations—Caspar Field dedicated to revealing a way to clear the mind of its horrific convolutions: the snake in the Garden of Eden writhing through the potential genius of every small child—

"Damn and blast!" said Peregrine, looking at his watch. "I'm due at the hotel for luncheon with the box wallahs at twelve thirty. Blasted bore about the presentation."

"We'll 'dove' on you from the air, as the Yanks say, Perry!" cried the Brig.

"And drive the blasted goats over the cliffs, I hope!"

Globe-Mornington came in with a syphon of soda-water, an excuse to say *sotto voce* to Miranda, "Your cob is ready when you are."

Peregrine, waiting on like a falcon, repeated, "In my opinion you're not fit to ride!"

"I feel ever so much better, thank you."

"Well, be in time to observe your pet Capella settling down with the rest of the herd to resume a normal occupation of destroying everything in sight. Where she goes after the handing over is nobody's business."

"I shall only see Cousin Melissa for a minute, then I'll come straight back."

"Now don't let her rope you in with that crowd of phonies in that bogus castle, or go to see that writing feller who claims to be our cousin."

The girl said distinctly, "Phillip is married to Lucy, who is my mother's cousin."

"Anyway, he's no good, like that other writing feller, that Yank Nilsson."

"Nilsson wrote a good book on fishing," said Brigadier Tarr.

"Maybe, Brig old boy. But I have no use for Americans, any more than you have, what?"

When the girl had gone 'Buster' said to Laura, "You might write to that young woman in Surrey, who is organising Glider Trials, and find out the form."

"Yes. By the way, you know we've got tickets for 'Yeoman of the Guard' tonight, don't you? Molly said she was bringing the cricketers' wives in a coach, so I reserved twenty-four seats."

The day was going to be even hotter thought 'Buster', climbing in a spiral above the incult valley. At a thousand feet he could hear voices distinctly; also little crackling noises which might be the bursting of furze pods. Drifts of air-borne seeds of rose-bay, willow-herb and thistle floated up past the cockpit. Strings of screaming swifts were cavorting above him, pursuing midges carried there on pulses of hot, dry air.

The troposphere lay plain up to thirty thousand feet: an unlimited container of the thunderbolts of Donner, the German god of thunder. Would the day come when scientists accepted that the ancients, who gave personalities to all natural phenomena, had divined the actual truth?

Down on the cricket ground, Jonathan was saying to David, "I hope it thunders. I love lightning. It pierces the air and the hole fills up so fast it gives a great crack. The crack echoes all over the clouds and that causes the rumble, 'Buster' told me."

Still climbing in narrow circles, 'Buster' saw a motorcoach driving down the valley road to the cricket field. Behind were motorcars, bicyclists, and little groups of pedestrians spread out all the way back to the east end of the valley. Hundreds more were already spread out around the field.

The Bucentaur family, of various aunts, uncles, and cousins, had been sent printed invitations. Two cattle floats and one horse-box were parked on the edge of the cricket field in front of a group headed by the Lord Lieutenant and High Sheriff of the county, with their ladies. Near this group, but not too close, stood lesser dignitaries—the Chairman and various members of two County Councils, together with the Mayor of Lynton in the robes and chain of office; members of the Rural District and Town Councils. Offset from both groups was a Town Crier hired from Brighton.

"He was attired", wrote Jack o' Lanthorn in *The Lynton Lantern*, "in all his historic habiliments and finery of black knee breeches, brocaded

coat, white stockings, black buckled shoes, yellow gloves, and tall
headgear of ancient shape."

As near to this figure as they could shift themselves while
sitting down, a group of boys was waiting. One of them had a
pea-shooter. Hidden behind a chum, he was attempting to hit the
Town Crier's hat. They were being watched, with some amusement, by Peregrine and his son Roger. Observing the apparent
approval of two of the gentry, the boy fired his first round. *Plip*
—a pea bounced off the top hat with its gold braided band.

"Go away you boys!" growled the Crier. "Be off."

"Us'v as much right yurr as you, you ould booger!" replied
the armed one.

The Crier pretended to gather himself to run; the boys arose
and fled, the shooter of peas taking up the rear as guard.

"Like the old days at Arnhem," remarked Peregrine to his
fourteen-year-old son, as he lolled on a shooting stick and glanced
around with an air of sardonic superiority towards the 'Box-
wallahs'.

"I wonder if anyone has briefed the feller from Brighton that
the cry of *Oyez* should never be yelled as the opposite of
Oh No. I doubt it. The feller will probably wag his bell and *not*
utter cries of *Oi-Oi-Oi*, which originally were used to penetrate
the noises of horse-shoes and wrought-iron rims of waggon wheels
on cobbles during a market assembly of beery carters and drovers
bawling at one another amidst the general lowing of cattle."

Presently he said, "I wonder what would happen if someone
inadvertently let-down the door of the horse-box wherein King
Billy is languishing? As you know, Roger, the old goat *loathes*
all self-advertising noises, and is liable to charge in their
direction."

Roger made an inarticulate throaty noise as he moved a few
feet away from his father, apprehensive of what might come next.

"My sense of humour doesn't appeal to you Roger, what?"

When the boy did not reply, Peregrine said, "The trouble with
you, my lad, is that you are still tied to your mother's apron
strings. And take your hands out of your trouser pockets!"

Roger moved away with head held down, dreading that others
had heard.

"Everywhere it's the same socialistic ideas of conformity, rot-
ting out the bloody country," Peregrine said to his son as he
passed him on the way to the horse-box.

Roger hid himself in the crowd.

At half-past two o'clock, the advertised time for the Ceremony of Presentation, the Crier, ringing his bell, advanced in the direction of a wooden platform erected in the centre of a roped-off square of grass. Arriving below a pole flying the Union Jack, he sang out as loudly as he could, "Oh Yes! Oh Yes!!! O Yes!!!"

A chant of "Oh No! Oh No! Oh No!" came from the boys, who had overheard what Peregrine had said to his son.

The Crier, climbing on to the platform, had got so far as, "Pray silence for the Right Honourable the Earl—" when shouts arose, and turning round, he saw a large horned apparition galloping straight for him. For it was true what Peregrine had told his son : the old goat was used to quiet and gentle voices (as indeed was Roger). Raucous human noises disturbed a social balance acquired on the broad acres of the Abbey park over which he had ruled, and where his sense of propriety had been formed.

The amused spectators saw King Billy leap upon the platform : the imported Town Crier of Brighton jumping off, to lose a buckled shoe as he landed below. The goat's mood changed when he saw the shoe; many times in the past King Billy had played *Hunt the Slipper* with the Bucentaur children. Picking up the gaudy object he made off in the direction of Castle Rock, pursued by the band of small boys led by the shooter of peas.

Meanwhile the Town Clerk of Lynton was hurrying forward to instruct the Crier to proceed. "We'll get your shoe back, don't you worry. It was they dalled boys who let that bisley animal go, I shouldn't wonder, the young limmers!"

The Crier, uncomfortable in ill-fitting hired finery, attempted to hide a hole in his sock with the remaining shoe, while yelling in a loud voice, "My lords, ladies, and gentlemen! Pray silence for Lieutenant-Colonel Pegerin Boo-Center, Commander of the Most Honourable Order of the Bath, Companion of the Distinguished Service Order!"

The anxious Mayor muttered to the Town Clerk, "He's got it in the wrong order!"

Peregrine got on the platform and said, "I now give, with whole-hearted satisfaction, every damned goat I possess to the Devon County Council, and may God have mercy on their vegetation!" Then he jumped down.

Nobody quite knew how to take this brief speech. Was it a

prayer for the safe-keeping of the goats, or for the local farmers'
crops, asked Jack o' Lanthorn in the afore-mentioned issue
of *The Lynton Lantern.*

Meanwhile the Crier had clambered back on the platform, to
announce the Lord Lieutenant of the County. He scrambled down
again, a Z-shaped figure worried about the hole in his sock, as
the nobleman—hair clipped short and moustache trimmed by
Van Tromp of Curzon Street, as befitted a Lancer who had commanded the Cavalry School at Camberley—said crisply, "I won't
detain you long on this fine summer afternoon—" glancing up
at the sky, where the two gliders were now circling at five
thousand feet—"to declare both my pleasure and my duty to
announce to you that Devon has been offered a most generous
gift from one of our very good neighbours in Somerset—Colonel
Bucentaur. The gift is both remarkable and unique. During four
centuries the herd of White Goats of Brockholes St. Boniface
Abbey has been famous. The herd has had its existence since
before the reign of Henry the Eighth—and may I say, in passing,
that it still appears to possess the bold, not to say dashing,
characteristics of the Elizabethan age!" (*Laughter.*) "I now have
very great pleasure in accepting the gift—a pleasure anticipated,
I may say, somewhat in advance by the leader of the herd, King
Billy—" (*clapping and loud laughter*)—"who has already betaken
himself into pastures new with, I am able reliably to inform you,
one of the buckled shoes of the Town Crier of the great watering-
place of Brighthelmstow—now known as Brighton—" (*Loudest
laughter and cheers*). "Mr. Mayor and Councillors of Lynton,
I now have the pleasant duty to accept, on behalf of all
Devonians, Colonel Bucentaur's most generous gift of the
immemorial Herd of Brockholes St. Boniface Goats, and long may
they remain to grace, Sirs—" he turned to the group of Devon
worthies—"your beautiful Valley of Rocks!"

Thirty released goats made for the figure of King Billy, now
silhouetted on a crag among other grey upstanding rocks. One
goat remained, Capella, to trot into the crowd of strollers, seeking
her friend and comforter, while uttering now and then little
bleats of distress at not finding her.

Rows of deck-chairs were set out before the pavilion, with
tables for the scorers. By this time the two gliders, familiar
sight to holiday-makers, were rising smaller and smaller in a
thermal lifting off the lichened rocks amidst bracken and furze

which bestrewed the wide valley. Both had sealed barographs; both pilots were after height records.

The two captains approached for the spinning of a coin, while the umpire, a tall elderly man with a drooping moustache and wearing a long white coat with a bandless yellow panama hat dating from 1902, stood by to pick up a silver crown-piece with the face of the young Queen Victoria almost worn away with the Royal coat-armour on the obverse side.

"Head," cried Peregrine, and won the toss. He decided to put in the opposing team. Let the Savages sweat it out in the hottest part of the day!

The articled clerk, a Saxon-headed man of about forty, went in to bat with a crony of the evening bar at the Club. Both were blue-capped. Their captain's directive was to break the esteem of the Bloody Redcapped Goats by stonewalling. Then, like Monty at Alamein, "Knock them for six!"

So the match dragged at first. Lucy sat with her small daughter between Melissa and Elizabeth, enjoying the feeling of having nothing to do. Very soon Mrs. Osgood Nilsson joined them.

"I thought perhaps I'd find you with Miranda and Molly Bucentaur. You are cousins, aren't you?"

"Oh," said Lucy, liking her cheery face. "They're in the pavilion seeing to the tea-things, I think."

"I always find cricket so boring, don't you? I mean the game itself—"

Lucy didn't know what to say to that; and soon the inquisitor departed for more amusing company.

The stonewalling persisted. Each ball was meticulously blocked. No runs were attempted.

For the third over, Peregrine put on another bowler. Six leaping, bounding hops; six times a yorker hurtling down the shortest distance between two points : *plop*, six times it was blocked, to come to rest a few yards down the pitch. And likewise, every ball of three more overs was either blocked or chopped.

"What, are these heathens on strike?" Peregrine asked the umpire, who shrugged the jersey partly tied round his neck and replied, a laconic "Oo-ah."

A party of onlookers along the road started a slow hand-clap. Peregrine stared furiously at them and gave the equivalent of Churchill's V-sign. Ironical cheers came back.

The first bowler was put on again. At his second ball, a yorker, the articled clerk sent it soaring up in a parabola, to drop over the boundary. Six! Clapping from Saxon Savages in a row grinning almost as wide as the peaks of their blue caps. And an odious, vulgar chortle reached Perry's ears—*Stuff to give'm!* Village cads, he thought; and decided to teach them a lesson.

Peregrine was an exceptionally cunning bowler. He knew how to knock down stone walls, which do not cricket make. When, before the war, he had played for his county, a chord of yellow horn-like skin had extended along the third finger of his right hand. The yellow corn had been built up by constant spinnings of a ball tossed vertically and curvaceously during many hours of practice. The ball could be made to swing and cut both ways, to break either to off or near stump on striking the turf. In his youth, while at Oxford he had been coached by Sidney Barnes, a great bowler who learned his art in Lancashire, home of great cricketers.

Observing who was now going to bowl, the grinning row of blue caps became as solemn as puffins.

The articled clerk, determined to do or die, stepped forward and sent Peregrine's first deceptive ball—a slow limer—skying over the pavilion. It fell in the rough. Seeing a familiar red object, King Billy came down from his rock to find out what was going on.

Peregrine did not discern what they were laughing at. He thought they were laughing at him. Another ball was tossed to him. He rubbed it on the grass before beginning an easy amble as though for another slow limer : two easy ambling steps : then a succession of springy strides : a long arm swinging vertically over and past a face set with *karata* intentness : flick of fingers and wrist which once could neatly chop in half a 9-inch Bridgewater brick by a concentration of will and spite—sustained and calculated hostility. The articled clerk dithered, playing off his foremost foot with a straight bat.

Anxiously he awaited the next ball, determined not to be confused by tricks. There followed a third off-breaking ball—was it *hissing?*—and then a fast leg-break—another, which also broke to leg : and thus softened up, speechless-thoughtless, the victim awaited the sixth ball, a hissing wobbler that swerved from legstump to off-stump, richochetting back to the leg.

Clean-bowled, mute and feeling witless, the tyro lawyer walked, puffin-nosed, to the pavilion.

During the interval, before the next batsman went out, Lucy saw the green Aston-Martin arriving with Phillip sitting beside Piers.

*   *   *

Leaving Beth resting in the hotel, Piers had driven up to the common where, following wheel-tracks, he came to Shep Cot. Phillip was round the corner by the corrugated iron lean-to, kneeling at the back of the jacked-up Silver Eagle, apparently examining a back wheel with a large-handled magnifying glass of the kind seen in libraries. A meshed chain lay across the worn tyre. The box body was loaded high with brushwood corded above six-foot lengths of oak poles extending beyond the rear. A small dog stood by, looking at him.

"Bodger, this is Piers," said Phillip; at which the small dog gave a single wag of its tail-stump.

"Moving house, Phil?"

"No, Piers. I haven't renewed the road-fund licence, or the insurance, so I'm going to use the old 'bus only on the moor, for collecting turf. I thought if I cut some now while it is dry, I can stack it in this shed. I'll need chains on the back-wheels to get up there," as he pointed to the southern skyline.

Piers helped to adjust the chain round the tyre of one rear wheel, thinking the while that his old friend seemed to fumble a lot at the fastening.

"Let me do it. I expect you've been working too long and too hard. Sit down and rest, Phil."

Having bolted on one wheel, the other was jacked-up, removed, chained, and replaced. "Shall I help you unload, Phil?"

"Thank you for the suggestion, but I think I can manage to take this load to the summit."

Piers was puzzled, but asked no questions. He picked up the magnifying glass. "I don't suppose you get many small flints in the tyres. Surely there aren't any on the moor? I thought the geological layers were shale and ironstone, or is it old red sandstone?"

"At times my sight isn't too good, so I use that glass."

"Overstrain, I expect. I don't know how you stick it here in winter. How's the magazine going?"

"I've had to close it down. Most of the old subscribers, when Christie had it, didn't renew their subscriptions; and the railway bookstalls took two thousand copies on sale or return. The first number sold about sixty. They refused to take any of the last number."

"Why?"

"Oh, I had a letter from 'The British Board of Traders' Protection', demanding an explanation of a paragraph I wrote in my editorial, that the free export of British capital, largely in the hands of cosmopolitan financiers before the war, should be legally forbidden. Would I define 'cosmopolitan'? Did I not mean Semitic?"

"You do tend to ram Birkin's ideas about 'international financiers' down people's throats, you know. Well, at least your loyalty can never be in question."

"I'm a failure."

"You've been too much alone. Can't I persuade you to leave off work for a spell, and come down and watch the cricket. You and me, and Melissa and Beth? I'd be like you without Beth. Every moment is alive for me nowadays." He hesitated. "I hope I'm not being selfish, but the weather's too good to be by yourself. In fact, almost too good. There's thunder about, I fancy. Look at the gulls, almost out of sight. I'm told they fly inland before a storm."

Over the hills and far away, above a sea cerulean and fused with sky along earth's horizon, other birds were flying, some too high to be seen by human eye alone. In lower airs the gulls were turning and changing direction as though without aim—stalling, flapping this way and then that as they criss-crossed the sky.

For this was the Day of the Ants. From miles around the Valley of Rocks, from every grass-grown ant-hump made of innumerable vegetarian and arboreal fragments compiled and tunnelled, chambered in food-storage caves and nurseries where young worker ants, white and sunless, lay within cocoons ready to break and release each its *imago* for a life of total work at highest speed—the chosen few, born with wings, were crawling to the light of day, to perform their brief, orgiastic fates.

What secret call made the winged females, future matriarchs of new colonies, to rise and shine together on their temporary wings? Only the spermed and ovaried ants alone received the impulse, to be borne into rising air. Those females returning shed their wings, each to seek a new habitation, bearing the sperm of a dead Icarus which should in due course launch a thousand ships for love of some dim, remote Helen of their perception.

The red-headed woodpeckers sloped from the oak-woods, each uttering yallery-greenery cries to announce claim to territory. And in due course each bird would leave its extraordinary little all-white cylinders, each one perfectly shaped, soon to dry in the sun. Those broken by inquisitive human fingers would reveal a faecal composition of black ant skeletons bound together in pure lime.

In a time-space of one hour, including the changing of leg-pads, the North Devon Savages were all out for eighty-seven runs; and the Crimson Ramblers went in to bat. By four o'clock they had lost two wickets, two balls, and had scored sixty-one runs; and the pitch was deserted for tea. Miranda, Rosamund, and other young girls attendant on their mothers carried round trays of tea and cakes first to the Savages, then to the Ramblers. Overhead every rook and jackdaw from the cliffs above the coast from Bull Point to the Quantocks was airborne, glutting itself on flying ants under a sky no longer of enamelled azurine, but flecked, at immense height, by little streamers of high cirrus. Over Dartmoor to the south 'Buster' saw cumulus forming. Thither flew Falcon One and Falcon Two; to return high in clear air to the Valley of Rocks. There they saw a storm brewing up over the sea.

Play was resumed, the Ramblers returning to bat. The air in the Valley of Rocks had become cooler. With the drop in temperature came the dropping down of ants. The first ball spread-eagled stumps. An ant had alighted on the moustache of the bats-man at the moment the ball was released : it started to crawl up and was about to enter a nostril. No use to protest! Out came another batsman, who promptly cut the ball and was caught by slip.

While the next man was going out, flights of swallows appeared twittering over the field, flying close to the grass. Ants were drop-ping everywhere. Hundreds of starlings alighted, to run about the pitch. The game was stopped, until the birds were chivvied away; then a fifth wicket was wrecked by the same bowler. Perry went in to stop the rot. He hit the next ball over the road. Six. The bowler was about to begin his run-down when the umpire held up a hand. All over his ancient panama hat ants were crawling and shedding wings. He cursed and swept them off. Play on ! The third ball went up into the sky, to fall over the boundary. More cheers from the Ramblers.

Miranda saw Phillip, while the fielding team was changing over, get up from where he had been sitting cross-legged and walk slowly past the pavilion to rising ground choked by furze and thorn which led to steep slopes to the sea below. She must speak to him. Lucy was beautiful, perhaps he still loved her; she could help him by telling him that she had not, as her father had told her, been 'running after him, tongue hanging out'. This was the holiday she had so looked forward to; and everything had turned out the wrong way. She must speak to Phillip. While she hesitated she saw that a man carrying a rolled umbrella had caught up with him and they had stopped together. What were they talking about? She waited until they had finished, too far away to hear what was being said.

"You are Captain Maddison?"

"Yes."

"I am from the paper of the times, in London. You've been a journalist, too, I know. So will you help me to get some facts right. By the way, I have a considerable admiration for the character of Sir Hereward Birkin. Have you see him lately?"

"No."

"And you are also a friend of Lord Cloudesley?"

"An acquaintance."

"Have you read the article in the New York *Herald-Tribune's* Sunday magazine, by Osgood Nilsson?"

"No."

"Mr. Nilsson has disclosed an idea to bring about the release of Rudolf Hess now serving a life sentence in Spandau prison. Do you know anything about it?"

When Phillip didn't reply, he withdrew a folded magazine from a pocket. "You know Mr. Osgood Nilsson, I think? I marked the passage where he suggests that the attempt to rescue Hess is to be made by gliders. Can you tell me if any, or all members of the Crimson Ramblers, visiting here today, served either as Commandos, or with the Parachute Corps at Arnhem?"

"I've no idea."

"But you must have heard of the project? Between you and me, as one old soldier to another, I've reached the conclusion that it never pays to allow vengeance to run its course. Churchill loathed the idea of the Nuremberg hangings, didn't he?"

" 'The grass grows green upon the battlefield, but upon the scaffold never.' "

"Did Hitler say that when you were his guest at the Parteitag at Nuremberg in nineteen thirty five?"

"My dear chap, it was said by Churchill in his prime of inspiration, that is, when a young man! Well, that's all I know, except

that I, too, used to work on *The Times*. Now, if you'll forgive me,
I'll be on my way."

Miranda watched the man with the rolled umbrella hurrying
back to the cricket ground; and making her way into the pavilion
she went through the main room to the door at the back of the
ladies' lavatory. Then through another door, and she was among
brambles and thorns, to tread a way through and up until, suddenly, she saw Capella. With a series of bounds her pet was beside
her. She knelt to put her arms round the goat while rubbing her
cheek on the coarse hair of its neck. "Darling, darling Cappy!"

Then she saw Phillip's little dog looking at her. She went on
and saw him sitting on a slab of rock.

"Don't you want to see me ever again, cousin Phillip?"

"Miranda! I haven't seen you for ages!"

She saw that his eyes were screwed up. "What's the matter?
Are you in pain?"

"My left eye sometimes feels as though it's been pierced by a
thorn, and then I can't open it. It's been like that off and on for
some weeks now."

"Then you didn't see me when you passed me in Lynmouth?"
"No."

"Oh, I'm so relieved, my darling Coz," she replied, as she put an
arm round his shoulders, desiring but not daring to lean her head
against his chest. She wanted to cry when he took her hand and
held it beside his cheek. They remained so until Bodger growled.

Phillip whispered, "I know that growl, just sit still, Miranda."
He shifted away from her, still holding her hand. "It may be my
fancy."

She moved her glance as though casually and saw the head and
shoulders of a man standing behind a brown furze bush. Bodger
was growling again.

After an interval the man began to shout, "I see'd what you got
this maid to do to 'ee! I'll gi'e in charge, won't I tho!"

"It was you who were doing it!"

"I see'd 'ee, di'n I tho! Yew wait till I tell your feyther!"

"I'll give you in charge," said Phillip, standing up. "Bodger, to
heel! Don't talk to the fellow, Miranda."

There was a crackling behind them as flames leapt up the dead
furze bush. Kedd followed them down a goat track through the
scrub, shouting as to an unseen companion, "Come yurr, Isaak,
come yurr and bear witness!"

"We weren't doing anything but talking," said Miranda, turning round. Flames were spreading.

"Yew wait until I zee the constable!"

They reached the north side of the pavilion, while Aaron Kedd continued to shout for all to hear. Faces were turned their way. The players were now walking over the pitch, depressing ants. Peregrine rested against the prop of his bat.

"Play on!" said the umpire.

The fast bowler of the Savages had the over. He started a long loping run and let fly a yorker. Peregrine moved forward, took a swipe and missed the ball; but reached for the crease just before the wicket keeper holding the ball whipped off the bails.

"HOWZATT?"

"Not out."

The umpire was now wearing his sweater like a sloppy white knitted umbrella over his head, while fanning away ants with his hat.

The bowler, a tall man, was all angles as he ran. His ball appeared to have knocked the bat out of the batsman's hands. But Peregrine had merely blocked the ball, then dropped the bat to leave the game and walk over to the pavilion. There, beside the table holding scoring sheets, he waited until the two came up to where he stood. He saw that Miranda had been crying, and with an upper cut to Phillip's jaw sent him to the ground. The on-lookers saw Phillip getting up slowly, and heard him say, "I beg your pardon, I didn't see you, sir."

"You filthy fascisti! Let that be a lesson to you!" He looked as though he was about to strike again, when his daughter ran forward and beat with impotent hands on her father's chest. They heard Molly say, "That was naughty of you, Perry. That creature over there is a well-known psychotic. Cousin Phillip, I am so sorry."

"Did you set fire to the furze?" Peregrine shouted, moving towards Phillip. "Answer me that!"

"Cousin Phillip has gone blind!" screamed Miranda. "That's why I was crying!" as she struggled against her father's hold. "I hate you, I hate you!"

King Billy, startled by fire, had jumped upon his rock, from where he looked down upon the figure of a man with white woolly face and head and carrying what looked like a cake. The old goat uttered a noise between bleat and rattle, being not altogether prepared to charge such an apparition, but the cake (which was the panama hat) looked eatable. King Billy had watched many cricket matches in his life, but this was the first for five seasons, and the spectacle brought to mind the heyday of his power. While he stood there, other goats which had seen flames and heard Peregrine shouting were appearing at various points overlooking the cricket field. Some uttered little grunts as they saw a red ball being lightly tossed from one hand as the bowler waited to continue.

Led by Capella, a dozen goats ran upon the pitch to share in the game.

In the meantime, Aaron Kedd had gone back into cover; to re-appear elsewhere shouting, "You'm all damned to hell fire, you'm all comed from Sodom and Gomorrah. And they bliddy goats ought to be kicked to flames! They'm bin and stole all my flat-poll cabbages!"

At the noise of shouting King Billy charged the umpire. That official promptly removed his jersey and used it as a cape. He kept off the animal, which succeeded in hooking it on a horn; where-upon King Billy retired to his rock with the trophy, which he attempted to eat.

Chapter 24

'THE SMOKE OF MY RESOLUTION'

In the sky alto-cirrus, those summer breast feathers of the dove of peace, gently hued in grey and pink, were about to be struck by swifter falcons of those winds which were bringers of blood and the pallors of death. One man alone, in the crowds which had been watching the cricket, saw what might be coming. Osgood Nilsson said to his wife, "You want to know something? That fire might trigger off a tornado. I've seen bush fires in Africa..."

Flames were spreading swiftly, fanned by a twirling wind induced by rising hot air and smoke. And, curiously, the hanging drift of strato-cirrus was being hidden by a milky gathering of flocculent cloud through which the orb of the sun appeared to be enlarged, deprived of its radiance, becoming a mere circle, pallid and dull, without heat or shine. All this change had occured, it seemed, while the game had been held up.

The umpire declared that it was no more than a land-drifting sea-mist following a day of torrid heat. But Osgood Nilsson, as he scanned the sky, remarked to Rosalie, "If we were way back in Florida, I'd say a bitch was on the way."

"But we're in England, not your beloved South, my dear!"

"The old British weather is passing away with the Empire, I guess, but they haven't caught up with the idea as of now. For one thing, the polar ice-cap is melting. The commies are planting eyed-ova in Siberian rivers, hoping to get runs of sockeye salmon. Also they're figuring out to grow a short-strawed wheat on land that fifty years ago was under ice all the year through. And shall I tell you something? That ice is now cold water streaming into the North Atlantic and pushing back the Gulf Stream two hundred miles west of Ireland. And that's only the beginning." He stood up. "I guess I'll go to The Marksman and draw my trailer way up above the river."

"I'll come with you, and give you a hand."

"Excuse me, Mr. Nilsson," said the reporter who had pretended

323

to Phillip that he was from *The Times*. "May I have a word with you?"

"On what?"

"Your article in this New York magazine, Mr. Nilsson."

"It speaks for itself."

"It certainly does, Mr. Nilsson. I've had a word about it with Captain Maddison, who spoke of Winston Churchill's generosity to defeated enemies, including Rudolf Hess, who flew against the Royal Flying Corps, with whom you served, I believe, in the First World War."

"I did."

"Would you agree, Mr Nilsson, that any attempt to kidnap Hess by gliders, on the lines of the abduction by Skorzeny of Mussolini at the end of the recent war, would fail?"

"I should say it's my opinion that it will fail today."

"Today?" cried the reporter. "You mean the attempt is to be made today? May I quote you as saying that?"

"May you hell!"

The man with the rolled umbrella ran to his motorcar, thinking, A scoop! A scoop!!

In the drift of flocculent cloud 'Buster' in Falcon One had lost touch with Falcon Two. And he had no idea where he himself was. Under the perspex hood he inhaled a steady hiss of sweetish-sick oxygen. Below him a whole mountain range of peaks and ravines was being formed and reformed as by the concealed giants of some new Valhalla : a shining new world in being, held on the back of a vast mythical terrapin—its movements heaving up new peaks around a central pattern—the tallest peaks being the centre of a strange and terrifying new universe—the globe turning on a new axis. A circular pyramid of reforming movement, pure white.

Was it an illusion, because he was flying in a wide circle? Hardly so.

He peered intently below. Massive cumulo-nimbus was definitely forming new peaks upon a central axis. He banked and turned, to be on the same spiral direction. He was keeping pace with the turning movement : it was a spiralling storm formation.

Then he flew across the diameter of the circle; and saw in the centre a deep hole, with cloud breaking away, whirling, filling the tunnel which sucked in more vapour by centrifugal force. The eye of a tornado!

Great dark clouds were opening slowly to form new patterns.

Banking to change direction he saw ragged cloud, rising up to swamp him. He turned back, to remain above the swirling funnel, and found himself in a vast blue hall of winds which bore him, ever circling higher in a rising spiral,—twenty-six thousand feet—then he was being flung about in a greenish darkness now at twenty-seven thousand feet—hail—and suddenly he was in blinding, shining light while just below the top of the cloud swirled and curled like a Medusa-head.

He could see below him, far right, the revolving suction of the hollow elephant-trunk which seemed to be the eye of the hurricane. He looked below and around and up for sight of Laura and The Brig, then removing the oxygen mask he sent out a call through the microphone.

"Falcon One calling—Falcon One calling Falcon Two—come in please—come in please—Falcon One calling Falcon Two—come in please—"

He switched over to receiving, but only an intense crackling abraded his ear-drums. He turned the switch again, and was leaning back in his seat when the sailplane was hurled over.

While Molly was sitting with her daughter within the pavilion, Phillip was walking away from the field accompanied by David holding his arm. "I am not hurt, David," he said to the boy by his side. "Thank you for your help. Perhaps you should go back, to look after Mother and the others. Don't worry about me, it is all a misunderstanding."

"Where are you going, Father?"

"Back to Shep Cot, to drive the Eagle up to The Chains, to light the pyre. I must get there before the storm, while the ground is fairly dry."

So David went back to his mother and the others, while Phillip followed Bodger partly by sound-echo: he could hear movements of the dog's feet and just discern the blur of the body a little way ahead. He began to feel pain; the blow had opened a scar on the flesh of the cheek-bone below the left eye, which for some days had been in a semi-fluid state, at times accompanied by pain so intense that it had been impossible to unclench the lids. How brave Jefferies had been, suffering internal pain until his body was almost a skeleton, while being told for months that his illness was imaginary: that hysteria was the sole cause of the body wasting away! Perhaps the deterioration of his own sight was due to suppressed hysteria—a condition of self-frustration, self-denial; of *cowardice.* Yes, that was the cause of every disaster and non-fulfilment in his life. As Osgood Nilsson said, *A no-good man. A failure ...*

He stopped, remembering that his father had once said to him, I am a failure. Poor Father, finally dreaming of resurrection with the girl called Myra—

His last words in the nursing home, *So you're against me, too, are you?*

Yes, I abandoned you, Father. 'He who is not with me, is against me.'

In the sky greyer, lower clouds were moving in, giving only glimpses, between gaps, of high strato-cirrus. These lower clouds began to turn the colour of copper, then darken to sullen nimbus moving along a curving course, vying away from the higher parnassian snows.

A heavy black wall was closing down on the Valley of Rocks, the bar clouds dreaded by airmen, packing the air below the twenty thousand feet level. A darkness to scare people, a cold shutting-down of the day, a reversal, a negation of summer's kindness.

"Darling, I must leave you now," said Molly in the pavilion. "I'll be back soon. I expect they'll shortly draw stumps. Just you rest and relax, and don't worry yourself. I understand how it all happened. You are not to blame, nor is Cousin Phillip. It is all a misunderstanding, Anda my pet."

"Oh Mummie, it is so unfair! Daddy should never have done that, he should have thought about himself, and know what he was doing to someone who was not like himself!"

Molly kept a smiling face, while wondering if there was more that the girl hadn't told her.

She looked at Miranda. Obviously the child was trying to keep back the tears from running down a face which had glowed with such joy and youth when Phillip had first come to see them—a face now hurt and desolate. "Darling, do not grieve. All will come right, I promise you."

As soon as she was alone again Miranda got up to look through the open door. Play had been resumed. Once again she climbed through the lavatory window and set out for The Eyrie along the path at the top of the cliff, followed by Capella. She meant to get her cob and ride up to Shep Cot. On the way through the oakwoods she passed 'the man from the paper of the times', who had started for The Eyrie, but changed his mind and turned back. He began to speak to her, but with set face the girl continued on her way.

Phillip was then on the road to Lynton, just before the ornate Town Hall. He was aware of the presence of his father, living again in the last walk they had gone together during the last year at Fawley, more than ten years before ... It was a wonderful walk, Father. We followed the Roman road over the downs, on the sward under which it lay buried. You told me how your father had taken you over the same way when you and your brothers were boys. When we came to arable fields, there the white-brown-black braided flints lay, turned and returned by the plough all during the centuries since the Romans had left. That was your country when you were a boy walking, walking, for miles happy and care-free in the open air, mile upon mile to far Cranborne Chace lying blue above the southern horizon when you had set out from Fawley at dawn. And you saw it again with me, on our only walk together since I was a small and disappointing boy on the edge of London.

He stopped to fasten the lead to Bodger's collar, for the sense of failure was returning, despite his knowledge that the direct cause of depression was lack of food. Even so—he would take a gun and two cartridges with him to The Chains, and there Bodger, Silver Eagle and he would go together.

Both spectators and players in the Valley of Rocks were taking occasional glances at the sky. A cold drift of air caused the umpire to untie the love-knotted arms of the woollen jersey—retrieved, in a somewhat chewed condition, from King Billy by the bold pea-shooting boy—in order to pull the garment over his head. In doing so, he forgot that he was wearing his panama hat. Thus he was not in a position to judge a fast ball which struck the padded leg of the batsman at the wicket. The interval be-tween temporary lack of sight and hearing was brief, due to the wool being pulled over his eyes at the same time that his ears were being pulled over their holes by a near-verticle hat-brim. Before he could recover or rather uncover there arose all around him a mass-cry of HOWZATT? co-incident with a hissing in the air which seemed to be all over the field at once, with many blue serpents arrived about the grass. The effect was queer: no one was burned, or received a feeling of being struck by this odd sort of lightning without detonation : but it was enough to end the game. A sickly pallor lay upon the valley. Soon little wisps of dusty wind were rising about the trees and rocks : stumps were drawn, a rapid making for motorcars, while players streamed towards the pavilion, looking at one another and seeing one another's faces in a clear gloom of light. Engines of the motorcoaches, which were to take them back to the Lyndale Hotel for the dinner dance to end Festival Week, were started.

Twenty thousand feet above the moor a strange wool-like clottage was moving across the black peaks of cumulo-nimbus, now ranged like a vast ampitheatre as though for the gods to appear in a final judgment before Götterdämmerung, 'Buster' was thinking : for the chains of the peaks might have been keeping guard all around the invaded summer heaven, ready for Donner to hurl his tremendous lightning bolts.

As he banked for the turn, 'Buster' saw many sea-birds whitely afloat above the vortex of clouds, tiny winged specks risen up out of danger of lower spinning winds that would suck them from the sea's surface and dislocate the joints of their wings.

The very air was waiting, while heavy bombards of nimbus clouds approached like a curtain of doom : among them a black whale floundering amidst sudden squalls of tearing, sea-whitening lesser winds which had crossed the bay between Hartland and Lundy and were now screaming over cultivated fields and coombes filled with primeval oakwoods; rocking slate roofs of isolated farmhouses and lifting the thatch of cottages—scattering, in the Valley of Rocks, a jangle of bicycles, whirling away banks of deck chairs, ripping canvas from wooden frames.

Confronting the storm like a quadruped Druid, King Billy remained on his rock, blown shaggy and not knowing which way to put his behind as he pattered on cloven feet shifting for security of tenure.

Puffs of hot air struck the cricket ground. And all of a sudden the roof of the pavilion, a jerry-built affair, was wracked off and sent, upended, over the bracken and rocky outcrops of the incult ground : to rest awhile, before being hurled up again and, after floating level for some seconds, to whirl upended and find rest among the rocks bordering the Severn Sea.

I suppose this is a breaking moment, I am leaving Shep Cot for ever. Have I really given up hope, except a black hope, a Tristan-like longing for the suns which have burned black after falling in rains of fire. A longing for Francis Thompson's 'after-sleeping.' Is it mere false pride, am I destroyed by the fear which is beyond pride, which seeks a 'noble' condition of a forlorn necessity?

Why do I dramatise myself? Because I have not dramatised my spiritual or true life in the service of others, by transmuting the marvellous scenes of my life, as I once intended? Good-bye, little shepherd's cot: here the children played, here sat Miranda by the open hearth when all life seemed to float in air, to be levitated as Piston would say, all grace and sweetness come into my life, a comradeship unbelievable between Miranda and myself living with an image that I felt I could not sustain.

The rear wheels of the Silver Eagle were ploughing furrows of sloppy black peat as the vehicle slid and yawed to the crest of The Chains. There the driver found himself in a sudden calm amidst queer little clusters of flickering blue discharges: silent and magnified skeleton-winged butterflies. Keeping the engine running, he lifted his legs over the low side of the body and felt without success for matches in the pocket of his leather flying-coat.

Bodger was curled on the floor by the pedals, shivering. The dog had shivered ever since seeing the gun put under the tonneau cover; for Bodger once had been shot at by his former master, Aaron Kedd, who owned a percussion-cap single-barrel gun firing black powder poured down the barrel, and rammed tight with paper wads before shot followed to be contained by more rammed paper.

Seeing that Bodger was apprehensive, Phillip withdrew the gun, removed barrel from stock, and put both back under the cover; whereupon Bodger's brown-toothed yawn signified relief.

Man and dog walked away from the motorcar. Phillip was think-ing. This must be like the electric storm in *Moby Dick*, masts and rigging of the ship frosted blue with St. Elmo's Fire. And suddenly he felt release from a dull acceptance of life being finished: and had reached the tumulus, where often he had stood to look over the Atlantic, when the sky appeared to split down a jagged line of violet light; and the obscuring vapours opened to reveal an immense copper-coloured cloud towering above other clouds moving, white-cowl-like, to smudge away the halo'd sun. A secon-dary drove of clouds, dark and thick, with ragged edges, trailed below the white hoods—but in the opposite direction.

These lower, darker cumulus clouds were fuming and tumbling in the skyey war between heat and cold : never could heat and cold, he thought, assimilate the other. The very efforts to come together caused friction leading to violence.

And violent it was, that war between opposites fought that afternoon on The Chains. Forked lightning hissed continuously; air-cleaving bolts released a smell of sulphurous oxide out of rain-pools instantaneously seeming to be made to boil and cool again in one stroke. Down flailed blobs of ice, to bounce on back and head of Phillip as he held Bodger under his coat.

After the barrage of hail came the bayonets of rain, stabbing thick and hard; but it was warm after the hail. And soon The Chains, fifteen hundred feet above the sea, was a glittering sheet of water from which a semblance of glassy thistles rose a foot high and side by side, so violent was the down-hurled rain. And the tops of the clumps of sedge-grass were linked by pale blue waving gossamers of St. Elmos Fire. Hurray! Hurray!

I am the only human spectator on The Chains who will know all the details of this moment in time!

The terrific purple flashes of lightning, followed by instant shocks of thunder as the nimbus clouds passed overhead at 3–400 feet : the water hissing down as upon a ragged lake : each flash lighting up the glassy thistles which are growing out of this lagoon, some nearly a foot high, to die and give place to others as the clouds shed their liquor!

I shall record all the details which my inborn visual gift, conjoined with that of the use of words—a clumsy phrase—will bring alive before some reader of the future!

How ironic, that I was nearly destroyed by the defects of what qualities I possess! No funeral pyre in this slashing, roaring, light-cracking battlefield night—the very elements at war among themselves, the old gods come together to thwart my cowardice, to bestow on me their gifts of courage!

Those curious rosy lights playing about below the senior flashes of the sky-cracking purple jags : fire-balls in play, shooting up from moor grass clumps and the wilted white tuffs of the cotton grass, to die away and be succeeded by others, each pink ball about two feet in diameter, and all gentle, a rosy play of infants while the giants fling their bolts in great angry veins of electric death!

I can go home after all this, I have a warm place to go to, I am free, this isn't Passchendaele—there all were homeless—I am free—

"I am free!" he shouted. "Brother Water and Sister Air! I am free with you! Never again shall I cower away from the elements, to mouch about inside a room with the death wish!"

A cloud directly above him was changing colour from a dirty grey-green to a ghastly swirling white as it heaved like a con-glomeration of enormous maggots. It had such a sinister appearance that he stood still upon the tumulus and stared up at it, a dis-coloured Chinese dragon: an Eskimo painter's idea of a tropical octopus. He picked up the shivering Bodger in his arms—

—then from one tentacle lowering upon the earth issued a stun-ning flash. He felt a blow on the top of his head, breaking body from legs as the earth rose up to his eyes. He thought, beyond an immense fear, that his heart was going to stop with his non-breathing against a stifling mass of horrible burning hair—

Black lashing rain was rattling on the perspex dome over the Brig's head and upon the wings of the two-seater, which was being hurled all ways, out of control. A dark cumulo-nimbus cloud, with a black top like the head of a colossal elephant with curving trunk moved slowly up to the shuddering glider, under the perspex dome of which were two pinched-in leather-capped heads, with wan faces. Laura did not understand what her companion was saying, for he spoke through teeth dentures rattling every time he exhaled frosted breath. When he stabbed with a finger towards the ugly black cloud, and then put his hands together as for prayer, and pointed them downwards, she understood that she must dive away from it.

Grey vapour rushing up and past caused the sailplane to judder, to bounce, to be thrown side-up and then on its tail. Hail rattled on a thick covering of ice which had enamel'd the wings to a depth of between one-and-a-half to two inches. This caused a turbulent slipstream to render the controls almost useless.

The sailplane rose up on its tail, and fell like a sodden shoe. Laura equalised elevator and rudder, hoping to gain flying speed by diving. And while falling, she saw the perspex dome burning white. She could not see. She felt her arms on the control half-wheel to be broken. Green sparks snapped about her, and when she put a gloved hand to her face one stabbed into her chin. Another blow struck her violently in the back. Some time after-wards she was aware as from a great distance that the Brig's head had struck her.

Lightning had run along the radio aerial trailing from the tail to the set and blown the valves. Travelling along the aluminium wings it burst free many of the rivets holding aluminium sheets to frame; but of this she was not aware at the moment.

The altimeter wasn't working, it had been burned out by the lightning strike. She extended the air-brakes and put the sailplane into a steep spiralling descent; and after some time was surprised by the sound of a voice come back after her ear-drums had clicked. As they moved out of the area of ionized air, she could hear what he was saying.

"I'm bailing out, Laura. To lighten the outfit. We'll crack up otherwise. You'll have a chance alone. Go down and find a break in the overcast. You'll have control without my dead weight. Put her nose down. I'm giving orders here! Keep her as steady as you can. God bless you, darling."

Having managed somehow to unfasten his safety belt he bumped up the hood, which was flung back, allowing him to dive head-first into obscurity, leaving Laura in an open cockpit after the hood had been torn away.

At first The Brig had fallen at about one hundred miles an hour through rain which was dropping at a little more than half his speed. He knew the danger of pulling the rip-cord : possibility of canopy tearing with extra weight of water. He turned over and over, seeing nothing beyond sudden flares of light. If only he knew the height at which he baled out. If ten thousand feet, it would take seventy two seconds to hit the deck. He began to count from ten to thirty—allowing ten seconds to have lapsed before he started counting. At *thirty* he opened up, not knowing that he had been dropping into a hundred-mile updraught. The fabric held; the shock caused him temporarily to lose consciousness; then he was aware of swinging wide sometimes with legs above his head, while feeling any moment he would be jerked out of his harness. He was buffeted until he felt the blows must burst the fabric of his umbrella. His face was cut by stinging hail and when above the cumulo-nimbus he was aware of an intense freezing cold.

He began to feel sleepy, to float in a drowse of green water-meadows, he saw mayflies in sunshine rising into the air after the dance of the drakes over the reeds by the river-bank. He let his mayfly float out on the thin, undressed line, and lightly touch the wimpling surface, it floated downstream, it disappeared; he struck; a trout was on, his first trout! splashing, splashing at the edge of the water while the net was placed behind the tail and then lifted, as Daddy has shown him. And he saw himself taking the trout home to show Mother, but Mother had gone away with another man and when Daddy was killed in the tank battle at Cambrai he was alone for ever and for ever—

The body of Phillip, beside that of Bodger partly charred by lightning, lay head down on the northern slope of the tumulus. He was unconscious and snoring irregularly. In a dark cave he was listening to hear the next beat of his heart, waiting in enormous fear that he had heard the last beat and was dead.

He lay in the dark cave of Time lost : wearing sailor suit with white skirt and no knickers underneath, pulling aside the fireguard he was forbidden to touch, with the shovel and coal in the hod, but he had to see what would happen when he pushed Mavis into the fire and she was screaming like he screamed when Daddy burned his bare bottom with the cane—bottom was a naughty word, it was really bee-tee-em.

As he waited for his heart to beat again in fear that he was dead, unable to breathe under the earth with his ears ringing . . . *thump!* . . . his heart had beat again and the Carabineer in woollen balaclava helmet was digging him out of the sulphurous stench of earth while his head was ringing and black-and-white zigzag snake flickering and darting out of his left eye. The windmill across the Messines road blazed until its arms dropped to pieces into running blazing tar until it became darker and darker . . .

Thump!

His heart had beaten, he was not dead ! His head was fixed to his elbow : stripe-vibrating eyes protruded from heavy skull of dazed marble, an all-red nightmare in which he was trying to drag monstrous clogged feet through mud suddenly became black-brilliant as in his roll of photographic-negative hung to dry in the dark-room at home lit by his red-lantern on a chest-of-drawers among boxes and travelling trunks.

While Phillip was lying unconscious upon the burial mound, a stag, walking stiffly after much running, was crossing The Chains, making for harbour in the Horrock valley. Antlers, body, legs were swathed in blue haze. It had been roused out of Summer House Hill that morning, and had run in a circle of thirty odd miles, several of them down stony streams, to throw off scent.

There followed silence of tongue and horn for some hours; it got up from under the shade of a rowan tree and headed north until bewildered by lightning and drenched by rain.

Two young hounds, entries of that season, had lost their way. They had been wandering about in the storm when the stag had appeared, an apparition surrounded by blue shimmer. They followed it docilely; and when the stag reached the raised mound and lay down they lay beside it, for comfort and warmth.

Thump!

He was riding his 3-speed Swift bike under flares rising in darkness and lighting the way into the wailing of Strombos gas-horns. From glittering shell-holes grew the lilies of the dead. Wailing sound and hovering green-white stalks were lost in a great livid light which bubbled out of the Salient's huge cauldron. He was floating on the light, floating above the duck-boards while the German howitzers were firing from the Gheluvelt plateau on his left. The duck-board led to Kansas Cross. If only he could get to Kansas Cross he would see Cousin Willie and the world would be saved.

The light was growing dim, the British 18-pounders on the line of the Steenbeke were firing shrapnel with red-burning fuses passing just over his head. His bike was going down, down into the morass, dragged down by the weight of the barrage. Down, down into darkness. Was he dying?

Thump!

He saw Cousin Willie beside him. Willie was lifting him up, he followed Willie floating before him towards a line of larger, oval orange-slower-burning flashes which must be from the line of British six-inch howitzers wheel-to-wheel on the Menin Road.

He could not see Willie : he could not move : he was drowning in a shell-hole, he would never see the white-dusty lanes of Kent again, he was between two great pulsings of Europe's blood running to waste in the light-as-day flashes of four thousand guns ringing the Salient, two pulsings of light in dying Europe's cauldron flaming to the zenith and making the slough of despond as plain as day, and yet in utter darkness because no one at home knew the truth.

Thump!

He was rising up from the morass, he was saved so that the truth should not be lost in death's dateless night. Only he could write it all, for he had seen Willie plain, as Willie saw Shelley plain. He must carry Europe's dead in his arms through the blood-weeping night.

Thump!

He had got through! He had reached the Town-major's office in the Old Prison of Ypres!

And his heart beat again, a great tongueless bell in the ruins of the Cathedral beside the Cloth Hall; and he was carrying his sister, small and burned in the fire, in his arms.

Thus the release of obsessional pictures among others filling millions of cells of one brain, messages fired electrically in normal times but now stimulated abnormally by a bolt of lightning. The brain cells were fed by more than four miles of veins containing blood; each cell a unit of intelligence, a nerve and its unit commander linked to an appropriate series of muscles, each one transmitting instructions in order to comply with demands.

The brain an entire G.H.Q. whence messages were dispatched electrically, as over a telephone system, to demand action ... a kaleidoscope of batteries firing on targets, co-ordinated by a Headquarters Staff ordering a ceaseless barrage of cross-fire and cross-signal; and sometimes to temporary destruction through over-organisation due to anxiety, to fear in all its sad forms.

And thus the release of living pictures out of Time past, composed of visual records which were of what once was called dead life; but which is not dead, only delayed in the slow corrosion of the body whence they would depart when the body was given up, to exist within the energy of the unseen world.

Phillip's eyes opened upon the visible world and he realised slowly that he was still alive; and dreadfully tired. He slept; and in a dream saw Melissa with his first wife Barley, insubstantial and diaphanous, moving among the phantoms of the past; and he wondered if the distance which seemed always to be between them, despite that they thought alike, was because the natural vital force in him had been burnt out by a dereliction of early life which had caused him to take an unnatural refuge in the Imagination.

And when his eyes opened again he lay there at rest, unfeeling wet and cold, and slowly his lost identity came back to him.

He was on The Chains; that was all.

Then supporting himself on an elbow, he saw Bodger lying beside him. All hair had been burned from face and body as the dog had been standing upon his fallen master, snout raised to utter a howl for help : heard by the two young hounds now lying close to him on one side, and beside the hounds lay a stag. They know, he thought, they know; and the poet knew, too, when he wrote, 'The lion shall lie down with the lamb'.

Phillip's habit of talking to himself in the cot, and to the tame robin, to deer seen on the horizon, to Bodger—now broke into lament. Getting to his feet shakily, he lifted the little bodged corpse and nursed it in his arms, crying out, "O Jesus God, this creature died for me!"

And memory brought back the scene on the Burrows by the estuary where he had walked with Laura earlier in the summer. And you, Bodger, were with us. Were you there, too, Willie, with your spaniel Billjohn? You died on your lonely pathway for the truth, you really did die, not make a mock of it as I have done. You, too, knew that every conquering war is lost until it gives back its revelation of truth. And you, Julian Warbeck, you were there. Are you dead as well? You said on that night of October, nineteen twenty three, when the spaniel was washed up with Willie on the sands of Crow Island, you said, We should give Maddison the honour and purity of fire. But it was only the spaniel the fishermen allowed us to burn. You thought it was the reward of ten shillings for a corpse they wanted, and so would not let Willie's body be taken from their boat. Surely it was pity for the dead boy, Julian, whose fame, like that of Keats, was writ in water? I liked you, arrogant Julian, when I saw your tears in the firelight as the swallows were flying over on their autumn migration. And you began to quote from your poet-god, Swinburne.

With that he fell face down in the water, hearing Julian's voice of grief crying,

> I the nightingale all spring through
> O swallow, sister, O changing swallow,
> All spring through till the spring be done
> Clothed with the light of the night on the dew
> Sing, while the hours and the wild birds follow,
> Take flight and follow and find the sun . . .
> O swallow, sister, O fleeting swallow,
> My heart in me is a molten ember
> And over my head the waves have met.

And getting to his feet, he ambled on, holding the dead dog

to him as though a sleeping child were being carried; and coming to the Silver Eagle, a shimmer of blue, laid the body on the near-side bucket seat. Matches, where were any not reduced to watery pulp? He was feeling in the flapped pocket beside the gear-handle when there was a shriving flash; the motorcar became bleak, shorn of its shimmer. It fumed sulkily amidst a stench of burning rubber. A smoky yellow flame licked the far side of the box body. Then other flames arose crackling : the faggots were on fire above the petrol tank.

Remembering the petrol cans, Phillip hastened away. He stood distant by a score of yards, watching while flames rose higher and higher until, with sudden roar, the tank blew up, inducing a greater roar of expanding flames as the cans exploded and burning petrol spread to water plashes all around the motorcar.

Laura, encased above the waist in frozen rain, hands without feeling, saw below a hole in the cloud break, and a fire which might have been lit as a beacon. She put the stick forward and dived into the rift, which widened as she lost height. She thought of stress, and eased out of the dive, to continue in a declining spiral until she was at an estimated height of four thousand feet.

Drifting cumulus covered the green area. She put down the nose again, hoping to find land somewhere, while wondering if the Brig had already landed. Otherwise she had no feelings for him, or for herself. She wondered if you felt a like indifference when you were dying.

And then she saw flames through grey mist and put forward the stick and made directly for the beacon. She dived through heavy rain, but didn't care if the wings fell off. She levelled out too early and made a pancake landing in what she thought must be a shallow lake. The craft bumped and tipped. A wing tore off. She slewed to rest among what looked like crimson Chinese lanterns being tossed into the air, only to disappear and be succeeded by others curving up and floating around until they seemed to puff out; while those that fell quickly to the ground appeared to explode.

Phillip sloshed to the broken glider, seeing that one seat was empty; and Laura, helmet'd head forward, immobile as though dead.

He touched her cheek; it was cold. She was breathing. He lifted one arm, then another, with no resistance. He stood there, knowing not what to do, until an eye opened, tremulously. He must get her to the fire, now a mass of bright oak flames about a gaunt chassis strangely rusted. He was putting his hands under her arms to heave her out when she murmured, "I—can't—find—my—legs."

"They're numb with cold," he replied, wondering what he should do if they were broken. If left there, she would die of exposure.

Having unfastened the belt he managed to lug her out of the cockpit. It took many attempts to heave the body over his left shoulder and then to rise; but he managed to get her more or less upright against the cockpit and then over his shoulder and stagger on towards the fire.

"I think—I—can—walk-now," she said between pauses to rest. "Why—is—everything—so—blue?"

"Electrical discharges. Some are red—look—ahead—"

A hesitant dance, as of crimson flares without vitality, mere wraiths of a war which was beyond them, was hovering about the burning motorcar—bulbous and hesitant, they vanished a moment after taking to the air.

He slid her off his shoulder, and all she said was, "I'm so cold."

"I'll soon get you warm by the fire, then we'll go down to the cot."

Some time later, as they walked hand in hand to the northern edge of the plateau they saw the stag about a hundred yards away, walking as though run stiff : or had it been struck by lighting? The two hounds still accompanied the animal.

Now below them lay the slope to the common, white with water gushing down everywhere.

Six miles above the earth Falcon One—that gay and near-living companion of skyey days—was upside down. 'Buster' managed to recover control, only to fall into a spin. After equalising the controls he was diving to regain flying speed when he moved unknowing into an updraught. The sudden shock cracked a wingroot. The wing was whirled away and up, while in expunging mist the pivotless craft was tossed about, to fall whirling at times like a sycamore seed, while the pilot saw below him the dark fuming trunk of the tornado.

In this fume the body of the Brig was spinning, frozen, all life departed. Then the third force flicked through the canopy of Falcon One to seek the steel-corset'd body of Hugh, twenty-third and last Baron Cloudesley of Lyonesse, in Cornwall.

Chapter 25

WATERSHED

The little runner of the West Lyn, where once Laura had sailed a paper boat, was a ten-foot-wide torrent leaping and foaming downhill with the speed of a trotting horse. When she stood beside Phillip just above the cot, she saw it to be an island, dividing the flood which was two feet up the walls. They were on what was now the bank of a river increasing its territory every minute.

They crossed the common, making for the farm at the beginning of the lane. He knocked on the door, which was opened by the farm-wife.

"This lady has crashed in her glider. Can you take her in, while I go on to Barbrook?"

"My husband has just come from there, sir. He said th' water be all auver th' road. The young leddy is welcome to stay wi' us, if her be a mind to't. Plaize to come in and set by th' vire. If her's sobbled wet, I could lend her my clothes—"

"Thank you, I must go on. Laura, will you accept this lady's kind invitation to stay here and rest?"

"Aw, 'tes Mr. Madd'zn and Miss Laura! I didden recognize 'ee before! You look proper tired people, if you'll excuse me zaying it, zur! Have 'ee th' little old dog with 'ee?"

"He was struck by lightning."

"Vancy that now! Was that your motorcar a' vire on The Chains? Us zeed vlames up there, and wondered what had happened, didn't us, mother?"

"That was struck, too."

"My dear soul! And you was saved?" cried the farmer.

Laura said, "Thank you, but I think I'll go with my friend. I feel better now."

They trudged up the narrow sunken lane, holding hands. The flash-daze was still behind Phillip's eyes, his head aching as he forced himself to push on, shoes squelching. Neither spoke; the evening was winter-dark though not yet seven o'clock. Move-

339

ment alone would keep Laura from breaking down, he thought, as with young soldiers coming out of battle.

It was a grinding walk through falling rain and the gulley a-run with water. The storm had moved away over the sea. From afar came a continuing rumble as of an artillery barrage. This, thought Phillip, is the war of the elements—Fire conscripting air to force turbulence between itself and its enemy, Water! Water rising as vapour to quell insurrection! Friction between the two elements calling into being a third force, which struck blindly at any object in air or on earth, so to escape from tyranny!

Aunt Dora in that sunny September of 1916: telling him of the Eyrines, the Furies of ancient Greek legend, called the Eumenides, the Kindly Ones in the hope of changing malice into magnanimity —and thus leading to the destruction of Hellas.

Mavis in Ionian Cottage: Elizabeth damned up with despair, like the swirling water behind the bridge at Barbrook. Mavis the dreaming girl with the large brown eyes, her spirit religio-poetical, then withdrawn, dependent in adult life on a mother for sustenance spiritual and material...a 'vulture' to her petrofact father. Love and the loveless—himself both generous and mean—a bravado coward among better men who had found peace together on the cornfields of Picardy and the wet, the treeless, the grave-set plain of Flanders.

I was the coward; but my Doppelgänger had desperate courage. Sister Elizabeth had no outlet for her corroding despair. A pale withdrawn face among thousands of others hurrying on the stone paving-stones of London Bridge: hurrying, hurrying through roar of iron-shod hoofs and iron-hooped wheels upon the cobbles spanning Thames: desperate-hoping pale faces becoming withdrawn above duckboards winding among the linked water-craters of the Salient, cringing at droning roar of howitzer shells descending— both effects of the same cause.

"We'll soon be there, Laura."

Water-roar under trees more insistent. Small lights flashing below. They went down the steep narrow lane above swirling river. Side eddies washing in pulses over the lane.

"Hold my hand."

They got through wading slowly, and came to an arched stone bridge beside a gaunt house with a monkey tree arising from a flooded front garden.

Small lights were flashing within one dimly-seen room. An old woman was standing in water to her knees, outside an open door of the house.

"My dear soul, 'tes turrible. The poor lady wor' all alone. 'Er were face down floating in her parlour, midears."

"We've just come down from the moor! Water is running everywhere!"

"Aye, 'twas comin' down like aught out of a sieve."

"I must cross the river, to get to the caravan site on Green Meadow."

"You bain't goin' vor cross thaccy bridge, midears? Thik watter be ravin' over th' wall like a local praicher!"

"My wife and children are camping down on the Green Meadow."

"God help 'ee, midear."

They stood beside the old woman. Water was moving in circular pulses before the bridge, revealing one drowned sheep after another, floating head down, in the eddy.

" 'Tes a loss, midears, 'tes a loss!" mourned the woman.

Figures waded out of the house, carrying a corpse. The rescuers were firemen, by their peaked caps. A policeman flashed a light.

"You can't get over the river!", he shouted. "The bridge will go any moment!"

The top of the wall of the upper parapet was just visible. Taking Laura's hand, Phillip pressed forward against water up to his waist.

"Come back, there! You'll be drowned!" yelled the policeman, shining torch on Laura, while someone tried to grab her. She cried out, "He wants to join his friend Plato! So do I! Buona Notte!!" and waded after him, water surging breast-high.

Upstream, against the stone cutwaters, the torrent tore into branches of trees lodged there with the body of an inverted bullock. The legs were visible in motorcar lights; red adorned with stems of balsam plants, strays from some water-side garden.

By the light Phillip and Laura got across to higher ground and sat down. A curious thing happened. The motorcar headlights began to turn blue, then purple as the vehicle was dragged away into darkness.

Soon the darkness became stellar with tiny flashes of hand torches. A sergeant of police stood there, holding a bicycle of which only the handle-bars were visible. He had to shout to make himself heard. "You and the lady were lucky, sir. The bridge may go any moment now. You're Captain Maddison, sir? Did you see a fire on The Chains above your place?"

"I went there in my motorcar, and lightning struck it, constable."

"Funny place to go for a car ride in a storm, sir."

"It was a beacon to help the gliders," Laura replied.

"Ah yes, there were gliders up from Porlock marshes." He peered at Laura. "Weren't you the lady secretary in one of them today? Speak up, miss, please!"

Laura yelled, "I went up with Brigadier Tarr! He baled out!"

"I'd like to ask you a few questions, sir. I suppose you know where he was due to land, or likely to land?"

Laura replied, "We were in turbulent overcast when he dropped!"

Phillip cried, "I'm sorry to interrupt, officer, but my wife and children are in a caravan on the Green Meadow!"

"This constable will take you down in his car. How did you hurt your eye, sir?"

The sergeant had heard about the cricket match in the Valley of Rocks.

"I—was—struck—by—lightning."

He felt a return of the white and hollow porcelain illusion of himself looking out blankly through vertical, flickering bars. As they were getting into the little Morris Minor there was an increased roar followed by leaping white waves as the bridge broke and released the dammed-up waters.

Down the Glen went the leaping West Lyn, rolling boulders of all weights up to ten tons, uprooting and sweeping trees into the deepening gorge. Some beech trees of twelve feet and more in girth were splintered, the bark ground off the boles in transit among rocks tumbling down, hundreds of tons of stone in overwhelming movement. The flood swept over the Green Meadow; and roaring seawards, pushed to pieces the arched road-bridge at the head of the village; and conjoining with the heavier surges of the East Lyn, toppled over part of a hotel in a grind of boulders, trees, motorcars, bodies animal and human, doors and roofs and entire walls of cottages into the Severn Sea.

Globe-Mornington was sitting before the fire in the butler's pantry, listening to the radio. Opposite him sat Corney, host of The Marksman Inn, in another arm-chair. A decanter of brandy stood on a Chippendale butler's tray, together with unused glasses and a plate of sandwiches covered by a second plate.

Rain beat against the french-windows. Three candles burned on a shelf above the open hearth.

High-speed Morse on the short wave-band sounded, rapid and irritable, from the loud-speaker on a table against the wall.

"I suppose, Mr. Corney, some tramp-skipper sending a message to his wife, telling her to have steak and french fried potatoes ready for his supper when he reaches Tiger Bay?"

"With respect to you, Mr. Mornington, my knowledge of the Morse code, indicates that the Amphibious Warfare little lot at Fremington is sending a DUKW with crew on the road to Lynton."

"Good weather for ducks, eh? Excuse my joke, but even Nero fiddled while Rome was burnin'. Can I offer you a drink, from my personal cellar?"

"Not at the moment thank you, Mr. Mornington. Excuse me, but I hope your hot-water system ain't about to blow up. I can 'ear it rumblin' away through the wall behind me."

"Perhaps it's that fellow from M.I.5. you were telling me about, Mr. Corney. After all, you never know who is who nowadays, do you?"

"You appear to want to query my information, Mr. Mornington. I tell you that he was around my 'ouse this morning, making enquiries about your gliding gentlemen."

"I'll go and shut the flap of the stove. Do you feel like a cup of tea?"

"Ah, I can always make do with a cup of char!"

" 'Char'! What memories that Hindustani word brings back!"

Globe-Mornington's memories were of a play in which he acted with George Arliss, *The Green Goddess*.

The telephone rang.

Corney sat uneasily still until the other man returned, saying, "You're right, Mr. Corney! It's a fellow from the Special Branch at Scotland Yard, wanting a word with his Lordship. Private matter, he said. I told him his Lordship wasn't back yet."

"No peace for the wicked," he exclaimed a moment later, when the telephone bell rang again. "That may be his Lordship! Sorry to keep having to leave you. The kettle's on, that's something positive, Mr. Corney, like Shakespeare's little candle in a naughty world."

He came back, saying, "It's the sergeant of our local police, reporting Miss Laura and Captain Maddison on their way here.

The river burst its banks when Barbrook bridge gave way. Would you believe it? Doesn't say much for local building does it? Still, it's been coming down cats and dogs for five hours now. Anyway, those two are safe, that's a relief. Patient you, Mr. Corney. I'll make the tea now."

The two men were sipping sweet strong tea laced with brandy when there came a banging on the front door.

"Welcome, Sir and Madam!" he said, leading them straight in. "Please to come into my parlour. Excuse this informality, but it's the only decent fire in the house. Tea with brown sugar, laced by Courvoisier is highly recommended. You know Mr. Corney, I think. Do sit down, now, miss, the tea was made this very minute. Brandy for you? And for you, sir?" After serving, he knelt to remove Laura's wet shoes.

She sat still, knees together, toes turned in, tears dripping down a vacant face.

"Eau-de-vie they call it, water of life. Tea too hot, miss? I'll pour some away." He jerked half the cup into the fire, topped it up with brandy. "That's better. How about you, sir?"

Phillip was sitting with eyes shut in a smoke-blackened face, hands gripping wooden arms of chair, broken skin of heavy bruise on one cheekbone, head nearly overborne by pain.

"He's shocked," Laura said in a whisper. "He was struck by lightning, which killed his little dog."

Mornington put finger to lips, and looked across at Corney.

"I'd like to run you both hot baths, miss."

"I must go down to Lynmouth," Phillip said hoarsely.

The telephone bell rang.

"Mrs. Bucentaur would like a word with you, sir. Let me give you an arm." He helped Phillip to the hall, while saying in a low voice, "I gather Miss Miranda is missing. I fancy her mother wants to ask if you've seen her."

Molly's voice was controlled. "Miranda was gone before I could stop her. Did you come across her at Shepcot? No? Well then, should she have gone to find you up there, will the door be unlocked do you think?"

"The door is unlocked, M—Molly."

By now the kitchen would be six feet under water. "Molly, a helicopter is on the way here, also a wheeled landing craft."

"You don't mean she may have wandered somewhere near the river? Mornington tells me it's broken its banks. Are you there, Phillip? Hullo—hullo. Phillip!"

"They are—getting organised—walkie talkie sets—police fire-men—on the the road—from Barbrook—to—Lynton."

"Firemen—in all this rain?"

"To pump—out—houses."

While Molly was saying how clever of them to think of that, Mr. Corney came into the room. His face was wan, desolate. He had seen his old master, Manfred, standing beside the hearth in Mr. Mornington's room. He knew he had come to fetch Master Hugh—

Laura took the telephone receiver. "Molly" she said in a low voice, "Mornington has told me about Miranda. Capella will be with her. She will be a visible mark for any helicopter. So don't worry. I'm sure she is all right. No, we couldn't see very far when we came down. Phillip's beacon saved my life. He drove up, after leaving the cricket match, to make a bonfire on The Chains. I saw the flames after the Brig bailed out to lighten the glider when our wings iced up. No; there's no news of 'Buster' either, I'm afraid."

"Keep your heart high, darling. Hugh is a very good pilot, and may have flown right out of the storm area. So he may yet have got the long-distance record after all!"

"He hoped to get to Redhill in Surrey!" The voice contained a dangerous euphoric excitement.

"How clever of him, darling. I'm keeping my fingers crossed for the Brig too. Now go and have a bath, and then to bed with a couple of hot-water bottles. The sun will be shining when you wake up! Now don't worry about the Brig. He's been in a worse jam than this, and come through. Did Lucy and the children get back all right? Any news of Peter, that dear child? Hullo! Can you hear me? Are you still there, Laura?"

Laura had gone down on the floor.

During six hours of rain, nine inches had fallen upon The Chains. From that lonely area under clouds three score runners had swelled into torrents leaping in creamy surge down both nor-thern and southern slopes of the watershed, bearing in their freshets the bodies of men, women, and children to both Severn Sea and English Channel—those western arms of Atlantic ocean which, since creation, has known four winds pouring across its wastes—names which were part of the very soul of Theodora Maddison, from her beloved Homer—Boreas whose home was the polar ice-fields: Euros, dry and bitter from the East, depressing

life in plant and mammal : Notos the South Wind, fanning wavelets in steady wan and wap upon shores of broken sea-shell and
crumbled rock : innocent and delinquent Zephyros, gentle in play
with leaf and feather, bringing peace to flower and bird and
cradled babe.

Shortly after ten o'clock that morning Peter had gone to the
meet of stag-hounds, and enjoyed the gay scene : the horses, the
riders, the cheerful faces, the crowds of summer visitors. He had
watched the two gliders soaring above the Valley of Rocks,
and wanted to go there to watch the cricket; but there was so
much to see that he lingered, while some old hounds, a few couples
of tufters, were taken into the wood to rouse the old stag which
harboured there.

At first the stag had refused to get up from its day-resting place.
The tufters had bayed it and the stag had seemed not to bother
much about them. At last it had got up and ran to the bed, or
harbour, a boy told Peter, of a smaller stag, which it tried to
get to run for it. A bit of a coward thought Peter, but the younger
stag wasn't a fool; it lay close in its bed of bracken, so the old
stag made off somewhere else, and eventually—after more than
an hour—got a hind to run for it. The old tufters knew it wasn't
the season for hind-hunting, so they were taken off the line of
the hind and laid on to the scent of the stag who had scarpered,
the boy—who had by now become Peter's friend—declared.

The stag having broken cover, the tufters were taken back to
the barn where the rest of the pack had been shut up, singing
mournfully.

Peter and his new friend didn't wait to see the hounds laid on
the line of scent where the old stag had run, but went on up to
The Chains hoping to see where the stag was making for. It was
a blazing hot climb, and they were soon puffed; but kept on,
eventually reaching the tumulus, which Peter knew well from
having walked there with Dad and his brothers two weeks before
—a period of time which now seemed to be part of another world
altogether, so pleasant was it camping on Green Meadow, paddling the canoe, fishing, and having all kinds of lovely things to do.

When the pack had gone over The Chains, and out of sight
of all riders except whippers-in and huntsmen, who wore scarlet
coats, while the field were in tweeds and bowler hats, the two
boys went down to Lynmouth. Peter wanted to show his new
friend the canoe; but, he said, he couldn't take him out until he

had asked his father's permission, as he had promised that he wouldn't. The tide was out, so they walked over slimy stones of the little harbour to look at it, and admire. There Peter's initials were, underneath the name painted in black, *Sea Rover*.

"It needs repainting all over" he said. "Do you like red? I think I do."

"Red shows up far away, don't it?" said the boy.

"You're right! Will you help me to carry it up the road?"

Which was done, the job being lightened by the promise of a double cornet ice-cream. "I'll ask Major Piston, who lives here, if I may keep 'Sea Rover' in his garden, for the time being."

It was a light affair, and the boys, with rests, got it into the garden of Shelley's Cottage. Major Piston said of course they could park it there, and they went happily into the cafe next to Bevan's hotel and had double vanilla ice cornets.

Afterwards they were standing by Glenlyn bridge when Mr. Osgood Nilsson drove up in his old motorcar, and stopped to talk to them.

"Do you see what I see in the sky, Peter? I see som'pn brewing. I guess we're going to have a twister. Want to come with me and help haul my trailer out of the meadow by The Marksman Inn? You're both welcome."

So up the long hill they went with Mr. Nilsson; and to the meadow in front of the Marksman, where they helped push the caravan and fasten it by a towing pin to the bar. Then down again by another way under Scob Hill and so to Watersmeet and Myrtleberry Cleave to Lynton, and over the East Lyn bridge and up the hill above the West Lyn to Lynton, where the caravan was parked in Mr. Nilsson's garden.

"Now I guess we'll go down again and tow out your mother's caravan, Peter. Do you see what I see up there?"

"It looks like a storm coming, sir."

"British under-statement, Peter!"

Towering sullen cumulo-nimbus was moving rapidly east, while, lower down, scarves of copper-coloured vapour were moving west. "I guess she's beginning to spin around, Peter. No time to lose, brother!"

When they got to Green Meadow heavy drops were coming through the canopy of green leaves of the beeches in the Glen. The owner of the site was already busy. Two motorcars with towing bars, one a jeep, were drawing caravans up the steep cause-way to the road, pushed by their owners and helpers. As soon as these were on the road they were unhitched well in to the right of the road and the towing vehicles returned for more. Meanwhile Osgood and the boys had hitched on Phillip's old, steel-sheeted caravan, which was hauled up to Nilsson's house up the hill to Lynton, through wind and rain which swirled across the windscreen and tossed the branches of roadside trees.

Motorcars were now passing through the town, bringing spectators from the Valley of Rocks, while thunder grumbled in the distance. The caravan was left outside the gate, for Lucy to see when she passed by. Nilsson asked both boys in, but Peter said, "Thank you sir, but I think the river might rise, and perhaps come over Major Piston's garden, so I think I'll go down and find a safer place for my canoe. May I come back later?"

"By all means, Peter. And if you see your mother, tell her you're all welcome to camp in the garden, and pick a bone with us tonight," said Mrs. Nilsson.

So Peter and his friend hurried down the hill again, and carried the canoe up the steep curve of hill, where they managed to heave it over the stone wall above the glen, and tie the painter to a tree before letting it down gently to rest against the bole of the tree.

"I suppose you didn't see Phillip on your way back?", Rosalie asked her husband. He replied that they had come down the East valley, and that Phillip would have gone up the road to Barbrook. "I guess he's back in his hide-out as of now."

"I wonder if Miranda is with him? She knows the way there, of course. I saw her going after him, with her goat. What a dreadful thing her father did, before all those people. My goodness, listen to the wind!"

Peter decided to wait for his father, lest he came down from the Cot and, finding the meadow under water and no caravans, would think that they had all been washed away. He wore his bicycling cape, and his friend, who had gone over the bridge to fetch his from his home near the electric light shed, stood beside him.

Major Piston, seeing them standing on the bridge, asked them in to have sausage rolls and cocoa. He said his mother was baking that day, so they could stuff themselves as much as they liked. Peter explained why he had taken his canoe higher up the hill.

Piston replied, "Wind up, laddie! It would be safe as houses with us. We're more than five feet above the river's winter-level, and this cottage has stood here since Shelley stayed here in

eighteen hundred and twelve. How about a game of draughts?
You two toss who starts off against me."

"I bestways should wait for my father by the bridge, sir, thank
you all the same."

"What, in all this rain?"

"My cape shoots it all off, sir. And the rain is quite warm."

"Bring your old man in for a drink when he comes, my lad."

"I will, thank you, sir."

Darkness. Peter had been waiting for hours it seemed. When
he heard a terrible grinding roar up the gorge, he couldn't think
what it was at first, it was like hundreds of thousands of sacks of
coal being emptied through the coal-hole in the pavement outside
the coal-cellar of Hill House all at once. He and his friend ran
in terror up the hill, turning their heads to stare a moment before
hurrying for dear life. A great plunging, leaping whiteness of
water roaring so loud that it was like a concentration of thunder
in a cavern. The water seemed as high as the cottages below
the bridge. Spray went right over some roofs and when the spray
stopped the roofs had disappeared.

Peter's friend began to cry, saying that his mother and father
would be drowned. The only thing Peter could think of to comfort
him was to say that it was only the West Lyn that was bringing
down all the water. He added that his friend could stay with
them in the caravan for the night if he liked. But the boy cried
all the same. Peter said, "Look, the flood is going down, perhaps
something blocked the bridge higher up, like a dam, and when the
dam burst all the water came down at once."

Many people were now gathered on the steep corner at the
bottom of the hill. Some carried paraffin-vapour lanterns.
There were policemen with short-wave transmitter sets. Firemen
with short axes in their belts, to each of which was hooked a
spare electric torch, Peter observed.

His friend was still crying, so he asked a policeman what he
should do. The policeman advised him to go home.

"But his home is beside the East Lyn," replied Peter.

"Then why not take your friend home with you? It will be
a kindness, and we're all in this together now. It's an emergency."

He took out a note-book. "May I have your friend's name and
address?"

The boy gave a gasping sob. "Don't be afraid, lad, you've done nothing wrong. I only want your name for the record, so that we can let your parents know you're safe and sound this side."

He wrote down particulars and then turned to Peter, who told him that they had been camping on the Green Meadow, but Mr. Osgood Nilsson had towed away the caravan in time, with all the other caravans.

"Splendid! I don't suppose you know the names of the other caravan dwellers? Yes, I know Mr. Osgood Nilsson is an American writer. I'll make a note that your mother and family are staying at his house. Your 'gen' is very important. I'll report to my Chief right away. Good show, my lad!"

The policeman's voice was a little like that of Field-Marshal Montgomery, Peter thought. Then he saw that he wore the riband of the Africa Star amongst others under his cloak.

"Your name? Any relation of Captain Maddison, who lives at Shep Cot? You're his son, are you. I suppose you don't know where he is to be found just now?"

"I've been waiting for Dad here, sir. He was with my mother and brothers and sisters at the cricket match this morning. I went to the meet of stag-hounds on Summer House Hill, so I don't bestways know where he is just now."

"You didn't see him upon the moor, in his motorcar?"

"No, sir."

Peter was toiling up the steep bend in the road, holding the arm of his weepy little friend, when the 'man from the paper of the times' stopped his motorcar and invited the two boys to get in, saying he was going up to Lynton. As he drove up the hill he asked Peter questions, starting off with, "Have you heard of Rudolf Hess?"

"Yes, sir."

"From your father? You did. And from Lord Cloudesley as well? Do you know of any plan to rescue Hess by glider? Lord Cloudesley's father knew him, didn't he, in those chivalrous days of the First World War, you know, dropping messages over each other's airfields and all that sort of thing. I thought so. Didn't your father also see Hess in Germany before the last war? Was it with Göring, did you know? Sir Piers Tofield went with your father, or rather the other way, wasn't it, for Sir Piers was then working in film production in Berlin. Your father went out to see Sir Piers, sailing in the *Bremen* from Southampton, as a matter of fact. Did they meet Birkin there, with Hitler, do you know? You're not sure? Oh, one more thing. Have you ever

heard your father speak of going to prison just after the First
World War?"

"I don't bestways know about that, sir" replied Peter, wondering if the man was a spy. He was pretty sure he was that when he
heard the last question.

"Your father is part German, isn't he?"

"You'd better ask him yourself, sir."

"I'll see you both safe and sound with your Mum," said the
fellow, "then I'll be on my way. And if I come across your father,
I'll tell him where you are."

"Thank you very much, sir, and also for the ride!"

The reporter asked to see Osgood Nilsson, who came out of
his study (which he was preparing as a bedroom, after putting
away all his papers, for other homeless people).

"I come from the paper of the times, sir—"

"You do, do you, you Fleet Street buzzard? Come in, and
I'll give you a drink, but this is a social visit, and off the record."

"I understand, Mr. Nilsson. Dog does not eat dog."

"What'je mean by that?"

"Only my little joke, Mr. Nilsson. I know very well that as a
foreign correspondent in Europe you're the top brass." You old
ham, he said to himself.

Both Lynmouth by the sea and Lynton on the hill were in
complete darkness. Part of the electric power house, wherein a
dynamo was worked by a turbine fed by water brought in a leat
down the wide and sombre valley of the East Lyn, was on its way
to the sea, with various fragmentated cottages. The flood, pouring
down the two valleys of East and West Lyn, was surging to the
harbour twenty feet above normal summer level of the combined
river-bed. It rushed eight feet above the street, lined with houses
on both sides, filling some cottages to their bedroom floors while
others had fallen entire.

One of the cottages which had, in part, withstood the flood
was Ionian Cottage. It may be remembered that it was built in
part over the river bed, rising ten feet above a mason'd wall when
the success of *Lorna Doone* had brought hundreds of summer
visitors, by coach and carriage, to the little fishing village already
known to the few for its association with the poets Shelley and
Southey.

The high river-wall was soundly built along the straight
course of the combined Lyns, permitting their flowings to pass

below without hindrance until this evening: when the eastern gable end of the cottage, built on to and above the river-wall, had given way in the first plunging roar of water released at Barbrook. Thus a bedroom was exposed to the weather. And in that bedroom, according to a short-wave radio message from a policeman standing on the east bank above the lapping edge of the flood, two women were marooned. He reported that he had seen a lighted oil-lamp carried across the disclosed bedroom, to and fro several times, as a signal. Then a far door had opened and two women went into what appeared to be an adjoining bedroom overlooking the street.

Then darkness.

The road through the trees steepened on the last half mile There were no lights by which Phillip could see the way. He fell more than once, losing co-ordination with his right hand and the rough top of the stone-wall built up from the side of the road. Behind the wall arose trees growing above the precipitous slope which ended at the river.

Stopping before the final downward sweep of the road he saw, while resting against the woodland wall, a long white object which on inspection he saw to be a canoe. Having neither matches nor torch he was unable to decide if it were Peter's. If it were Peter's, then it had either been stolen, or, more likely, put there above possible flood. So Peter might be alive!

With return of hope he went on down the hill to get help to carry the canoe. The East Lyn was now running with less turmoil but with great surge of white water over masses of rock and uprooted trees carried down with motorcars, cattle, mason'd walls and wooden floors of cottages. Men in steel helmets were lying down, one had a Lewis gun, the water gleamed with German flares across the marsh, where the enemy held the left bank of the Ancre below Thiepval. The R.S.M. said Jerry had broken through, but why was he talking about the effects of the flow of water?

Phillip tried to hold on to words describing how slabs of rock had been detached from the old river bed after being under-cut by water-streams so rapid that they appeared to have been rolled down the Glen only a little less in speed than that of the spate.

"It required only two such sections of displaced rock to arrive together under the bridge to crack the masoned structure, which then gave way, releasing a secondary volume of water which carried with it sufficient force to destroy walls of some of the boarding houses and cottages lining the street below."

"Then you'd say that the chief factors causing the disaster are :— (a) the steep descent of gorge; (b) the dislocation of rocks and boulders already part of the river-bed, which got wedged under the bridge and caused a battering-ram effect of rock and water together?"

Hallucination passed. He remembered with stony despair where and what he was. He recognized the questioner as 'the man from the paper of the times'.

He said to the sergeant of police, "My sister and a friend are marooned in a cottage about sixty yards down the street. There is an eddy or backflow coming *up* the street, caused by back-pressure of the main flood in front of us. Will you help me to get down a canoe, please?"

"Afraid not, sir. You'd never make it. There are trees under the white water down there, and great boulders, even motorcars."

"I must get across to my sister."

"Sorry, sir. But I'd like to say this : the flood is receding, and those houses which are damaged are likely to stand up. Your ladies are on the upper floor, where they'll be safe. May I enquire your name, sir?"

"Maddison."

"Captain Phillip Maddison? Then this gentleman of the press has some good news for you. Your son Peter is safe, together with his mother and the other children, and staying in the Lynton house of Mr. Osgood Nilsson, whom I think you know."

"That's right," said the reporter. "Mr. Nilsson managed to get to the camping site in good time, to tow out your caravan, with others, from Green Meadow, before the main force of the flood arrived there."

"That is correct," said the police sergeant. "This gentleman took up your son, Peter I think he is called, with a chum of his to the house, earlier this evening. Catch him! He's all-in. Let him down gently. Here, put him on my cloak. He's wet through poor sod. Come from off the moor, got across Barbrook bridge with a young woman just before it gave way."

"Who was the girl?" persisted the reporter.

"Secretary to Lord Cloudesley, a Miss Laura Wissilcraft."

"Funny name. Is it her own?"

"So far as we know. She's been with his Lordship some time. She brought down her glider on The Chains. Captain Maddison went up apparently to make a beacon to guide both gliders down. Only one arrived."

"Does anyone else know this? Any other reporter, I mean?"

"Not that I know of."

"There will be a fiver for you, old boy. I'll get on the blower to Fleet Street! See you later!"

Phillip was wondering why the two men were speaking in dialect.

"All they poor souls to Shelley's cottage, them' dade, I reckon."

"Aye, them' all dade, surenuff."

"This one be a visitor, I reckon."

"Noomye, 'tes the gennulmun what lives by issell in thaccy shep cot up to Vuzzle."

"He with thaccy li'l ole dog of Aaron Kedd's ?"

"Aye."

A white and shimmering radiance broke in the sky. Above it, in a circle, moved a helicopter, showing a small red light.

"What be thaccy?"

"Tes a light, I reckon."

"Mebbe a rocket."

"Tidden no rocket, else us'd zin'n goin' up, like."

"Aye. Tidden no maroon vor th' live-boat, else us'd'v heard'n."

"Tidden no maroon, midear, no live-boat cud get past they rockses scat abroad when the Rannish tower went."

"Aye. Th' watter be up to th' Risin' Zin, they'm tellin'. My Gor, 'tes a loss'."

The solitary parachute flare wavered as it sank slowly down.

The Germans were across the Ancre Valley. Why had all his men left him?

Piers kneeling beside him. Had he been hit? He heard his own voice saying, from a rent in an immense darkness of fear, "Don't leave me!"

"You're all right now Phil," said the voice of Piers.

"How long have I been here?"

"Oh, some time. Now just relax, we've sent for transport."

Piers put a rolled coat under his head.

Phillip awakened to a sense of dolour which became ease and well-being when Lucy came in to tell him the good news that both his sister and Melissa seemed to be none the worse for the night's ordeal.

"In fact, my dear, I think it's done Elizabeth a world of good. I've never seen her quite like this before. Melissa said she behaved calmly after the first shock, and able to cope cheerfully with the little dogs, who slept in her bedroom, afraid of the lightning and thunder, all together in a large clothes basket."

"What, Aunt Mavis and the dogs?", cried Jonathan.

"No, the little dogs, darling," said Roz, coming in, "Anyway, I wouldn't mind sleeping with them. Where's Bodger, Dad?"

Lucy said, "Well, he was ill, wasn't he?"

"Mum," said Peter, downstairs. "What will Dad say when he learns about his little house—"

Peter was sad for his father; but happy for his new friend, the boy whose parents had survived the flood.

Later in the morning they walked down Mars Hill to Lynmouth, and picked their way over and through obstacles to the cottage. Elizabeth and Melissa had cleared the kitchen and the sitting room of most of the debris and mud. Phillip went to his sister and kissed her on both cheeks. She felt his tears on her cheek.

"There now," said Elizabeth, "don't worry."

Later she said, when they were alone, "I did mean to look after Dads, you know. Only I couldn't get two nurses, it was a terrible time. I did try."

"It was just after the war, dear sister, and everyone young was with the Forces. And Bournemouth must have had more elderly invalids than any other place in England."

"You can come and live here, if you want to, when the place is rebuilt. I hear that a Fund has been started, to help everyone."

"Thank you, my dear."

"You know your little cot is gone, don't you?"

"I thought it might."

"You don't seem very worried."

"I'm not. I shouldn't have needed all my notes, anyway. They were preliminary clearance, only. They were emotion recollected without tranquillity. May I look upstairs?"

"Of course! It's your house for as long as you like."

Melissa was looking down at the wreckage which spread away in all directions as far as could be seen. She took his hand. "Elizabeth was thinking of you, so often. I told her what happened at the cricket match, and do you know what she said? 'It isn't fair!' You see, while we were all on the beach here, with Lucy and the children, Lucy told her a lot about you, and Elizabeth's eyes were opened."

"I think I needed some shock before things could come into adjustment."

"The angels are trying all the time, Phillip."

Elizabeth called up the stairs, "Come down and have some coffee. Mr. Mornington has just called."

He had come down Mars Hill to tell Phillip that Miss Laura had gone to hospital; and that neither Lord Cloudesley nor the Brig had returned to The Eyrie.

"No news of their whereabouts has been reported by either police or coastguards. I hope you won't mind if I accompany you on the beach, sir?"

"You are one of my best friends, Mornington."

It was possible to cross over a light Bailey bridge erected by the sappers below the wreckage of the West Lyn Bridge. Great beech trees lay upon boulders and stones which spread fanwise from the changed course of the two rivers : trunks, branches, lesser branches even twigs—all white. Bark scaled in the frantic trituration of racing sand, grit, pebbles, stones, boulders; the frantic grind of rocks whirled, bashing and rebashing, dragging, scraping, paring, shredding. A wide new estuary of grey stone had arisen above the old narrow watercourse; a levelled valley of bricks and broken walls upon which rested a vast litter of planks, doors, rafters, smashed furniture, beams and joists—enough to build half the beacons of the West Country, thought Phillip. Pyres for the dead—speckles of fire arising on hill beyond hill across the West Country to far Cranborne Chace, under starlight !

Motorcars lay upon the desert of grey stones, some half buried. Ancient little Austin Sevens and cumbrous taxicabs of the 'twenties, wide wings crumpled and compressed, abraded of all rust and paint, new-burnished in action between rock and water until some had become cigar-shaped, save for rubber tyres bulging sullen and contorted.

Trees stuck out of the stained sea a hundred yards from the tide-line. In one tree was lodged a bedraggled white object, shapeless and still. The three brothers went down to the water's edge to get a clearer view. Jonathan's sharp eyes detected a crimson collar below an unmoving head.

Two military frogmen, in black suits were flapping down the beach towards the sea.

The three-score runners feeding the East and West arms of the Lyn river had, between them, swept away or broken nearly half that number of bridges. The Lynmouth sewerage system was destroyed, so nearly a thousand people were to be evacuated at once. A new wide water-course, it was already being said, must be built east of the old and narrow river-bed.

Rest centres had already been set-up in Lynton. A missing Persons Bureau was opened by the Devon Constabulary. To this office came telephone calls from all over England and Scotland. Some were from the Continent of Europe, since the flood had been classified by Whitehall as a National Disaster, and thus covered by the Press of the World.

At various points some miles inland from the coast, police road-blocks had been placed. The general public, arriving in a succession of motorcars, pony traps, motor-bicycles and pedal cycles were stopped from further progress north; and asked to return. Only those holding official positions in the Army, Ministry of Food, Civil Defence, British Red Cross, etc. were permitted to enter the area of devastation. Some had been present the previous afternoon, in an official capacity, including the Lord Lieutenant, the G.O.C. South-Western Command, the Chief Constable of Devon, and Lt-Col. and Mrs. Peregrine Bucentaur.

Now, as Authority moved in little groups about the ruinous scene, Phillip kept his distance along the low-tide-line. Mornington followed, on guard. His immediate concern was to prevent a confrontation between Phillip and Colonel Bucentaur. For by now what had happened on the cricket field was common knowledge.

So Mornington followed beside the wet lash of distained wavelets breaking upon boulders, now scoured of green algae, until Phillip, seeing Lucy and Melissa talking to the Bucentaurs, decided to return.

"Would you do that, sir?"

When there was no reply Mornington said, "I understand from the police that Miss Miranda's name is posted among the *Missing.*"

He followed, still keeping his distance, until he saw that the Colonel, ("a ramrod type waiting with one knee bent, as though standing at ease during a rehearsal of Trooping the Colour," as he said later to Mr. Corney) had turned his back on Phillip's approach.

Phillip went to Molly and said, "Your sweet child is never out of my thoughts."

Peregrine about-turned and Mornington heard him say, "Did you abduct my daughter from the cricket field?"

"No, sir."

"That smallholder, Kedd, told me he saw you with her!"

"Oh no," said Lucy. "Rosamund saw Miranda walking up the cliff path to Lynton, while Phillip went the other way."

Thank God, Mornington said to himself. He observed that two press-men were approaching. One with a camera said, "Excuse me. Colonel Bucentaur, but I think I'm right when I say your daughter went about with one of your white goats?"

"Well?"

"There's a white goat hanging in a tree out there, and it's got a red collar."

Peregrine shouted, "Do not attempt to take any photographs!"

Frogmen were wading into the water towards the tree. They submerged; to return with the body of a young girl with long black hair.

Later, when Peregrine was asked by the Chief Constable to go with him to the sea verge, Phillip took Molly's hand, while a voice seemed to be whispering under the azure sky, *Ariel from Miranda hear, This message that the sea-waves bear—*

While Peregrine was with the Chief Constable and a doctor, Molly said to Lucy, "What a sad end to your holiday, my dear. You must all come back with us"—thus seeking relief from remote terror growing in her mind. To Melissa she said, "Go to Phillip, my dear, he needs you", for he was now walking alone towards the Foreland cliffs, at the base of which waves were breaking.

If only I had remained at the cricket field, and given of my true self to Miranda, and Peregrine, by behaving as though nothing had happened—for nothing ever happens if one remains true to oneself—

The waves are the tears of Christ breaking on the stones of the world.

No! Christ was real, I am an escapist—a romantic: untrue to myself.

When Melissa came to him he was sitting with arms held across the front of his crumpled jacket, the sea-wind blowing the silvery hairs of the bowed head . . . a figure almost of stone, she thought, conscious of life's beginning in the rocks fused by fire, eroded by water and air—creating the soil for which life had left the sea, to arise and fall in 'the ceaseless flow of the fountain'.

She sat beside him, he was shivering. "Come with me to Old-stone, where I'll be able to look after you. Lucy and the children have gone home with Molly, and Elizabeth is returning to her Dorset cottage."

There followed an anxious week for Melissa. Pneumonia developed in both his lungs. She was with him during most of the nights and days, resting on a couch in the bedroom, seldom leaving him. And as the fever abated he felt himself to be floating blessedly in her presence. There were moments of recrudescence, when he would cry, the face wrinkled, the voice self-accusing.

"Darling, it is wrong for us to be too hard on ourselves—"

"My father clung to his roll of lavatory paper, but they took it away!"

What could it mean? When he was calmer he said, "If only I had remained with that poor, lost creature!", and told her about the nursing home. She was relieved, having feared that the lightning stroke might have hurt the brain.

That night she lay beside him, facing him as to an anxious small child who may so easily feel lost when the mother's back is turned upon it. Then as he dropped into sleep quietly she turned over to ease her cramped body, but keeping touch by the palms of her feet held against his legs. And her virtue flowed into him, giving a feeling of peace which he had not known since his first wife Barley had died after the birth of his son Billy.

In the mellow sun of September he sat in the garden at Old-stone, once visited by Mornington and Laura; then he was strong enough to go for a walk; but not into Lynmouth, not under The Chains. Melissa took him by bus across the moor, and down to the shallow coast by the estuary of the Two Rivers.

One morning as they walked through the sand-hills wild sweet calls came down from the sky as a gathering of curlews passed overhead to feed at the tide-line—survivors of the storm upon the moor, crying delight at the gleaming sands below.

"The curlews recognise you, Phillip. You kept the crows away from their young."

"They're calling to Bodger—"

She took his arm, he felt the little dog was near him as they sat on the shingle by Airy Point, above a white bicker of cross little waves under the sky's windless blue. "Willie is safe, too," he said. "The dead are safely over." He got up and wandered over wet pebbles, trying in vain to recall the end of Birkin's book, the one composed in prison during the war. He went back to her.

"Melissa, I used to know the peroration by heart, but now—"

"I remember it."

"You do?"

She quoted, " 'It is the age of decision in which the long striving of the European soul will reach fulfilment, or plunge to final death'."

"I remember!" he cried, " 'Great it is to live in this moment of Fate, because it means that this generation is summoned to greatness in the service of high purpose'."

She moved close to him, " 'From the dust we rise to see a vision that came not before'."

" 'All things are now possible'." He kissed a scarred cheek lightly.

" 'And all will be achieved by the final order of the European'."

"Yes," he said. "And I hope, in a very small way, to complement Birkin's dream by writing my novels. What trials that man has endured for his country. He is a statesman at present without state in the seen world. I must reveal the past of our generation to your generation, indirectly; to reveal truth by a study of the past—the truth, overlaid in nearly all those I have known, yet also invisible and neglected— Will you help me?"

She took his hand. " 'Whithersoever thou goest—' " She felt his tears on her forehead as he stammered, "I – I saw my past life while I was l – lying there, on The Chains— I felt I was being led back out of Hades— Never leave me," he whispered, hiding his face against her breast.

"I never have, Phillip."

"With you I shall be able to begin my chronicle! Do you know, I'm glad I didn't write the novels before. They would probably have been angry and satirical if written in the 'thirties. Now I think I can understand every kind of man and woman. Particularly my father. Yes!" he cried, getting up and walking about on the sand. "I shall start my chronicle in the mid-nineties, on a spring night, with that reserved, shy young man walking up the hill at Wakenham. He was carrying his dark lantern, eager to see what moths were on his 'strips', as he called them—pieces of old flannel steeped in a mixture of rum and treacle pinned to the bark of one of the elms. And one night in the beam of the lantern, he saw a rare Camberwell Beauty! My father must have felt it was an omen, for the girl he loved was born in Camberwell, then a village. She became my mother. She was dark and intuitive, like Miranda—"

"Weep no more, old soldier," she whispered, but her tears, too, were flowing. Then they were smiling and walking hand in hand down the shore.

"You remember Blake's lines—'When the stars threw down their spears/Watering Heaven with their tears—' I know now what that old poet meant. And you have brought love to me, and to my sister—love which dissolves arrogance and hatred— love by which one can see all things as the sun sees them; without shadows." He held up his arms, crying, "O my friends! My friends in ancient sunlight!"

1964 – 1968

Devon.